PRAISE FOR
Out of the Clear Blue Sky

"The perfect beach read. *Out of the Clear Blue Sky* provides the kind of heartwarming tale of hard-fought growth, crazy family, and welcoming community that will linger with you long after the final page." —#1 *New York Times* bestselling author Lisa Gardner

"Reading a Kristan Higgins novel is like spending time with a dear friend, one who understands your soul, captivates your senses . . . and every now and then makes you snort with laughter. Higgins never disappoints! If you're looking for a novel brimming with heart and humor, look no further than *Out of the Clear Blue Sky*. Each time I opened this book, it felt like reuniting with a dear friend. With her trademark wit, Higgins tackles tough issues, and does so with sensitivity and heart. *Out of the Clear Blue Sky* is everything I love in women's fiction—smart, hilarious, and brimming with heart and hope."

—Lori Nelson Spielman, *New York Times* bestselling author of *The Star-Crossed Sisters of Tuscany*

"Your big summer read has arrived! Book after book, Kristan Higgins is a can't-miss author who always serves up stories that are fresh, relevant, and deeply involving."

—#1 *New York Times* bestselling author Susan Wiggs

"From the first page, I was deeply invested in Lillie's plight and desperate to keep turning pages. Kristan Higgins nails it with this laugh-oud-loud, pitch-perfect, heartfelt novel about a woman's life upended and the unexpected ways she finds her way forward. Full of hope, positive messages, and humor, *Out of the Clear Blue Sky* is the perfect book for summer, or any time!"

—Elyssa Friedland, author of *Last Summer at the Golden Hotel*

"A fantastic journey with a brave, delightful, and mischievous heroine who will keep you laughing and rooting for her from page one. I did not want this book to end!"

—Jane L. Rosen, author of *Eliza Starts a Rumor*

"With a blend of humor and poignancy reminiscent of Nora Ephron's *Heartburn*. . . . [*Out of the Clear Blue Sky* is] a beautifully told blend of grief, hope, and humor that showcases Higgins at her best."
—*Kirkus Reviews* (starred review)

"Higgins has created an accomplished protagonist with strong values, a good heart, and an enviable network of friends. Everyone in the community is on her side; take that, ex-husband! This will be satisfying for readers who like to see a strong woman thrive during times of trial."
—*Library Journal*

"Higgins is known for her emotionally potent novels about characters whose lives are in transition. . . . A bighearted treat for relationship-fiction readers."
—*Booklist*

"An emotional, funny tale of second chances."
—*Woman's World*

PRAISE FOR
Pack Up the Moon

"A gorgeous study of love, life, and grief, this book broke my heart—and then stitched me back together again. Kristan Higgins is a masterful storyteller."
—*New York Times* bestselling author Colleen Oakley

"A moving and life-affirming portrait of grief that's sure to bring the tears."
—*Kirkus Reviews* (starred review)

"Higgins is a master of snappy dialogue, and her characters are authentic and relatable—a must for this type of novel. The heart of the story is tragic, but just like real life, there's humor hidden in the darkest moments. This warm, bighearted story about grief, family, and the redemptive power of love will appeal to fans of Katherine Center and Jennifer Weiner." —*Booklist* (starred review)

"Perfect pacing and plotting lift Higgins's masterly latest. This is going to break (and restore) plenty of hearts."
—*Publishers Weekly* (starred review)

"*New York Times* bestselling author Kristan Higgins tells a heartwarming—and heartbreaking—story about young love, loss, and the lingering effects of grief. . . . A story about resilience and everlasting love, this stunningly written tale is a true tearjerker."
—*Good Morning America*

"Kristan Higgins is beloved for her rich, heartwarming sagas—which her latest novel delivers." —*Woman's World*

"Higgins has crafted one of the most beautiful love stories I have ever read. It will make you cry but also leave you breathless and aching for a love like Joshua and Lauren's." —Bookreporter

PRAISE FOR
Always the Last to Know

"A thoroughly entertaining exploration of families' complexities—from bitter disappointment to quiet strengths."
—*People*, Pick of the Week

"Filled with hilarious honesty and heartwarming moments. . . . A moving portrait of a family putting their differences aside in favor of love." —*Woman's World*

"This sparkling story is perfect summer reading."

—*Publishers Weekly*

BERKLEY BOOKS BY KRISTAN HIGGINS

Good Luck with That
Life and Other Inconveniences
Always the Last to Know
Pack Up the Moon
Out of the Clear Blue Sky
A Little Ray of Sunshine

For a list of Kristan's other novels,
please visit kristanhiggins.com

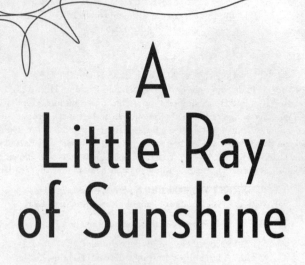

A
Little Ray
of Sunshine

Kristan Higgins

Berkley
New York

BERKLEY
An imprint of Penguin Random House LLC
penguinrandomhouse.com

Copyright © 2023 by Kristan Higgins
Readers Guide copyright © 2023 by Penguin Random House LLC
Penguin Random House supports copyright. Copyright fuels creativity,
encourages diverse voices, promotes free speech, and creates a vibrant culture.
Thank you for buying an authorized edition of this book and for complying with
copyright laws by not reproducing, scanning, or distributing any part of it in
any form without permission. You are supporting writers and allowing
Penguin Random House to continue to publish books for every reader.

BERKLEY and the BERKLEY & B colophon
are registered trademarks of Penguin Random House LLC.

Library of Congress Cataloging-in-Publication Data

Names: Higgins, Kristan, author.
Title: A little ray of sunshine / Kristan Higgins.
Description: First edition. | New York: Berkley, 2023.
Identifiers: LCCN 2022056151 (print) | LCCN 2022056152 (ebook) |
ISBN 9780593547601 (hardcover) | ISBN 9780593547618 (trade paperback) |
ISBN 9780593547625 (ebook)
Classification: LCC PS3608.I3657 L58 2023 (print) |
LCC PS3608.I3657 (ebook) | DDC 813/.6—dc23/20221125
LC record available at https://lccn.loc.gov/2022056151
LC ebook record available at https://lccn.loc.gov/2022056152

First Edition: June 2023

Printed in the United States of America
1st Printing

Book design by Elke Sigal

This book is dedicated to you, Hilly Bean. I have loved you before I had memory, and I love you more than words can say. Thank you for the dance nights, the bongos, the long phone calls, for always having my back and always bringing something good to eat. You are, without a doubt, the best sister in the world.

A
Little Ray
of Sunshine

ONE

HARLOW

I didn't ask for this," I said. "Why are you tormenting me, Addie?"

"It's a lunch date," my sister said. "Don't be such a gutless wonder."

"Cancel him." I continued placing books on the new releases table of Open Book, the store I owned with my grandfather. It was the second week of June, and the Cape Cod tourism season was just about to explode. "I'm very busy."

"Addison, stunning shoes," said Destiny, the one employee not related to me, and our resident fashionista. I glanced at my sister's shoes . . . pink leather ankle boots with snakeskin straps. Tacky, if you asked me, but I tended to wear Converse most of the time.

"Gucci," Addison said proudly. "Fifteen hundred dollars. Anyway, Harlow, he's already on his way to the Ice House. It's too late to back out. I'm doing you a favor. You want what I have. Everyone does."

Destiny gave me a pained look and went to the back to get more boxes of books.

"Goggy?" asked Imogen, my two-year-old niece. "Goggy!" She was strapped in her stroller more securely than an astronaut at countdown. Her pudgy little hands reached toward my dog. Ollie was our resident literary mascot (full name: Oliver Twist), a black-and-tan little mutt I'd rescued. He whined, rightfully wary of my niece.

"Doggy is dirty, Imogen," Addie said. "Dirty dog. Nasty."

"Oliver is *not* dirty," I said, slicing open another box. Oh, good, the new Susan Elizabeth Phillips book! "He's afraid of your demon child."

"She's an angel," Addie lied cheerfully. "Harlow, I'm happily married, have two beautiful daughters and live in a stunning home."

"Yay for you."

"You're dying of envy. You too, Cynthia," she said to our cousin, the third partner of Open Book. Cynthia hissed in response. For once, I agreed with her. "You need to take action to fulfill your dreams," Addie continued. "Put on some lipstick." She pulled out a tube and offered it to me. "You can't stand him up. What would that do to his ego?"

I looked down at myself, clad in my usual jeans and snarky T-shirt (*Books: Because people are horrible*, a bestseller at my store). Dressing up for me meant combing my curly blond hair so it didn't drift into the snarl zone. "Lipstick, Addie? I haven't worn lipstick since high school. And why would I care about his ego? You go. Explain that you're a pushy, irritating sister who thinks she found the secret to happiness."

"I have, though."

I sighed. Once, I had indeed pictured myself married with a few kids. Then adulthood hit, and I wised up. That being said, I *was* starving, and the Ice House had the best burgers on the East Coast.

"Go," said Addison. "I can hear your stomach growling. You can eat and maybe meet your future husband."

"Some of us are happily single, Addie. Right, Cynthia?"

"I prefer not to discuss my private life, but yes, I'm fine with my own company." My brother had suggested that Cynthia ate her first husband, praying mantis style. Given the perpetually sour expression on our sixty-something-year-old cousin's face, her general hatred of humanity and her resemblance to Dolores Umbridge from *Harry Potter*, I could definitely agree.

My stomach growled again. The image of a massive, juicy burger tipped the scales. "Okay. But he's normal, right?"

"He seemed normal enough on his profile. If he's a serial killer, he hid it well."

"They *all* hide it well," I said. "That's the reason they're serial killers."

"You read too much," said my sister.

"I own a bookstore, and it's hardly a character flaw."

Cynthia stomped past. "That baby is chewing on a sixty-five-dollar book," she said. Imogen had wriggled a shoulder free and was laying waste to a book on photography.

"She's very advanced," Addie said. "Aren't you, Imogen?"

"Is she rich, though?" I asked. "Can she afford what she's eating?"

My niece smiled at me, then spit out some paper. Imogen was my sister's biological baby, the image of her (and our sister Lark, since she and Addie were identical twins). Straight blond hair, big green eyes, adorable little nose, entitled attitude. Addie's other daughter, Esme, was her wife's biological child, age five. Addison and Nicole used the same sperm donor, so the girls were half sisters, all according to Addie's plan. The universe would never defy her.

While my job had me interact with children quite a bit, I wasn't the most baby-oriented person. I'd probably like my nieces more when they were teenagers. At least the girls had my sisters—sweet, sensitive Lark; and Winnie, crusty on the surface but with a gooey center. Robbie, our brother, who was ten years younger than I, liked to see how high he could toss a kid, hopefully catching them on the way down. Add to that our parents and sweet grandfather, and the kids were all set. I didn't need to be aunt of the year.

"Did I hear someone say I had a date for lunch?" Grandpop asked, wandering in from the back room. "Wonderful!"

"Can you all just go?" Cynthia asked. "This is hardly a professional discussion. And try not to take too long. The rest of us are also entitled to a lunch break."

"Go ahead," said Destiny, coming back into the room with a box in her arms. She set it down with a thud. "Hardcover James Patterson," she said. "Cynthia and I can unpack and arrange."

"Wish Auntie Harlow luck, Imogen," Addie said. "Tell her not to bite the nice man."

"Pay for that book," I told my sister, grabbing my backpack from under the counter.

"I love lunch!" Grandpop said merrily. "And I'm *famished*! What should I have?"

"A cheeseburger," I said.

"Too much fat and salt," Cynthia said.

"So? He's ninety," I said, pushing the door open. Grandpop could eat whatever he wanted. My grandmother had been gone for three years now, and if a cheeseburger killed Grandpop, well, was there a better way to go? "Come on, Grandpop."

The screen door banged behind us. Open Book was that store people dreamed of owning. Housed in the three-story Victorian that had been in the family since 1843, the store had been founded in the 1980s by my grandmother. Inside, it was cheery and snug with lots of alcoves and cozy corners, a fireplace and places to sit, a little coffee bar and gift area. The children's section was in the sunny, enclosed front porch.

Outside, the garden burst with hostas and ferns, columbine and astilbe and little blue forget-me-nots. We had a couple of granite benches for scenic reading spots, and a brick pathway led to the street. It was an unofficial law that businesses in Wellfleet, Massachusetts, had glorious window boxes, gardens and, whenever possible, a resident dog. We hit all those notes, plus we had Grandpop, Wellfleet's most-loved citizen.

I slid my arm through my grandfather's, since he tended to wander. Grandpop was my favorite person, and it truly was a beautiful day to be out—clear blue sky, a breeze off the water. Main Street was in peak form . . . pink, red and white rhododendrons just now coming into full glory, the crooked old buildings awash in character and charm.

Wellfleet was my hometown, and my three sisters and brother all lived in the area. Our parents owned Long Pond Arts, a well-respected gallery that featured Mom's paintings and a few from other local artists. We Smiths knew all the locals, and most of the regular summer people, who were always so glad to be on the Cape. Robbie was a boat mechanic. Winnie had just bought into an event planning business. Lark was doing her residency at Hyannis Hospital. And Addison, the only one of us who had gotten married so far, was a stay-at-home mom, living comfortably on her wife's wealth. Nicole, Addison's soulmate in materialism, superiority and self-love, worked for her family's foundation.

I was the quiet one. The eldest. The responsible one. The one who'd cook for you if you were sick, drive if you needed a ride. I was the one who was always around—ironic, given that I'd gone to college out West and lived in Los Angeles for a few years. For the past decade, though, I'd lived in an apartment over the bookstore,

kept an eye on Grandpop and was happily turning into the cli-
chéd bookish spinster. It was a quiet, good life, and I planned to
keep it that way.

"Speaking of dates," Grandpop said, "I think I want to get
married again. I do! Yesterday, I took a nap under the porch for
two hours, and no one even missed me."

"I wondered where you'd gone," I said. "Why under the
porch?"

"It looked *very* cozy."

I nodded, understanding the allure. Dark, private, cool . . . I
might have to give it a try.

"Will you help me find someone?" he asked.

"Sure!"

Grandpop and Grammy had been very happily married for
more than six decades, setting the bar high. My parents, too, had
an idyllic marriage, to the point where their five children and two
grandchildren were very much afterthoughts in their day-to-day
lives. If Grandpop wanted my help, he'd get it. When Grammy
died and left me fifty percent of the store, he and I became closer
than ever.

"What are you looking for in a person?" I asked.

"Someone who can talk loud enough for me to hear, first
of all."

"If you wore your hearing aids, we could widen the net," I
said. He chuckled. "You're serious about this, Grandpop?"

"Why not? Life is short! Actually, life is horribly long, Harlow! I thought I'd be dead and buried at least twenty years ago."

"Well, I'm glad you're not," I said.

"Did you know," Grandpop said, "last week, I went for a
drive and forgot where I was!" He announced it as if it were a

delightful surprise. "I got lunch somewhere . . . Orleans, maybe? That crowded place with all the signs?"

"The Land Ho! probably," I said.

"Yes! That one! Anyway, after I ate, I was feeling a little sleepy, so I got in my car and took a nap. But it turns out it wasn't my car! The owners were very nice, though. A little surprised to find me, but they were very friendly."

"Didn't we talk about you not driving anymore, Grandpop?" I asked. "Cynthia and I can take you wherever you want to go." He was her godfather, and we called her our cousin, though how she was related was a mystery. She called Grandpop "Uncle Robert," and Grandpop actually liked her, because he liked everyone.

"We did talk about it," he said. "I just felt like taking a spin. Gosh, it's a lovely day, isn't it?" Grandpop asked. "I just love August."

"Me too," I said. "But it's June."

"Is that right? Goodness. Time flies." He smiled at me, making me glad he was coming along. Always dressed in trousers and a shirt, vest and tie and still standing at six feet tall, Grandpop was a dapper gentleman, and his kindness shone from his faded blue eyes.

We got to the Ice House, and Beth, the owner and a member of my book club, waved to me. "Just you and your handsome grandfather today, Harlow?" she asked.

"Oh, aren't you a *charmer*, Beth," Grandpop said. "Are you making a pass at me? I *am* looking to get married again."

"Are you?" Beth said, grinning. "Well, if my husband leaves me, you'd be my first choice. Where would you two like to sit?"

"Actually, I'm meeting someone," I said, grimacing. "Grandpop, would you like to sit at the bar and flirt with Beth here?"

"I would *love* that!" Grandpop exclaimed. "I so enjoy talking to pretty girls!"

"And *I* love talking to charming older men," Beth answered. "Sit wherever you want, Harlow, and Tanner will be over in a few."

I took a seat facing the door so I could see . . . oh, shoot. I didn't know his name. I took out my phone to text Addison, but she'd beat me to it.

Pete Schultz, data analyst, divorced, no kids, likes fishing, boating, the Patriots. He knows you have four incredibly attractive siblings and dropped out of law school. Should be worth a second date.

We'd see about that. Thus far in my adult life, I had not had a meaningful, committed relationship. I wasn't averse to one, but I wasn't looking, either. If, say, Keanu Reeves dropped into the bookstore one day and begged me to marry him, I would definitely consider it.

But dating? I'd tried it in my late twenties. Ugh. The work, the profiles, the texting, then calling, then meeting, only to find you didn't hit it off. The longest I'd dated someone was two and a half weeks—Jake, a plumber from Hyannis. That ended when he had to go on an emergency call for an overflowing toilet and left me with his seven-year-old child (previously unmentioned), who needed babysitting because his wife (also unmentioned) was out.

Tanner, Beth's nephew and my server, came over with menus. I ordered a glass of prosecco to make this meeting more pleasant and the cheeseburger du jour. No need to wait for my, uh, companion. My stomach growled with appreciation.

"Got it," he said.

Destiny texted me. Anything to report?

He's not here, I texted back. Praying for a no-show. Only in this for the cheeseburger.

Ah. My parents had just walked in, holding hands, looking like an ad for Cape Cod living—Mom with her long, curly blond hair streaked with gray, sparkling brown eyes, and Dad tall and with a tan that made his blue eyes stand out, still with a great head of salt-and-pepper hair. I waved. They didn't wave back but walked right past me. This was not uncommon, as they were usually wrapped up in each other and the cloud of satisfaction that engulfed them. "Hello, Mother, Father," I said. Mom jumped.

"Oh! Harlow. We didn't see you there," Mom said.

"Hello, honey," Dad said. "Having lunch?"

"Yes," I said. "And you?"

"Also lunch." We smiled at each other.

"Well. Have a good time," Mom said, and off they went to a table in the back where they could play footsies and coo at each other.

Growing up with parents who were so blatantly in love had been . . . impactful. On the one hand, they really liked and loved each other, were openly and sometimes horrifyingly affectionate and were always a united front as parents. As an adult, I couldn't quite figure them out. The whole town was infatuated with my parents' marriage. *I saw your parents kissing in the Memorial Garden*, a customer or friend might say. *So romantic.* Or *I cannot believe your parents still hold hands. So romantic.* Or *Your father just bought your mom a necklace. So romantic.* "Showing off" was what Winnie, my youngest sister, called it, and she had a point. It was a little attention-grabbing. That time they were trying for a quickie in the coatroom at church just before Esme's baptism, for example.

An average-looking man came into the restaurant. Khaki pants, blue button-down, Nikes. His hair was light brown. He'd make a *great* serial killer, I decided, going with my original instinct. No one would be able to remember that face. "Pete?" I called. "Hi." I gave a little wave.

"Hey!" he said. "Pete Schultz. Great to meet you, Harper."

"It's Harlow, actually, but hi. Nice to meet you, too."

"Harlow, right, right," he said. "How are you?"

"Doing fine. How are you?" My brain emptied of small talk, something I was usually quite good at behind the counter of my store.

"I'm good. Cool place." He looked around appreciatively. "Was it once actually an icehouse?"

"Yes. Mm-hm." The building's history was printed on the menu. Pete could read it himself. From the corner, I heard my mom give a sultry laugh at something Dad had said.

"This was indeed an icehouse, young man," said my grandfather, walking over. "Back in the day, the ponds on the Cape would have ten or twelve inches of ice come winter. The iceman would cut great chunks of it and store them here, then put them on a cart and go around town. The ladies of the house would leave a number in their windows, letting him know how many pounds of ice they needed! Isn't that interesting?"

"I guess," said Pete, scratching his head, then examining his fingernails. He flicked a little scalp out of his ring fingernail. Nasty.

"This is my grandfather," I said. "He's a whiz with history. You should see him at trivia night." Yes, yes, I was that dork who loved trivia nights. My team had been All-Cape champs last year, though we'd lost our strongest science guy to a Florida retirement. But Grady Byrne, a marine biologist and a former elementary and high school classmate, had replaced him in January. I was confident we would win the trophy (again).

"Here's a dating tip, Harlow," Grandpop continued. "Talk about topics of general interest. Stay away from money, politics and sexual preferences."

"Good advice. Thanks, Grandpop," I said, accustomed to these little tidbits. Beth called him back to the bar, and Grandpop tipped an imaginary hat and left us.

"Your grandfather's a little . . . unfiltered," Pete said.

"My grandfather is *perfect*."

Luckily, Tanner arrived with my beautiful, mouthwatering cheeseburger. I took an enormous bite and moaned in pleasure, eyes closed.

"Uh, I'll have a salad," Pete said, his voice tinged with disapproval. I looked him in the eye and took another bite. "So you own a bookstore?" he asked as he watched me eat. "It said so in your profile."

"Mm-hm," I said, wiping my mouth with my napkin. "Open Book."

"Great name."

"Thanks." I swallowed. "Um, do you like your job, Pete?"

The next fifteen minutes were filled with Pete's description of data integrity as he ate his salad. I tried. I did. Not too hard, because that burger was way more interesting, but I gave it a shot. "I'm kind of known for statistical inference," he finished up, and I noticed a fleck of carrot stuck to the left side of his lip. "Not to brag, but I'm kind of famous in my world. My predictive modeling is world-class."

"Wow," I said.

"I know." He smiled proudly.

We chewed in silence. Well, I did, anyway. He sounded like a horse. Ten more minutes? Sadly, Pete wasn't ready to call time of death just yet. "What do you do for fun?" he asked.

"I kayak and paddleboard," I said. "Almost every day. I have a dog. Trivia night, as I said. And of course, I read a lot."

He didn't answer, just kept chomping on the salad.

"How about you?" I asked. "What do you like to read?"

"I'm not much of a reader," he said. So he was dead inside. Got it. "But I do write."

"Most writers I know love to read."

"I dabble in poetry."

Unexpected. "Who are some of your favorites?"

"Gosh. Hard to say." He offered a shy smile.

"I love Mary Oliver," I said. "Amanda Gorman, Robert Frost. I'm on a Rumi kick these days."

Pete tilted his head. "I guess I'd have to say *I'm* my favorite poet, to be honest."

"Oh. Um . . . that's great." From behind me, my parents' murmured sweet talk stopped and I guessed they were eavesdropping (or kissing). Grandpop had just left—he may have forgotten to pay, as was his habit, so I'd have to check with Beth. I ate a french fry.

"Can I read you something I wrote?" Pete asked. "I'd love to have your take on it, since you're in the business."

"We just sell books." You'd be amazed at how many people thought I could help them get published. And yes, we did occasionally sell self-published books by local authors, but it wasn't like we could make anyone a national sensation. "I'm not involved with publishing."

"Sure you are," Pete said. "Let's see if you think this is something your customers would enjoy. Maybe I could do a reading at your store." He lifted his eyebrows suggestively.

Not gonna happen, pal. "Fire away." I drained my prosecco.

Pete reached into his pocket and pulled out a worn-looking piece of paper. "I call this one 'Despair.'"

"Catchy," I said. The date had suddenly gotten more interesting.

"It's about my ex," he said.

Did I have time to fish out my phone and record this? Rosie, my best friend, would love it. "Go for it," I said.

Pete cleared his throat. "'You ruined my life. I thought you'd be my forever wife.'"

Definitely should've asked to record it.

"'But you brought me strife. Like a sharp and hacking knife. Cutting through my heart. Instead of cherishing it like a piece of art. And pierced it with a dart.'" He glanced at me to see if I was paying attention. I was. "'You are still in my head. But now I dream of you dead.'"

I almost cracked on the last line, but kept my expression neutral. After all, the serial killer odds had skyrocketed.

He put the paper away and looked at me expectantly.

"Tanner? Check, please!" I called. "Very powerful, Pete. And terrifying. You might want to reconsider that last line."

"Too harsh?" he said.

"I'd get a restraining order if I were in her shoes."

"But what about the rhyming? It took me a really long time to find words that rhyme."

"It does rhyme. You are correct about that. Tanner? We're all set here."

Pete shrugged. "I guess it doesn't matter," he said. "My ex, I mean. She'll be super jealous that I've moved on. When do you want kids, by the way? I'm totally ready. I'd like us to get pregnant within the year. That would really chap her ass."

"Sorry. We're not really a good match, Pete," I said. "I don't want kids."

"Shit," he said. "Think you could've said that in your profile?"

"My sister wrote it. I don't even know what's in it, to be honest."

"Great. Thanks for totally wasting my time." He tossed a ten down on the table and stomped off.

"My time was also totally wasted," I called. "And your salad cost sixteen dollars." He didn't pause.

My parents were instantly at my side, wheezing with laughter. "We won't let you marry an awful poet," Mom managed. "You can do better."

"Blame Addison. She found him."

"You'll find someone," Mom said. "We do want more grand-children."

"Talk to Robbie. He has an entire stable of women."

They were already disinterested. "Ellie," Dad said, "what do you say we skip dessert and head home for a nap?"

"I love naps," she said coyly. "Even more than dessert."

"Okay, kids," I said. "There are children present. Me. I'm your child."

Mom grinned. "Aren't you glad your parents have a healthy sexual enjoyment of each other?"

I made a strangled noise, and they left the restaurant, laugh-ing, arms around each other. I settled up with Beth, paying for Grandpop's lunch, too. *Still single*, I thought as I walked home. Which was far better than being with a homicidal poet. Besides, I had an arrangement with a guy named James, who taught cello and violin in Harwich. Once or twice a month, I'd drive to his place so we could fool around.

James was talented and attractive, but also that kind of tortured artist guy prone to a lot of *I could've been somebody* mono-logues. In other words, he wasn't the next Yo-Yo Ma, had been married twice and would die in debt. We had no pretenscs. He served a purpose, and so did I. It wasn't the worst scenario in the world. My best friend, Rosie, on the other hand, had a habit of falling for married men, only to discover they weren't going to leave their wives (shocking, I know). In the past five years, I'd flown to LA four times to console her, which meant ordering Chinese food, cleaning her apartment and lying in her bed while telling her how wonderful she was. Because she was.

My only life goals were to make Open Book the best book-store on the Cape and win every trivia game I ever entered. I couldn't see myself married at this point. Kids? Out of the question.

My phone started blowing up with texts from my siblings, since the parents had clearly updated the troops.

Sorry, said Addison. It was more apology than I usually got.

Finding a spouse is almost impossible after 30, and you're 35. It's not Addison's fault. This from Nicole, Addie's wife. No sense of humor.

At least he didn't write a crappy poem about YOU. 😌 This from Lark. Not yet, anyway. 😊 💜 💜 💜

You don't HAVE to be with someone. Winnie. But if this is your kink, you do you.

I fail to see the problem here, Robbie said. Sounds like you were perfect for each other.

I texted an emoji of a laughing face and a middle finger to Robbie and left the rest for later.

"How was your date, which lasted more than an hour?" Cynthia asked sharply when I returned to the bookshop. *Her* lunch breaks were twenty minutes of joyless salad eating.

"Lunch was delicious," I said. "Thanks for asking."

"I already heard," Destiny said. "But you can tell me all the details later."

"News travels fast," I said, bending to pet Oliver's silky fur and gaze into his beautiful eyes. "I don't need anyone but you, Ollie," I said, kissing his perfect head. "Did Grandpop come back?"

"He went to take a nap," Destiny said.

"Am I the only person who works here full-time?" Cynthia snapped.

Destiny and I exchanged a look. Cynthia had come to the Cape three weeks after Grammy died with a chip on her shoulder and a snarl on her face. Divorced, childless, angry at the world. Some people had resting bitch face. Cynthia had resting bitch soul. But Grandpop had given her twenty-five percent of the business, cutting his share in half. Why, I wasn't sure.

A woman was in the back, perusing our teeny, tiny erotica selection. "Hi, Ms. Henderson!" I called. "Looking for something new?"

"Just browsing. Getting inspiration," she said. She picked up a book called *Super Sex After Sixty* and thumbed through it. "Heh. I could've written this one."

"Oh, we got a new book in," Destiny said. "It's not in your usual BDSM vein, but I think you'll love it, Karen." Hand-selling like a champ, our Destiny. She knew how things worked.

As a small business in a small town, we made our livelihood book by book. Every once in a while, someone would drop in and spend a couple thousand—new homeowners who wanted to fill their shelves. Melissa Spencer, for example, had bought every novel with a blue spine so her bookcases would match her throw pillows. It had pained me, sending books into a house where they were only décor. Maybe Ophelia, her niece, would read them, since she was a frequent flyer here. But mostly, we had to know what our customers liked and get them to read new stuff, too.

Karen bought Destiny's recommendation, plus two more. I rang her up and told her to have a great day. I saw that Grady Byrne had ordered another marine biology book. This one cost $204. *Good on you, Gray,* I thought, and sent him a quick note thanking him for using us. *See you Friday!* I added. Trivia night.

Father's Day was coming, so I went through the store, grabbing books for the window display. Red Sox triumphs. World War II. James Patterson and Michael Connelly. The most recent Colson Whitehead novel. Some Robert Bly poetry. *This Old House* how-to manuals. Cookbooks that featured meat, beer and fire. One on baking, since I knew a few guys who loved to make dessert.

Outside, the June day beckoned. I'd probably take my paddleboard to Marconi Beach after work, since it didn't get dark until almost ten o'clock.

The window display could use a little something else. "Do we have any dad-like objects lying around?" I asked. "Maybe some sporty stuff?"

"You're asking the wrong person," Destiny said, giving a little twirl so her dress swirled around her. I smiled, went to the back closet and rummaged around. Ah. A baseball mitt. A hammer. My Red Sox cap. I could get my rolling pin for the bakers and would raid Grandpop's place later for other masculine touches, like his Panama hat and a shaving brush.

The bell over the door rang. I looked up to see two men— one in his forties or early fifties, and his son, I assumed, who wore droopy jeans and a hoodie. The man had salt-and-pepper hair and a solid build. He picked up a book and said something to the boy, and the boy smiled. I couldn't quite see their faces, because the light was behind them.

I started to say hello, then stopped. A weird, prickling feeling started in my knees, almost painful. The air seemed to change and grow too thick to breathe.

The older man turned, and I saw his profile. I *knew* him. Sure, I knew many customers. But he wasn't a regular. No. My mind skipped like a stone on the water. I knew him. Once, I'd known him very well, but my mind wasn't letting me place him.

Then the younger one turned, and I saw more of his face. My stomach dropped like I was in an express elevator.

He was about five-ten. Lanky. Unkempt, curly dark hair. He glanced at me surreptitiously, not long enough for me to see his face clearly, then looked down at the book he'd grabbed off the shelf. *The Enduring Shore.* He was holding it upside down.

My heart was banging against my ribs like it wanted to burst out and run down the street, and yet my brain couldn't gather a single coherent thought.

Then the boy moved away from the window, and I could see his face now, and once again, he looked at me. Our eyes met. He smiled, and the floor dropped away.

I took a step forward, but my knees were made of water, and I staggered. The older man looked up. I reached out to steady myself on a table, missed and took another wobbling, unsure step.

"Are you all right?" said the older man, starting toward me. He was Indian. Oh, yes, I *knew* him.

"Harlow?" said Destiny.

"Oh, crap," said the boy, his smile fading.

I was falling and my vision was shutting down.

He looked so much like my brother with his dark curly hair and brown eyes . . . he looked like Robbie because he was related to Robbie. He . . . he was . . . Robbie's nephew.

In other words, he was my son.

TWO

HARLOW

I was lying on the floor with something cold and wet pressed against my head. My eyes were still closed, and I felt weird and light. Ollie was licking my ear, and I reached up to touch his silky head. I had to order that book for Grady Byrne. And finish the Father's Day display. Cynthia was irritable, as usual. What else? There was something else. Should I open my eyes? I probably should, so I did.

"Harlow? Sweetie? Are you okay?" asked Destiny. Her face was worried.

A nice-looking Indian man with a kind face looked at me from behind Des. He also looked concerned.

"Hi," I said, scooching up.

"Hello," he said. "Why don't you stay put for a moment, okay? You fainted."

"Right," I said. I put my arm around Oliver, who seemed worried, and gently pushed his muzzle away from my ear. Did I forget to eat today? No, I'd had lunch at the Ice House, and . . .

Oh, my God.

I scrambled to my feet. There he was. The teenager. The boy who, in about six weeks, would be eighteen.

It wasn't a dream. Oh, my God, he *was* here. He was *here*.

I wanted to say something, but my vocal cords weren't working.

"Hi," said the boy. Man. Man-boy. Young man. Whatever. His voice was so deep, and his hair was shaggy and he needed to shave, maybe. He was . . . he was beautiful.

I reached out a shaking hand to touch him, but then pulled back.

"Hi," he said. "I'm so sorry. I . . . it was stupid. I should've called or messaged you."

"You didn't *call*? Dear God, Matthew!" His father looked truly shocked.

Matthew. *Matthew.*

"Um . . . well, hi. I'm Matthew." He grimaced and came a little closer.

"You're so . . . grown up," I whispered, and then we were hugging. He was skinny and as tall as I was, not the soft, helpless baby he'd been when I last saw him, obviously. Tears were streaming down my face, and I had to struggle not to sob. My *son*. My *baby*. He was here, and he was so *perfect*. I did sob then.

Matthew hugged me back, harder, and I could tell he was crying, too. Oliver barked once, twining around our legs. The room swam again, and I let go, staggering back. Luckily, the couch was behind me, and I fell onto it. Oliver jumped up next to me, excited and wagging.

Destiny pressed a bottle of cold water into my hand. "Close the store and go home," I whispered.

"Are you sure?" she whispered back.

I nodded. "Take Cynthia, too," I added.

"I am so very sorry about this," said Matthew's father, and I remembered his accent and how much I'd liked it. Sanjay Patel and his wife, Monica Patel. Sanjay and Monica.

The couple I chose to raise my son.

"Cynthia, we're closing early," Destiny called.

"Why?"

"Because something is happening, and it's none of our business," Destiny said. "Call me later, Harlow." She dropped a box of tissues next to me and touched my shoulder, then was gone.

"I better get paid for these hours," Cynthia said.

Matthew sat in the chair across from me and pulled it closer so our knees almost touched. His eyes were also wet. Brown eyes, pure brown eyes with long, thick lashes. He was beautiful. Objectively beautiful. My *son* was here. This couldn't be a coincidence, could it?

It is very hard to play it cool when your child, whom you haven't seen since the day of his birth, walks into your life. Apparently, I wasn't even trying for cool. I was shaking so hard, I sloshed the water onto my pants.

"Surprise?" Matthew said, and I laugh-sobbed.

"Okay," Sanjay said. "Um . . . should we . . . go somewhere else?"

"No! No, this . . . it's . . . good. This is fine. Please stay." I may have been having an out-of-body experience, because I couldn't feel my limbs. I tried to take a steadying breath, but it wasn't even close. I was here with my son and his father. My son, who had *found* me. Oliver nudged my arm. Sanjay sat in the other chair and looked at his son. Our son. My son.

I sure hadn't seen this coming.

My heart was throbbing, pulsing in huge, rolling beats, and I was hot all over. I grabbed a tissue and mopped my face. "Look at you," I said, and more tears spilled out. "You're so big."

Sanjay Patel laughed. It had been almost eighteen years since

I had seen him, but abruptly, I remembered him in minute detail, his kindness, his smile, his . . . his heart. "Nice to see you again," he said with a grimace. "I am so, so sorry. My son here failed to mention he had planned a reunion. Because it is not a coincidence that you chose Cape Cod for our vacation, is it, Matthew?"

"No," said my son, looking at his hands. "I'm really sorry."

"No, it's fine. It's great!" I said. Another shuddering sob. I drank some water and blew my nose.

The two of them turned away for a heated-whisper exchange, and I heard the words *terrible way to handle this* and *you should've thought this through* and *kicked a baby rabbit.* I think that last one was in reference to me.

"Perhaps we should come back tomorrow," Sanjay said. "Would you like to call someone?"

"No! No. Don't go." All I could do was stare at my boy. "You're named Matthew?" I asked.

"Yeah," he said. "Matthew Rohan Patel."

They had kept the name I'd picked out. Matthew. Matthew.

"I'm so happy to see you," I managed to whisper. His hands were man hands. Big and strong with square nails. The last time I'd seen those hands, they were the impossibly soft and beautiful hands of a newborn.

"Okay, Matt," Sanjay said, "you clearly owe Harlow an apology, buddy. This was not very considerate, appearing out of the blue like this."

"No, it's great!" I said. "I'm so happy. I—" *I love you,* I wanted to say, but maybe I shouldn't. Was there protocol for this kind of situation? We had books on adoption in the store. I would read them all tonight. "Please stay."

"I'm really sorry," Matthew said. He sounded . . . was it my imagination, or did he sound like my dad? "I—well, I thought you might not want to see me," he went on, "so I just . . . showed up. Shit. Mom is going to kill me."

Mom. He meant the woman who raised him. Monica. Oh, God, I had loved her!

A thought occurred to me. I was hallucinating. Or dreaming. Yes. That made more sense. My head hurt, because I may have thunked it while fainting, and I was sweating profusely. Did you sweat in dreams? If so, that didn't seem fair.

"Is this a dream?" I asked, looking at them both.

Matthew's eyes filled at that.

"No, this is actually happening," Sanjay said. "We could have been more graceful about it, but here we are."

The infant I'd given away when he was only minutes old, to Sanjay and Monica Patel, tearing my heart out in the process, was sitting in front of me.

I never imagined it this way. I never let myself imagine it completely at all, really. I wished I had, so I'd know what to say. "You look so much like my brother" was all I managed.

"You certainly do!" came Grandpop's voice as he came in the door that led to his house. "And also like myself in my prime, I don't mind saying. You're a good-looking lad! Hello, there, I'm Robert Smith, proprietor of this fine store along with my granddaughter here, right, honey? Where's the other one? Cynthia? Where are you, dear?"

"She went home," I said, not taking my eyes off Matthew Rohan Patel. "Destiny, too."

"Ah. And who are these fine people?"

Matthew looked at him, dark eyes wide with wonder. Holy crap, he was meeting his great-grandfather.

"Grandpop," I said, my voice breathy and weird. "This is Matthew Patel and his father, Sanjay."

Grandpop didn't say anything for a second. "Wonderful to meet you," he said, and his voice was normal. "What brings you here today?"

"Grandpop, um . . . this . . . I . . . I'm going to talk to you later," I said. This would require some finesse. "For now, can we have some privacy?"

"Of course," Grandpop said. "Have a *wonderful* afternoon." I wondered what he guessed. It was hard to know with a man who wasn't sure what month it was.

"It was great to meet you, sir," Matthew said. "Um . . . I hope we'll see each other again, too." Was he about to tell Grandpop who he was? Sanjay and I looked at each other, my uncertainty palpable.

"A pleasure, Mr. Smith," said Sanjay.

"What nice manners you both have," Grandpop said. "Most teenagers today can't string three words together when they're talking to an ancient soul like myself. Harlow, sweetie, you're cooking tonight, right? Remember how I set fire to the hot dogs last time? Oh, that was a hoot! Nice meeting you, gentlemen! Ollie, want to come with me, boy? Come on, puppy!"

My dog jumped off the couch and followed my grandfather. Silence settled around the three of us. My head still felt light and strange, and I blinked hard to try to focus.

"Your grandfather dresses very nicely," Sanjay said. "A very dapper gentleman."

"Yes! Yes, he does. So. Um . . . well, that was your great-grandfather," I said to Matthew. "He's a little . . . forgetful? But very nice."

Matthew looked confused. "He doesn't know about me?"

My mouth opened. "Uh . . . yeah. I . . . um . . . I never . . ." I swallowed. "No, my family doesn't know."

Matthew and his father looked at each other. Oh, God. Did they hate me now? Did my son . . . I could not finish a thought.

"If I may suggest something," Sanjay said, and I remembered how formal he had sometimes sounded. His voice was deep and warm, but he spoke somewhat formally and with authority. Well, he *was* in charge. Matthew was his son. "Why don't we reassemble tomorrow? Harlow, you've had quite the shock, and my son has some explaining to do. However, to summarize, we are here for the summer. I am a teacher, if you remember, and every summer, our family takes a vacation so the children can experience life in a different area. Matt and I were looking at colleges on the East Coast, so we came out early. Monica and our daughter are coming when her school year finishes."

Matthew had a *sister*. He was a big brother. Oh, God, that was so nice! He had a sibling!

"But you'll come back?" I asked, tears starting again.

"Absolutely," they said in unison.

I stood up on shaky legs. My son reached out, a little awkwardly, and we hugged, hard and long, and I bit down on the sobs that tried to wrestle their way out.

My son. My baby. My little pal. God, how I've missed you.

"We will see you very soon," Sanjay said. "Again, very sorry to have handled it this way."

"Totally," Matthew said, looking contrite.

"No! I'm so happy! This is the best day of my life! Just . . . you know. A shock. Right? I mean, I just had a crappy date at lunch, and then my son walks in, and . . . It's fine. It's wonderful!" I sounded unbalanced. I *was* unbalanced.

"Well. That's good," Sanjay said.

"Oh, wait, do you have my phone number? You don't, do you?"

"Tell me what yours is, and I'll text you," Matthew said.

My son wanted my *phone number*. He would *text* me. It sounded so normal.

"Right!" I recited off the numbers, hoping they were right, and he typed them into his phone.

"Got it. Thanks." He smiled, and my heart nearly tumbled out onto the floor.

"Bye," I remembered to say as they left the store together, Sanjay's hand firmly on Matthew's shoulder. I fought the urge to run after them, to grab Matthew and drag him back into the store, up to my place, to lock the doors and keep him with me. To hug him and stare at his face, to kiss his cheeks and feel his hair and gaze into his eyes.

Would he forgive me for not telling my family? It had made so much sense back then not to say a word. Shit. Matthew *would* come back, wouldn't he? They'd promised.

A second later, my phone dinged.

Great meeting you, First Mama. ☺

My legs gave out once more, and I was back on the couch, staring at the message.

He didn't hate me. He sent me a smiley face emoji. He called me *mama*.

I had met him. He was *here*. I would see him again very soon, Sanjay said. My hands were shaking violently, and it took me three tries to find my best friend's name.

He found me h ecame to the ftore toady, I typed, then hit send, then retyped. To the store today.

I didn't need to tell her who I was talking about.

A few seconds later, Rosie's answer appeared. In Vietnam right now. I'll be there asap. Hang in there.

THREE

HARLOW

I sat on the battered leather couch for a long time, adrift on an ocean of feelings. Joy made me buoyant, loss pulled like a riptide, and waves of grief, shock and love hit me from every direction. But outside, the sky shimmered with deep blue joy.

It was fair to say that my safe, carefully curated life would never be the same again, and I didn't care.

Since I had returned to Cape Cod ten years ago, I had been living on the surface of life. I knew there was an ocean of unaddressed issues beneath me, but like a bug skittering on the surface of the water, I'd carefully stuck to the safe parts of life and ignored the depths below. Eighteen years ago, I had been broken, and it had taken a long, long time to put myself back together. I felt the echoes of my son every single day. I knew love was the most dangerous thing on earth. Love had ruined me and defined me, and the last thing I had ever wanted was to be so horrifyingly vulnerable again.

I had given my son away. *Relinquished* was the word they used now. Seventeen years ago, when I was a freshman in college, the idea of keeping him, raising him, had felt impossible. Wrong. I hadn't even been close to adulthood. I had wanted more for my child. Two parents. Adoration. I had wanted him to be seen, and not just another Smith kid, just another kid raised in the blur of life with my family. I didn't want him to be the kid with a teen-aged mother, no father, where he might be viewed as just another chore.

So I'd given him to Monica and Sanjay when he was just a few minutes old. And now here he was.

He was okay. He was *beautiful.* So beautiful! I wanted to breathe him in as I had when he was first born. I wanted him to know how much I loved him. How I had loved him every day of his life. Was he a good kid? Was he dating anyone? He *seemed* like a good kid. Was he smart? Was he kind? How could he not be? He sure had been nice to me, accepting my blubbering, stunned exclama-tions and hugging me hard.

Oh, that hug! That hug!

The thoughts ran through my mind like debris in a flash flood.

Here's the thing. When I'd handed my child to another woman, a vital part of me had been torn away. No—shattered. But I'd glued myself back together, at least well enough so that I man-aged a functioning, happy life as long as I didn't think too hard or open myself up too much.

When I'd given Matthew to the Patels, I had destroyed any fantasy of a little family of two. I gave away the one I had loved so fiercely, so fully—my little pal, my companion every second of every day for nine months, one week and three days. I had handed him to someone else, never to feel him hiccup again, never to hear him cry, never to say, "Shh, honey, Mommy's here." I gave up the chance to rock him at night, sing to him, laugh with him, wipe his nose, teach him the ABCs. He never gripped my finger, looked up at me with dark eyes. He never reached for me when he was scared, or cuddled next to me when I read to him. He never mouthed off to me as a teenager, then asked me to drive him to a party or make spaghetti and meatballs for supper.

Sanjay and Monica had had all that. I had given my son to them because I hadn't been up for the job. Or maybe I had been. Maybe I'd been selfish. I would never know for sure, because we don't get to relive our lives, no matter how much we might want to.

For seventeen years, ten months and two weeks, the loss of my child had been a black hole, always trying to suck me in and crush me into nothing —and one time, succeeding. I had tried so hard to pretend the black hole wasn't there, carefully tiptoeing around, never speaking of it to anyone but Rosie.

Hugging him today, hearing his voice, touching his hair . . . it was joy, but it was also the grief of everything I had lost.

Balled-up tissues surrounded me, making me glad Grandpop had taken Oliver with him, because Ollie liked to eat paper goods. I drank water, pretty sure I was dehydrated from crying. My hands were still shaking.

My thoughts stuttered and sped by. My family was about to have a bomb dropped on them the size of Texas. Did I have to tell them right away? Would Matthew want to meet them? Probably. Would the Patels let him? How long were they staying on the Cape? They told me, but I forgot. How many times could I see Matthew before they went home? Did they still live in California, in the sweetly named town of Pleasanton? I couldn't wait to see Monica again. She had loved me once. But would that be different now? Matthew had a sister now, too. Gosh, how fantastic. Was she adopted as well?

When would my son text me? How many more hours till I saw him again?

I felt sick. I felt jubilant. I was drowning in love, but I was drowning just the same.

Rosie couldn't get here fast enough. She was the one person still in my life who knew everything about Matthew, who'd been there while I was pregnant, and afterward, and during the devastation.

My phone dinged, and I jumped as if I'd been shot.

Where are you??? Addison demanded. It's Esme's kindergarten graduation party! Everyone else is here already. Even Lark made it, and she's a fucking doctor. Get moving. The caterers just dropped off the food.

Ah. A bit of normalcy. Addie really should've been the dictator of a small country. Always eager to show off the Perfect Life in the Perfect House, she and Nicole hosted many events, some of them nonsensical . . . such as a kindergarten graduation party. But Esme was my niece, and it would be easier to go than to endure the interrogation Addie would give me if I didn't show up.

Esme had a *cousin*. As of today, she was no longer the eldest grandchild. Addie and Nicole would kill me for that, no doubt. My whole family would be at the kindergarten graduation party. I could tell them there. Or not.

Moving automatically, I went through Open Book (the name of which now struck me as incredibly ironic, although I hadn't chosen it) and turned off the lights, checked the door, closed down the computer system and chose a gift for Esme—a boxed set of the Poppleton Pig series by Cynthia Rylant.

Fifteen minutes later, I arrived at Addison and Nicole's—a gorgeous, sprawling house on Lieutenant Island, which was a little chunk of land connected to the rest of Wellfleet by a bridge. My knees felt sick and wobbly as I walked in.

"Auntie Harlow!" Esme cried. "You're late!"

I took a breath and tried to sound normal. "Hi, there, graduate. Congratulations on not flunking out."

Addison sent me a dark look, and Nicole pretended not to hear, though her face soured a bit. "There are still some appetizers in the kitchen, even though you're almost an hour late," my sister said. "Tacos and burritos are in the dining room. Mango, watermelon and classic margaritas on the sideboard."

Because no kindergarten graduation would be complete without margaritas. However, I could definitely use some liquid courage; that was for sure. My body was overloaded with adrenaline, and I still felt a little faint. I went into the dining room, vaguely noting Addie and Nicole's extreme good taste—their house was expensively furnished with sleek mid-century furniture, beautiful paintings from Mom and Dad's gallery, and best of all, a gorgeous view of the bay. The sunset was gearing up to be glorious, a fat bank of cumulus clouds just above the horizon that would catch the light and transform the sky.

It seemed fitting that the sky would be glorious this night, and not because of Esme's milestone. Because of Matthew. I hoped he would see it, too.

"Harlot," Robbie said, graciously pouring me a margarita from the colorful pitcher. Oh, no, that was for himself. "Did you have a special, special day, sis?"

My head jerked. Did he know? "What?"

"The poet?" he asked. "Are you marrying him?"

Oh, thank God. "No. Now move so I can get a drink. You should've poured me one, since I'm your big sister and changed your diapers. Also, you're the harlot, not me." Robbie was a very popular lad on the Cape, sowing his wild oats as he slutted about the peninsula.

"True, true," he said. God. He was an *uncle*. Well, of course he was Esme and Imogen's uncle, but he'd also been an uncle when he was only *eight*. He had a nephew. I bet Matthew would like him. They'd hang out together, maybe, and—

"Hello, my darling girl," said Grandpop. "Would you like a gummy? Robbie just gave me one. I feel nice and floaty."

"Robbie," I sighed before taking a slug of my drink. Marijuana was legal in our fair state, and you couldn't swing a cat without hitting a dispensary, but getting our elderly grandfather stoned . . .

"Grandpop deserves to get high," Robbie said. "Helps with his back pain, right, Pop?"

"Let's put it this way," Grandpop said. "It makes me care less about things like pain. Am I making sense? I feel smarter when I'm stoned. And funnier. Am I?"

Robbie laughed. "You definitely are," he said.

It was easy for me to fade into the background of my family. I'd been doing it all my life, after all. Tonight, I was grateful. My hands still trembled, and I couldn't keep a single thought in my head. How would I tell them? I had to tell them, though, didn't I? Did it have to be tonight? It probably did. Had Cynthia heard anything? If so, she was the type to tell everyone in the store. Destiny was not a concern, since she was a true and loyal person. Was Cynthia here? No, Addie never remembered to include her.

Winnie jerked her chin at me as a hello, opened the liquor cabinet and poured herself a finger or two of Woodford's Bourbon, then sat down in an easy chair to watch the rest of us. Of all my sisters, she'd probably be the most understanding. Or not. Or she'd say, "Jesus, Harlow, how could you *do* that? You abandoned your child!" Which I hadn't, of course, but there had been so many days when it felt that way.

I took another slug of margarita, hoping it would calm me down a little.

Lark came in from the kitchen, still wearing her scrubs, holding a giant burrito in one hand. She dropped a kiss on my cheek, smiled at Winnie and sat on the floor, stuffing half the burrito in her mouth. "I haven't eaten all day," she mumbled through the beans and rice, some of it falling from her mouth.

"Great," I said. "I mean, that's too bad." *Stay focused, Harlow.*

As Esme opened her presents, I picked up the torn wrapping paper and tucked it in a bag for recycling. Nicole bounced Imogen, told me Esme already had the Poppleton series so could I just return it myself? Addie filmed, photographed and posted. The sunset deepened, growing more intense, more flamboyant. Someone turned the gas fireplace on. Mom and Dad stood in the doorway, leaning into each other. Esme played with her graduation gifts; Imogen chewed on the corner of a box, then offered a chunk of wet cardboard to my mother.

"Thank you, precious," Mom said, holding it up to the light to admire it. "I love it." My God. She was Matthew's grandmother.

"Gerald, we need more grandchildren," Mom said. "Girls, Robbie, get on that."

My face flamed with heat, and my heart rolled and bucked.

"Pass," said Winnie.

"Maybe someday, when I'm not trembling with exhaustion," said Lark, who was lying on the floor, eyes closed.

"Okay," Robbie said. "As long as I don't have to raise anyone."

"Given that you're a child yourself," Winnie said, "please keep using condoms."

"Shall do, Winston."

"Windsor, idiot."

"Don't say 'condoms' in front of the girls," Addison hissed. "And try to be a better example for the girls, Robbie, and not such a slut."

"Don't say 'slut' in front of the girls," Robbie said, imitating her, then added in a normal voice, "I can't help it. Women are all over me like Tiny Tim on a Christmas ham."

"Like *E. coli* on room temperature beef," Lark added.

"Like Jean Valjean at a bakery," I said, easily tapping into the bookish part of my brain.

"Like shit on Velcro," Winnie said, making us all laugh.

"Can we bring the attention back to Esme?" Nicole said, her voice sharp.

Matthew. Matthew Rohan Patel. A beautiful name. Rohan was a kingdom in *The Lord of the Rings*, and the Riders of Rohan were some kick-ass warriors. I'd googled it at the store and found that it meant "ascending," and I loved that. Black curly hair, dark chocolate eyes, still gangly in that sweet teenage boy way. His smile was so pure, so perfect. I glanced at my phone. Still no text from him. One from Rosie, saying she was on her way. I wished she could teleport here right now.

I'm okay, I texted. You be safe. Love you.

Love you, too, Lolo.

"Snap out of it," Addison muttered as she set out an elaborate cake from Cottage Street Bakery. "This is Esme's night."

"Oh, wow, that cake is . . . um . . ." said Winnie, her eyes widening. I glanced, did a double take. Um . . .

"Beautiful, isn't it?" Addie said. "Geodes, because Esme loves them."

The pink frosted cake had three layers that split open, revealing a darker pink, rock candy interior, the split lined with gold piping. It looked . . . well, once you saw it, you couldn't unsee it.

"No one is thinking of geodes, Adds," Robbie said.

"What are you talking about?" Addie asked. "It's called a geode cake. Crystals? She makes them out of rock candy, dummy."

"Looks like my gynecological rotation," Lark said.

Nicole was holding Imogen in her arms, frowning in confusion. Dad's face was bright red, and he was bent over, wheezing with laughter.

"What are you all saying?" Addison asked. "What?"

"Sweetheart, the cake looks like a vagina," said Mom calmly.

"No it doesn't!" she yelped. "No! It's a geode cake! They're very popular!"

"I can see why!" Grandpop said, and I barked with laughter.

"Stop it!" Addie said. "You're ruining Esme's big day!"

"You know, Addison, you're one of those mothers everyone hates," Robbie said. "I mean, *we* love you. A little. For now, anyway. It's fading fast."

Then Esme walked up and, with one finger, scooped up some rock candy from the very center with her fingers and popped it in her mouth, which made Robbie cover his eyes and stagger back as the rest of us cried with laughter.

Would my son laugh at this, too? Did he have a good sense of humor?

"What's funny?" Esme asked, her teeth pink with sugar.

"Shit, you're all right," said Addison, sagging a little. "I can't believe I didn't see it."

The cake was delicious; we had to give it that. There were pink macarons as well, and after a few more rounds of gyno humor, we settled down.

I could picture Matthew here, standing next to Robbie, maybe blushing at all the girl-part references. I was going to have to tell them. Maybe the sooner the better. But no, I needed to calm down, to let this most incredible day feel a little more real.

Also, eighteen years is a long time to keep a human being a secret. After they knew, I would be a different person in the eyes of everyone here.

The girls ran around, shrieking on their sugar high, Esme pretending she couldn't catch her little sister. Grandpop was dozing in a recliner, hands folded on his stomach.

Robbie picked up his coat. "Gotta run," he said. "Hot date."

"Use a condom," Mom said, because she was that kind of mother.

"Yes, Mommy Dearest." Robbie caught my eye and grimaced.

"I have to go, too," said Lark with a yawn. "I need sleep."

"Me too," said Winnie. "Thanks, Addison, thanks, Nicole."

There. The decision had been taken out of my hands. Passive, yes, but I'd take it.

"Hold on," said Grandpop, lurching upright in the chair. "Aren't we going to talk about that boy?"

My eyes widened, and I shook my head slightly, but Grandpop didn't see.

"Did anyone else meet him? The young man in the store today? Or was it just me? It was today, wasn't it? I always have the hardest time remembering time when I'm stoned."

"Don't say 'stoned' in front of the girls," Nicole admonished.

"It *was* today, right, Harlow? When your son came in? He looks just like you, aside from the hair color. So wonderful, having another member of our family! Now, where are my shoes?"

I lunged for the shoes, then handed them to Grandpop. "Not right now, okay?" I whispered.

"Oh, dear," he said. "Was I not supposed to say anything?"

"What are you talking about, Dad?" my father asked.

"Her son," Grandpop said. I cringed. Grandpop noticed, then said, "I mean, nothing! Nothing yet, I should say. And certainly not my news to tell. Harlow can tell you when she's ready. I should stop talking, shouldn't I? Who's driving me?"

"Tell us what, Harlow?" Mom asked, her eyes narrowing.

"Whoopsie. I seem to have let the *cat* out of the *bag*," Grandpop said.

The room had gone very quiet, and I felt the gaze of my family settling on me like lead.

"Maybe the girls could go to bed," I said, my mouth dry. "I do have some news."

"Bedtime takes at *least* an hour," Addison said. "They both need baths and stories and fifteen minutes of Bach's cello suites."

"Again," said Robbie. "The kind of mother we all hate."

"Harlow." My mother's voice was both hard and scared. I opened my mouth but nothing came out. For the second time that day, my vision grayed. I reached out and grabbed the back of a chair to steady myself. Took a deep breath, then another. The grayness disappeared.

"I had a baby in college," I said. "I put him up for adoption."

No one moved. No one even breathed. Well, except for the girls, who were now smooshing macarons in each other's hair, laughing merrily.

"Girls, bedtime," said Nicole. She swooped Imogen under one arm, Esme under another, and hauled them out of the room.

I swallowed. Wished I'd had another margarita or one of Grandpop's gummies. The wind gusted against the house, the only noise I could hear.

"You didn't have a baby in college," Mom said. "Of course you didn't." She shook her head at the absurdity of the idea.

"A baby?" Dad said.

"*I'm* the only one who had a baby," Addison said, sinking to the floor next to Lark. "Me and Nicole. How can *you* have a baby?"

"Sperm meets egg," Robbie said. "That's how."

"Let her talk!" barked Winnie, and everyone shut up.

Well, I had their attention now, didn't I?

"I had a baby in college," I said again, straightening up a bit. My son had found me today, and I was over the moon about it. Mostly. "Summer of my freshman year. I . . . I chose adoption. And today he . . . found me."

"Holy shit," Robbie murmured. "You are so in trouble."

There was suddenly a roar of questions. *You never, you didn't, why would you, never said, don't believe, can't believe, should've, would've, could've.* The urge to flee was wicked strong, but as Grandpop said, the cat was out of the bag. Or rather, the baby.

"Okay, I'm going to say this once," I said loudly, trying to sound in control. "So shush, everyone." Addie was crying. Lark held her hand. Mom's eyes were too wide and her face was white, and for once, Dad wasn't paying attention to her, just staring at me, his face slack. Winnie looked like she'd just swallowed a brick, and my idiot brother rubbed his hands together in anticipation.

Nicole came back into the room—she must have thrown the girls into their beds like Tom Brady landing a touchdown pass. I felt a warm, dry hand in mine. Grandpop.

I swallowed. "Okay. Well, when I was a freshman in college, I got pregnant. It was November. I decided to . . . place him for adoption, which I did, with a very nice couple from California. He's seventeen, almost eighteen now, and he came into the store today."

"Handsome boy," said Grandpop. "Nice manners, too."

"I didn't know he was coming," I went on. "So it was quite a shock. I know you all have questions, but that's . . . that's what's going on with me. I met my son today. I'll see him again soon. But for now, I'm . . . I'm leaving. Sorry. Sorry for the shock."

With that, I left.

FOUR

MONICA

Monica Walker Patel ended the call with her husband and sank to the floor in their vast bedroom. The California sun streamed through the windows with ruthless golden light, but Monica saw nothing.

Matthew had found his birth mother. Without discussion, without a word, without a hint. He'd just walked into that woman's place of work and blown up her world, his world, their world. Nothing would ever be the same again.

Why? She and Sanjay had always been so open about his adoption. Way back when, Harlow Smith had said that when he turned eighteen—less than two months from now—Matthew would be welcome to write to the adoption agency and get her contact information. That would've been the right way. The kinder way.

But showing up at her place of work? Tricking the entire family by choosing Cape Cod for their vacation so he could pull off this stunt? What about Meena? How would the summer be for his little sister as he discovered his birth mother? It was completely selfish. What about Harlow? Sanjay had said she'd fainted. Fainted! What if she had other children by now? Didn't Matthew think about these things?

Not for the first time, Monica wondered what other secrets her son was keeping.

And Sanjay was being the nice parent, as usual, which irked her even more. "It's done, my love," he said. "Now we will make the best of it."

Their marriage had always been a little . . . lopsided. She was the serious one, the rule-maker and breadwinner. As an IT security specialist at one of the biggest companies of its kind, she worked long, draining hours and earned a very comfortable salary.

Sanjay, a fourth-grade teacher, was the more present parent. He and the kids got home at the same time, spent the afternoons together, Sanjay doing pickups and drop-offs for the kids' extracurriculars. They made dinner together, and he oversaw the start of homework. His tight-knit family lived within ten miles of them—his parents, two older brothers, older sister, their spouses and children. Every weekend, it seemed, there was a celebration of some kind, which was wonderful, if exhausting.

Her family . . . not so much. Her parents and sister lived in Idaho and viewed her as an oddity, from her attendance at Stanford to her PhD from Caltech to her marrying an Indian man. "Won't it be hard?" her mother had asked when she told them she was dating Sanjay Patel, a fellow student at Stanford. "Will his parents accept you?" (Sita and Ishan most certainly had, with great warmth and enthusiasm; more than her own parents had shown Sanjay at first, anyway.)

And then, adopting Matthew. "You should try for your own baby a little longer," Mom had said.

"An adopted baby *will* be my own baby," Monica had said.

"You know what I mean," Mom had said, the hurt in her voice loud and clear. And then after the adoption, there had been that "told you so" tone every time Monica told her mother that Matthew was going through something. She quickly learned to paint a rosy picture rather than have her mother sigh knowingly.

They had been young when they adopted Matthew . . . well, youngish. Thirty. Monica had always known her girl parts were faulty. When she was seventeen and her periods were so painful she would pass out in class, she finally went to a specialist and was diagnosed with severe endometriosis. And because she was a science geek, she learned everything there was to know about it. Like an evil fungus, it grew and spread throughout her pelvis and was likely to cause at least some difficulties in getting and staying pregnant. By the time she was twenty-four, an ultrasound showed that one of her ovaries was choked off completely, the other on its way.

Being a planner, she figured adoption would be the most likely way for her to become a mom. Sanjay had known this well before they were even engaged, and said he'd always wanted to be a father, however that came about. Infant adoption? Sure. Foster-to-adopt? Sure. Foreign adoption? "Whatever you want, my queen." So carefree, so easygoing, the yin to her yang.

She and Sanjay had been serious from the start and, given her odds of pregnancy, decided not to use birth control six months after they began sleeping together. By the time they got married, Monica had never gotten pregnant. Not even for a few weeks. *Sorry,* her ovaries and uterus seemed to be saying. *We just can't. We're exhausted.*

And so she and Sanjay registered on adoption sites, were cleared by social workers. They took classes and read books about adoption. Their family and friends and colleagues were interviewed. There were several home visits. It could take years, they were warned. It might well never happen, especially with an infant. She and Sanjay decided that if they didn't have a child by the time they were thirty-five, they'd accept their childless state and breed golden retrievers or live in Nepal and Venice, Japan and Ecuador.

Instead, a year after they'd posted their video at half a dozen agencies, they were informed that someone wanted to talk to them.

Harlow, a first-year college student in Colorado.

A few months later, they were parents. Matthew Rohan Patel, her joy, her pride, her little mystery. A child who was deeply loved not just by her and Sanjay, but by the entire Patel family and, yes, hers too. Her sister, age twenty-four, already had three daughters by the time they got Matthew, but they welcomed him. Though her dad just couldn't stop introducing Matthew as "my adopted grandson," he loved Matthew, the only boy in the family, and took him fishing and taught him to use a drill.

Matthew was loved. He was *adored*, even. She and Sanjay had thoroughly researched adoption before, during and after the process. They read the books that told them their child would always feel the wound of his birth mother giving him away, would always have certain insecurities and fears they couldn't understand. They joined online and in-person groups for adoptive families and made sure Matthew had friends who'd also been adopted. His adoption was discussed in positive terms, and his feelings were validated when he felt sad or lonely for his birth mother. When Matthew was twelve and seemed depressed and angry, they found him a therapist who specialized in adopted kids.

But in terms of *love*, the fact that he was adopted made no difference . . . except, of course, it did to him. He was not Monica's biological child, and all the research said that no matter how good a mom she was, she would never be enough. Fathers didn't seem to be so accused in the literature.

Now Matthew had gone and found Harlow behind their backs, and the whole family would have to deal with it. It was as if he'd shoved his parents and sister off a cliff, and he'd done it with a smile.

It had been a beautiful reunion, Sanjay had reported. Tears, hugging, shock and wonder. Even he had cried a little.

Monica would have liked to have been there. Good God, she wished she had been. Of course Sanjay, the favorite parent, had been the anointed one, while she was three thousand miles away and completely in the dark. The familiar surge of anger and love for her teenage son stabbed at her. Her boy, her beautiful, precious son, had not included her in one of the most important moments of his life.

The little shit.

"Mommy?"

Monica dashed her tears away. Wonderful. Now she had to tell Meena that her big brother had found his other family. Or maybe she should make Matthew do that. After all, Monica had no *fucking* idea why this had happened now.

"Hey, pumpkin," she said. "Guess what? We're going to the Cape a little early."

"Hooray!" said Meena, who, at twelve, was still Monica's sweet little angel. She skipped into Monica's arms for a hug, and Monica dropped a kiss on her head. She caught a glimpse of them in the mirror—both with black hair (though Monica was going gray and wondering if she should start coloring it—not only was she a woman in tech, she was middle-aged at forty-seven, practically dead by industry standards). She and Meena were on the small side. Meena and Matthew even looked a bit alike, though his hair was curly and Meena's was straight, like Monica's. Sanjay's hair was wavy. Monica was the only one in the family with blue eyes. No one ever asked if Matthew was adopted, something that pleased him unless it irritated him. Depended on the day.

"Let's pack, okay?" she said to her daughter. "I'll call the school and tell them you're playing hooky for the last week."

"Okay. Can we make pancakes for supper? Since it's girls' night?" Meena's big eyes sparkled up at Monica, knowing the answer was just a technicality.

"Absolutely. And we can watch whatever you want on TV."

"*America's Next Top Model*?" Meena asked.

"Except for that. Please. We Patels have standards." She didn't mention that the show was one of her guilty pleasures. (She watched it on the computer, but only when she had insomnia. Which she'd had a lot lately.)

She'd always prided herself on knowing when Matthew needed something, when he was edgy or down or bursting to tell her something. Not this time. She hadn't sensed a thing. She regularly checked her kids' computers, had blocks on porn and extremist sites. But Matthew had erased his search history, or used a VPN, or the disallow feature, or had gone incognito, or had done any one of a hundred things she knew people could do to cover up their internet tracks.

At least he listened to her sometimes.

Meena trotted off to finish a paper on the National Parks, and Monica went down the hall into Matthew's bedroom. They'd redone it when he started high school, erasing the little boy feel the room had once had, with its Pokémon cards and *Star Wars* Lego projects. Now, wooden planks were mounted on the navy blue wall behind his bed, which was queen-size, not twin. A denim duvet cover, red beanbag chairs, a desk with a brown leather chair.

She sat on the bed and smoothed the pillow. Matthew had been so excited when they'd done the room over. It was maybe the last time he had seemed to really enjoy time with her. When all the major work had been done, she shooed him from the room, straightened up, made the bed, moved the desk, arranged the bookshelves, then invited him in for the reveal.

"Wow, Mom! I love it!" he'd said, hugging her. Still her little boy. Not the sneak who'd just sabotaged their vacation.

For the past eight or nine years, the Patels had gone away for the summer. Because he was a teacher, Sanjay had the time off. And because Monica earned so much, they could go just about anywhere for six weeks or two months. Well, Sanjay and the kids could. They took turns choosing the place they'd stay for the summer. This year, Matthew had chosen Cape Cod. His private boys' school finished earlier than Meena's public school, so he and Sanjay had left six days ago and had visited NYU, Columbia, Dartmouth and Harvard before going to the Cape a bit early.

Technically, Monica had four weeks of vacation plus comp time, but there was an unspoken rule that Guardian Security employees didn't take those weeks consecutively. Peter Bidwell, her direct boss and the owner of the company, was the only exception, taking six weeks each summer, something Caroline Xiao, the only other female in the department and Monica's work wife, had discussed on the rare occasion they went out for a drink to commiserate about the boys' club. The poker nights they were never invited to. The golf games with prospective clients, even though Caroline had taken golf lessons for years for just this eventuality.

And so, while Sanjay and the kids enjoyed two months of vacation in Glacier National Park or on Assateague Island or the Upper Peninsula of Michigan, Monica would fly out for five or

six days, then go back home to Pleasanton for a week or two to
work and catch up, repeat as necessary, then fly back to be with
the family for their last week of vacation.

Cape Cod, which had seemed like such a delightful place to
spend the summer, was now overhung with a sense of foreboding.
Meeting his birth mother . . . that was fine. It was important.
Necessary to Matthew's development as a person, the answer to
the many questions he would doubtlessly ask. But the secretive
way he'd gone about doing it, the fact that it had already happened and she'd been completely left out of the process . . . that
hurt. Deeply.

Her Apple watch vibrated with a text. Sanjay.

Are you doing okay, babe? I'm so very sorry it happened this
way. Do you want to talk? I have already spoken very firmly to
Matthew for stunning everyone, including Harlow, and he's feeling
appropriately ashamed. He's going to call you later, but I wanted
to touch base first. I love you, and you're a wonderful mother,
Moni. Everyone knows that. Everything will be okay. Just a slight
adjustment in our mindset for the summer, right?

She could almost hear his voice. Sanjay was a good husband,
a *wonderful* husband. Steady, handsome, loyal, loving, intelligent.
But he had a way of reducing any crisis to such a calm and rea-
sonable state that it could be infuriating. It was one of the things
she loved best about him, and one of the things she hated. Problem, solution. Problem, solution. "Water under the bridge" was
one of his favorite sayings. He rarely got angry. Why would he?
He had a great life. He worked hard as a teacher, and she was in
awe of how well he did his job.

But she was the one who carried the burden of providing

for the family financially, faced the pressures of a career based around security crises. Taking a two-year leave of absence when Matthew had come home had set back her career, a sacrifice she was glad to make. When Meena was born, she took her three months' paid maternity leave, but Sanjay's generous, state-funded parental leave made him much better positioned to be the parent at home. So she handled her job, juggled business travel and weekly emergencies in internet security, stayed on top of a field that could change by the week, and dealt with the reality that she had to be better, smarter and faster than any man in the same position. Everyone was competing at Guardian, and Peter Bidwell liked it that way. "Keeps you hungry," he'd say when announcing bonuses or potential promotions. Monica rather hated him, but the money was too good to turn down.

Sanjay, meanwhile, was a rock star at his school. Parents requested him when their kids were in *kindergarten*. He'd been named California Teacher of the Year two years ago, and the Patels couldn't venture out in public without kids—some of them now grown—or parents stopping them to say what a great person he was, how wonderful that year of school had been, how their kid had learned so much.

Then they'd look at her and give a nod. That was it. A nod. No one acknowledged that she was the one who supported them because a teacher's salary would not cover the cost of living in California, let alone their beautiful home, two electric cars, private school tuition and college funds for the kids, summer vacations wherever they liked. None of Sanjay's fans asked about the pressures of her job, the late hours she'd have to pull if something went wrong, the way she never had a true weekend. It seemed that no one, not even Sanjay, really wanted to know.

Being a fourth-grade teacher had its burdens, of course. He

was enriching their young minds. He had to endure active shooter drills, and she knew he'd die for those kids in such a hellish scenario. The administration could be ridiculously shortsighted and even stupid, changing policies at the whim of an angry Karen or the threat of a lawsuit. He worked during the school hours and after school as well. But he was home by three thirty every day and got to spend more time with their kids than she did. Those summers off. The holidays and breaks. She could swear the school calendar had only three weeks a year when school was in session all five days.

And Sanjay was also Matthew's favorite parent. How could it be otherwise? Even though she'd taken two years off to make sure he felt secure and safe as a baby, even though she'd worked half-time from home (a special sort of hell) until Meena was in kindergarten to be present for both kids. Even though she tried so hard to be there for him, to let him know he could tell her anything, to tell him she was proud of him, to be sure he knew she loved his company, to leave notes under the kids' pillows when she had to be away and did all the holiday shopping and bought all the presents . . . still, Sanjay came out as the hero parent. Mom . . . Mom was kind of a pain in the ass. A great provider, but not someone Matthew wanted to hang out with. The little ingrate. Yet here she was, sitting on his bed in order to feel closer to him, smoothing his pillow like he was Harry Styles and she was a teenage girl.

At least Meena liked her, and the thought made Monica feel guilty, because Meena was her biological child, and she didn't ever want Matthew to think that because he wasn't genetically related to them he was loved any less. And she didn't love him less. She just *liked* Meena a hell of a lot more.

Matthew was pushing it these days. For the past three years, he'd gone from a pretty good kid to a problem child. Broken cur-fews, shoplifting (even though he had a generous allowance), cut-ting classes, even getting drunk at least twice, lying about where he was to the point where she swiped his phone while he was in the shower and installed a tracking device he wouldn't be able to see.

And now, this. This huge disruption to their whole family's life, making a decision that would affect them all with no regard for anyone but himself. Not even his birth mother.

It was too much. But Monica would have to get her feelings under control, or at least fake it for Meena's sake. She'd have to wait until she could ask Matthew directly what the hell he'd been thinking, doing it now, this way, when in just six weeks, he'd turn eighteen and could've done it the *right* way. But she'd have to tamp down her anger and not show her hurt and be calm and happy so he wouldn't feel defensive or misunderstood or unloved, not to drive him away when, in just a year, he'd be leaving anyway.

Sometimes Monica just wanted to be alone in the house and howl. For an hour. Until her vocal cords gave out.

The phone rang, and the screen showed a photo of her beau-tiful boy, smiling, his dimple showing. At least he'd had the de-cency to FaceTime instead of text. She slid her finger over the screen to accept the call and forced a big smile.

"Hello, sweetheart! How are you? What an incredible day for you! Tell me everything."

Motherhood. Not for sissies.

FIVE

HARLOW

Getting away from my family was easier said than done, since my grandfather lived in the same house as I did. Also, my parents were hot on my tail. Four minutes after I got home, the three of them were knocking on my apartment door. I let them in. After all, I owed my parents an explanation. Grandpop, too. No point putting off the inevitable anymore.

Ollie pranced around, delighted by the visit. Mom's hair, curly like my own, was standing out at all angles, and Dad's eyes were ringed with white, his lips invisible since his mouth was clamped so tight.

"Have a seat," I said.

Grandpop smiled as Oliver put his front paws against his knee, then put his arm around me.

"It'll be all right, sweetheart," he said. "You're still you." Then he lowered his voice to a whisper. "But I have to go to bed now. This is between you and your parents, and besides, I took another gummy, and I'm not sure I know where we are right now." He looked at my parents. "You go easy on her," he said. "She's my number one gal."

My parents didn't answer.

"I'll be right back," I told Mom and Dad, and led Grandpop

downstairs to his bedroom. I had laid his pajamas on the neatly made bed this morning, as I did every day.

"Oh, perfect!" he said. "Thanks, honey, I've got it from here. Just set the door alarm so I don't wander off."

"Will do. Love you, Grandpop." I kissed his cheek.

"Don't tell anyone," he said, "but you're my favorite."

My eyes filled. "Thanks. You're mine, too."

He chucked me under the chin and sat on his bed, bending to take off his shoes.

My sweet, dotty grandpa had once again said just the words I needed to hear. I took a deep breath and felt a teeny bit braver.

I set the alarm—I'd installed it last year when Grandpop started taking nighttime strolls, and it would send me an alert if he opened the door. Back up to my apartment I went, feeling like I was walking the green mile.

My parents were parked on the couch like two statues, ignoring my dog, who was lying in front of them, belly exposed, waiting for one of them to rub it.

"I would prefer that we sleep on this," I said, clasping my hands in front of me.

"Absolutely not," said my mother. "Harlow, you can't lob a grenade like that and just leave."

"Well, I can. And I did." But I sat in my beloved blue chair like the obedient child I'd always been. Oliver jumped up with me, nuzzling his nose under my arm until I stroked his fur. My heart was thudding.

Dad took a deep breath. "Tell us, Harlow."

I nodded. "It's not a long story," I lied. "I . . . I was young and stupid, I got pregnant and, after thinking about it for a few weeks, talked to an adoption agency. They helped me find a nice couple, and I . . . I stayed in Boulder that summer, if you remember, and had the baby, and . . . that's it."

Mom began to sob.

"We can't *believe* you went through this alone," Dad said.

"Right."

"What's his name?" Mom asked, wiping her eyes.

"Matthew. Matthew Rohan Patel. His father is Indian—they moved here when he was young. His mother is white. She works in tech. Or she did. He's a teacher."

"Go on," said Dad, his voice uncharacteristically stern.

"There's not a lot to tell. It was a closed adoption. That was my choice. The Patels are great. I . . . I thought they'd make fantastic parents." I was nodding, willing them to agree with my choices.

"Who got you pregnant?" Mom asked, her voice shrill. "You weren't assaulted, were you?"

"No, Mom, I wasn't raped."

"So *this* is why you didn't come home that summer," Mom said. "You didn't have a great internship. You had a baby. A baby! You hid that from us!"

"Yes. I did." I nodded, started to bite a nail, then stopped. "He was born on July twenty-fifth. The Patels were in the room with me. And then . . . you know . . . they took him." My lower eyelid quivered, but I held it together. No need to go back to that moment, the worst in my life. I cleared my throat. "So anyway, Matthew"—it felt so strange and wonderful to say his name—"was touring colleges on the East Coast, and I guess his family decided to rent a place here on the Cape, and . . . well . . . he came into the store today. To meet me." I was nodding again and forced myself to stop. "I'm not a hundred percent clear on the details yet."

There was a long silence. The clock ticked loudly from the kitchen. I heard Grandpop's toilet flush downstairs.

"Jesus God in heaven," Dad said. "Harlow, why the *hell* didn't you tell us?"

"Yes, Harlow," said my mother, her voice thick with despair. "You went through this *alone*, honey? Why? We would have supported you no matter what. Were we such awful parents that you couldn't confide in us? I can't believe you kept this from us. My heart is completely shattered!"

I nodded, trying not to cry. Parental disapproval was something I'd only encountered once before, when I dropped out of law school.

"I thought we were closer than that," Dad said, sending a dart into my heart.

More nodding. "We were close," I said, trying to stop the bobblehead action. "We are close."

"No, we're not," Mom snapped. "You had a *child* and you never said a word, Harlow. That is not close."

"You guys are great. Um . . . I just didn't want to disappoint you. I felt really stupid, getting pregnant by accident."

"It *was* stupid," Mom said. "I'm *sure* I told you all about birth control. I put a condom on a *zucchini* so you kids would know how to do it. Didn't I?"

"You did. Yep," I said, starting to nod before I caught myself. "You did tell me, Mom, and we used condoms, but neither one of us was very experienced." Ollie nudged me, my only ally in the room.

"I can see why you wouldn't want to tell your mother," Dad said. "But Harlow, baby, come on. You and I have a special bond."

"She's my firstborn, Gerald," Mom snapped. "I have a special bond with her, too!"

"We all have special bonds," I said. "Please don't fight."

"We can fight if we want to!" Mom said, her voice teetering on hysteria. "But we were always here for you, damn it, Harlow." She buried her face in a ragged tissue.

"Were you really so scared of your parents that you went through this huge life event with no one? Was that to prove a point, Harlow?" Dad asked. "And if so, what? What could possibly be gained by that?"

"We would have helped," Mom said. "You didn't have to give him away. We could have helped you raise him. My God, Gerald, we've been grandparents for seventeen years!"

I took a breath that bordered on a sob. "Um . . . listen, it's been a day. I can't . . . I have a lot to think about, and I don't want you to sit here and yell at me or each other. I'm thirty-five now. I got pregnant a few months after I turned seventeen."

"Wouldn't you have been eighteen?" Dad asked.

"She skipped third grade, Gerald," Mom said. "Will you ever remember that?" She turned back to me. "How could you keep us out of this? No matter what you decided, you shouldn't have gone through this alone."

"I wasn't alone. I had Rosie."

Dad threw his hands up.

"Rosie? Rosie? Your *friend*?" Mom asked. "Your college *roommate*? Is Rosie somehow better than the mother who has loved you since conception? You've kept this secret all these years . . . why? How could you do that to me? To us? We deserved better."

I swallowed. "I love you both very, very much, but you're kind of missing the point."

"What *is* the point, then, Harlow?" Dad asked. "We're in shock. We just learned we have a grandson, a grandson who could've been raised by *us*. All of us. You know that. Instead, you made all these decisions without so much as a goddamn phone call."

"You know what?" I said, abruptly angry. "I met my *son* today. I've thought of him every single day of his life. Today, I saw him. I hugged him. Your feelings are going to have to stand in line, because right now, mine are more important. So thanks for coming over, but now you need to go."

With that, Oliver and I showed them to the door.

Once my parents had left, I stood a moment, unsure of what to do. Call a friend? But which friend? Rosie was the only one I could really talk to about this, and she was somewhere in Asia.

Most of my friends were also my sisters, so they were out. Destiny? She was definitely a friend, but also worked for me, so maybe that wasn't fair. Lillie Silva, maybe? We played on the same trivia team, and she was lovely. Once, years before, I'd gone to her for a pap smear, and she'd asked, "How many times have you been pregnant?" I was shocked by her question, but figured a midwife could tell. All I said was, "Once."

"Full term?"

"Yes." She didn't ask anything else and never mentioned it again, and I loved her for it. She *was* a friend . . . not a super-close friend, but a friend still. The truth was, I didn't have a wide circle. I mean, I had a lot of people I liked well enough. Regular bookstore customers, a few friends from high school—Megan, who lived on the Cape. We didn't see each other much, since she'd had twins a few years ago. Grady, I guess, since he was back now and I'd known him literally all my life, and Alexa, who was in New York. But Rosie was the best friend I'd ever had. A soulmate friend.

I took Oliver's leash off the hook by the door. He sprang from the couch, looking like a flying squirrel in midair, joy in every molecule of his body.

"Yes," I said. "It's true. We're taking a walk." Because if any-one ever needed a walk to clear their head, it was me. I grabbed the flashlight I kept by the door, pulled on a Sox cap and went down the creaky stairs. Checked on Grandpop, saw that he was fast asleep and went out the door.

I looked at my phone yet again in case Matthew had texted me. Not yet. Messages from all four of my siblings, as well as Des-tiny, expressing concern. There was also one from Cynthia, who asked if the store would be open tomorrow or if "your fainting problems" would force us to be closed again. I answered hers with only We will be open, then assured Destiny I was okay. The rest I left for later.

I hadn't expected my parents to be *angry* with me. I mean, I hadn't had a lot of time to picture how they'd react, but . . . well. Clearing my head meant not thinking about those things. And I was good at that, wasn't I? That's how I got through my twenties and half my thirties, after all.

Ollie and I walked down Main Street, now quiet, since tour-ism season hadn't really begun. I wanted to sit somewhere and breathe the good salt air and not run into anyone I knew, which would be hard. The light tended to linger at the edges in June, unwilling to give over to night, so it wasn't full dark yet. I went past Preservation Hall, which had benches in the vast, pretty yard, but it was closed after dark. The gorgeous Memorial Garden was a little too visible, so I kept going. Across the street, Winslow's Tavern glowed with lights—people were on the patio, even though the night was getting chilly. I walked faster in case anyone I knew saw me—I was a regular there and knew the whole staff.

Ollie and I continued past the quaint little shops, turned past Wellfleet Marketplace and headed down Bank Street, where my parents' gallery sat in quiet grace. I could have gone to the courtyard behind the gallery, which had a garden, benches and a view of the water, but given that I was irked with them, I passed. This was the second-most important day of my life, after all. They might have waited on the guilt trip.

Oliver trotted happily at my side, his feathery tail swishing in delight. Like me, he was a fixture in Wellfleet, but tonight, we were lucky, and no one stopped to pet him or say hello.

We headed for Uncle Tim's Bridge, one of the most photographed spots in Wellfleet. In the olden days, the folks from South Wellfleet would come to regular Wellfleet via this bridge, and no one saw a good reason to change that. Uncle Tim, as the town had fondly called him, had been a shopkeeper some two hundred years ago. The bridge stretched out over Duck Creek to Hamblen Island, its official name. It was a rare night that you didn't see a blue heron stalking fish along the edge of the marsh, a Canada goose or swan gliding silently on the water. The tide was high, and I heard little splashes, indicating a school of fish had come in from the bay. Oliver snuffled happily, his ears alert, nails clicking on the wood.

Once on the island, I kept walking. The trails were well-worn and clear even at night, the sand easily visible against the dark of trees. My footsteps were soft, and Ollie stopped every few yards to sniff. Otherwise, there was just the shushing of the wind and the occasional splash of a small wave.

Here. A bench that would do nicely for a little thinking. I sat, unclipped Oliver's leash and told him to be a good boy, then watched as he trotted off to explore and, if he was lucky and I was not, find a dead bird to roll in.

There was a tiny slice of moon in the sky, so thin I didn't notice it at first. A seagull called and was answered. I inhaled slowly.

Thinking about Matthew wasn't new, but it wasn't as if I thought, *I wonder what my son's doing.* It was more like he was an ingrained part of me, like my hand or my heart. Everything about me seemed to be because of him, as if my DNA had been rewritten during my pregnancy. The fact that I hadn't told anyone about him had been self-preservation. My family, especially my mother, would have picked apart every experience and feeling I'd had during those nine months, sucking them dry until they were dust.

Of course, there were days when Matthew's memory stabbed me like ragged shards of glass . . . I tended to avoid babies for that reason, even opting not to visit Addie and Nicole in the hospital when they had theirs. Matthew was the most important person in my life, the one I loved the most, even more than Lark or Winnie or Robbie. I was his *mother.* I didn't raise my child, but I was still his mother, and the fact was both indescribably precious and painful. I had hoped he would contact me someday, but I sure hadn't pictured him walking into my store unannounced.

"First Mama," he had called me. God, that was so kind! So affectionate and even playful. I hoped he'd like me. I hoped he would forgive me. When I was pregnant, I had read hundreds of articles written by people who were adopted. The questions. The biological yearning to connect. Sometimes, the anger and feelings of betrayal, too. *You didn't want me.*

There were also plenty of articles about adopted kids loving their birth parents and *not* being tormented. Some had reasons for not wanting to find their biological family. But speaking generally, it did seem that many adopted kids wanted to meet their birth parents. Especially their mothers, who had carried them and given birth to them. It wasn't that they were looking for a replacement. Just answers.

I would give them. I'd been waiting to give them. Dreading it, too. I supposed I should check with Monica and Sanjay and learn what he already knew.

I had missed them, too. For the last half of my pregnancy, Sanjay and Monica and I had Skyped and emailed and talked on the phone almost daily. They'd been . . . well, like the most wonderful older siblings a person could have. They'd cared about my feelings and told me they would understand if I changed my mind. And they'd been in the room when Matthew was born and my heart was destroyed.

For a second, it felt like I was seventeen again, alone in a near-empty dorm the summer after my first year of college, awkward and clumsy, my body not my own. Once again, I could feel the ache in my back, constant since the fifth month. My hair sticking to my sweaty neck, my distant toes. The ridiculousness I felt taking a shower in the echoing dorm bathroom. Lumbering across the vast CU Boulder campus to my summer job, where I would slide into a windowless room and answer the phone and file in the financial aid department, a bit of a freak with my belly.

Matthew. They had kept the name. More tears flooded my eyes.

"Harlow?" said a voice, and I yelped in fright. "Sorry. It's Grady."

"Grady! You scared me." I dashed a hand across my eyes, clicked the flashlight back on. It was indeed Grady, my trivia teammate and former classmate, now a marine biologist.

He flinched from the harsh light in his eyes, but only said "Sorry" again. I turned off the flashlight. "I saw Oliver and thought he might've run off, so I was going to bring him to your house. I didn't know you were here."

"Oh. That's nice of you." Oliver jumped up next to me and

shoved his wet muzzle in my ear. I put my arm around him. "Are you working?"

"Yeah. Studying the loss of oceanic nitrogen deposits from the creek to see how it affects the sediment of the ocean floor."

"Same," I said.

"Really?"

"No. Not really, Grady. No one studies that stuff except you, brainiac."

"Oh. A joke, then." He had always been on the somber side, more so since he'd returned last fall, three-year-old in tow, divorced, looking older than he was. Only during our trivia games did Gray seem to smile. And sometimes at the bookstore with his daughter, Luna, during Story Time with Grandpop, our most popular event.

"Want to sit down?" I asked.

"You seem sad," he said at the same time.

"I do?"

"Yes." He sat next to me. "Were you worried about Oliver?"

"Oh, no. He wasn't lost. I let him off the leash so he could explore."

"Got it."

We sat in silence for a minute. Grady was good people, and I'd known him since elementary school. We'd been lab partners and friendly academic rivals in high school. We'd even gone to the prom together as friends. He went to Harvard and then MIT, becoming a marine biologist, working in Mexico and Texas.

Though his daughter was only four, she could read already and wasn't shy. I liked talking to her about books as Grady watched, always in the background, the kind of person you might not invite to a party but it was always nice to see.

A lot like me, now that I thought of it.

A bird called, a trembling, sweet sound. "Screech owl?" I asked.

"Yep," Grady confirmed. "It uses its whole body when it calls. Looks like it's shivering."

"We had one in the big tree in my parents' backyard when I was a kid," I said. "I tried to tame it by leaving it chunks of raw hot dogs."

"Did it work?" he asked.

"It did not." I stroked Oliver's head. He put his paws on my legs and yawned. The screech owl called again and was answered. My hands were cold.

"I met my son today," I said.

Grady's head turned toward me, but I couldn't see his expression, thanks to the dark. He didn't say anything.

"I gave him up for adoption when I was in college. He's seventeen. Almost eighteen now."

Grady was silent for a minute, then, "Wow."

"Yeah."

Another call from the screech owl. "Are you okay?" Grady asked.

There was a sudden lump in my throat. Had anyone else asked that today? Certainly no one in my family. I cleared my throat. "I'm not a hundred percent sure."

We sat there another minute, listening to the owl, the gentle lapping of the tide. It was getting chilly, but the sky was so deep and beautiful, I didn't want to go.

"What's his name, your son?" Grady asked.

"Matthew," I whispered.

Grady shifted, and then, hesitantly, put his arm around me. "Big day for you."

I gave a laugh that sounded a lot like a sob. "That's one way of putting it."

It was not unpleasant, sitting here with my sort-of friend. I didn't know much about Grady's last fifteen years, and he didn't know much about mine, but I appreciated that arm around me more than I could say. I guessed that Grady Byrne knew a thing or two about heartbreak and devastation. The broken part of me sensed the broken part of him this night, here in the dark and quiet.

In another minute, I would start bawling. "Well," I said, standing up abruptly. "Guess I'll head back." I switched on the light, breaking the gentle dark with its coldness.

"Want me to walk you home?" he asked.

"No, but thanks, Gray." Somewhere in high school, I'd started calling him that. It beat Gravy, which had been his middle-school nickname.

He nodded and stood as well. "See you around."

"Yeah. Your book should be in by the end of the week, by the way."

"I'll stop by."

I started down the path, then stopped and turned back to him. "You're the first person I told," I said. "About my son. Outside of my family, that is."

He nodded. "Well. Thank you. And, uh . . . congratulations."

I stood another moment, then gave a nod, and Oliver and I headed off.

SIX

CYNTHIA

News trickled down to Cynthia that the reason for Harlow's melodramatic faint was that she'd had a secret baby who was now a teenager. Destiny had filled Cynthia in (with Harlow's permission, she was quick to say). This irked Cynthia, because she was supposedly family—not that anyone but Uncle Robert treated her that way. It was so annoying.

Harlow *herself* was annoying. For years and years, Cynthia had heard via Louisa, Uncle Robert's wife and Harlow's grandmother, how *smart* Harlow was. How *helpful*, how *sweet*. Harlow skipped a grade! Harlow got a perfect score on the SAT! Harlow got a full scholarship! Harlow was going to law school!

First, it was as if Harlow were the only child who'd ever been born. Cynthia's own mother had been proud of Cynthia, but bragging was uncouth. Besides, so what if Harlow was book smart? She'd dropped out of law school and come crawling home (although, to be fair, Cynthia had come crawling here to Cape Cod, too).

Second, having Harlow's "son" breeze into the store and cause a scene . . . honestly, they could have picked somewhere else for the reunion. Oh, and Harlow just deciding the store was closed, like Cynthia was just some clerk and not a quarter owner? Good-bye, sales for the day! The little trio could've gone, who knew, maybe up the stairs to Harlow's apartment? Which would've been a perfect place for Cynthia to live, but Harlow got here first.

The day after the boy had come in and Harlow fainted, the bookstore was full at 10:01, because someone in the Smith family (Addison, probably) had blabbed. Everyone wanted to see the long-lost prince—Matthew, such a common name—and talk to Harlow. It was a wonder they didn't throw her a baby shower. So what. She'd put her child up for adoption. Big deal, he came to find her. It happened all the time. There was even an irritating television show about it, which Cynthia hate-watched religiously.

After all, *she* was adopted. No one had ever made a fuss like this over her. Granted, she hadn't known she was adopted. Back then, more than sixty years ago, most women didn't want to advertise that they couldn't have children. And most didn't want to broadcast the fact that they'd been foolish enough to get pregnant accidentally. There was no shame anymore.

Unlike this Matthew person, Cynthia didn't know the identities of her birth mother or the man who'd impregnated her. Why would she want to? They'd given her to a better life, end of story. She had wondered about them, of course, but only occasionally. Her *parents* were the people who'd raised her. No need for more than that.

"Have you met him?" Nicole asked in a low voice.

Cynthia noted that Nicole was wearing a bezel cut diamond pendant set in rose gold, similar to one Cynthia had sold after Henry divorced her. Irritating on all fronts—Henry divorcing her, her subsequent poverty and Nicole with her effortless wealth. Now that Cynthia had no money, she hated people who did.

Still, it was rather fun being asked to spill the gossip tea.

"I suppose I have," Cynthia said, hoping Nicole would pry for more.

"And?" Nicole asked, riveted (for once).

"He was ordinary. Curly hair, black—"

"His father was Black?"

"No," Cynthia said with exaggerated patience. "His *hair* is black. He looked like any other teenager. Poorly dressed, unkempt hair."

"Last night was Esme's graduation," Nicole said, irritatingly changing the subject. "Harlow completely upstaged her with the news that she had a kid. I had to put the girls to bed so they wouldn't overhear. Now I'll have to tell Esme she's not the oldest grandchild anymore."

Nicole and Addison were truly the most obnoxious parents, parading their girls around like purebred dogs. And really, a kindergarten graduation party? Cynthia heard it had been catered. Those two sure loved to show off their money. Not that Cynthia would know, since she hadn't even been invited.

"Well, it certainly was dramatic," Cynthia said. "Harlow fainted. Or pretended to faint."

"You're kidding me. What else?"

"I don't like to gossip," Cynthia said. She *loved* gossiping and hated those sanctimonious liars who denied they did. But Nicole shouldn't get the goods for free. "Maybe we could have lunch at Winslow's, and I could catch you up."

"Never mind," Nicole said, and Cynthia's mouth tightened. "Someone else will know more. No one in this family can keep a secret."

"Obviously, Harlow can," Cynthia said. "Now, please excuse me, since I have work to do." What she wanted to say was, *Nicole, I was rich once, too. You should treat me with more respect. Oh, and by the way, I was also adopted, and the world didn't stop spinning.*

Nicole left the counter to gossip with someone else. There

were a dozen people here, and most of them were dying to hear about Harlow. Didn't people know what bookstores were for? For quietly browsing and purchasing books. Not hanging around, chatting or perusing cards or buying a magnet or fancy napkins, which Open Book shouldn't even carry. It was a bookstore, not a souvenir stand. If Nicole had her way, the store would be more like the old-fashioned library of her youth. A temple for books and silence. Not this overly friendly place where people popped in when they were bored.

"So you met him?" asked Alissa DeJonge. She was the principal of the only school in town and, as such, had considerable rank in Wellfleet. And to her credit, her young son, Pierce, actually read books. Not manga or comic books, but actual *books*. "What's he like?"

Cynthia took her time answering, relishing the moment. Harlow wasn't in today, leaving Cynthia with Destiny, who was dressed as if she were Meghan Markle, as usual. Uncle Robert was nowhere to be found at the moment. She held up her finger to Alissa, as if she were finishing something important, then looked at her. "I'm sorry, what was that, Alissa?"

"Harlow's son. I'm sure he's lovely."

"Mm." Let Alissa work for it.

"What a shock. Poor Harlow. But how wonderful, too."

"Well," Cynthia said, lowering her voice. "He certainly had no problem creating a scene. And at her place of work, too. Not very considerate."

Alissa fixed her with a look. "He's only a kid, I hear."

"Old enough to know not to air the family's dirty laundry in public." Cynthia leaned forward. "The father . . . the one who adopted him . . . is quite attractive. Indian, I think. He had an accent."

It was the wrong thing to say, and Alissa's expression tightened. "Give Harlow my best," she said. "Tell her I'm thinking of her."

"I will," Cynthia said. She wouldn't. She adjusted her own tone to be cool and brisk. "Any purchases today?"

"Pierce? Do you want that book, sweetheart?"

"Yes, please," said Pierce, approaching the counter with a book about bridges. "Thank you."

He had nice manners and was a smart and pleasant boy, but Cynthia wasn't about to compliment him, not after Alissa had just cold-shouldered her. She rang up the purchase and handed the boy his book. "Have a nice day."

"You too," said Alissa, and they left. The other people in the store were Smiths or Smith friends, all of them in clumps, talking about Harlow, Harlow, Harlow.

"Hey, there," said Bertie Baines. Cynthia sighed. Bertie was *not* a welcome presence in the bookstore, not to her. Harlow, of course, loved him, and so did Uncle Robert. Cynthia thought he looked like a grade A hobo, dressed in stained jeans and a ragged flannel shirt, left open over a grubby T-shirt. Men on Cape Cod did not know how to dress. She felt a pang for Henry and his fine suits, followed by the spurt of stomach acid that always followed any memory of her ex-husband.

"What can I help you with, Albert?" Cynthia asked, keeping her voice cold.

"Just wanted to say hello," he said.

"Hello. Any purchases today?"

He tilted his head. "Dunno. You read anything good lately?" He had that wretched Cape Cod accent that was akin to nails on a chalkboard to Cynthia.

"I read good books every day," she answered tartly. Was there any point to reading a bad book?

"Got any recommendations?"

"Yes. Here." In order to make the transaction as quick as possible, because Bertie Baines would talk for an hour if she let him, she handed him the nearest paperback. It was actually a very good book.

"*Where the Crawdads Sing*," he read. "I've heard of this."

So has everyone, she thought. "It's about the power of solitude," Cynthia said, hoping he'd get the hint. "It makes a person want to be left alone for years at a time."

"I'll take it," he said. Good, because she was going to gag if he didn't get out in the next minute or two. His hygiene left much to be desired. "Hey," he said, looking at her with faded blue eyes. "I hear Harlow had quite a shock. How's she doing?" He leaned on the counter, bringing that odor closer. Sweat and salt and God knew what else.

"She's fine."

"Her kid, huh? Who knew?"

"No one. That'll be ten forty-nine."

He fished out a ten and a single from his pocket, and she took the bills by the corner, as they no doubt smelled like body odor and low tide. She gave him two quarters and a penny, making sure to drop the coins into his hand and not touch him.

"See you soon, Cynthia."

"Yes." Unfortunately. Yet another person came in looking for Harlow, and Destiny turned to talk to her. How did Destiny afford such nice clothes? Family money? Certainly it wasn't her salary, because even Cynthia couldn't afford to dress as she once did.

Honestly. All this fuss for a nearly adult child. It was so irritating. Cynthia's parents had never told her she was adopted at all. Her mother, Miriam, had been desperate to have a child.

Cynthia learned this when she was a teen and found the trunk that contained her mother's diaries, faithfully kept since her wedding day. The diaries all had locks on them, but a safety pin took care of that. She had been sixteen at the time and couldn't resist learning more about her mother, the person she most admired in the world. The majority of the diaries had been standard stuff about planning meals, shopping, talking with friends . . . and then Cynthia read about the inability to get pregnant. The doctor's appointments. The heartache, month after month after year after year. And then . . .

At last, we were approved to go to St. Joseph's. I knew the minute I saw her. She was the prettiest baby in the entire orphanage, and the minute she saw me, she smiled.

It was a shock, yes, but after thinking about it for an hour or so, Cynthia decided it didn't matter. Her birth mother (and father) hadn't wanted her, but her actual parents had. End of story. She'd never told her parents she knew. They'd cared for her, provided for her and loved her. If anything, the knowledge that she wasn't their flesh and blood made her love them all the more. They had *chosen* her, the prettiest baby in the entire orphanage. She'd smiled at her mother. It was meant to be. She went home with them that same day. Those were the good old days, to be sure.

Those reunion stories. Ugh. Cynthia certainly didn't want some strange woman bursting into her life saying, "Surprise! I'm your mother! Sorry to ignore you for all these decades!" And Cynthia would never inflict that kind of "reunion" on anyone else. She'd had the perfect family—two doting parents, no siblings. They'd lived in a large sunny home in Kansas City, Missouri. Mother was a homemaker; Daddy was a banker. It was just the three of them, and that was lovely. Uncle Robert, who wasn't actually her uncle but her father's second or third cousin, *was* her godfather, and he and his wife, Louisa, had visited every other year or so, which was always a special time, when Cynthia wore her best dresses and was allowed to eat with the adults.

Every so often, Cynthia would play with Janet, a girl about her age from down the street who had two younger brothers. Cynthia didn't like going to her house. The boys were noisy and messy and loud, and the mother always seemed frazzled. Janet was tolerable, but Cynthia's favorite person was her mother, who was so capable, putting up jam, arranging flowers, embroidering napkins. They had a maid named Kimberly, who wore a uniform, and she and Mother took wonderful care of the house. Kimberly went to the market with Mother's list, and Mother cooked dinner after Kimberly went home each day. Mother was always perfect, lipstick always on, perfume freshened before Daddy came home. She wore a dress or blouse and skirt every day. Pumps with a two-inch heel. Pearls. She could make an aspic ring with tomato juice, Swedish meatballs and beef bourguignon, same as Julia Child. She instructed Kimberly to make a bed so tightly you could bounce a quarter off it, and knew to use lemon juice for stained linens. She taught Cynthia the proper way to set and clear a table.

It was the 1960s. The people her parents knew lived the same way. No women's lib for them. No, thank you. Not like their more liberal relatives, the Smiths of Cape Cod. Even so, Aunt Louisa was very nice, though she was more of a hippie, wearing floral print pants in loud colors, her hair hanging loose. She was younger than Cynthia's mom by a good measure, and it was almost as if she were Cynthia's friend, because Louisa asked her questions about what she liked and listened when she answered. On one visit, she taught Cynthia to French braid her own hair. Robert and Louisa sent her lovely, whimsical books for her birthday and Christmas—*The Wolves of Willoughby Chase* and *The White Stone*, *The Trumpet of the Swan* and *The Children of Green Knowe.*

Gerald, their son, was almost the same age as Cynthia, but he was loud and liked jumping off the swing in the backyard and laughed too loudly. She was glad when he started staying with his grandparents instead of visiting. He was too . . . happy. When she started school, Cynthia realized something. She was better than these other children, many of whom formed instant packs. Also, no other girl was wearing a dress with petticoats. "Is that your Easter dress?" asked one girl, who towered over Cynthia. "It's not even springtime, dummy."

Cynthia gritted her teeth. Her outfit was the prettiest one here by *far*. She scanned the tall girl critically. Rust-colored corduroy pants, an ugly mustard-colored shirt with a huge, flopping collar. "My mother wants me to look pretty. Not like a boy."

This remark earned her a shove. Cynthia grabbed the girl's arm and bit it, hard, causing the girl to howl in pain before the teacher separated them.

"What is going on here?" Mrs. Green had asked.

"She's jealous of my dress," Cynthia had answered.

"She bit me!" said the taller girl.

"You deserved it," Cynthia said. Her mother had instructed her to speak up if other children treated her poorly, and it came easily with these inferior beings.

Thus, her role was cast. Snooty, sharp-tongued, surprisingly good in a fight. She didn't mind. In fact, she rather liked it.

But the differences didn't end there. The other parents were so . . . young. They all looked like hippies or hobos. Some wore peace sign jewelry and tacky bell-bottoms, the mothers with long, unsecured hair, the fathers with thick mustaches and long sideburns. *Her* mother wore pants only when she was working in the garden, and her father wore a suit every day, except on weekends, when he wore trousers and a starched oxford. This new species of parent, Cynthia observed, shouted and played with their kids, tackling them, tickling them, messing up their hair, kissing and hugging them. "Some people just love drawing attention to themselves," said Mother tightly.

Cynthia went through grade school with her hair neatly combed, wearing penny loafers and ironed dresses. She knew she was better than these loud, ill-mannered children who didn't know to say "Yes, sir" and "No, ma'am." Her teachers praised her manners and reading abilities, but her classmates mocked or ignored her. She didn't care.

At home, the Kansas City Smiths sat down to eat at the table every single night. Another cocktail for her father, water for her mother, milk for Cynthia. Kimberly would stay late and serve dinner if they had company.

And so, Cynthia never felt comfortable in her own era. Why would she? The world was godless and chaotic, its people overly personal and loud. The only people she really liked were Mother and Daddy, Uncle Robert and Aunt Louisa. And herself, of course. Better to be aloof and superior than try to fit in.

Obviously, she never thought she'd end up *here*, lost and bitter at the turns life had thrown her. She certainly hadn't envisioned needing to *lie* to get the least little bit of security, that was for sure.

But a woman did what a woman had to do.

SEVEN

HARLOW

At 4:43 the morning after I re-met my son, I got up early. Might as well, since I hadn't slept a bit. I looked at Ollie's sweet face and whispered, "Kayak?" He leaped off the bed and ran to the door.

I kept my kayak in a rack at Mayo Beach, just a quick walk from my place. Ollie trotted by my side, no leash necessary this early. The sun was just about to rise, and the birds weren't waiting—the robins tweeted in the trees and the chickadees were already busy. Blue jays alerted the world to my presence with their raucous blurt, "Thief, thief!" according to Thornton Burgess in those delightful Old Mother West Wind books I'd read as a kid.

The sky was lightening in the east when we got to the beach. I pulled on my life jacket, then dragged my cheery blue kayak to the edge of the water. Took the paddle out, got in and said, "Ollie!" He raced over and neatly leaped onto the deck. The kayak bobbled a bit, and Ollie sat down, ready for our ride. I dipped one side of the oar into the water, then the other, the rocking and bobbing feeling as familiar and comforting as my bed. Now the seagulls were awake, laughing their raspy laughs. The piping plovers ran and scattered over the sand, theirs the sweetest little peep of all the shorebirds.

The morning clouds were beginning to come alive—first gray,

then golden as the light strengthened. The ocean was dark blue, but as the sun rose, it turned violet and green. The world felt so still and yet so alive, my sweet dog keeping lookout. For a moment, it felt like God was putting his hand on the back of my head and saying, "I've got you. Everything will be fine."

I paddled out past the channel marker and then just sat. Off to my right, a school of stripers flapped in the water, feeding. Then the sun rose higher, the colors faded and the beautiful day began.

My first day of motherhood, in a way. It felt . . . miraculous.

Back home, I dusted and tidied the entire apartment in anticipation of Rosie's arrival, which would hopefully be tomorrow, depending on her ability to get a last-minute flight. I put clean sheets on the bed for her. Ironed her pillowcases. Went out back and picked some flowers for her room. Cleaned the guest bathroom, put more flowers in there. Baked muffins.

At 10:01 a.m., eyes gritty, buzzed on caffeine, my apartment sparkling, the phone dinged, and I nearly leaped out of my skin. It was a text from Sanjay.

Good morning, Harlow. I hope you are well after yesterday's shock. Monica will be here Friday with our daughter, and there is much to be discussed, as you can imagine. We would like to approach this the right way, now that Matthew has . . . how shall I put this? . . . gone rogue. Are you free to meet with Monica and me on Saturday? We would like to talk before you and Matthew reconnect. Is that acceptable?

Crap. They were being sensible, not leaping into this, which, while disappointing in this moment, was just one of the reasons that had made me choose them in the first place.

Yes, of course, I wrote back.

The three dots appeared, and then, Wonderful. Are you free at 3:00 p.m. Saturday afternoon? Here is our address.

I said that it would work perfectly. Of course it would. Cynthia would be irritated that I'd be taking a Saturday afternoon off, but who cared? Nothing was more important than this. But Saturday seemed years away, and while my brain knew this was a wise plan, my heart sank just the same.

I now had thirty-nine texts from my family. Guess I wasn't the boring one anymore. My plan on the family front was . . . well . . . to lie low.

Growing up the oldest of five children, you become one of two things: the adored, spoiled, fascinating firstborn who can do no wrong; or the responsible, quiet one who never caused anyone a second's worry.

I was the latter. In a family of five kids, my claim to fame was simply that I was the helpful oldest. And I liked helping. We had home movies of me, nearly three, going between the crying twins with a bottle, sticking it in Addie's mouth until she stopped crying, then pulling it out and giving it to Lark. Winnie came along three years after that, a colicky, demanding baby who needed constant attention the first six months of her life, and even at just six myself, I had a knack for soothing her. By the time Robbie was born when I was nine, it seemed I knew as much about taking care of kids as my parents did.

Don't get me wrong. I had a happy childhood. My parents were in love, which set the tone for our happy, chaotic household, the two of them always exchanging a kiss or caress as they cooked or handed over a baby or went out the door. I loved being a big sister. By the time I was eleven, I could start dinner, give the twins their baths, read bedtime stories, sing lullabies, walk the dog, water the garden and clean up the kitchen, and most nights, I did at least four of these. My parents needed the help, after all. Dad was a nurse at Hyannis Hospital, coming home with stories of severed fingers or festering wounds or a baby born in the emergency room. Mom had her art, which she pounced on the minute she had a little free time, the pleasant smell of oil paint wafting down from the attic.

In church or the grocery store or library, adults told my parents how lucky they were to have such a responsible, levelheaded child. Then they'd bend down to admire Lark and Addie, who were angelically beautiful, or try to cajole a smile from Winnie, or comment on Robbie's sparkling eyes and dimples. Even before I understood the full meaning of *role* or *identity*, I knew who I was in the family. The responsible one. Reliable. Dutiful. Patient. Uncomplaining. Some very dull adjectives, in other words.

My parents said I had to set a good example for "the Littles," as we called them, and I took that job to heart. Straight A's, quiet voice, switching the laundry or wiping down a counter without being asked, reading a book to someone or braiding a sister's hair. My reward for being the oldest was that my bedtime was a half hour later than the Littles, and I could read uninterrupted in the living room while my parents watched TV or talked in the kitchen over a cup of coffee. Sometimes, that half hour would stretch longer until Mom or Dad discovered me and said, "Harlow! I forgot you were there! Go to bed, honey."

The only time I could remember feeling special was when I got a sleepover at Grammy and Grandpop's house. Grammy and I would bake whatever I requested—apple pie or chocolate cake or cinnamon cookies. She'd ask me what kinds of animals were my favorite, which books I loved the most, why I liked a certain teacher. She'd tell me about her childhood and her mother, how she was the best baker on the Cape. Then Grandpop would come home, by then working part-time for the law firm in Boston, and he'd tell me about his cases as we sat on the porch. They'd let me stay up late, snuggled up with Grandpop in his big chair, and I'd doze off with the nice smell of him, wool and the minty scent of Ben-Gay. He would carry me up the stairs to the guest room, and Grammy would kiss my head. In hindsight, those were the only times I ever felt like a child myself. Cuddled and cared for and . . . well . . . cherished.

We had an old piano in the basement, and it quickly became apparent that Lark had talent, so she was given lessons. Addie kicked up a fuss, so she got piano lessons, too. When I asked if I could take them as well, Dad explained that money was tight, and besides, I was smart enough to teach myself off the twins' beginner books (or by helping them practice). Winnie needed speech therapy. Robbie was an imp, always getting into trouble for something adorably naughty—stealing the neighbor's cat because it looked sad, or asking every girl in his preschool to marry him and causing a fight over who would actually become his bride. Even then, he had a way with females.

I wasn't musical. I wasn't artistic. I wasn't a diva like Addie or a sulker like Winnie or achingly sensitive like Lark. I wasn't particularly beautiful, not compared with the twins, and I wasn't delightful like Robbie. I just . . . was. My value came from being useful. Otherwise, I was pretty much invisible.

"Thank God for you, Harlow," Mom would sigh once in a while. "I never have to spare you a thought." It might have been a compliment.

When Mom opened Long Pond Arts, her gallery, it became her sixth child, as she liked to say. It quickly became successful; Mom was talented, and she had a good eye for special art. By the time the Littles were in school all day, business was booming. I'd herd my siblings home, giving a piggyback ride or racing some-one, always pretending to lose so they could win. I'd give them a snack and help with homework as I did my own, and maybe start dinner per the instructions Mom or Dad left on the counter. But I was never lonely. Not really.

It was only in high school that I started to take form. I knew my parents wouldn't be able to provide much for college. They made a decent living, but the Cape is an expensive place to live, and they owned the house and the gallery and had five children. Grammy and Grandpop had started a college fund for each of us at birth, but it wouldn't alleviate the need for loans and schol-arships. If I was going to go to college, I'd need to make good grades.

And so, like the dutiful, responsible girl I was, I made myself a schedule for studying. I mapped out my projects and papers the minute they were assigned. I studied on the school bus, and used the time I had before the Littles came home from their school. After dinner and helping the kids get settled down, I'd stay up late, studying more.

I loved high school—the learning part, at least. Maybe it was because Nauset High was a regional school, and I didn't know everyone there. But suddenly, I was one of the smart kids and considered nice. I was too quiet to be popular, and interaction with boys felt like visiting a foreign country without knowing the language. I was not quite thirteen when I started high school, since my birthday was in September and I'd skipped third grade. At least I was tall, so my age didn't come up too often.

I did some quiet extracurriculars—Best Buddies, where I was paired with a sweet boy named Rory, who had Down syndrome. Twice a week, we'd draw superheroes after school and chat. I joined the Mock Trial Team, which was a bit rowdier, and loved that, too.

Megan Nickerson, Jessica Demers and I ate lunch together in the cafeteria. After sophomore year, when it was apparent we were both nerds before it was cool, Grady Byrne and I chose each other for lab partners. Sometimes, Megan, Jessica and I went to the movies. In the summers, I worked at PJ's and cleaned rooms at the Blue Dolphin Inn (which was actually a motel) and helped out at Open Book.

High school was pleasant. Not exciting, not turbulent, not romantic, not at all like the movies I saw about teenagers in high school. I read and studied, asked Grady to tutor me in chemistry so I could ace that class. I started applying to colleges in the fall of my senior year, scored perfectly on the SAT (as did Grady) and spent weeks on my college essay. Sure enough, in the spring, I got a letter announcing a huge scholarship and enrollment in the honors program at a lovely university.

In Colorado.

If you're born and raised on Cape Cod, the land gets its sea-grass into you early. It's a wonderful place to live—mild winters with the occasional wild, romantic snowstorm; a spring so filled with flowers, you feel drunk with it; sunny summers that rarely have a day over 90 degrees; and long, lazy autumn days, the abundant poison ivy turning brilliant red, the locust trees showering down yellow leaves. The ocean is everywhere, along with the smell of salt and fresh air.

And yet, for years, my secret plan had been to leave home.

Obviously, I loved my family. But as I got older, I felt myself . . . disappearing. The good child, the easy teenager, the strong student. My siblings outgrew their need for a sitter/shepherd. High school hadn't given me a new identity, though it came as a surprise to me and my schoolmates that I'd somehow squeaked past Grady to become valedictorian.

It's hard to know who you are when you've been assigned a role so young. If your identity comes from what you do for other people, who are you when you're alone? I had always been "the oldest Smith kid" or "Gerry and Elsbeth's kid" or "the twins' sister" or "Robbie's sister." It was time to find out who I was without those titles.

In a college far away, I'd be just me—Harlow Grace Smith. I loved my name (though my siblings called me Harlot far too often, and ironically, since I hadn't even been kissed yet). I thought Harlow Grace Smith from a little town no one in Colorado had ever heard of could be someone kind of cool. Maybe she was more interesting than I myself currently was. Maybe she just needed some mountain air and a couple thousand miles between her and home. After all, if ever there was a time to live far away, it was college. If it didn't work out, I could always transfer. But the West sounded so romantic with its mountains and bears and moose. I'd never seen a moose before.

The University of Colorado Boulder gave me a very generous scholarship and a work-study job, and with the nest egg my grandparents had set aside for me, I could get through college with almost no debt. All of a sudden, I *was* interesting, though perhaps not in the best way. My parents were stunned and upset that I hadn't discussed this with them. Lark cried, Addie was jealous, Winnie slammed her door, Robbie asked if he could come with me. Only Grandpop and Grammy were delighted that I was "spreading my wings."

I stood firm, and in late August, I packed my bags and left, my entire family sobbing (except for Winnie, who scowled). I sobbed, too. Walking into Logan International Airport all by myself was terrifying, and for a second, I almost turned and shouted, "Wait! Come back! I can't do it." Robbie was only seven! How could I do this to him? I was abruptly terrified by the idea of going so far away. I didn't know anyone out there. Not a single soul.

But once I'd walked through Logan and got to my gate, elation bubbled in my chest. I'd done it. The grades, the applications, the scholarship, the packing and organizing and emailing my roommate to introduce myself . . . I had done something big, something interesting, something even a little risky.

When the plane landed, I took a shuttle to my college and instantly fell in love. There were more eighteen-to-twenty-two-year-olds here than on all of the Outer Cape, including Orleans. The trees, the buildings, the green grass and beautiful trees felt so *invigorating*. The quad and Norlin Library . . . for *me*. The astrophysics building . . . I could become an astrophysicist! I was part of the CU Buffalo Herd now. Our mascot was an actual buffalo, and I got to pet her and everything.

And the *mountains*. The Flatirons rose raw and strong around us. So pretty, so full of danger, grace and beauty. In the distance were the Rockies, and I couldn't wait to hike there. I was grateful for the proximity to nature. Being able to trek into the Flatirons once or twice a week was necessary for me, unused to such big crowds. Those hikes were like taking a walk with God, the air so dry and pure, the aspen leaves aglow.

And then there was Rosie Wolfe. My roommate.

She was all energy and sass, sloppy where I was neat, a night owl to my early bird.

"Hey!" she said when I walked in. "You're Harlow? I'm Rosie. We're gonna have so much fun."

And we did. If I felt a little awkward at putting my best, most cheerful and engaging self forward, Rosie's rocket fuel personality swept me up with her. By the end of our freshman orientation, we'd been invited to two parties, joined the Alpine Club and Buffs Against Bullying, and been approached by three sororities asking us to pledge. After all these years of being in the background, I was suddenly, unbelievably *popular*. Me. The boring one. But I wasn't boring anymore. I talked to everyone on my hall, and before long, the effort of being outgoing faded, and the friendliness became natural.

I was undeclared and figured I'd get my core classes out of the way. Rosie's dad was an entertainment lawyer, and she thought she might want to become a screenwriter. Since I loved to read, I figured I'd lean into history, political science and English, maybe become an environmental lawyer. Rosie and I had two classes in common, and we ate together nearly every night, took walks around the vast campus, talking about our lives, our hopes for the future, our experience (or in my case, the lack thereof) with romance.

"It's so easy to talk to you, Harlow," Rosie said a few weeks into the semester. "You make me feel . . . okay, this is weird, but I feel *safe* with you. Like, I know you're a truly good person. I've never had a best friend before, but I think you're it."

"Really?" I said. "Because I feel the exact same way." I smiled and linked my arm through hers. "Best friends. Sounds about right."

Rosie was an only child who grew up between Los Angeles (Dad the lawyer) and Phoenix (Mom the plastic surgeon). She'd traveled all over the world, had regular dinners with the Will Smith family, called Robert Downey Jr. "Uncle Bob" and had delicious gossip about the celebrities who were nipped and tucked by her mother, whose computer password Rosie had hacked. She was fluent in Spanish and French, had a black Amex card and wore clothes by designers so elite, I'd never heard of them. In other words, we were complete opposites. Why the roommate algorithm put us together, we didn't know, but we were grateful.

In addition to being friends with everyone, Rosie and I were determined to graduate "at *least* magna cum laude," so we were those students who sat in the front row of every classroom. We organized study groups, found our place in Norlin Library, were content to flop down on the grass on a sunny day with our books and laptops. I reminded her to drink water and eat enough, since she was a bit of a butterfly, taking a bite there, three fries here. She supervised me after I had my first alcoholic beverage.

By the end of October, high school was a distant memory. I kept in touch with Megan and Jessica a little, and Grady Byrne emailed me from Harvard to check in, but it was like I barely remembered my old self. This new me was so much better.

Rosie advised me on wardrobe and told me not to touch my hair when I contemplated coloring it red. "People spend *thousands* to get hair like yours. Don't be an idiot." I tutored her in chemistry and math. When a guy down the hall started sniffing around her, I told her he gave me a bad vibe. She shut him down, and a month later he was arrested for possession of child pornography. "Jesus," Rosie said. "Thank God you warned me off. I wouldn't have been able to live with myself if I hooked up with him."

We decided she should come to the Cape at summer break and stay with my family. Neither of us was going home for Thanksgiving, since traveling that week was too chaotic (and in my case, too expensive). Besides, Christmas was right around the corner.

I was becoming the person I'd imagined—Harlow Grace Smith, funny, smart, calm, wise, generous with her time and actually rather pretty. It was almost a shock. The Colorado sun and dry air cured my frizz and streaked my hair with white-gold strands. I was five-ten and started appreciating my height, and I slimmed down and muscled up from all the hiking and gymming. I smiled at everyone I passed or met, simply because I was so happy.

Sometimes, I rallied the other freshmen on our hall and initiated adventure hikes or goofy games, such as a campus treasure hunt. I started trivia night (which stuck). Rosie dared me to make out with the campus statue of Robert Frost, and I did with glee and gusto (sorry, sir) while she cackled and took pictures. We sat on the buffalo statue and went to football games.

I'd never felt so vibrant and committed and clear. My professors knew my name. People brightened when they saw me, because I was nice and fun and kind. I had Rosie, and I had all these other friends, too. Classmates asked to study with me. Boys checked me out. I had weekend plans, flitting from party to party or just hanging out in the common room with a group, watching a movie.

It was magical. Golden. How did I get so lucky? How did I instinctively land here, in Colorado, a place so far from home but home already? Rosie and I affirmed that we'd been put together by the universe.

"I would've found you anyway," she said one night. "We're kindred spirits, Harlow."

"Sisters," I said, and her eyes filled with tears.

We talked about our future, which would obviously involve each other. We'd go to grad school in the same area and share a beautiful apartment. We'd take vacations together, go to Spain our junior year. She couldn't wait to meet my large family, and I couldn't wait to meet her impressive parents. We'd be each other's maids of honor, and that way I wouldn't have to pick one sister over another. We'd be godmother to each other's kids.

It was the happiest time of my life thus far.

And then I met Zach Baser, and that bright, golden world, still so new, changed completely.

EIGHT

MONICA

Monica was finding it very difficult to feign normalcy. Matthew's decision to meet his birth mother had thrown the week into chaos. No, the entire summer. But as a mother, she had to contain her emotions so as not to alarm Meena. She had to get everything done faster and sooner so she and Meena could fly out to the East Coast ten days earlier than planned. Peter, her boss, wasn't happy, and she'd had to stay up till 2 a.m. for four nights running to finish the Billings project. Meena's school had piled on work to make sure she finished everything before the school year ended (as if Meena needed to prove anything; she was the smartest kid in school).

Monica asked the house sitter if she was available earlier and, when she wasn't, found another one, then had them both come over to instruct them on looking after the cat and the houseplants. Before she left, she made up the guest room with fresh sheets and new toiletries. Sanjay had made the travel arrangements, but he'd booked them a flight that left at 5 a.m., which meant getting to San Francisco at 3 a.m., so she'd rebooked it to a more civilized hour.

And then there was speaking to Matthew. She'd had to be all cheerful and excited for him, asking questions that showed she was interested but not prying, asking him to share his feelings without discussing hers, being careful not to let any hint of disapproval or censure creep into her voice or words. Being a parent was a lopsided relationship.

"So how do you think she felt after you left?" she'd asked a day after he'd met Harlow. It was just a call, not FaceTime, and she felt guilty that she was relieved they didn't have to look at each other.

"Great, I think. I mean, she said it was the happiest day of her life. Mine too."

Her stomach flinched at the knife he'd just stuck there. "Wow. You must feel amazing."

"Well, yeah." There it was, the sullen teen accusation in his voice. *Don't tell me how I feel. You don't know what it's like. You weren't adopted.* A familiar refrain these past three years or so.

"I'm excited to see her again," Monica said.

Matthew grunted.

"Honey . . . I really am happy for you. And for her. I can't imagine how much this means to you." Did she dare say it? She was his mother, goddamnit. She shouldn't have to pussyfoot around. "I just wish you'd said something beforehand. This is a huge development, and it affects all of us."

"I *knew* you'd say that, which is exactly why I kept it to myself. This was mine. My decision, my life, my mother." At least he sounded slightly guilty at that. "I mean, you know. My birth mother. Besides, I'm gonna be eighteen next month. An adult."

"Yes, Matthew, I know when your birthday is." She smiled to soften the words. "But we're your family. We've never been against you reconnecting with Harlow. It would have been nice to talk about it, that's all."

"Yeah, well, water under the bridge. Is Meena around?"

"She's in her room." Monica went down the hall and handed the phone to Meena. "Your brother," she said.

"Hi!" Meena said, grabbing the phone. "Put me on Face-Time so I can see your ugly face. What was she like? Is she pretty? Did you tell her about me?"

Monica smoothed her hand over her daughter's hair.

"Ma?" asked Matthew. "Can I talk to Meena alone?"

"You bet. See you Friday, honey. I love you."

"Love you, too."

She took the phone from Meena and looked at her son, her beautiful boy. "I love you, Matthew Rohan Patel," she said again, making sure he heard the smile in her voice.

It worked. His voice softened. "I love you, too, Monica Nicole Walker Patel."

"That's Mommy to you."

"Love you, too, Mom."

Good enough. She handed the phone back to Meena, simultaneously proud that her kids were so close and jealous because she was being left out, then went back to her bedroom, closed the door, went into the bathroom, closed that door, turned on the shower and let it run so Meena wouldn't hear her cry.

NINE

HARLOW

I opted not to read any of the texts from my family. Instead, I went to Open Book on Wednesday afternoon (having hidden in my apartment the day before) and called a staff meeting in the back room, so I wouldn't have to see the public, as it were. We three women crammed in there amid the boxes. It was a small space, piled with advance review copies of books, notices of bookseller events, handwritten reminders to the staff. *Make it a great day!* (Destiny). *You are all wonderful!!!* (Grandpop). *Don't forget your staff recommendations!* (me). *Clean your own coffee cups* (Cynthia).

Destiny touched my arm and smiled. That was all. She was such a kind person.

"Staff meetings are usually on Tuesdays," Cynthia said.

"And yet one is needed today. Grandpop?"

"Coming, sweetheart," he said, emerging from the office. "How's my girl today?"

"Doing okay."

Cynthia stood with her arms folded, lips tight. Grandpop and Destiny sat on the two office chairs. Oliver put his front paws on Destiny's knee, and she politely removed them.

"This skirt is cashmere, doggy," she whispered.

"I guess it's public knowledge that I had a son in college," I said. "I'm going to be taking a lot of time off, it seems, and I'm sorry if that inconveniences you."

"It does," Cynthia said.

"Well, I haven't taken a vacation in three years, Cynthia, so consider this balancing the scales," I said tightly.

"Some things are *far* more important than work," Grandpop said.

"Not a problem," Destiny added. "I can always use more hours. Besides, your boy! Harlow, how wonderful that he found you, honey." Destiny had a rich and lovely voice, and my eyes filled at the kindness in her tone.

"If we need to hire part-time help, let me know," I said.

"We can't afford it," Cynthia said. "It hasn't exactly been a banner year."

"Then I'll take it out of my pay, Cynthia." But we should be able to swing it. Cynthia was just being her mean old self. She muttered something under her breath, and I chose not to ask her to repeat it.

"I'm sure people have been asking about my son, and I'd appreciate it if the official answer is that it's a family matter. Okay?" I looked pointedly at Cynthia.

"Of course," Destiny said. "That's what I've been saying all day."

"What was the question?" asked Grandpop. "Sorry, dear, my mind was wandering."

"I'd rather not have anyone talk about Matthew in the store."

"Well, of course not!" Grandpop said. "It's no one's business but yours. And his. Handsome boy, though, isn't he?"

My eyes filled again. "He is," I said.

"Can we get back to work?" Cynthia asked. "If this install-ment of the soap opera is finished?"

"Cynthia, let me make you a cup of tea," Destiny said. "You seem upset." I shot Destiny a grateful look. "How about you, Robert? Tea?"

"I never say no to a pretty lady," he said, following the ladies out of the office.

Time to face the music. I started a group text that included my siblings, parents and Grandpop.

I would like to talk to you all about my son and what has happened. Family dinner, maybe at Addie and Nicole's (please?) Sunday? They did love to entertain.

My mother answered immediately. I don't want to have to wait that long.

Me: Please see the message above.

Mom: I am your mother, Harlow Grace. I deserve to speak to you alone.

I thought about that. No, I decided, she didn't. I mean, she did, but I wasn't going to do it. Not after the way she'd blown up at me.

Me: Please see the above message and don't make me block you, Mom. xox

Standing up for myself. That was kind of new.

Happily, another event intervened in "my drama," as Cyn-thia put it. Winnie had sent out a text—All unmarried Smith family members will show up at Truro Vineyards tonight for a singles event. You will behave. You will be polite. See you at 6:30.

It was her latest event party, and no one dared disobey her. And why not? I could use the distraction.

Last year, Winnie had bought Hannah Chapman's event planning business. Once, the company had done excruciatingly expensive and gorgeous weddings and elaborate parties for the 1 percent. Winnie had toned it down a bit and expanded the business to include smaller celebrations. A baby shower, for example. Poetry readings at Preservation Hall. Food festivals, wine tastings, kids' parties, cocktail parties, author talks at my bookstore with refreshments. She did weddings, sure, but not the crazy-expensive kind, because she said she'd end up punching someone in the face, which wouldn't be good for business.

And now, singles nights, apparently.

That evening, six members of the Smith family pulled into the parking lot of Truro Vineyards in five different vehicles. Winnie was in her Hyundai (all electric, the lucky thing), Grandpop and me in my car, Robbie in his pickup, Lark in her little Honda hybrid and Cynthia in her aging BMW, a gift from her ex-husband. She saw us and frowned.

"What's Dolores Umbridge doing here?" Robbie muttered to me. "Oh, and hey, scarlet woman. Can't wait to hear about your slutty ways."

"Don't make me hit you, Robbie."

"Cynthia, my dear!" said Grandpop. "Aren't you pretty!"

"Is Grandpop going blind?" Robbie whispered.

By now we were standing in a group in the parking lot.

"First rule," Winnie said, "no one asks Harlow a goddamn question about her kid. Second rule, you all charm the pants off everyone you talk to. You too, Cynthia. I need your demographic. Third, Robbie, flirt with everyone. I'm low on straight males."

"I'd say no, but you scare the poop out of me."

"Like your chubby thighs, Robbie, we need to stick together," Winnie said, checking her phone.

"I'll be your wingman, Robbie," Grandpop said. "Do people still use that term?"

"They do," Robbie said. "I'll be yours, too, Pop. By the way, you're welcome, Winifred."

"Windsor. Take a second and learn your sister's name." She smacked him on the side of the head.

"Thanks for being *my* wingman," I murmured to Winnie. "I'm a little . . . discombobulated."

"Yeah, well, you met your son yesterday. You get to be discombobulated. Listen." She folded her arms and looked over my shoulder. "I just want to say that I'm sorry you had to carry this on your own all these years. You could've told me. I wouldn't have judged you."

I looked at her, my youngest sister, her face always so serious. "Thanks, sweetheart," I said. "But you were eleven at the time."

She considered this. "True. But you could've told me in all the years since."

"You're right. I could have. It was just . . ." I took a deep breath. "It was not something I wanted to revisit."

"I guess I get that." She patted my shoulder, always awkward with physical affection. "By the way, this costs thirty dollars a head. You can pay Manuel at the front of the tent."

"We have to pay?" I asked.

She gave me a look. "Yes, Harlow. There's wine and food. It costs money."

"I'm sure it will be *well* worth it, sweetheart," Grandpop said. "I'll pay for Lark, since she's poor."

"Thanks, Grandpop," Lark said, standing on her tiptoes to kiss his cheek.

"Oh, drat, I don't have any cash," Grandpop said, looking into his empty wallet. "Harlow, do you mind, honey?"

"As long as they take Venmo or credit cards," I said.

"Can you cover me, too, Harlot?" Robbie asked.

"No," I said.

We walked across the grass, herded by Winnie, to a white tent, smaller than the one for regular visitors. Truro Vineyards, just down Route 6 from Wellfleet, was idyllic with rolling fields and lush grounds. Since summer wasn't in full swing yet, it wasn't as mobbed as it usually was.

Weird, that I was having all these normal thoughts when my whole heart throbbed at the thought of seeing my son again. He wanted to get to know me. It made me euphoric and terrified at the same time. The last time I'd seen him . . . Oh, God. Remembering that day in any sort of detail would just about kill me.

Lark grabbed my hand as if reading my thoughts and squeezed it, giving me her sweet smile, the one thing that differentiated her physically from Addison. "Nice to see you out of scrubs," I said.

"Nice to be out of them," she said. "Are you doing okay? I won't ask anything else. Just are you okay."

"I'm . . . yeah. I'm okay. Happy, even."

"I'm excited for you. He must be great, if he's yours. Whoops! Sorry. I won't say another word."

I felt the familiar sting of tears. "Thanks, sweetie," I whispered.

"Of course. Hey, keep an eye on me in case I fall asleep, okay? I've been working for the past thirty hours."

"You got it."

A sign in front of the tent said, "Welcome, Cape Cod Singles!" in case we didn't feel uncomfortable enough. There were about twenty people here, not counting the Smiths—Reverend White from the Congregational Church (reputedly a bit of a manwhore, but judge not, of course). Lucy Greene, who worked at

Blue Willow Fine Foods and Bakery (I'd marry her just for her cranberry orange muffins). Louisa from Chequessett Chocolate, which I sold at Open Book. Oh, goody, there was Destiny. She'd been looking for love for a long time now. She blew me a kiss. But oh, shoot. Also present was Pete, my date from the Ice House the other day. He was currently glaring at me. I waved. He did not.

There was wine, of course, and I grabbed a glass and drank it fast enough to make it go to my head. Some nice appetizers. I ate a mozzarella ball covered in pesto, then a little hot dog wrapped in filo dough (delicious). People mingled and ate. Most people looked to be between thirty-five and fifty, with a few sixty-to-seventy-somethings tossed in. There was my Girl Scout leader, Mrs. Perry. Maybe she'd be interested in Grandpop. I tried to catch Robbie's eye so he could facilitate something there, but he was flirting with Destiny.

"Hey," said a voice.

I turned. "Grady! Hey. What are you doing here?" The penny dropped. "Oh. Right. Sorry. Are you . . . um, on the market again? Oh, gosh. Cringey. Sorry."

His eyes crinkled in amusement. "It's okay, and yeah. Figured it's time to start dating again."

"Who's looking after Luna? Your mom and dad, or your nanny?"

"She's with the nanny. Probably asleep by now."

"Got it." What time had Matthew gone to bed when he was four? Had he been a good sleeper?

"You looking to date, Harlow?" Grady asked.

"Me? Oh, God, no," I said. "I mean, no judgment, of course . . . I'm just here because Winnie summoned me. I think she needed bodies." I was not doing a great job selling my sister's event. "I think it's great to meet in person instead of on the apps, though. But for me, you know, my life is in a bit of turmoil. On account of . . . my son." God. Those two words. "I think I'll be spending some time with him next week," I said, hoping it was true.

Grady handed me a napkin, and I wiped my eyes. "You okay?" he asked.

"Oh, sure. Crying is my resting state since I . . . you know."

"Understandable." His green eyes stayed on mine for a minute. Then he looked over my head, surveying the crowd. He'd have no problem tonight. Meaningful job, devoted dad, rather brilliant, great trivia player and not bad-looking, either. Funny, I'd known him so long, I'd never really noticed that before.

"Okay, people!" Winnie said in her drill sergeant voice, and I jumped. "Thank you for coming to Outer Cape Singles Night. We'll do this speed-dating style, so take a seat, and you lucky people on this side"—she indicated one side of a long table—"move one seat over every time the bell rings. People on that side, stay put. You have five minutes to talk. Everyone can talk to everyone. It doesn't have to be a romantic connection. Maybe you just want a new friend."

"I do not," Robbie said at the same time Grandpop said, "What a *wonderful* thought!"

Winnie continued, "If you want someone's number, you write down their name. If you match, I'll provide phone numbers. It's not rocket science, is it? Everyone sit down, and we'll get started."

"Good luck, Gray," I said. "You're a catch." Another cringey statement, but he didn't seem to mind. I went to find Grandpop.

"Where are we sitting, Grandpop?" I asked.

"Let's start right here," he said, plunking himself down on

the "stay put" side of the table. He was across from a very cute thirty-something guy with lots of gel in his hair and very long eyelashes. I was across from an attractive woman with short gray hair and many tattoos on her sculpted arms.

"Five minutes starting now!" Winnie said.

"I'm Kate," my person said. "You smell amazing. Jo Malone?"

"Um . . . no. Deep Woods Off." I laughed. She did, too. "Listen, Kate, I'm not actually looking for someone. I'm here with my grandfather. Also, I'm straight. Sorry."

"Oh," she said. "Super." She leaned back in her chair and waved to a waiter, who was carrying a tray of wine-filled glasses.

"I'll have one, too," I said to the server. "Um, Kate, do you want to practice with me?"

"Not really." She took another sip of wine, her eyes wandering to other, eligible people. I felt guilty, as was my way.

"Hello!" said my grandfather to the young man. "I'll go first. I'm looking for someone to take care of me in my dotage. Not quite there yet, though!"

"Cool!" said the young man. "I'm Drummer. Are you wealthy?"

"Okay," said I, leaning against Grandpop so Drummer would know my grandfather was chaperoned. "At least you're direct. I'm his granddaughter and wingman. There will be no sugar daddy situations here." I looked back at Kate, who looked extremely bored. "Um, Kate, what do you do for a living?"

"I'm a bartender."

"Cool! That must be fun!"

She gave me a *please stop* look, so I did.

"You're a drummer!" exclaimed Grandpop. "How wonderful!"

"No," he said, "my name is Drummer, and I'm not at all against having a sugar daddy."

"What did I just say, Drummer?" I asked, rapping my knuckles on the table.

"Do you play other instruments?" Grandpop asked.

"Nope. My name, not my gig."

"I see. Do you have any experience in nursing, sponge baths or cooking soft food?" Grandpop asked.

"I could learn, I guess," Drummer said.

"You'd be her step-grandfather if things work out," Kate told him, gesturing to me.

"You know," said Drummer, "I have, like, mad respect for the greatest generation? World War II heroes, saving the world, am I right?"

"He's just a bit younger than that," I said, "but he did serve in Korea."

"We had a war with Korea?" Drummer asked. "Oh, you're joking. I get it. Do you like K-pop, sir?"

"God, kids are dumb today," said Kate, draining her wine.

"We certainly *did* have a war with Korea, young man!" said Grandpop. "Now, listen, Cymbal. I've never been with anyone but my wife, God rest her soul. Not sure I can even function in that respect anymore, no offense to yourself. You're a very handsome boy—"

"Next!" Winnie yelled.

"Sorry again," I said to Kate.

"Whatever," she said.

"You're very attractive," I added. She rolled her eyes, but fondly, I thought. "I have a friend you might like—"

"Move it, people!" Winnie barked. The other side of the table shuffled a few steps down, some people skipping others (like Grandpop and me).

Grandpop was now seated across from Cynthia.

"For God's sake, Winnie," Cynthia said, twisting her neck around to glare. "He's my uncle."

"Yeah, I vaguely recognize him," said Winnie. "Just practice flirting and exchanging information. Harlow, you do the same."

"Well, now, *you're* a very pretty girl!" Grandpop said to Cynthia. "You look just like my goddaughter!" He laughed merrily.

A man sat across from me. Pete the Poet. Not my night. "Hello again," I said.

"I wrote a poem about you," he said, his face tight as he took out a folded piece of paper.

"I'm excited," I said. "Bring it."

"'There once was a woman named Harlow, who met me for lunch but left solo.'" Another glare. "'She looked in my eye, I felt myself die, but Harlow, she was a liar and wasn't even interested.'"

"Kind of lost the beat there," I said. "Maybe 'but Harlow didn't budge from her no-go?'"

He didn't respond, just folded his arms and literally stuck out his bottom lip.

Down the table, a woman took a picture of Robbie and giggled.

"What are the qualities you're looking for in a partner?" Cynthia asked Grandpop, which, to her credit, was a great question.

"Well, Cynthia, I'm glad you asked," said Grandpop. "I'd like someone who enjoys short walks, because my knees aren't what they used to be. Someone who can cook and clean and isn't averse to changing adult diapers."

I laughed out loud. "Maybe save that last bit for the second date, Pop," I said, grinning at Cynthia. She didn't smile back.

"Next!" Winnie yelled.

A gorgeous, dark-haired woman around forty slid into the

chair across from Grandpop. "Hello, papi," she said with a slight Latin accent, grinning.

"Well, aren't you *lovely*! Do you like old men?"

"Let's find out," she said. Oh, yeah. Grandpop would have a great time with her. Across from me was Grady. "Hey, there," I said with a smile.

"Hi." He smiled back, just a little, his green eyes creasing attractively. I could hardly see the skinny boy who'd been my friend all those years ago, because the man in front of me was . . . well, manly. Tall. Wicked nice shoulders.

"I'll be your guinea pig," I said, clearing my throat. "What qualities are you looking for in a partner, Gray?"

He gave a nod, eyes down, a little smile. "Kindness would be the first. Intelligence. Someone who loves kids, as I have a four-year-old daughter."

"Well, that rules me out," I said. "I'm terrified of children."

"No, you're not," he said.

"I'm terrified of most children," I corrected. "Your child is quite nice. Anyway, what are your hobbies, kind sir?"

"I like trivia nights," he said, smiling again.

"Have you heard of the Kingslayers?" I asked. Our team.

"Their reputation is terrifying," he answered. "Also, I love being on the water and love swimming, being out in my boat, snorkeling and scuba diving."

"Imagine if you didn't. It would make your job much harder."

Another appealing smile. "I also love doing things with my daughter."

"Like what?" I asked.

"Reading to her. Going to Story Time with Grandpop."

"Fabulous answer."

"Taking her on hikes, doing art projects. She loves to be

pushed on the swing. We go to the beach every day, and she picks up shells and rocks, and we put them in a big glass bowl on the coffee table."

Is that what it would've been like if I'd kept Matthew? All those wholesome activities the Cape offered? My eyes were suddenly stinging. Again.

"Next!"

"See you, Gray," I said, swallowing.

The next guy in front of me was Reverend White. "Pass," I said. "No offense, Reverend."

"None taken. I've always wondered why you've never been married, Harlow," he said, leaning back in his chair and accepting a stuffed clam from one of the servers. "You're such a wonderful person."

"And how do you know that, Reverend? I could be a shrivel-hearted miser."

"Oh, please," he said. "You're here with your grandfather. That's all the proof I need. Besides, you should be presenting your best qualities, not turning away compliments."

"Point taken. Thank you for the compliment, Reverend White."

"You are. You're smart, pretty and nice to people, which is a lovely quality."

"Thank you. And you're . . . um, a very good ego booster."

He looked pleased. "I hear you have a bastard son in town."

I jerked. "Okay, first, don't ever call him a bastard again."

"I know, I know. It's my age. We used terms like that back then."

"Still not acceptable."

"But you do, right?" the not-so-good reverend asked. "Have a son?"

I looked away. "Yes."

"Shocking, that you kept him a secret all these years."

"None of your business, Reverend."

"Well, Harlow, people *have* been talking. It's rather monumental news. How are you handling it?"

"Next!" Winnie bellowed. The reverend mercifully switched seats. If he knew, he'd have told everyone he came across. Such a gossip, that guy.

Robbie plunked down in front of me, and a fifty-something woman sat across from Grandpop.

"You are so my type," Robbie said. "I feel like I already love you."

"Shut up," I said, laughing.

"Hello!" Grandpop said, he of the indefatigable energy. "I'm Robert J. Smith, Esquire. And you are, my dear?"

"I'm Lisa B. Townsend, MD," she said, smiling.

Grandpop practically gasped at his good luck. "Can you tell me why my left calf muscle cramps every night at nine forty-five? Wakes me out of a sound sleep."

"Pop, you definitely have game," Robbie said.

The doctor laughed. "Lots of people get those, especially as we get older."

"Should I hire a masseuse? I know there's a little place in Orleans, but the windows are papered over with palm tree posters, and I can't see inside."

"Those massage therapists are actually sex workers, Grandpop," Robbie said.

"How do you know?" I asked.

"No comment."

"Massage can help, but make sure you get a certified massage therapist," said Dr. Lisa. "Make sure you're eating a lot of fruits and veggies. You can also have a gin and tonic every night. Quinine, which is in tonic water, can help a lot."

"Oh, I like *that* suggestion very much!" Grandpop said. "Now. Do you think you'd like to date me?"

"I'm looking for someone a little closer to my age, but if I were thirty years older, definitely," she said.

"What about this mole on my neck?" Grandpop asked, pulling his collar down. "It has *hair* growing out of it!"

"Next!" called Winnie.

An hour later, we were done. Grandpop had four numbers, three from age-appropriate women, one from the woman who'd called him papi. Robbie had sixteen from males and females alike, Lark had five, and I had none, as per my wishes. I wondered how many Grady had . . . he was talking with someone I'd never met before. Good for him.

Turning toward my car, I saw Destiny and waved her over. Just as she reached me, Kate the tattooed bartender walked by us, heading to her own car.

"Hey, Kate," I said, "it was nice meeting you. Um, did you get a chance to meet Destiny here?" They both stopped, looked at each other and then at me. "Destiny, this is Kate, a bartender with a great sense of humor. Kate, meet Destiny, a brilliant former school librarian who works at a charming bookstore."

"Love your name," Kate said.

"Thanks. I picked it myself." She paused, not too subtly looking Kate over. "I'm sorry we didn't meet. I must've missed you when I took a phone call from my sister."

They eyed each other more.

"I'll let you ladies chat," I said, backing away. I couldn't help smiling. Look at me, being an awesome matchmaker.

Just then, my phone chimed. It was from Matthew!

sorry we have to wait for my mom to lecture me before we can meet
up again. hope we can see each other soon.

"No capitalization?" I said through a glaze of happy tears.

I'm great, I typed. Hope you're enjoying the Cape so far. I sent the
message, then I thought about what to say next. I love you? I miss
you? I haven't stopped thinking of you? Please remind your
mother that I'm a good person?

I'm really looking forward to seeing you again, too. Sleep tight!

I deleted "Sleep tight!" and just used a smiley face, then hit
the arrow. He sent back a thumbs-up.

My son was thinking of me. He hoped to see me soon.

TEN

HARLOW

At 8 a.m. on Thursday morning, Rosie Wolfe burst into my kitchen and wrapped her arms around me.

"Hello, Mama," she said, and I immediately began crying. "Oh, ick, stop," she said fondly, patting my back. "Or at least make me a drink while you sob. I don't know what time it is wherever I was last, but it's definitely cocktail hour." She pulled back. "You look awful." She scanned my outfit—jeans and a T-shirt with a logo that said *Arya's Meat Pies, Westeros*—and shook her head.

"Hi," I said, laughing and wiping my eyes. "I'm so, so glad you're here. Thank you for coming. Do you want coffee? I made muffins. Third batch this week. I'm stress-eating."

"First of all, you're my best friend. I had no choice but to come at the most exciting and terrifying moment of your life. Second, please, no more coffee. It's all I've put in my stomach in the past twenty-four hours. But yes to a muffin and alcohol, babe."

"You got it. What would you like?"

"Got orange juice and vodka?" she asked. "Breakfast of champions?"

"I do." I went to the fridge, pulled out some orange juice, poured her a big glass and added a splash of vodka. "Screwdriver, right?"

"Yes. Like the one in my head right now." She sat down in the kitchen chair, bending to pet Ollie, who had his paws on her knee and was whining with love and deep devotion.

"Hello, Oliver. You've only gotten more handsome since the last time I saw you. Will you sleep on my bed while I'm here? You will?"

I set down a blueberry muffin and sat across from her. Rosie looked exhausted, which was common among people who spend two days flying across the planet. Even so, she wore a great outfit—brown plaid pants with a cropped green silk shirt and a long gold cashmere sweater that my dog was baptizing with his drool. There were circles under her eyes and a faint tremor in her hands.

"You okay?" I asked. "I mean, how are you, other than whipped?"

"Overcaffeinated. Delirious with fatigue. Filthy dirty. Can I entertain you with tales of monsoon season in Bangladesh and how it affects flight patterns? Or what it's like to sleep on the floor of an airport in Romania? I was so tired, I lay down, my head on my carry-on, and I wake up, and there's a man lying with his face right next to me, and he's jerking off. Jerking off, Harlow!"

"Oh no!"

"Right? So I scream and jump up, and I'm flapping my arms, completely freaked out. Security comes, but they're not taking me seriously, because it turns out I have a piece of paper stuck in my hair and my makeup is all smeared, and I don't speak Romanian, and they don't speak English . . ." She gulped the drink and held out the glass for another. I obeyed, pouring her the fresh drink, which she sipped more delicately. "Then we were somewhere in Mexico after we were diverted from *Miami* for reasons they didn't tell us, and this family gets on. Six of them and . . . wait for it . . .

their goat. They're German, I think, and they say the goat is their emotional support animal, but Harlow, this goat was basically only good for a pagan sacrifice. It was filthy. Clumps of dirt in its fur, rolling those Satanic eyes, big gray nasty teats hanging down, little poop pellets stuck to its butt and this head like a hunk of concrete, and it's bleating and bucking and shitting everywhere . . ."

I was crying with laughter, and God, it felt good. Rosie. She was my person.

"I have been awake for a year," she said. "I probably smell that way, too. Is there any goat shit on me? Or worse?"

"Go take a shower," I said, "and a nap. There are fresh sheets on your bed and clean towels in the bathroom. When you wake up, I'll tell you about my son." Predictably, my eyes filled with tears. "Rosie . . . I love him."

"I'm not taking a nap," she said indignantly. "The most important thing in your entire life just happened. Let me grab a shower, though. You have a point. I can't imagine how I smell. Oh, crap, I just got a whiff. *Is* there goat shit on me?"

"It's actually semen from that guy in Romania."

"No!" She checked herself. "Oh, damn you, Harlow. Not funny."

A half hour later, she came out, her black hair wet, smelling like the jasmine body wash I'd bought for her. "The flowers in my room are absolutely gorgeous. Thank you," she said. "And look at this breakfast! You should run an inn, Lolo." She fell upon the omelet (spinach, feta and red onion with a side of crisp bacon and toasted rye bread). "God, I'm in heaven. Okay, tell me everything."

I did. From my fainting at the sight of Matthew to hugging him for the second time in my life to my mother's rage, I told her everything. "I still can't believe it," I said. "After all this time, he just walked in. It's like a dream."

"I wish he'd called you first. Given you a minute to prepare."

"I know. He said he didn't think I'd recognize him and just wanted to see me first. But Rosie, it was like my cells knew him before I could figure anything out. And we look alike! Except his hair is black, but it's curly. Same exact nose and chin, and the same dimple Lark has."

"What do his parents think about all this?"

I paused. "Well, they were shocked, too. He didn't tell them about meeting me, and they're . . . I don't know. Concerned? Protective? Freaked out a little? Plus, Monica's not even here yet." I used the edge of my fork to break the toast crust in thirds. "I can't believe he came to find me. I always worried he'd hate me."

"Why, hon?"

"Because some adopted kids do. They feel like their mothers—because it's always the mothers, since we were the ones who were pregnant—abandoned them. There's a theory that every adopted kid is traumatized because they were adopted. No matter if she was a drug addict or in an abusive relationship or a kid herself."

"That sounds like some serious bullshit to me," Rosie said. "It's not like you threw him out a car window."

"But he was a baby. He didn't know that. He just knew I wasn't there, I guess."

Rosie made a face. "Monica was there. Before he was ten minutes old, she was there. Don't go guilt-tripping yourself quite so hard, Harlow. You wanted the best for him, and you came through."

It was easy for her to say. Neither of us was adopted.

"Well," I said, "let's change the subject. How are you? You still dating the cinematographer?"

"Nope. He and his wife reconciled. Again. How's your family, aside from the big bombshell? Will I get to hang out with everyone?"

"Of course," I said. "You're everyone's favorite."

"Except Addison's."

"Except hers. Come on now, it's nap time for you, missy." I stood up and led her upstairs, pulled the shades and folded down the bedcovers. "Those sheets are line dried, I'll have you know," I said.

"I love how you take care of me," she said. "Will you marry my father and adopt me?"

"Absolutely," I said. "Anything for you, Rosie."

ELEVEN

CYNTHIA

If there's anything else, Albert," Cynthia said, not bothering to keep the irritation from her voice. "It's nearly closing."

Bertie Baines glanced at his watch. At least he didn't have to check the time by pulling out his phone, like every other human on earth (except her). Watches were becoming extinct. Such a shame. It was the one thing to appreciate about Bertie Baines's appearance. His thinning, too-long white hair was hideous, and his clothes were stained. Did people not realize that clothing made an impression?

"Guess I lost track of the time," Bertie said.

"Yes. It's four fifty-eight."

He smiled a little. "Got weekend plans, Cynthier?" That accent.

"I do." She didn't elaborate. She had to work, since Harlow was taking so much time off. Otherwise, it was none of Bertie's business. "Did you care to purchase something, or shall we say good night?"

"Sure. Did you read this?" He held up a copy of *Inheritance* by Dani Shapiro, the type of book Cynthia hated the most. A paternity memoir or some such thing. *Oh no! My father wasn't my father!*

Look at me and my insecurity! This obsession with genetics was ridiculous.

"I have not, nor do I intend to. It's now five oh-one, Albert." She didn't want to call him Bertie, the way everyone else did, lest he think they were close enough for nicknames.

"I'll let you know how it is, then."

"Fine." It was more than twenty dollars after tax. Cynthia resisted the urge to tell Bertie Baines to stop spending what little money he had on books and invest in some decent clothing and a haircut.

"Thanks so much," he said.

"You're very welcome." Finally, he was gone.

Why did the raggedy man insist on coming in three times a week? Didn't he have a family? A job? He was probably too old to work, but nonetheless, Cynthia wished some other age-appropriate man would come in to talk to her. Someone who bathed.

If there were rich men on Cape Cod, she had not been able to find them. That singles night had been a complete waste of time. Cynthia had come here because she'd had to, and because Uncle Robert was the only family she had (it didn't hurt that he was wealthy). But she hadn't planned on working in a bookstore, for heaven's sake! She'd *planned* to meet an erudite older man, marry him and live out the rest of her life in comfort, since her idiot ex-husband had stolen her future from her.

It was supposed to have been so different. Damn the whole feminist movement for making things so hard for her. She had been trained to be a gracious housewife and hostess . . . and nothing more. Here on Cape Cod, with all these liberals, all these unsupervised children and sloppy families (Hello, Cousin Gerald!) . . . how was someone like Cynthia supposed to fit in?

She hadn't gone to college, not able to find any subject she was that interested in. She hadn't wanted to live away from home. After all, home had been so lovely! The coolness of the stone house, the stained glass windows, the gracious yard and glorious garden. Kimberly, who seemed ageless, continued to work for them, and Mother and Cynthia found plenty to do together—flower arranging, tending to the garden, card night with Mrs. Cumberland and her daughter, Nancy, who was unmarried and in her forties but very funny. Cynthia sang in the church choir and became a member of the Junior League of Kansas City, that bastion of civility in an unpleasant world.

She took some courses at the junior college, where she made several casual friends, and they would go to the movies or out to a restaurant from time to time. She dated one boy in her sociology class, but on the third date, when he put his hand on her breast, she slapped his face and ordered him to take her home.

Her father asked her if she had plans for the future. "To take care of you, Daddy," she said, and he pinched her cheek. The man had already had two heart attacks, so her offer might be necessary. Mother was delighted to have her at home, and now that Cynthia was older, they became confidantes. Best friends, really. Occasionally, Mother would fix her up with the son of one of her friends, but they either didn't call or only took her out once. It seemed Cynthia had a reputation for being too picky, which was ridiculous. She simply had high standards.

What Cynthia wanted was the same life her mother had—to live in a beautiful house with a maid, and a husband who provided well and appreciated her domestic skills and talent for entertaining (not yet proven, but something Cynthia felt more than capable of). She didn't want to care about the world outside—no war protesting; no causes that were too unpleasant, like hungry children or civil rights. Just Cynthia, her husband and her attractive, spacious home. She wanted to wear high heels and a fancy dress on Saturday nights, when her husband would take her to the country club dance. The maid could stay with her one well-behaved daughter—perhaps one chosen from the orphanage, the prettiest baby there—and the three of them would live in a private little world and be better off for it.

It wasn't how things had turned out.

Instead, Mother was diagnosed with pancreatic cancer just after Cynthia's twenty-fifth birthday and spent the next year shriveling and shrinking, sometimes screaming in pain, which made Cynthia sob. When Mother finally, mercifully, died, Uncle Robert and Aunt Louisa came from Cape Cod for the funeral, hugged Cynthia long and tenderly and stayed for a few days. Only then did Cynthia feel supported. Daddy had taken to the bottle.

The days were long and lonely without Mother. Then Daddy had his third heart attack, as predicted, and needed her to do everything, from pouring him a Scotch to hiring a male nurse to help him bathe. By then, Cynthia was thirty-one, unmarried, only five college courses under her belt. She'd never had a job.

Daddy died from his final heart attack when Cynthia was thirty-five. By then, her father had become a different man from the one she remembered with such reverence, and she couldn't say she was sorry he'd died. Better to have him gone than forgetting who she was or, horribly, soiling himself. Of course she was sad, but also relieved.

Cynthia had assumed she'd get the house and a comfortable inheritance. She was wrong. To her shock, the house was mortgaged to the hilt, all the money going to her parents' medical bills. It was a horrible betrayal. Daddy had been a banker, after all. He should've planned more carefully. At the very least he could have warned her.

At the funeral, when she asked Uncle Robert what she was going to do, he seemed confused. "Well, honey, you're certainly old enough to get a job," he said unhelpfully.

"You're so bright," Aunt Louisa said. "You'll find something that suits you."

Cynthia did *not* find anything that suited her. After all, she was used to a certain lifestyle. She wasn't going to peck away at a word processor or file papers. She stayed in the house, almost daring the bank—the same bank Daddy had worked for—to kick her out. She had to let Kimberly go, and oddly, Kimberly didn't even seem to mind.

After some months, Cynthia found work at a florist. At least she was surrounded by something beautiful, rather than sitting in a stuffy office with men who smoked cigarettes and thought they knew everything. Like her father.

More than ever, Cynthia realized she'd have to marry money. She hated dating, hated having to practically hand out a list of what she would and wouldn't do at the end of the night. She hated bars and couldn't afford places like the opera or ballet anymore. Besides, not many young, unmarried men went to those. She hated being set up by a well-meaning friend of her parents, only to find that her date was a car mechanic or a mailman. For heaven's sake! Who did they think she was?

When the bank finally evicted her, Cynthia found a place to live by agreeing to be a nighttime companion to Gertrude Hanson, a wealthy old woman who went to bed at eight and slept a solid twelve hours, thanks to the Benadryl that Cynthia gave her each night. The house had the sharp smell of old age and stagnation, but it was a gracious older home in a prestigious neighborhood, better than anything she could afford.

The years slid by. Gertrude got more and more forgetful but didn't die, which was a relief. Cynthia still had a place to live and a little spending money. She did enjoy flower arranging, but hers was hardly a fulfilling existence. Cynthia didn't want to change, however. She wanted the change to come to her.

And finally, it did.

One day, a neatly dressed, rather plain-faced man came into the flower shop and stopped to fondle the orchids in the front. His shoes were shined to a high gleam, and his trousers were light wool, the kind her father used to wear. He had on a sharp white shirt with crisp collar points and a wool vest in an argyle pattern. His hair was brown and thinning, and he had a very close shave—refreshing in this day of stubble.

Cynthia, now in her mid-forties, was wearing a dress (as she did every day, still hoping to make the right impression on the right person). She had on her mother's pearls, because otherwise the female patrons treated her like the help. Which she was, tragically.

"I need some flowers for my mother," the man said, and she could just tell he was upper-class. "Anything but orange, please. She despises orange," he added with a grin.

Cynthia smiled. "I'll be happy to take care of that for you." His watch looked expensive. She took a chance, aware of the fact that she hadn't been on a date in more than two years. "I love seeing a man who cares about how he dresses," she said. "It's so rare these days."

"Thank you. And the same to you, miss. I sometimes think I was born in the wrong era."

Cynthia nearly gasped. "So do I! I wish I *had* been born at a different time, frankly. I've always felt a little . . . dismayed that I landed here."

"I would've been a perfect nineteen-forties husband," he said easily. "Postwar, preferably."

"Do you know," she said, lowering her voice, "that I've never worn jeans in public? I think they look crass on a woman."

He smiled. "I don't suppose you'd meet me for dinner one night, would you?"

She was surprised by the invitation, which seemed a bit sudden, but she couldn't deny being pleased, too. She paused as if to consider it. "I'd love to," she answered with a coy smile.

His name was Henry Millstone, and he had money, all right. Family money, the best kind. His home was in a good neighborhood, though rather plain. She could work with it, she supposed.

They dated the old-fashioned way . . . in other words, he paid, and she didn't put out. Some Saturdays, they would stroll the various parks and museums of Kansas City, then stop somewhere for a cocktail. He took her to the opera. She prepared a picnic for him. She told him about her childhood, mentioning the country club, the season tickets to the opera and ballet, the Junior League. As for Gertrude, Cynthia said she was an aunt who doted on her, and a soft heart was the reason Cynthia lived there.

Henry was heir to a wallpaper company founded by his mother. Apparently, the Saudis and Russians adored her work, and the paper couldn't be printed fast enough. Henry also wanted to design wallpaper, but his mother was resistant, so he was the de facto manager of the company.

"I'd quit and start my own business," Henry said, "but the money is just too good."

"I understand completely," Cynthia said. "You value security.

There's nothing wrong with that. Your day will come." According to the internet, his mother's company was worth $25 million. He'd be an *idiot* to quit, since he was her only child. His mother was in her eighties now, still working every day . . . but she *was* in her eighties.

Seven months after they met, Henry presented her with 1.78 carat emerald-cut diamond flanked by sapphires, net worth $18,000 according to the jeweler who appraised it the next day. She'd already said yes . . . she just wanted to make sure he wasn't being cheap. Henry's mother insisted on a prenup, but divorce was unlikely, Cynthia thought, and even if that happened, the prenup allowed her to get a healthy percentage of Henry's net worth. In a surprise to both of them, Henry's mother gave them her beautiful brick Tudor as a wedding gift, saying the house was too much for her. It was dazzling (ugly wallpaper aside). Cynthia told Henry her "Aunt Gertrude" had gone to live with another relative in Upstate New York and left Mrs. Hanson's.

Their wedding itself was small and tasteful. Uncle Robert and Aunt Louisa came, her only family. She hadn't invited Cousin Gerald and his wife, who had a brood of children by this time. She asked Robert to walk her down the aisle and wore her mother's gown, shedding a few tears that Mother wasn't here to share the day. It was all so elegant. Finally, Cynthia felt as if she'd landed where she was meant to be.

Like Queen Elizabeth and the Duke of Edinburgh, she and Henry had adjoining bedrooms, because Henry snored, and Cynthia was a light sleeper. Sex was tolerable, and Henry was quick, at least. It was embarrassing, all that grunting and moaning. But she enjoyed her husband's company. He was more of a friend than anyone had ever been—except Mother, of course—and finally, Cynthia could live the life she had been trained for.

It was with great glee that they stripped the house of his mother's wallpaper and painted the rooms instead. They spent huge sums of money on new furniture, paintings and beautiful things. Henry was someone in Kansas City society—or at least, his mother was—and so Cynthia was adopted into the world of fundraisers, galas and boards. Her husband loved hearing about the petty politics involved—they both loved gossip—and she loved hearing about his tyrannical mother. They had many deliciously bitter talks about her narcissism, her outdated taste. Soon, however, Joan would be dead, and Henry would get everything.

At home, Cynthia dedicated herself to living as her mother had taught her—working in the garden, transforming it into an oasis. They entertained Henry's business colleagues at various restaurants and had the occasional dinner party, hosting their neighbors or acquaintances.

Neither of them wanted children. At this point, Cynthia was too old to want to care for someone else. They mocked the people who worshipped their children. "We considered being childless," someone might say, "but that was before we had Melanoma." Or "We'd sure have a lot more money without Linen, Latin and Lakota! But you can't put a price on children." She and Henry would exchange a look across the table, silently congratulating themselves.

She kept up her friendship with Louisa, once meeting her in Philadelphia for the flower show. They had stayed pen pals and talked on the phone several times a year, though she was completely uninterested in hearing about Louisa's grandchildren, all with ridiculous names (except the boy). Still, Louisa was the only friend she'd had all her life, and they discussed books and authors, Louisa telling her about the occasional event at her little bookstore.

"You must come visit!" Louisa said. "I'm dying for you to meet my grandchildren. They're growing so fast."

Cynthia had no desire to meet those grandchildren, or reconnect with Gerald. Oh, Cape Cod sounded pretty enough, but she and Henry traveled to more . . . well, more elegant places on their vacations. London, Vancouver, Venice.

When Henry's mother *finally* gave up the ghost at the age of ninety-one, he did indeed inherit her business and her vast fortune. Finally, Henry could live his dream and take Millstone Décor in a new direction. Did Cynthia like his wallpaper? No, but she hadn't liked his mother's, either. She pretended to admire his designs, of course, and listened to him drone on about business and accounts and competitors, hoping he didn't sense her boredom. He'd been a lot more interesting fuming about his mother.

Did she love Henry? In a way. Had Mother loved Daddy? Did it matter? Henry worked, and Cynthia made a home, listened to him talk, murmured in the right places, and played the dead starfish twice a month . . . that is, spread her limbs and let her husband climb aboard.

Every once in a while, someone they knew would adopt a child, or she'd hear a news story related to adoption, and she'd remember that she, too, was adopted. Strange, how much it meant to some people. Most people, it seemed. The only thing Cynthia felt for her birth mother was a faint tinge of pity. Stupid of her to get pregnant when she had no way to support a child. And heavens, if she had been raped, all the more pity, but Cynthia certainly didn't want to know if her conception had been the result of violence.

She was happy. She loved home, loved sitting with a book in

their beautiful sunroom, picking flowers from her own garden and having a cocktail at six o'clock every night, especially when Henry worked late, which was more and more these days.

One evening over dinner (leg of lamb, one of his favorites), she was filling him in on the fashion show the Junior League was planning. "And there was Jill Sheffield, lecturing the rest of us on fashion when she was wearing a purple rayon dress that looked like it came out of the Goodwill bin, Henry!" She laughed merrily. This was where they really connected . . . mocking other people.

But to her surprise, he said, "Does it really matter, Cynthia? There are more important things in the world than what's-her-name's ugly dress."

Her mouth snapped closed in irritation, and she took a sip of water. "Is that so. Do you want to discuss terrorism, then? Or the famine in Africa? I was just trying to share a part of my day with my husband."

"I can't deal with your stupid little fashion show," he said. "I have a lot going on at the company."

She rolled her eyes, but he didn't notice. Henry thought he was a titan of industry, but it wasn't as if he'd invented the iPhone, for heaven's sake. Ugly wallpaper . . . how hard could it be?

Her fiftieth birthday came and went unnoticed by her once-thoughtful husband. She'd been expecting a party, or at least an expensive gift. She didn't even get a card. As revenge, she bought herself an Elsa Peretti gold cuff bracelet from Tiffany's for $20,000. That got his attention, all right. They fought harshly, her accusing him of forgetting one of the most significant days of her life, him accusing her of being self-indulgent and wasteful.

It was almost inevitable that Henry would have an affair.

Their tepid sex life had dwindled to a biannual event. Still, when he told her, she was stunned . . . not by the affair, but by the fact that Henry had the balls to go for it. He was in *love*, he said, which made her laugh out loud.

"Congratulations," she said, sarcasm oozing. At this point in her life and their marriage, divorce was preferable. Her prenup said she'd get 25 percent of his net worth, and he'd inherited a company worth $29 million at the time of Joan's death. She could live off $7.25 million. She could live off that quite well. "I want the house," she said. "Otherwise, I won't fight you."

"This house has been in my family for two generations."

"We'll see. A case can be made that I restored this entire place."

"Painting a few rooms and planting tulips is hardly restoration, Cynthia," he snapped.

"Well, I'll certainly get the contents I bought," she said. After all, she'd spent tens of thousands of dollars on this house . . . his money, of course. But that had to be worth something. She loved this place almost as much as her childhood home.

"The court will decide what you get," he said. "I'm going to bed."

A chill ran down Cynthia's spine. She hadn't brought any money to the marriage. There were no children.

For the next few weeks, Cynthia was on fire, squirreling away whatever she could. All her jewelry, of course. The ugly Tiffany vase Joan had acquired. Everything Henry had given her as a gift, including a painting that looked like graffiti, which turned out to be worth $40,000. Certainly, all her designer clothes, shoes and purses—Armani, Gucci, Carolina Herrera.

It was when they sat down with the lawyers that Cynthia

learned Henry had run Millstone Décor into the ground. To get back at his mother, Henry had discontinued all her designs and featured only his own. The company was now worth $1.2 million, thanks only to the factory space it occupied. She shouldn't have been surprised.

"Your mother knew this would happen," she hissed, knowing the words were a knife in his liver. "How satisfied she'd be to know she was right about your incompetence."

"Doesn't matter," Henry said. "Nadia and I are in love, and that's priceless. And we have the house." That burned.

Oh, and Nadia? A thirty-five-year-old Venezuelan widow with three children under ten years of age. She wasn't even pretty. And the children! Henry didn't *like* children! Well, Nadia would be in for a surprise if she thought she was marrying money. If she was relying on Henry's business acumen, they'd all be on the streets in a year.

Cynthia's takeaway sum would be somewhere around $400,000, including the sale of essentially everything she owned. Foolishly, she'd believed Mother's credo of "less is more" where jewelry was concerned, that bracelet aside. Four hundred thousand sounded like a lot to most people, but most people hadn't married someone once worth nearly $30 million.

Cynthia listed her purses and gowns on a website that sold used designer wear. The Tiffany vase . . . $1,200. Even the ugly painting had depreciated.

It was so humiliating. She couldn't stay in Kansas City, not when she'd been so high and was now so low. It was possible that she'd find another wealthy man to marry, but she was in her fifties now, and rich men her age were dating women a generation younger. She'd have to move. Somewhere cheap.

As she was packing up her things, weeping over the home she'd have to leave behind, the phone rang. The caller ID said *Louisa Smith*. Good. She could pour out her heart to Louisa, tell her how awful Henry had been. She grabbed the phone.

"Hello, Louisa, I'm so glad you called," she said. "I'm having an awful time of it."

"Cynthia, dear, it's Uncle Robert."

"Oh. Hello, Uncle Robert. How are you?"

"I'm afraid I have some sad news," he said, and his voice thickened. "My dear Louisa died two days ago. The cancer finally got her."

"Oh no!" Cynthia said, genuinely stricken. Another blow. The only friend she really had. Of *course* it had to happen now, because life just kept on kicking her in the stomach. Louisa had been fighting cancer for ages, but the last time they'd talked, four or five months ago, she'd sounded chipper. It wasn't exactly a surprise, but even so. "I'm very sorry, Uncle Robert."

"Thank you, dear. I know you and she were close. I thought you might want to come to her funeral."

Cynthia looked around at the boxes and tissue paper, the suitcases. "Uncle Robert, I'm so sorry, but I can't. I'm getting divorced, and everything is chaos. My husband is kicking me to the street, marrying a younger—"

"I'm sorry, dear, I should go," Uncle Robert said. "We'll talk again soon, but I have arrangements to make."

She paused. "Of course. I'm so sorry for your loss."

"Yes. Well. Take care of yourself, dear."

"You too, Uncle Robert. I'll call soon."

She hadn't seen them since her wedding day. Poor Uncle Robert!

And then, a mercenary but intelligent thought crept into her brain. Uncle Robert was well-off. He'd been a lawyer and had old Yankee money . . . Suddenly, the future was clear.

A week later, Cynthia walked through her beautiful house once more, crying at her misfortune. Goodbye, walnut paneling and slate roof, mullioned windows and oak floors. Goodbye, stone fireplace and butler's pantry. She would not miss Henry one bit. Men. First her father, now Henry, ruining everything.

Cynthia drove across the country, her BMW pulling a tacky U-Haul with a cowboy painted on the side. She stayed in inexpensive hotel chains on the way, mourning her former life. But she also made plans for what was to come. Her money wouldn't last forever.

Uncle Robert would help her. After all, Louisa had been Cynthia's lifelong friend. Uncle Robert was her godfather. Didn't he walk her down the aisle? But she was not so naïve as to trust another man to take care of her. Uncle Robert had a son of his own and all those grandchildren. It was doubtful he'd just write her a check.

Somewhere along Interstate 90 in Pennsylvania, Cynthia had an idea.

She had saved all those letters from Louisa in a pretty box, a habit from a more civilized time. Louisa would want the best for her, wouldn't she? She would, Cynthia decided. When she crossed the Cape Cod Canal at last, she checked into a grotty motel and rummaged through the U-Haul until she found the box of letters. Back in her musty little room, she studied the handwriting. Copied it. Spent a couple of days perfecting it, then went into Hyannis and hunted down the thick kind of paper Louisa had used—red Florentine from Crane.

It took her several tries to get the wording and handwriting just right.

Dear Cynthia,

   How wonderful to hear from you! We are so alike in so many ways, I often feel you are the daughter I never had. Oh, how I hope you'll come to the Cape and take over my share of the bookstore, just as we've discussed so many times. You'd be such a wonderful addition, and it would be my dream come true. I miss you so, dear friend. I know my Robert would love having you there, especially after I pass away. You've always been so special to him. Please consider it!

   Lots of love,

   Louisa

Maybe because his grief was fresh, maybe because he was an old man, it worked. Uncle Robert signed over 25 percent of the store to her. Apparently Harlow, his oldest granddaughter, had already swooped in and claimed 50 percent.

And so, with a down payment from her divorce settlement and because Cynthia was a co-owner of a local business, the bank gave her a mortgage large enough for her to buy a tiny place. The housing market on Cape Cod was ridiculous, and all she could afford was this two-bedroom "condo." Ha. A shack was more like it, with red laminate kitchen counters and a cracked linoleum floor, a bathroom so small she could barely squeeze past the toilet to the shower. It made her furious.

However, her shack was right on the water, and every night, she fell asleep to the sound of the ocean just a few yards away. The sunsets were pretty, of course, but it didn't make up for anything.

The pangs of guilt faded. So what if she'd lied to Uncle Robert? He was her godfather. He should've looked out for her when Daddy was sick. Besides, he had it to give.

Forging that letter had been the only thing to do. She had to look out for herself, because no one else would. The pay and profits from the bookstore were hardly what she was used to, but she had her ways. She deserved more, and she'd make sure she got it.

TWELVE

HARLOW

I say this with great authority," Rosie said Friday morning as I poured her a cup of coffee at Open Book before we opened. "This is the prettiest bookstore in the world."

Had Matthew liked it? Would he come back here? I'd bet Monica would like it. The thought of seeing her again had me shaking in my sandals.

"Thanks, pal," I said. It was true. "I never knew I wanted to run a bookstore until I was running a bookstore."

"It suits you," Rosie said.

"Just like your job suits you," I said. "The coolest job for the coolest chick."

"I don't know. Location scouting is travel all the time. I think I should quit and move here."

"Don't get my hopes up," I said. "But just in case you're serious, we already know we're great roommates. Have a muffin. Blue Willow delivers them every morning, but be forewarned. They're even better than mine. I think the baker's a witch."

Rosie broke off a hunk and put it in her mouth, closed her eyes and groaned. "I see what you mean," she said. "There are more of these, yes?"

"Yes," I said. "Eat two. I have to open and do a few things, but you're welcome to hang out here. Grab a book, make yourself comfy. But if you want to wander around town or go to the beach, that's fine, too."

"I'm staying right here," she said. "Oh, shoot, I forgot my phone. Be right back." She darted out the back, and I heard her footsteps on the stairs. A few minutes later, she returned, cheeks flushed, looking fresh and pretty as . . . well, as a rose. "And now, I shall relax," she announced. "Because I'm on Cape Cod, and it's what we do here."

I laughed. Rosie had visited many times, from the summer between our sophomore and junior years to just last January. I loved seeing my hometown from her eyes, and hey, if she wanted to move here, it would be a dream come true.

When I'd come home from California, humbled and unsure of my future, I moved in with my grandparents rather than Mom and Dad. The cancer my grandmother had been fighting had come back, and it made sense for me to move into their house and be a de facto caregiver. I'd always helped out at Open Book, so it was a natural progression for me to work there full-time. By then, my grandparents had converted their first floor in order to save Grammy's knees from the stairs, so Grammy suggested I take the upper two floors and make them an apartment.

In the years of Grammy's cancer battles, the store had stagnated a bit, becoming a dusty, quiet place filled with classic literature and used books, a few new releases from big authors, like James Patterson and Nora Roberts. It made my grandmother a bit sad, but she lacked the energy to revive it.

I did not. *This* was a project I could handle. The store was a gem waiting to happen. The first thing I did was ask my grandparents if I could close the place down for a month or two. They agreed, pleased that I was excited to join the business.

The thing about bookstores is that the best ones appear peaceful and mysterious, offering a quiet way to spend an hour or two, to browse and read a few pages, away from the world. Buy a few books and the soul was soothed. The reality was, for this to happen, a thousand things took place behind the scenes.

Open Book had had a lot going for it—the building was appropriately creaky and rich with character. Formerly the home of Captain Jedediah Smith, it had been built to house the good captain's sixteen children. When Grammy started the store in the 1980s, they'd divided the first floor of the house and put on an addition with a new kitchen and full bathroom. The rest of the first floor—the drawing room, the library, a bedroom, the enclosed front porch and the entryway—was the bookstore. It had always been delightfully crowded, cozy and dark . . . and unprofitable. Dust and cobwebs had accumulated, and there were books on the shelves that had been there since I was a kid. The lighting was poor and the windows let in the cold.

With the money I'd banked during my law school summers in LA, working fourteen-hour days at one of the biggest firms in the city, I could afford to sink in some cash.

"Yes, yes, bring this place into the new century!" Grammy had said. "I've always wanted to and just never managed."

The two of us had discussed which walls to take down; where various genres should be placed; how to keep the essence of the cozy, charming place but invigorate it, too. We'd keep the faded Persian rug but rip up the carpeting my great-grandmother had put in over honey-colored oak floors. The register should be along this side, the children's section on the porch. New releases on a table in front; classics in the back; romance, mystery, general fiction and thrillers lining the walls or tucked into an alcove.

Grammy loved making it over—well, she loved me making it

over, and I think it gave her a little kick of energy, seeing her sweet little business blossoming with new ideas. I found a battered leather couch for in front of the fireplace, bought a few wing chairs and refreshed an old trunk to use as a coffee table. Mom pitched in and painted the ceiling and walls of the kids' section with blue skies and clouds, Cape birds flying above the bright blue sea.

We started holding events—Story Time with Grandpop, Romance Lovers Book Club, Mystery Lovers Book Club, YA Book Club. We had a Valentine's Day night for singletons, and at least three people who'd met at our store ended up married. We had Scary Stories Afternoon the day before Halloween. At Christmas, Santa, who looked a lot like my dad, stopped by. We asked local authors to do signings and talks, because you couldn't swing a cat on Cape Cod without hitting an author. I joined the Independent Booksellers Association and yearned to have events the way RJ Julia in Connecticut did . . . they had just about every single big-name author and celebrity in America at their store for a new release. But they were conveniently located midway between New York City and Boston. The Cape was out of the way, and our traffic was notorious.

I reached out to schools to see if teachers would order their books through us and gave students, teachers, first responders and medical professionals a 15 percent discount. I approached local businesses to let them know we'd love to supply any books they might need for training or seminars. If your book club purchased more than ten of the same title, you'd get a free goodie basket for one of your members—coffee from Beanstock Roasters, an array of Chequessett chocolates, a journal, a lovely pen, a box of stationery.

I lost myself there, working twelve hours or more every day, unpacking inventory every Monday night before the new releases came out on Tuesdays, glazing the old windows, talking with publisher reps, asking customers what they liked and adjusting inventory according to what sold best. I plunged the toilet, fixed the leak in the roof, ran the cash register, joined the Chamber of Commerce.

By the end of the first year, I hired Destiny part-time. In her previous life, she'd been a school librarian. The kids especially adored her, since she could always find a book for even the most reluctant reader. She started a teen writing club, held at the store on Saturday mornings. At the holidays, we beefed up our gift section and hired wrappers, and in the summer, we'd employ a couple of wonderfully bookish kids to help out as well.

I loved it. I *needed* it, too . . . a purpose, something to take my mind away from the child who wasn't mine anymore and focus on something positive, something for the town, something I loved. I sent out a newsletter with staff book recommendations, event listings and fun facts about famous authors. *Did you know that Sherry Thomas, author of the Lady Sherlock series, taught herself English by reading romance novels? Or Roald Dahl, author of* Charlie and the Chocolate Factory, *once worked at Cadbury as a taste-tester.* Grammy would offer one of her recipes, and Destiny would list research websites other than Wikipedia for kids.

At night, I'd fall into bed, exhausted and eager to do it all again the next day. It wasn't what I had planned to do with my life, but I think it was what I was *meant* to do. All around me, I had books, my constant friends. They helped me through the sad days, kept me company when I was lonely, brought me to places I'd never seen and introduced me to characters who felt like friends. When Grammy died three years ago, I know she was proud of what we'd done with her store. Destiny came on full-time, and Cynthia joined the staff, taking over the accounting, my least favorite part of the job.

Open Book was the heart of our little town, in fact. I hoped my son would see that.

As if on cue, my phone dinged with a text from an unknown number.

Hi, Harlow, it's Monica Patel. Just confirming that tomorrow at 3:00 still works.

My nerves buzzed. Yes, that's great. Hope your trip went smoothly. Three dots, then: Thanks, it did. See you tomorrow.

What a strange relationship—two women, almost strangers, mothers to the same child. When I was pregnant, my relationship with Monica was probably the most intimate I had ever been with someone, even Rosie. I had given her my son and trusted her with his life.

"Harlow!"

I looked up from my phone. "Hey, Cynthia."

"I've been talking to you for a solid minute and you haven't even acknowledged me," she said.

"Sorry. What is it?"

She complained about the lack of space in the storeroom (which was filled with books; kind of our purpose, but she could complain about anything). "Sure, I'll make some room, but technically, I'm on vacation."

"Lest we forget," she sniped.

At ten fifteen, in came Grandpop. "Rosie!" he exclaimed. "The prettiest girl in the world after my granddaughters!"

"Mr. Smith," she said, standing up and hugging him. "My future husband. So wonderful to see you."

"Oh, aren't you *delightful*," he said, holding her by the shoulders to take a look. "I should be so lucky. Did Harlow tell you I'm dating again?"

Rosie turned to me. "How could you let him date anyone but me, Harlow?" she said, and Grandpop threw his head back and laughed. They chatted amiably about her job for a minute or two before Rosie decided she needed another nap to counteract her jet lag.

A couple hours later, I went up to my apartment to find Rosie awake. "Want to go to the beach?" I asked.

"Hell yes," she said.

"Go change, and I'll put some snacks together," I said.

A few minutes later, she came down in a bikini that resembled a few Band-Aids and strings. "The waves are going to pull that right off you," I said. My own suit was a very sensible tankini.

"I know, but how much longer are we going to look like this?" she said. "Even if I am a little bony."

"I've got the sunscreen. Fifty factor, apply every two hours," I said.

She laughed. "Yes, dear."

We drove to Nauset Light Beach in Eastham, just over the town line. For one, it had the incredibly picturesque lighthouse, the unofficial mascot of the Cape. For two, it was in Eastham, where my son and his family were staying for the summer. If we ran into them, well, those things happened all the time, right?

We didn't run into them. But we found a place on the sand not too far from the lifeguard stand and spread our blanket, set up the umbrella. I'd packed us a picnic with sandwiches and bottles of iced tea and some cherries. It was a perfect beach day— dry and sunny with big waves and a cool breeze off the water.

I slathered sunscreen on Rosie—so much skin showing, all so white—and she returned the favor for the inch of skin I couldn't reach. For a little while, we just sat, listening to the waves and the snatches of conversation and music that the breeze brought us.

"I never go to the beach back home," Rosie said.

"Why not?"

"Just seems like too much work." She sounded somber.

I looked at her a minute. "Being by the water is good for your soul," I said. "Even on the days I don't really feel like it, I'm never sorry that I came."

She smiled at me. "Yeah. Self-care and all that."

"Yes. Self-care and all that. You look wrung out, and I'm going to take good care of you while you're here."

"Good. Then I'll never leave."

"Good. And I'll always take care of you."

"Damn it, woman," she said, standing up. "You're the love of my life. If we were gay, everything would be so simple. Come on, let's go swimming."

Rosie always forgot how cold the water was here, so I grabbed her hand and ran toward the water so she couldn't back out. The second a wave hit her, she shrieked with laughter.

"It's so cold!" she yelled. "How are we still alive when it's this cold?"

"Dive under," I said. "Trust me, it's easier this way."

"That's what he said." But she did it, and we went out a bit farther.

"What's the plan if we see a shark?" she asked, clutching my hand as a wave picked us up.

"You run onto the beach and preemptively get a tourniquet while I engage the great white, saving your life."

"I'm gonna write you the best eulogy ever."

When we could no longer feel our feet and several gray seals had popped up a wee bit too close, we went back to shore.

Rosie paused. "I love a good father," she said, watching a guy pick up his child and swing her above the waves. "So hot. Look at those abs. Hello, Daddy."

"That's my friend," I said. "Grady Byrne. And his daughter, Luna."

"Is he single?" Rosie asked.

"He is. Divorced."

"And you're not climbing him like a tree because . . . ?"

I laughed. "Because he's . . . well, he's still raw, I think. And the kid thing. He's a serious guy looking for a stepmother for his little girl." But he did look wicked appealing there, laughing with his kid, tossing her up in the air. Gorgeous arms.

He turned and saw us, and I waved. Bending down, he said something to Luna, and she came running over to me.

"Miss Harlow! I didn't know you came to the beach. Don't you have to stay at the bookstore?"

"They let me out once in a while," I said. "Luna, this is my friend, Miss Rosie."

"Hello," she said. Then Grady joined us, and she wrapped her arm around his leg.

"Hey," he said. "I'm Gray." He stuck out his hand to Rosie. "Harlow and I went to high school together."

"And prom, if I remember correctly," she said, offering her hand as if he should kiss it.

"Rosie and I were college roommates, and we shared an apartment in Los Angeles for a couple years. She knows everything about me," I said. "Grady Byrne, meet Rosie Wolfe. Rosie, not only was Gray my prom date, he is also on our trivia team, totally elevating our science game."

"The whole package," Rosie murmured appreciatively.

Gray looked at me. His nose had a slight burn on it, and there were droplets of water in his stubbly beard. A few freckles. His green eyes were somber. "How are you, Harlow?"

He was asking about my son. "Good. I'm seeing his parents tomorrow. You know, to talk about how things are going to go from here."

He nodded. "Hope it goes well."

"Thanks, Gray. Me too."

"Daddy, can you take me back in the water?" Luna asked.

"You bet," he said. "Nice meeting you, Rosie. See you both tonight?"

"Absolutely," I said. "Kingslayers forever."

He grinned, and sure, I felt a little . . . tug. Who wouldn't? Gray took Luna's hand, then they walked back down the beach to where they'd been before, in front of their blanket and towels.

"That man should be on a calendar of Hot Dads," Rosie said as we went back to our blanket. "Did I sense a little zing there, Miss Smith?"

"He's a good guy," I said, sitting down. "And yes, nice-looking. A high school dork turned hottie, just like in all the books." I lowered my voice. "But he's a single dad."

"And?"

I hesitated. "Well, I don't think I should date anyone with kids. It always seems more serious that way."

"As opposed to what?"

"I don't know," I said, grabbing the sunscreen to reapply. "James, I guess."

"Your fuck buddy?"

"Inside voice, please. Yeah. Like James."

"Who is basically a vibrator in human form."

"Well, he's a good cellist, too."

"I don't know," Rosie said. "I feel like *I'm* more the fuck buddy type, and you should be baking a little kid oatmeal raisin cookies. I bet that little girl would love you for a stepmother."

"Nah. I don't think I should help raise someone else's kid when . . . you know. When I didn't raise my own."

"You know, putting a kid up for adoption when you're not even eighteen is not something that needs punishment," she said. I didn't answer. "Well," she added, mercifully letting it go, "if I was staying here, the hot dad would be on my list. Speaking of hot guys, will we see your brother anytime soon?"

"My *baby* brother, you mean? He's the DJ tonight. You can see him then."

I spent two hours looking at Monica's social media when Rosie and I got back from the beach and Rosie was upstairs, working. Tomorrow, I would see Sanjay and Monica again, and maybe— the thought made my knees weak with nerves—and maybe my son, too.

Her Facebook and Instagram accounts were careful . . . pictures of food and pretty views from vacations, a lot of her and Sanjay. She didn't post any of her children unless their faces were hard to identify. There was a shot from behind . . . Matthew and Meena walking on a beach with huge boulders, his arm around her shoulders. A long shot of them on horseback in what looked like Glacier National Park or the Canadian Rockies.

The years had been good to Monica. She had always been pretty, but now she was beautiful. In a picture from her company's website, she looked both approachable and regal. Her shiny black hair was cut in a chin-length bob, and her subtle makeup accented her blue eyes. I'd bet the diamond studs in her ears were real, and not the cheapies I bought in P-town.

The last time I'd seen Monica, I'd just pushed a baby out of me. She'd been thirty at the time, I thought. So now, close to fifty. A mother to a girl, too. Would she welcome me back into their lives? Would she resent the fact that Matthew had found me? Some adoptive parents felt threatened by that, even subconsciously. I couldn't blame them, really. They'd done all the hard work, and suddenly there was someone else, someone their kid was dying to get to know. A new and shiny mother.

All I could do was hope for the best.

At six thirty, I went downstairs and knocked on Grandpop's door, then went in. He was sleeping in his recliner. "Grandpop? Wake up. Time for trivia."

"Where am I?" he asked. "Oh, yes! Hello, Harlow, my dear! You look very pretty today."

Every man should be like my grandfather, I thought. Never a bad word about anyone, always cheerful, always sneaking in some wisdom just when you thought his mind was slipping. I kissed him on the head. "Ready for another winning season?"

"The Kingslayers return!" he said. "And we shall vanquish our foes!"

Rosie, Grandpop and I walked down to the Ice House, which was packed with us trivia nerds and a few innocent tourists. Robbie was our DJ and master of ceremonies for the night. A second after he saw us, "Someone to Watch Over Me" started playing.

Grammy and Grandpop's favorite song. Just when a person thought Robbie was a wastrel youth, too. Grandpop pretended to tip his hat to his namesake, then put his hands over his heart.

"Robbie!" Rosie cried, and cantered over to hug him as I made my way through the crowd. Something happened to me when I played trivia. My killer instinct came out. It was the one place in my life where I was competitive and bent on global domination. I loved the regular trivia teams with our dumb names and trash talk, but I was here to win.

"Heard you had a big surprise, Harlow," said Pedro Silva, who had recently joined the I See Dumb People team.

"Yes, I did," I said. "But I have nothing to report."

"That's okay," he said, patting my hand. "Just wanted to acknowledge his existence."

"Thank you." I'd always liked Mr. Silva, who came into the bookstore and bought disaster-at-sea books whenever possible. Also on the team was his on-again, off-again wife, who terrified me, and my friend Lillie Silva's honey, Ben, who was also Mr. Silva's longtime first mate. Or, no, Ben was the captain now. (Barkhad Abdi, *Captain Phillips*, Academy Award nomination, *Look at me, I am the captain now*, said my trivia brain). Happily, Lillie's loyalties were to the Kingslayers (which was great, because we'd be left hanging in the medical department otherwise).

I walked over to where Robbie and Rosie were laughing and tousled my brother's hair. Same as Matthew's hair. There was that adrenaline, spearing my stomach.

"Why wasn't I told that Rosie was in town?" Robbie asked.

"Why do you think you're important enough to know these things?" I asked.

"Oh, sibling bickering," Rosie said. "I love it."

"Let's go sit down," I said. "It's about to start."

"She's so pathetic," Robbie said to my friend. "This is the most exciting thing she does. Ever. Except when she's out having secret babies."

That earned him a smack on the head. "No adoption jokes. Too soon."

"Got it. Sorry." He gave me a sweet smile, the same one that let him get away with petty crimes, and Rosie and I went to our table. Lillie was already there, and Grady was at the bar, getting what I assumed was our usual pitcher of Sam Adams.

"Hey, you guys!" Lillie said, standing up to hug me. "You doing okay?" she asked in a low voice.

"I am," I said. "The news is out. No secrets in my family or this town."

"Tell me about it. Hi, I'm Lillie," she said. "Harlow's friend."

"Rosie Wolfe," she said. "Thanks for letting me crash."

"Rosie will help us in the pop culture department," I said. "She works in the movie industry."

"How cool," Lillie said, and they got chatting.

Our answer sheets and pencils were on the table already. Tanner the waiter came over and we ordered nachos, as we did every week, with a quesadilla for Grandpop.

"Ready to do what we do best, Kingslayers?" I said as Grady approached with the pitcher and some napkins.

He glanced at me. "Hey."

"Hi."

Rosie kicked me under the table. She didn't understand our New England ways, where one-word answers were the norm and perfectly acceptable. However, she had a point.

"How was the rest of your afternoon?" I asked.

"Really nice, thanks."

I looked at Rosie, who somehow had procured a martini.

"Welcome to the Jungle" by Guns N' Roses started playing over the speakers.

"Time to get it started, trivia geeks!" said my brother, and we all cheered. "Let's welcome our regular teams . . . The Beach Bums; Blood, Sweat and Beers; Sherlock Homies; I See Dumb People; and our reigning All-Cape champions, the Kingslayers!"

My team cheered (though Grady had not been around last year), and the other teams booed.

The first category was sports. I watched the Sox religiously, so I had a leg up on baseball. Otherwise, we relied on Grandpop for hockey and football. Basketball was our weakness, but Rosie had once dated an NBA player, so hopefully she could help us out.

"Our question tonight," said Robbie into the mic. "This legendary baseball player had more hits at the end of his career than any other shortstop in history. Your choices are (A) Nomar Garciaparra"—a cheer went up for the former Sox legend, along with a few cries of *Nomah!* since we were Red Sox Nation—"(B) Honus Wagner, (C) Derek Jeter"—that name got boos, obviously—"and (D) Cal Ripken Jr. You have five minutes to bring your answers up, folks."

We leaned in, our heads almost touching.

"It's Jeter," I whispered.

"Seriously? What about Cal Ripken?" said Lillie. "It has to be."

"Wouldn't it be Lou Gehrig?" said Grandpop.

"He played first base," Rosie said. "I've seen *Pride of the Yankees* four times." She took a sip of her martini.

"Yankees fans have to sit in the corner," Grady said with a grin at Rosie. "Let's go with our hearts. Nomar."

"I wish," I whispered. "He's not even close, though. It's Derek Jeter. Give the handsome devil his due."

"I'll go with Harlow," Grandpop said.

"Okay, me too," said Grady, and I smiled at him. Lillie nodded, so I circled C on our card and ran it up to Robbie.

The other teams followed suit, and after a minute, my brother said in his DJ voice, "And the answer is C, Derek Jeter!" Frank Sinatra's voice came over the speakers, singing "New York, New York," and the crowd booed cheerfully.

Someone shouted, "Yankees suck!" and a brave tourist said in a singsong voice, "Let's go, Captain!"

We Kingslayers high-fived, but I See Dumb People and Blood, Sweat and Beers also had the right answer.

Our beautiful nachos came, and we had a few, sipping beer, and insulted Sherlock Homies for picking Honus Wagner. Such was the good-natured blood sport of trivia night.

The next question was in literature, and my teammates grinned at me.

"Which American author has written the most books?" called my brother. "Is it (A) Stephen King, (B) Nora Roberts, (C) Barbara Cartland, or (D) L. Ron Hubbard?"

Another huddle. "It's D, but let's pretend we don't know and wait," I whispered. We had strategies, oh, yes.

Beach Bums went up immediately. Blood, Sweat and Beers did the same. Ben Hallowell went up with his answer, stopping to touch Lillie's cheek on the way back. She blushed.

At the last minute, I turned ours in.

"And the answer is . . . D, L. Ron Hubbard!" said Robbie, and "Superfreak" began to play. I did love my little brother. "Well done, Kingslayers."

Grady won us extra points when the write-in answer was Sea of Marmara for the smallest sea on earth. No one else knew that one. We were in the lead by twenty points. Lillie knew that the human hand had twenty-seven bones. But we missed the longest-running number one single of 1973; we guessed "Tie a Yellow Ribbon," but shockingly, it was "Killing Me Softly."

"Roberta Flack?" Rosie said. "I had no idea."

"Who *could* know?" Grandpop said. "I felt very confident with our guess. And unlike you young people, I was alive back then!"

"We'll be taking a fifteen-minute break, guys," said Robbie. "Get another drink, but please, drink responsibly. Order some food to soak up that alcohol, and yes, I'm talking to you, Sherlock Homies. We don't want another drunk librarian situation, do we?" Everyone laughed . . . the team was made up of our two librarians and the former librarian, Mrs. Yu.

Lillie got up to insult our fellow teams and smooch her honey. Grandpop said he'd stretch his legs "so I don't get an embolism," and Grady went to call his nanny to check in.

"This is fun," Rosie said, waving to Tanner for another drink. I had never mastered that move—I was invisible to servers. Tanner practically ran over with a second martini for my friend, because she had that effect on men.

"I'm so glad you're here," I told her. "Everything is more fun with you around."

"It's true," she said. "Tanner, hon"—she already knew his name—"bring my friend another beer, would you?"

"No thanks, Tanner," I said. "I have to stay sharp in case Grandpop falls asleep."

Rosie laughed and ate another nacho, and Gray returned from his phone call.

"All good on the home front?" I asked.

"Yes," he said. "She's already in bed." He took out his phone and showed me an image—his daughter, asleep, arms curled around a large stuffed animal.

"Is that a live feed?" I asked.

"Yep."

"Kind of creepy, but also so smart for you parents."

"Yeah, it's definitely a Big Brother device, but it's good for peace of mind. And when I just miss her."

"You're a good dad, Gray," I said.

Rosie gave me a nod of approval, then excused herself to go to the bathroom. Which left just Grady and me at the table.

When he'd moved back last November, with a three-year-old and no wife, we'd sort of renewed our friendship. He came to Story Time with Grandpop, and I recommended books for Luna. But it was only the past few months, at trivia night, that I'd seen him socially, so to speak.

I wondered, not for the first time, what I would have done if Zach Baser had responded differently when I told him I was pregnant. What if he'd proposed? It still happened—my electrician and his wife eloped as soon as they found out she was pregnant. What if Zach had said, "If you keep the baby, I'll be here for you both." Would I have gone along with it? I never had a chance to wonder, because the conversation we'd had instead when I told him I was pregnant had killed any affection I'd had for Zach. I never looked him up after I left Boulder. Never wanted to. Never had so much as an ounce of desire to find out what happened to him. He may as well be dead as far as I was concerned.

But if I'd gotten pregnant with someone like Grady Byrne, the story might have ended very differently.

Someone brushed the back of my chair, and I jumped.

"You okay?" Gray asked, his brow furrowing.

"Yes," I said a little too loudly. "Just . . . a lot on my mind."

My grandfather was back, a glass of whiskey in his hand. He pressed the backs of his fingers to my forehead. "She doesn't have a fever," he said.

"I'm fine, I'm fine," I said. "Just . . . yeah. Distracted."

"Grady, did you know Harlow had a *baby*?" Grandpop said. "It was you, honey, wasn't it? Well, of course, Addison had a baby, too."

Luckily, Rosie plunked down next to Grandpop and Lillie rejoined us.

Robbie read the next question. "Which president was assassinated in 1901?"

"McKinley," Grandpop whispered. "I remember it like it was yesterday."

We all laughed, and things fell back into the realm of normal.

At the end of the game, the Kingslayers had crushed our foes. We spent a few minutes pretending to be gracious and claimed our prize—a plastic lobster and a $30 gift card for the Ice House.

"Your turn for the winnings, Gray," I said. "Hope your daughter likes the lobster." I paused. "But don't let her chew on it. It might be toxic."

He looked at me steadily, and I felt my cheeks warm. Grady didn't need to learn parenting skills from me, and I was the last person who had the right to dole out advice on raising a kid.

THIRTEEN

MONICA

At 2:51 on Saturday afternoon, Monica took a last look in the mirror. She had dressed carefully—sleeveless rose-colored silk shirt with a cowl neckline, white cropped linen pants, leopard print suede sandals, an artfully tangled multistrand pearl necklace and gold hoop earrings. A little spritz of Jo Malone, some pale pink lip gloss. Careful makeup, with extra concealer under the eyes, because she'd barely slept since Sanjay had called with the news that their son had found his birth mother.

Without a word to her. It was still a knife in her side.

Well, if clothes were armor, hers was in place. It was a classic weekend look for her, because Sanjay's mother and sisters always dressed so beautifully—richly colored tunics and saris, salwar kameez outfits and statement jewelry. Also, she had to dress the part for work—successful, hip, stylish tech goddess, not to be replaced by some child just out of MIT. Gone were the days when she wore loose-fitting jeans soft from years of duty and an ironic T-shirt.

Today, though . . . what was she trying to prove to Harlow Smith? That she was worthy of having raised Matthew? That she was a good mother and had provided well for her children? And this house, good God. Yes, Monica had chosen it, as she always did for their summer vacations, but it was even more stunning in person than online. A three-story modern house hidden from the road by a long driveway. Salt Pond Bay was just at the edge of their yard, leading all the way to the ocean. The beautifully land-scaped yard, a koi pond, surprising little destinations throughout the yard—an arbor with a wooden glider underneath, a stone firepit, a bench among the rhododendrons in the front.

The first floor of the house had a bedroom suite, a gym and an entertainment room with a huge TV and multiple consoles. On the second floor were four huge bedrooms, all with their own bathrooms. Their master suite had a little alcove for an office. And on the third floor, making good use of the vast and breath-taking views, were the living room, kitchen, dining room, family room and screened-in porch complete with its own bar. There was also a rooftop deck, accessible by a spiral staircase, from which you could see the old Coast Guard station and the crash-ing waves of the ocean in the distance.

It was a vast and impressive house and property, wonderful for entertaining but also lovely for just the four of them. Or three of them, since Monica still had to put in time at the office. Some years, members of their families would visit them during their vacations, though Monica's parents had already pronounced it too far for them this year, and Sanjay's sister was once again ex-pecting a baby and couldn't fly at this late stage. A big house was usually necessary. But today, it felt like too much. It felt . . . embarrassing. Like they were showing off.

Harlow would be thirty-five now, not the trembling seventeen-year-old Monica had felt so protective of. Thirty-five, an adult, and one who had been, by all accounts, overjoyed to have Matthew walk in off the street and detonate a bomb in all their lives.

Matthew had been on his absolute best behavior last night when she and Meena pulled up in their rented car. He gave them both long hugs and carried their luggage upstairs, showed Meena the house while Sanjay made cocktails for the two of them. Then Matthew acknowledged that he should have handled the whole thing better, and he was sorry for the shock and secrecy. He cleaned up the kitchen after dinner and suggested they play cards before Meena went to bed.

It was impossible to be mad at him when he was like this. Which he knew very well. Was he manipulative or just charming?

It was now 2:56. If Monica could guess, Harlow would be exactly on time.

"How are you, my love?" asked Sanjay, coming up behind her and putting his arms around her waist. She leaned back into him a little, savoring his warmth and solidity, and knew once again that marrying him had been the best decision of her life.

"I'm okay. How about you?"

"Just fine. This will be a good summer, Monica. A different summer from what we had imagined, but good just the same."

Right on the heels of that warm squishy feeling came a twinge of irritation, completely unjustified. It wasn't always easy to be married to someone so endlessly calm.

"Are the kids gone?" she asked.

"Yes. They left for the beach while you were in the shower, and I told Matt we'd text him when it was time to come home." That was the plan—kids out of the house, adults talking, then . . . well, then Matthew could see his birth mother again.

You raised him, said the voice in her head. *You are his mother. You've taken care of him for eighteen years. She can't take that away.* It didn't do much to calm the fear and anxiety slipping like a snake through her heart.

They both stiffened at the sound of a car in the driveway and looked out the window. It was 2:59. Harlow drove a blue Subaru. So down-to-earth, that car, with a rack on top for a kayak. Probably plastered with bumper stickers of the Cape and various social justice issues. Monica's own car was a Tesla, white and pristine, back in the garage at home.

Eighteen years ago, Harlow Smith had been the most important person in Monica's life. She had loved the girl. Today, she wasn't so sure.

"Showtime," Sanjay said. He turned her around, kissed her forehead and went to greet Harlow.

"Let me do it," Monica said, slipping past him. "Okay? You've already seen her. Let me answer the door."

"Yes, my queen," Sanjay said, but Monica wasn't in the mood for a smile. She ran lightly down the unfamiliar stairs to the ground floor and vast, airy entryway. Waited for the doorbell to ring, then counted to five and opened the door.

The girl who had been pretty had become utterly beautiful. Her blond hair was the same, long and curly, streaked lighter by the sun. Cheeks pink and glowing with health. Not a drop of makeup, and none needed. Matthew's big brown eyes looked out at her from Harlow's face.

"Harlow," Monica breathed, and spontaneously opened her arms. Harlow stepped in and they hugged, close and hard. Monica could smell the sunshine on her hair, felt the toned muscles of her shoulders. She was shaking. Or Monica was. Maybe they both were.

They broke apart, not making eye contact.

"Come on up," Monica said, her voice shaky. "Sanjay is waiting."

"This is an amazing house," Harlow said, following Monica up the stairs to the living room.

"Yes, isn't it lovely? We were so lucky to find it." Small talk. It felt so bizarre.

"Hello, Harlow," Sanjay said, standing to greet her. "Very good to see you again."

"Hi," she said, twisting her hands together. "Nice to see you, too." Harlow wore jeans, flip-flops and a plain white sleeveless shirt and somehow looked like an ad for summer. "Thanks for having me. Um . . . is Matthew here? And your daughter?"

"No," Sanjay said. "They've been sent to the beach with instructions not to come back until we text them."

"Can I get you some tea, Harlow?" Monica asked. "We have some cookies, too."

Sanjay had baked nankhatai yesterday, quick and easy spice cookies the whole family loved. Monica had eaten six last night when she couldn't sleep.

"Sure. Thank you."

"Have a seat," Sanjay said, and Monica went into the kitchen. Goodness, why hadn't she planned ahead to serve tea? Now she felt frazzled. Where was the tea in this kitchen? Sanjay was very particular about his personal take on chai, so there were his favorite brand of cloves, cinnamon sticks, cardamom, his mortar and pestle. But you know what? She didn't have time for that. Instead, she found the box of Bigelow chai bags, turned on the electric kettle (a necessary appliance when married to a tea drinker) and arranged the cookies on a plate. She found a tray in the fourth cabinet she tried, placed the mugs and spoons and creamer and sugar bowl on it, added the plate of cookies and a few napkins, poured the boiling water into the teapot. Then, stomach jangling with nerves, she carried the tray into the living room.

Sanjay was laughing at something, sitting opposite Harlow. She looked maybe twenty, not thirty-five. Monica would bet good money she got carded regularly.

"That smells lovely," Harlow said.

"Yes. It's chai, I hope that's okay. These are nankhatai. Homemade spice cookies. The guys made them yesterday. Matthew and Meena can't get enough of them, and Sanjay is a great baker."

It was the first shot across the bow, the acknowledgment of their family. *We are happy. We have a family culture. We do nice things together.* She poured Harlow a cup, then one for Sanjay and finally herself.

Harlow took a cookie and nibbled on the edge. "Delicious," she said.

"How is your family, Harlow?" Sanjay asked.

"Oh . . . they're fine. Um, my grandmother died three years ago. She and I were close."

"So sorry to hear that."

"And my sister Addison—she's one of the twins—she got married, and she and her wife have two little girls."

"Congratulations," Monica said. "How nice that you have children in your life."

Sanjay gave her a quick look but said nothing. He better not.

Harlow was breaking the cookie into little crumbs. "How are your families?" she asked. "Everyone doing well?"

"Indeed, yes, they are," Sanjay said. He didn't mention the three-hour conversation he'd had with his parents that he'd told Monica about last night, the one that had left him with a pounding headache. Sita had essentially suggested they all go into witness protection so Harlow wouldn't "steal her baby back." Ishan had unhelpfully stated he'd known this would happen and they should've kept the adoption sealed.

"I remember you had a few nieces and nephews," Harlow said.

"We do, yes," said her husband. "There are fourteen in all now, eleven from my side of the family, three from Monica's. Our oldest nephew just graduated from medical school, and our youngest niece is six."

"Oh, wow. How . . . how great. That's nice. A big family. I mean, with all the cousins and aunts and uncles."

"It is quite wonderful," Sanjay said. "We're still very close geographically as well, except for Monica's parents, who live in Idaho still, despite our efforts to get them to move to California."

Okay, Sanjay could make small talk for weeks at a time. Monica would have to get things going, which she always did when difficult conversations were required. She set her mug down on the coffee table harder than she'd intended. "Harlow, we're very sorry for the way Matthew came back into your life. From what they both told me, it was a terrible shock. You fainted?"

Harlow's face colored. "Yes, but it was a wonderful shock, too."

"You're aware that we knew nothing about this, I hope. I apologize for my son's lack of consideration." Her language tended to get more formal when she was nervous, a by-product of life with an eloquent husband and in-laws who spoke more beautiful English than most, herself included. Sanjay took her hand, recognizing her signs of stress. "I hope it hasn't caused you too much distress."

"No! No, it's fine. I always hoped he'd . . . reach out."

"He's an idiot teenager," Sanjay said warmly. "This could've been handled a thousand different ways, and each would've been better than the one he chose. You have our sincere apologies."

"No more apologies, okay?" Harlow said, glancing between the two of them. "I can't tell you what it means to see him again." Her hands were shaking. "So . . . what have you decided about this summer?"

Monica and Sanjay looked at each other. He gave a slight nod, letting her take the lead. "As you know, of course, Harlow," she said, "Matthew turns eighteen next month. He'll be a senior this coming year. We put him in kindergarten a year after he qualified so he wouldn't be too immature when he started college."

Sanjay squeezed her hand lightly. Shit. Harlow hadn't even been seventeen when she'd started college. Sure enough, Harlow's cheeks darkened once again, but she said nothing.

"Once he's eighteen," Sanjay said, picking up the thread, "he will be able to do what he likes. But we hope that he's also the type of young man who doesn't want to . . ." He waved his hand vaguely.

"Turn anyone's life inside out," Monica said. "Cause harm by his thoughtlessness. Bring up feelings you're not ready to handle." Harlow blinked. "But now that he's done all that, we figured we'd talk to you first about how you feel. We have some concerns, of course."

Harlow nodded. "Sure. Yep. I would, too." Tears filled her eyes. "I would very much like to spend time with him," she said, her voice wobbling. "I'm so happy that he found me, and I . . . I'd like to get to know him as much as possible while you're here."

Monica's toes clenched in her sandals, but she tried to keep her face neutral. "How does your family feel about all this?" she asked.

Harlow took a deep breath. "Well . . . they're surprised. Very surprised. I never told them about my pregnancy, so this is the first they're learning about . . . about my freshman year. You remember I wanted a closed adoption because . . . well. For a lot of reasons. But partly because I thought my family . . . my parents . . . would try to talk me out of it."

Sanjay leaned forward. "So they knew nothing?" he asked at the same time Monica said, "You kept him a secret?"

Harlow looked out the window, and her throat worked. "I was . . . it wasn't that I was ashamed of having Matthew," she said. "It was that I didn't want to cause the kind of chaos I knew it would have. If my parents had known, they would've pressured me to keep him so they could help raise him. And that would've . . . well, it wouldn't have been horrible or anything. But I wanted him to have two parents who adored him, not a committee of teenage aunts, an uncle who was eight, overtired grandparents and . . . me. I didn't want him to be lost or overlooked."

"Even so," Monica said, "there's no shame in giving up a baby for adoption, Harlow."

"Oh, there can be," she said, and there was some bitterness in her voice. "There definitely is in my case, at least."

"Well, to us, you're very much a superhero," Sanjay said. "There should be a shrine to birth mothers somewhere." Laying it on a little thick, Monica thought, but she knew he was sincere.

"I transferred colleges after Matthew was born and tried to put the experience behind me, because thinking about it . . . about him . . ." She swallowed audibly. "It was really hard, and yet I knew I did the right thing, so I tried to be . . . normal. A regular college student, not the dumb teenager who got knocked up."

That was exactly what she looked like right now. The scared teenager who'd talked to them over that early version of Skype, so overwhelmed by the huge choices in front of her.

Monica got up and went to sit next to Harlow, putting her arm around the younger woman's shoulders. "You weren't dumb,

Harlow. You aren't. You were incredibly generous and brave, and we've told Matthew that all his life." Nevertheless, this was going to hit Matthew hard, learning that his birth mother had never breathed a word about him. Or maybe not. Maybe he'd just shrug and say he could see why Harlow had done that. They were about to enter the honeymoon phase of their reunion, according to the literature. Already, he'd been waxing poetic about how cool and great she was, how much they looked alike.

"It just never seemed like the right time to say something," Harlow said. "Telling them about a baby they'd never meet seemed . . . cruel."

"Well, this is something you'll have to talk about with Matthew," Monica said. She didn't want to sit next to Harlow anymore, but wouldn't moving be worse? She stood up, poured more tea into her already full cup and sat back down next to her husband. Awkward, but it did the job.

"Can I ask you about Matthew?" Harlow said.

"Of course. That's the whole point of our meeting," Monica said.

"How did he feel about being adopted? How old was he when you told him?"

"He always knew," Sanjay said. "I don't know that there was ever that one time. When my brother's wife got pregnant for the third time, he was about two."

"Almost three," Monica said.

"Right. He asked if he'd grown in Mommy's tummy the way his cousin was now, and we said no, that families come together in a lot of different ways. We told him the truth—he was given to us by a young woman who wasn't ready to be a parent and chose us to raise him. We told him that we'd met you, and that you were very, very careful to give him to a family who would take good care of him, and that you would always love him."

Her husband had a gift when it came to talking to people, all right. Small wonder he was such a beloved teacher. Harlow took a napkin and wiped her eyes.

"Of course, he was curious about you," Monica said, "but we respected your wishes and told him only about the interactions we had with you. We didn't speculate."

"Did he read my letter?" Harlow asked.

Ah, the letter. "You had asked us to give it to him on his eighteenth birthday, so no," Monica said. "But I brought it with me." She stood up, went to the table at the top of the stairs, pulled an envelope from her purse and held it a minute.

She had never read it. Oh, she had wanted to, a hundred times, especially when Matthew was in one of his angry phases, blaming her and Sanjay for whatever was bothering him, whether it was not going varsity as a freshman or when her sister's older daughter told him he wasn't her "real" cousin. Monica would have *loved* to have read the letter, not just because she had longed to hear what Harlow had said, but in case it could've helped her son feel better.

But she had respected Harlow's wishes. The letter was for Matthew when he turned eighteen. Period. She went back to the living room and handed it to Harlow. "Here you go. You can give it to him yourself." And he would read it and probably never tell her what it said.

Just another secret he kept from her.

FOURTEEN

HARLOW

Seeing the envelope again was like a punch in the heart. My handwriting at seventeen had been rounder, sweeter, more innocent. *For my baby*, it said. I took it with shaking hands.

"As for how he feels about being adopted," Monica said, her voice calm and unreadable, "we know it's multilayered. He loves us and his sister, and he knows we're his family. We were careful not to make him feel he had to be extra special because he was adopted. We made sure he knew he was completely part of our family, ours in every way except genetically. We told him his feelings were valid, and if he felt sad or out of sorts because he was adopted, we understood. If you remember, we went to an adoption counselor before he was born. We've read dozens of books about raising an adopted child, and we know many families with adopted children."

"Was he sad?" I said. "Or upset or . . . angry?"

Monica sat back against the couch and was quiet for a moment. Sanjay stared at the floor. "Yes," she said. "Sometimes, when he was little, he would cry because he was afraid you might be lonely. I would tell him that you would always miss him and think of him, but that you had other people who loved you, and that maybe someday, he would get to meet you."

My son had cried over me. The image of a little dark-haired boy, sitting on his bed, tears in his eyes . . . "Excuse me a second," I said, standing abruptly. "Um . . . bathroom?"

"Of course," Monica said, standing up. "Just down the hall on the left."

In the tasteful bathroom, I sat on the edge of the tub and buried my face in a thick towel so they wouldn't hear me crying. When I could inhale without sobbing, I stood up and blew my nose. They had the nice kind of tissues, the kind with lotion, and I went through a few of them. Then I splashed cold water on my face and held my wet hands against my eyes, which were red and puffy.

It had never been easy. There was no reason it would be now. There would never be the definitive answer—should I have done it or not? Because the answer was both yes and no. I *could* have raised Matthew. Maybe I'd been completely selfish, giving him to the Patels. I hadn't wanted to be a teenage mother. I hadn't wanted to be such a cliché . . . a girl who had trusted her boyfriend to put the condom on before Mr. Happy touched Miss Vagine.

But mostly, I hadn't wanted my child to be seen as a mistake. An accident. I knew how too many people looked at teenage mothers, contemptuous of our carelessness, viewing us as a drain on the system. Hell, I'd thought that myself, the last time I'd been to the mall in Hyannis. There'd been a girl who couldn't have been older than eighteen, scrolling idly through her phone, three disjointed tattoos visible on her arms. A toddler had been yanking at her hand, saying, "Mommy, watch me! Watch me! Watch me!" She gave him a sip from her vat of Dunkin's iced coffee and didn't look away from the phone.

I had told myself both that I could make it work and also that he'd be better off with two adoring parents. Both choices were right. Both choices were wrong.

I took another look in the mirror and told myself to get my shit together. I went back to the living room, where Sanjay and Monica were murmuring.

"All you all right?" Sanjay asked. "You're probably not. This is very . . . emotional, of course." He smiled to soften the words. Monica said nothing.

I sat back down. "You were telling me what you did to make sure Matthew felt comfortable with his adoption," I said. I took another cookie, just so I wouldn't pick at my cuticles.

"Right. Well, we made sure he knew other adopted kids," Sanjay said. "We joined an adoption network in the area and became friends with a few families. We'd have cookouts and beach days and stuff like that, so he was around other kids in his shoes."

"How did he feel when Meena came along?" I asked.

"Fine. Very happy," Monica said.

Sanjay gave his ex-wife a look. "He was only five. He was a little nervous that we wouldn't love him as much," he said. "That we wouldn't need him, because we would have a biological child." Monica's eyes filled with tears. Mine, too. "I told him that was not going to happen, but we understood that he'd have those thoughts. It didn't make them true. When Meena was born, we made a big deal about him being a big brother, and we always called Meena 'our' baby. Like, 'Wow, Matt, our baby had the nastiest diaper! I think she ate a pigeon! Come see!'"

I sputtered on a laugh, and Monica smiled and took her husband's hand. They still loved each other. That was clear.

"He saw a therapist for a few years," Sanjay said. "When he was, what, Moni? Eleven?"

"Twelve to fifteen," she said. "He said it was fun to talk about himself and complain about us. Eventually, he stopped going. It was his own choice."

So they'd done everything adoptive parents could do, it seemed. They'd gotten counseling, read the books, joined a network, gotten him a therapist. And clearly, they loved him.

"Eat your cookie," Sanjay said, and I did. We sat in silence for a few minutes, me trying to absorb all this information.

"How was it, when you took him . . . home? From the hospital?"

"It was amazing. Wonderful," Monica said. "He was a very loved baby. Our parents came to see him right away, and all the cousins were so excited to have a new baby in the family."

"Okay, good," I said.

"He cried a lot," Sanjay said.

"He had *colic*," Monica said sharply. "He was our joy, Harlow. He still is. We've loved him since before he was born. Just as you have."

I nodded, remembering that. Their excitement, their love, their generosity toward me and my feelings. I had to keep that memory in the forefront of my mind. Taking a deep breath, I asked, "So how do you picture this summer?"

Monica folded her arms across her chest. That blouse was absolutely stunning. "The three of us talked about the expectations he might have of you and your family. That none of you were prepared for this, and he'd have to tread more gently." She paused, then looked right at me. "Every adopted child is curious about his birth family, but I want to make this clear, Harlow. Matthew is *our* son. We have no problem with him getting to know you and spending some time with you, meeting your family, but at the end of the summer, we're going home. Whatever relationship you and Matthew have established by then will play out as it does, but he is our son and Meena's brother."

"I know all that," I said, feeling chastened by her words. "Believe me, I know. It is literally the story of my life."

No one said anything for a moment. "Harlow, forgive me for asking such personal questions," Sanjay said, "but are you married? Living with someone? Do you have other children?"

"Oh, God, no," I blurted out. "Um . . . no. I never really . . . connected with anybody." James, my occasional one-hour stand, didn't count. "No other children."

"Good," Monica said. "That makes things less complicated for Matthew. It would be harder if he had to see you raising another child when you gave him to us."

I sucked in a sharp breath. "True." God. I felt like I was being sliced up, even though she and Sanjay had not said one untrue thing. But me being single and childless, never having had a serious romantic relationship? I wasn't sure that was good. My social life consisted of Ollie, the bookstore, trivia night and family gatherings. The very thought of having a baby brought on panic attacks. It wasn't *good*.

"Harlow," Monica said, her voice gentler now, "you gave Matthew to us because you trusted us to raise him well. And we have. He is very loved and has had a lot of advantages and opportunities. We will always be grateful you gave us our son. We're glad he's meeting you this summer, despite the way he initiated it. But . . . well, I'm just going to say it. You're a stranger. Someone very glamorous to him right now, almost mythological. But *we* are his parents."

The lump in my throat had become a shard of glass. "Got it."

Sanjay leaned forward, resting his elbows on his knees. "Let's do this," he said. "I'll call Matt and have him and Meena come home, and we'll take Meena out and let you and Matthew have some time together. He's six weeks away from being a legal adult, so the two of you can decide how to interact this summer. But please keep in mind that this is our family vacation, the last summer before he graduates, and this time is special for us also."

"I understand."

"Excuse me for a moment, then, and I'll give him a call."

He left the room, which suddenly seemed much bigger without him. Monica was fiddling with her earring. She was nervous, I realized. Of course she was. Her son was meeting the woman who'd carried him, whose genes he shared, and I was a bright and shiny new toy.

"Monica, I want to say something to you," I said, winging it.

Her hands dropped to her lap, and she sat up straighter. "Go ahead."

I swallowed, and even though my eyes were full of tears, I looked right at her. "Thank you for raising my baby. For loving him and taking care of him and being his mother."

Her face flickered, but God, she was amazing with self-control. "Raising my son and daughter is the greatest privilege of my life," she said. Such grace and dignity. My own nose was running.

"I'm not going to steal him from you," I said, trying to smile.

She gave me a look from those cool blue eyes. "You couldn't if you tried."

Fifteen minutes later, Matthew Rohan Patel, my son and the Patels' son, stuck his head in the living room. "Hey. I'm gonna wash up and change, okay?" he said, disappearing before I could fully process his presence.

There was a girl standing there, also. Meena. She was dark-eyed like her dad, but otherwise, she was all Monica.

"Hi," I said. "I'm Harlow."

"I know," she said. "You're all we've talked about since Tuesday. I had to wear my noise-canceling headphones on the plane because Mom wouldn't stop obsessing. I'm Meena Jane Patel, the second-favorite child."

"Meena!" Monica chided, but I smiled.

"You guys are all my family's been talking about, too," I said.

"I wish I had a birth mother, too," Meena said. "For those times when you drive me crazy, Mom. You too, Daddy."

"We never drive you crazy," Monica said, her voice rich with love. It was the first time she seemed to relax since I got here.

"You are a terribly spoiled and insolent child," Sanjay said, kissing her head.

"I got a B+ once," Meena said in a loud whisper. "Bringing shame to my family for generations to come." Her father smiled.

"How old are you?" I asked the girl.

"Twelve."

"Going on forty," Sanjay said. "Breaking her father's heart every day by growing up."

"Do you like to read?" I asked.

"A hundred percent," she said.

"I own a bookstore in Wellfleet," I said. "I know a girl about your age who volunteers in the store. I can introduce you, if you want a friend for the summer."

"I *totally* want a friend for the summer. HRH gets a whole new family, so I should at least get a friend."

"HRH?"

"His Royal Highness," Meena said, and I smiled.

"As if you're not a princess," Sanjay said.

Meena turned to her father. "Daddy, there's an awesome bike trail here," she said. "Do you think you could buy me a bike for the summer? One with a basket and a bell and a really comfy seat?"

"Of course, honey." He glanced at me. "Because I want to, and not just because I am wrapped around her little finger."

"Why don't we take out those kayaks?" Monica suggested. "Give Matthew and Harlow some privacy?"

"Nice meeting you," Meena said.

"You too, Meena. Hope to see you again."

Then the three of them left.

I stood up, took in the view without really seeing it.

Then Matthew came into the room.

"Hello, Birth Mother," he said with a grin.

"Hi!" My heart rolled and skittered, and it seemed like every cell in my body reached out for him. I felt hot and shaky and . . . and dazzled. My son was beautiful. Perfect. "Um . . . can I hug you?"

"Sure."

He came across the room, smiling, and wrapped his long arms around me. We were almost the same height—five-ten—but he'd be taller soon, I suspected. He smelled clean, like Dove soap, and his hair was silky and springy under my hand.

Oh, my little pal. I remember you. It was like we'd never been apart, it felt so natural.

When the hug had gone on for way too long but not long enough, he stepped back. "I just wanna look at you, you know?" he said, and his eyes were wet.

"I do know. Same here."

"Our eyes are the same shape," he said, and they were, the

rather pretty round eyes of my mom's side of the family. Winnie had them, too, and Robbie.

"Our noses, too," I said.

"Thanks for that," he said, grinning, and my heart grew three sizes.

"Wait till you meet my brother," I said. "You're a ringer for him."

"Cool. Do I look like my bio-dad, too?" he asked.

I ignored the jolt of animosity that flashed. "Well, a little. His hair was black, too."

"Is he dead?"

"Oh! Um, I don't know. Sorry."

"It's okay. I can find him easily enough."

"By the way, how did you find me?"

He tilted his head at me and smiled with pity at my naïveté, no doubt. "It took me, like, half an hour on Google."

"Speedy."

Matthew sat down on the couch, and I did as well, turning so I could continue to look at him. "Well, I knew your first name was Harlow, that you were a student at CU Boulder and that your family was from the East Coast."

"But our last name is Smith."

"That's why it took thirty minutes. If it had been something a little more colorful, it would've only taken ten." He smiled again, his dark, dark eyes on me. "Then I saw a picture of you on Instagram."

"I don't have Instagram." Open Book had a page, but Destiny ran it.

"Your sister? Addison? She posts all the time and her account is public."

"Right. She's a social media whore."

He smiled. "I mean, it wasn't a great picture, because you were off to the side? But I felt this . . . I don't know. This weird current of electricity or something. You know?"

I was already nodding. "That's how I felt when you came into the store. I mean, I sure wasn't expecting you, but I felt this . . . buzz, even before I could see your face. When you turned and smiled, I . . ." My voice broke. "I knew exactly who you were." I wiped my eyes. "I'm so glad to meet you, Matthew," I whispered. "I've thought of you every day of your life."

"Yeah. Same here." He grabbed a cookie from the tray and ate it in one bite. "So maybe you could tell me about yourself."

"Sure, honey. Whatever you want to know."

"Already with the honey." He sounded like Sanjay, and he was grinning the same way. Nature and nurture. He leaned forward, elbows on his knees, the way my dad often did. Well, lots of people did. But still.

He was so beautiful. I had made this beautiful human.

I cleared my throat. "Okay. Um, I'm the oldest of five kids. Me, then three years later the twins, Addie and Lark. They're identical, by the way. Three years after that came Winnie, and then three years later, Robbie, the only boy, when I was nine. We all have kind of weird names. Harlow, Addison, Larkby, Windsor and then Robbie, who has a normal name. My father's a retired nurse, and he and my mom own a gallery in Wellfleet. She's an artist."

Matthew nodded, processing the fact that he had three aunts and an uncle. Another set of grandparents. "So what else? You run the bookstore?"

"Yep. My grandfather and I, and my cousin, Cynthia. Um, I have an apartment in the same building. My grandfather lives downstairs, and I have the second and third floors. It's cute. You'll have to come see it."

"So you have a big family, and you guys are close?"

"Pretty much, yeah."

"What else do you like?" he asked.

"Well, I love being near the water. I kayak and paddle-board—"

"Me too! I love the water, which drives my parents crazy, because it takes a good hour to get to a beach on any given week-end. And they're more, like, lake people. Me, I love the ocean. Guess I know where I got that." He looked smug. "What else?"

"Um, I read a ton, obviously."

"Okay, we're different there. Other hobbies?"

"I have a dog. Oh, right, you met him. Um . . . I bake." He looked a little disappointed. "My mom's a great artist. Wait till you see her gallery."

Matthew's mouth hung open. "Seriously? I paint, too! I mean, this is so weird, because my parents are so not artistic. Mom can do a basic stick figure, and Dad's students make fun of him because they can never tell what his pictures are supposed to be. And Meena is more right-brained? She draws, but it's always a picture of a building or something. Our grandfather's an archi-tect. And my mom, well . . . you know she works in IT."

I nodded, feeling a strange weightlessness. I was talking to my *son*. My heart was still thudding, and I hoped I wasn't about to faint again, but it was dazzling. We had things in common. I was part of him, even though I hadn't raised him.

"So why didn't you keep me?" he asked, and it was like a kick in the heart, the question I had dreaded for nearly eighteen years.

I took a steadying breath and looked into his dark eyes. "It wasn't an easy choice. Um . . ." I had tucked the letter between the cushions of the couch, and I pulled it out now. "This is a letter

I wrote you a couple of weeks before you were born. Your parents were going to give it to you once you turned eighteen, but Mon— your mother brought it with her so I could give it to you now."

"Can I read it? Right now?"

"Sure." I handed it over.

"Should I read it out loud? So you can remember what it says?"

I'd never forget what it said. "Whatever you want," I answered, my voice husky.

He studied my handwriting, then opened the envelope. I swallowed and folded my hands together, holding them hard.

Matthew cleared his throat, grinned at me and began reading.

Dear Matthew,

Hello. I am your birth mother.

You might not be named Matthew anymore. I found out you were a boy at one of the ultrasounds, and I didn't want to just call you "baby," so I looked up some names and picked Matthew.

When you read this, you'll be eighteen years old. Right now, you are not born, just kicking and pushing inside me. I love that feeling. I love being pregnant with you. I don't know how I'm going to go through with your adoption, but I know that I will.

I'm not sure what to tell you. I'm sorry? I am sorry. There is no good answer here, because I love you so much, and I'm also not quite eighteen years old. I'm too scared that you would pay the price for me keeping you when I'm not completely grown up. I wasn't sure what kind of future I would have as a single mom, but I know it would be harder for both of us. Please don't think I

didn't want you or love you. I did. I do. I just can't raise you,
Matthew. You deserve a real family, two parents, a home with
real adults who can take care of you.

Matthew stopped for a minute and wiped his eyes on his
sleeve.

Your birth father was not a bad guy. He had (has) black hair
and green eyes and is about six feet tall. He played golf. We
dated for about two months my freshman year, and then I got
pregnant. When I told him I thought it would be best if you were
adopted, he agreed. His name is not on your original birth
certificate, but I can tell you who he is if you want someday. You
should have both our medical histories, which are clear, except for
my grandmother, who has breast cancer.
I want you to know I picked your parents as best I could.
The adoption agency let me watch videos from prospective
couples. I watched probably a hundred of them. When I saw
Sanjay and Monica, something in my heart said, "Here they are.
You found them." And at that moment, I felt you move for the
first time, like you wanted them to be your parents.

Another pause. He grabbed a tissue, handed it to me and
took one for himself, then resumed reading.

They seem so kind and smart and happy together. Their video
was a little dorky, and that made me smile, too. When we met,
they were so kind to me, and so excited about you.
I hope they love you with all their hearts. I hope you are
happy and safe and healthy. I hope you love your mom and dad,
and I hope they did a good job raising you. I will pray every

*day that they do, even though I'm not super religious. But I will
ask the universe and God and every deity out there to watch
over you, Matthew. To help you be happy and healthy and full
of life.*

*Right now, you are still my baby. I can still change my mind.
I love you more every minute, and I'm not sure I can give you
away, but I'm writing this letter, so I guess my brain knows
what my heart doesn't want to admit—you belong with Sanjay
and Monica, and they'll be better parents than I could ever be.*

*Pretty soon, you'll be here. I'm so excited to see you, but I'm
so scared of that day, too, because I'll have to say goodbye to you,
my little pal for these past nine months. I don't know how I can
do that, except by believing that it's the best thing for you. You,
my baby. That's what a mother is supposed to do—whatever is
best for her child. In a week or ten days, you'll be born, and no
matter what, you'll be perfect in my eyes.*

His voice caught, and it took him a minute to recover. Tears
were streaming from my own eyes, and I was glad for the box of
tissues.

*I gave Monica and Sanjay a picture of me while I was
pregnant, and there's one of the three of us the first day we
met. They said they'll take a picture of you and me once you're
born, so you can see that I loved you. If you ever get sick or need
a kidney or something, I will give it in a heartbeat. The
adoption agency will always have my contact information if
you need it.*

*It's strange to think that as you read this, you'll be the same
age as I am now. I hope you'll forgive me for not keeping you,
Matthew. I hope it was the right choice.*

I wanted you to wait until you were eighteen to read this letter so you could have a full and real childhood. But now that you are reading it, if you ever want to find me, please know that I'll be so, so happy to see you again.

I'll never be sorry I had you, and I'll think of you every day. I will always hold you in my heart. I love you, and I always will. Your name means "gift from God," because that's what you are to me.

Love,
Your first mother

By the end of the letter, I had my hands over my mouth to hide the ugly-cry face. He was crying, too.

Then my son stood up, came over to me and hugged me.

"I love you, too," he said. "I always have. I always knew a piece of me was missing, and it was you."

FIFTEEN

HARLOW

I got pregnant twenty-three days after I lost my virginity.

Zach Baser was at college on a golf scholarship. He had straight black hair, green eyes and olive skin. He lived in my dorm, and we ran into each other a lot, it seemed. Then, one day in October during an absolutely stunning and surprise snowstorm, we found ourselves in the common room.

"Hey," he said.

"Hi." I smiled easily.

"Okay if I study here, too?" he asked.

"Sure thing. I'm Harlow Smith, by the way. I live on the third floor with Rosie Wolfe."

"Zach Baser. Yeah, I've seen you around," he said, and he gave me a crooked grin. "How's it going? You like school so far?"

I had seen him around, too. He was a freshman too, had grown up in the Chicago suburbs, was undeclared and hoped to be a golf pro. We studied for an hour or so before he asked if I wanted to grab some food. I said yes, and we went out into the snow, the fat, wet flakes making the already beautiful campus look ethereal and magical.

Because I was the new, outgoing, fun me, I scooped up some snow, packed it into a snowball and threw it at him, and then we were cavorting like puppies, trying to stuff snow down each other's coats, slipping and sliding and chasing each other. He tackled me gently and lay on top of me, brushed some snow off my cheeks, then kissed me.

It was the most romantic moment of my life. We got pizza, held hands on the way back, and he walked me to my room. I introduced him to Rosie. He asked for my number, then kissed me goodbye, right in front of her.

"Well, well, well," Rosie said after he'd left. "My girl has met a guy."

Sixteen days later, Zach and I slept together, because I was seventeen and horny, and this version of myself was ready to lose her virginity. Why not? I really liked Zach. Sure, it had been only two weeks, but he'd taken me to dinner and called me his girlfriend in front of the other guys on the golf team. During a call to my family the week before, on speaker, I told everyone I was dating a nice guy, and they were delighted (except my father, who pretended to cry, and Robbie, who made gagging noises and left the conversation).

Mom said, "I don't imagine you'll stay a virgin until your wedding night, Harlow, sweetie. Just make sure he uses a condom. Sex is a wonderful part of life at every age." I heard my sisters all groaning, and Mom and Dad laughed their special *we love horrifying the kids* laugh.

"We can't wait till you Littles all get out of the house," Dad added. "We're going to have sex in all your bedrooms."

"Daddy!" the twins shrieked in unison.

"But Harlow," he went on, "Daddy would be very happy if you just came home to take care of me in my old age."

"Don't listen to him," Mom said. "Live your life. Just make sure this Zach person is good to you. And don't get pregnant or get an STD." More shrieks from my sisters, more laughter from the parents.

So that was that. My parents weren't holding me to puritanical standards of chastity. Sex was normal. I was above the age of consent, and so was Zach. He'd had sex before (twice). I had not, and admitted this.

I had envisioned being on the pill, but the side effects scared me off. Migraines, which I'd had a few times in high school. Weight gain, nausea, sore breasts, depression. I didn't want to take anything if I could avoid it. Condoms were 98 percent effective, the nice nurse at Planned Parenthood told me, as long as they were used correctly.

Yeah.

The first time was predictably awkward, uncomfortable and quick. The second time, things improved. The third time, I found out that sex was wicked fun. How cool I was, having sex with my boyfriend in college! How delightful to be in a relationship!

Zach was very good-looking, with an easy physical grace and laid-back manner. We talked about school, our planned futures, our families. He had a sister and a brother and was a devoted White Sox fan (alas). Like me, he'd enjoyed a relatively normal, happy life. He loved his parents and was especially close to his dad, who'd taught him to golf. Though he'd never been to the Cape before, he said it sounded great.

Was I in love? I wasn't sure (no, in other words). I didn't think he was, either, but maybe it would grow into something more. For now, it was just right—fun, light, consistent, sweet. A bit shallow, but in the good way, since we weren't about to get married or anything.

"You guys are adorable," a girl on my floor said one night.

I'd heard the stories of hookups and drunken sex, waking up

not knowing where you were, and yes, I felt lucky for doing it this way. Zach and I went to a concert and a football game, fooled around a few times a week. It was a very happy, fun month. My first boyfriend, and it had all been so easy.

And then, for the first time since I was twelve and a half, my period was late. You could have set your watch by my period—mega cramps and weepiness the day before announcing its arrival like a billboard every twenty-nine days.

I didn't notice right away. But then Rosie got hers, and I realized I was late. I told myself it was probably because I was . . . uh . . . more hormonal? Because of the increased activity down there? That could happen, right?

Six days later, I borrowed a bike and rode to the Walgreens on Baseline Road, rather than the one nearer to campus. Bought a pregnancy test with shaking hands, avoided eye contact with the clerk and rode back to campus.

I couldn't take the test in the dorm bathroom, which was shared by far too many girls, so I headed for the Germanic and Slavic Languages building. I was taking Intro to Ukrainian to satisfy the foreign language requirement and had class there on Mondays and Wednesdays. The bottom floor bathroom was private. I sat on the toilet and peed on the stick. Then I watched as two pink lines appeared.

Oh, God.

How could this have happened? I asked myself as I wept. We'd used condoms every single time! Christmas break was coming. I'd be going home. My parents would be so disappointed in me. And the Littles . . . I couldn't bear to picture their faces. I slammed my hand against the metal stall. This had to be a mistake. Condoms, every time!

But yeah, there was that second or third time when Zach had just started, and I said, "You have a condom on, right?" and he said, "Oh, yeah, hang on a sec." But that was before ejaculation. The chance of pregnancy was teeny!

But not nonexistent.

My sobs were sharp and ragged.

I called Rosie and asked her to meet me here, and be discreet about it.

"What's up, roomie?" she said fifteen minutes later as she came in the door. "You sick, hon?"

I opened the door of my stall and held up the stick.

"Oh, shit," she said. "Oh no."

I started to cry again, and she did, too. Later that night, I took the second test. Also positive. I googled "pregnancy without ejaculation" and found out that yep, it was possible. Guess I'd inherited my mother's fertility. Yay for me.

I told Zach to meet me the next day at a grimy diner way off campus, so we wouldn't run into anyone we knew. It was in a strip mall along with a nail salon, a car parts store and an empty mega-gym, just as depressing and bleak as it sounded. Zach knew something was up the second he saw me, since my eyes were swollen from crying.

"What happened? Did your grandmother die?" he asked, because I'd told him Grammy was fighting cancer, and for a second, I was touched that he'd thought of her.

"No. Um . . ."

"Coffee?" the waitress asked, and we each nodded.

"Decaf for me," I added hastily. Mom had never had caffeine while pregnant.

"Dude, what's up?" Zach asked.

I waited till the server came back and asked her to give us a little privacy. Then, with my toes clenched and my legs shaking, I said, "Zach, I'm pregnant."

His face drained of color. "Oh, fuck."

"Yeah."

"Fucking fuck. Oh, Jesus." His head fell back against the booth. "No way."

"Way." Tears slid down my face.

He did not reach across the table to hold my hands. He didn't sit next to me or put his arm around me.

"But we used condoms," he protested. I didn't answer, too busy suppressing sobs. "Well, obviously, I'll pay for the abortion," he said. "If you want, I can go with you."

With those words, my first relationship died. Oh, I hadn't expected him to propose, but come on. *If you want, I can go with you.* Was that really the best he could do?

"Wow. Big of you."

"Well, you're not gonna *keep* it, right? You can't keep it." His voice rose with panic.

"I just found out, Zach. I haven't made any decisions. I'm in shock, okay? Obviously, I had to tell you."

"I wish you hadn't. Christ."

That would have hurt, too, if he wasn't already dead to me. "Look," I snapped. "This is happening to me a lot more than it is to you."

"Yeah, whatever. I get it. But shit, Harlow. We used condoms."

"Nothing is foolproof." Tears pricked my eyes once again. The waitress glanced over, her face worn and sympathetic. That could be me, ten years from now, struggling to support a baby, waiting tables or cleaning motel rooms. I had no life skills. I'd have to drop out.

Suddenly, Zach's jaw clenched. He looked at me, eyes cold. "Is this because I'm gonna be a golf pro?"

"What?"

"Are you trying to stick me with a kid because I'm gonna make a lot of money at golf?"

"Are you kidding me?" My voice echoed through the diner. "No," I said more quietly. "You could end up working at a car wash for all I know."

"Yeah, right. It's like when the guys are recruited for the NBA in high school, and all of a sudden their girlfriends are pregnant."

"Shut your mouth right now, Zach," I hissed. "I am not pregnant because you have a snowball's chance in hell of going pro. I'm pregnant because you didn't wrap up soon enough. Remember?"

"Now you're trying to pin this on me?"

"You *are* the sperm donor."

He ran a hand through his thick black hair. "Look. I'm sorry. I'm just . . . shocked, that's all. I'm sorry." His mouth trembled. "I didn't expect this."

My anger dropped a few notches. "Neither did I." We sat in silence for a few minutes, looking at anything but each other.

"Are you, like, super religious or anything?" Zach asked. In other words, was I morally opposed to abortion?

"No, we're sort of Episcopalian, but not really."

"You're barely pregnant right now. It's just a clump of cells, right?"

"I . . . I need to think. But I'll let you know, of course."

"Yeah. Sure. Great." He grabbed his wallet and threw a ten on the table. "Did you want anything else?" he asked belatedly. "Food?"

"No. I'm good. I . . . I'm just gonna sit here awhile longer," I said.

"Do you want me to stay?"

Already, he was itching to get away from me. "No."

"Let me know what you need, then." With that, he was gone, a gust of cold air blowing in behind him.

Later that week, Rosie and I went to Planned Parenthood together.

"They'll have all kinds of information," she said. "It's not just for abortions."

Like most women, I wanted abortion to be safe and legal . . . and never, ever to be in the position to need one. The nurse there was great, kind and efficient. She had me take another pregnancy test and felt my abdomen. She asked me about dates and birth control. Zach was right . . . I was only a couple of weeks along. Three at the most.

"So how can we help you today, Harlow?" the nurse asked, and her voice was gentle.

"I don't know," I said, my voice husky. I swallowed. "I really like babies. I have four younger siblings. But I'm only seventeen. A freshman at CU." Rosie squeezed my hand.

The nurse nodded kindly. "Well," she said, "you know the options, honey. There's abortion, as I'm sure you know. If you want to stay pregnant, we can get you started on prenatal vitamins and refer you to a midwife practice. If you're considering adoption, we can recommend some great agencies."

I nodded but said nothing.

"Here," she said. "I'll give you information on everything, how's that? Be back in a sec." She left the exam room, and Rosie and I looked at each other.

Realistically, I had three options. Option one . . . abortion. I could make the case for that, sure. I hadn't been careless. We'd used birth control. I'd been sexually active for all of four weeks. An abortion would let me continue with college, and I had worked so hard to get this scholarship. If I went that route, all I'd be left with would be a sad memory from a cold winter's day. A reminder to be more careful with my body and my partners.

Option two, I could give the baby to a couple who were legitimate grown-ups. Just the fact that I still thought of adults as grown-ups made me feel like a little kid. A little kid with a fully engaged reproductive system.

Option three, keep the baby and go back to the Cape. My family would help, though they'd never look at me the same way again. I certainly knew my way around kids. But I'd be completely dependent on my parents. I'd get a job waitressing or doing some landscaping, maybe. Eventually, maybe I'd save enough to take classes at Cape Cod Community College and learn a trade. Or I could chip away at a four-year online degree and maybe get it in . . . what? Eight years? Ten? By the time my kid was in fourth grade? And then what?

My Nauset High classmates would wonder how their valedictorian could've been so dumb. Grady Byrne would look at me with kind, sad eyes and go back to being brilliant, and my girlfriends would distance themselves when they came home on break. My siblings would have to help change diapers and burp the baby, and my parents would be exhausted. The baby would be raised by committee as I tried to earn enough to cover our costs: Health care. Food. Clothes. A car seat and all the other gear.

What if the baby was born with problems? What if it was twins? What if the baby *died*? A child was not a cute accessory. I would be responsible for a human life. Forever. My parents occasionally called us terrorists—they said we held them hostage in fear. I abruptly understood what they were talking about.

My second cousin, Julianna, had gotten pregnant in high school, also at age seventeen. She was now in her forties, still living with her mother and Axl, named for the lead singer of Guns N' Roses. He was, what . . . twenty-three? Twenty-five? He'd never gone to college. According to the family grapevine, he smoked weed, played video games in the basement and had screaming matches with his mother. I'd met him two years ago at a funeral. He was covered in tattoos and had shaved his head.

I wouldn't want my kid to turn out like that. And certainly I knew not all children of single mothers did. But it still scared me.

After the diner talk, Zach avoided me. He texted a few days later, asking if I'd made a decision. I knew he was hoping for the abortion option. But I was frozen. Three weeks after taking that test, I went home for Christmas break, crying when the Littles swarmed me, hugging my parents so long and hard.

"Our pride and joy is here!" Grandpop announced when I walked in their door the next day. "How's the best girl in the world? Learning a lot?"

"Oh, honey, tell me everything," Grammy said, and her eyes were bright even though the radiation had sapped her energy. "Do you think you'll be a sorority girl? Oh, my goodness! So many adventures in front of you!"

I told them about all the good things that had happened at CU so far. It seemed like I was describing someone else's life, a dream from long ago.

"And that young man you're dating?" Grandpop asked.

"Oh, we broke up," I said easily.

"Probably for the best. You don't want anything interfering with your studies, now, do you?" Grammy said.

I baked Christmas cookies and took Winnie gift shopping in P-town, helped Robbie with homework, listened as the twins complained about the same teachers I'd complained about. My family had saved decorating the tree for when I was home, and we spent a night singing along to carols and amicably bickering over who got to hang which ornaments. At times, I could almost forget I was pregnant.

I blamed my incredible fatigue on jet lag and the hours I'd put in for finals. When I threw up (just once, thank God), I told Mom I'd had coffee on top of fried clams and coleslaw for lunch at the Land Ho! with the girls.

"Bad combo," she said, and her maternal instincts didn't so much as twitch.

My father (the nurse) told me I was prettier than ever. So much for his medical expertise.

On New Year's Eve, when Winnie and Robbie were in bed and the twins were at a sleepover, Mom, Dad and I sat in the living room, eating popcorn and watching TV. Mom stretched, putting her feet on Dad's lap so he could rub them.

"I love the holidays," she said, "but they are exhausting. I'm so glad you kids are older now. I was this close to telling Robbie the truth about Santa."

"Eleven years till an empty nest, babe," Dad said. "We can make it. Harlow, are you still thinking about law school, sweetie? A lawyer in the family will come in handy, because I know your brother is going to be a career criminal."

My parents laughed, and I fake-laughed along with them and made my decision.

I wouldn't tell them. I'd make excuses for why I couldn't come home this summer, I'd have the baby and give it away to a wonderful couple, and then tuck the memories away and carry on, just like my tea mug said. Keep calm and carry on. I wasn't the first stupid teenager to get pregnant, and I wouldn't be the last, but I could give this baby a good life.

Yes. Next year, my baby would be enjoying its first Christmas with two parents in a lovely home somewhere. There'd be many presents under the tree for this much-wanted baby. My life would stay on course, and when the baby did cross my mind, I'd picture him or her with that stellar family and smile, proud of myself for being such a hero, so selfless, so noble.

"Harlow, are you crying?" Mom asked.

She was right. Tears were hot and wet on my cheeks. "Oh. Just missed you guys so much, you know?" I smiled and wiped my eyes. "I'm so happy to be home again."

I went back to Boulder at the end of January, called Planned Parenthood and asked them to recommend an adoption agency. Later that week, I went to my first appointment there and was assigned to Jen, an adoption counselor. Her warmth and kindness were evident the second I met her.

"This isn't just about placing your baby," she said. "This is about you wanting the best possible future for your child. It's one hundred percent okay that you're not in the position to create that yet." I felt a tiny bit better. "We're here for you just as much as we're here for your baby, no matter what your final decision is."

I burst into tears, and she hugged me.

Jen told me most birth mothers wanted at least some contact with the adoptive family after the baby was born. I pictured my little brother, what it would be like to say goodbye to him over and over, leaving him with someone else, his sweet little face in the window as I drove away.

"I don't think I will," I said after a minute. "It sounds like torture for both of us, to be honest."

"You don't have to decide now. But just the fact that you're thinking about adoption shows a lot of emotional maturity. There's no pressure here. You can change your mind at any time in the process."

Changing my mind was exactly what I was afraid of. I was now just out of my first trimester, and I already loved my child. I thought it was a boy, but it was too soon to find out.

When I told Zach the baby would be adopted, he sagged with relief. "Thank you, Jesus!" he said. "Do I have to, like, do anything?"

"You'll have to sign away your parental rights." My voice was cold and hard.

"Awesome. Not a problem. Man! I literally dodged a bullet."

This, I told myself, was why I should date someone for a long, long time before sleeping with him. So I could know what kind of person I was letting into my life and my body. Zach was a boy; a spoiled, self-centered child in a man's body. Not once had he asked how I was. Also, he didn't understand the meaning of "literally."

It was winter and I was barely showing, so I just wore leggings and big sweaters like everyone else. I could see a slight bulge in my abdomen. One night, as Rosie and I were lying in bed in the dark, she asked, "Did you ever wish you were adopted when you were little?"

"No. Did you?"

She was quiet a minute. "I did, actually. I mean, both of my parents are great in their own way. But sometimes I wonder why they even had me. I had a nanny from day one. My mother went back to work three weeks after I was born. Full-time. My dad . . . I barely remember him being home."

"How old were you when they got divorced?"

"Four. First I was with Mom, but then she wanted to move her practice to Arizona, where there's more skin cancer and wrinkles for her to treat. I guess Dad wanted me more, because he was the custodial parent. I visited her plenty, but I don't think she ever really missed me. I'd call, tell her about school and ballet, and that was that. She was nice, of course. But more like an aunt or a family friend than a mother."

No wonder Rosie had only given the highlights of her childhood before. "Was your dad around more after the divorce?"

"Yeah. I mean, he tried. He would even show up at a school event once in a while. When I got older, sometimes he'd take me out with one of his girlfriends and have me weigh in on her." She laughed. "I hated them all. When I was fourteen, my nanny retired, and after that, I had an au pair in the summer, and the housekeeper would look after me when I got home from school."

"It sounds lonely," I said.

"It was." I heard the rustle of her covers. "Lolo, you get to pick out the best parents in the world for your kid. I used to wish I could do the same thing, but for myself. Parents who would raise me, not just 'enjoy' me here and there."

She had a point. I *would* be choosing them and I *would* find the best. I promised my baby he'd get the absolute best. Jen sent me the links to the videos made by hopeful parents. If I liked them, she'd give me more information . . . jobs, family, education, religion, hobbies. "What if I make the wrong choice?" I had asked her.

"We've screened everyone," she said. "Background checks, home visits, interviews with psychologists. But most of our birth mothers say something just clicks. Trust me. You'll know."

I watched the videos, crying, hormonal, sad. It was *so* hard . . .

all those couples, seeming so wonderful and eager, many of them acknowledging the heartbreak of infertility. They showed off their homes, yards, pets, nieces and nephews. Talked about how grateful they'd feel, what devoted parents they yearned to become.

I felt for them all and ruled them all out.

I watched dozens of videos, then dozens more. Some of the couples were almost right, some of them completely wrong. Sometimes, a minuscule thing would put me off . . . the guy who wore an orange hunting cap in his interview (could he have at least tried to look nice when making the pitch for a baby?). The woman whose teeth were too white, nails too long, lashes too fake. Clearly, she was too vain to be a good mom, I thought heartlessly. Would my child have to go to a babysitter during her spa days? Next! Okay, that couple had a cross big enough for a real-life crucifixion hanging in their *bedroom*. Next! How about this gay couple? They seemed nice, but did I want my kid growing up in that cramped little house? That woman looked too thin. Was she sick? Would she die and leave my baby motherless? Oh, my God, the ridiculous hair on that guy. Next!

This couple was too young, I thought, and that couple was too old. These folks already had a kid. Did I want my baby to have older siblings, or be a worshipped only child? I didn't think one couple looked in love enough. What if they got divorced? Then the whole point of a two-parent family would be erased. This couple was way too far apart in age and had both been divorced before. I didn't like their odds. Here was a couple who had obviously hired a videographer for their profile video . . . was that an unfair advantage, or did it speak well of them, that they'd spend the money to make a good impression?

They all wanted a baby so much, and I hated that I'd be the

one to crush their dreams. I told that to Jen, who smiled. "Don't worry, Harlow. They all know the deal . . . nothing is guaranteed. If you talk with them and don't like them, you'll never have to talk to them again."

"It's just such an important choice," I said, wiping my eyes.

"It absolutely is. I promise, something will click."

And then, in April after I'd watched more than a hundred videos, I was sitting in my dorm room midday, poring over the computer as Rosie slept—she'd been out till 4 a.m., come back from her morning class and crashed in her bed, still a little hungover, snoring and drooling into her pillow.

One more video, I thought, and then I'd have to go to class.

The words *Monica and Sanjay* floated on the screen. He was Indian, she was white, and they were rather gorgeous. He had inky black hair and gorgeous brown eyes; she also had black hair, a huge smile and clear blue eyes. The first thing their video showed was Sanjay turning on the video camera and sitting on the couch next to Monica.

"Does my head look too big?" he asked, and Monica rolled her eyes and laughed.

"Your head *is* too big," she said.

It didn't seem staged. They'd been together since college, and they looked young, but not childlike. Sanjay was a fourth-grade teacher; Monica was an IT security specialist. As they sat there, telling me why they'd be great parents, there was a sense of humor between them. Most of the videos were saturated with earnestness and poorly disguised longing, but theirs . . . theirs was kind of fun.

"We would absolutely *love* to be your baby's parents," Monica said. "Adoption is something we've planned on since we met."

Sanjay replied, "My queen speaks the truth. Did we bring it

up on the third date or the fourth?" He had an accent, and I found it warm and lovely.

"The second, actually," Monica said. "I have a history of endometriosis, and my doctor said it wouldn't be easy to get pregnant. I've always assumed my kids would be adopted. We didn't want to spend a hundred thousand dollars and ten years trying for a biological baby, because we want to have kids while we're still young."

"I'm young," said Sanjay. "She's older."

"By three months," Monica said, shoving him fondly.

Oh, yes, I liked them. And I liked their rationale, too.

"This is our garden," Sanjay said, showing a small, shady backyard. "I call it *garden* because it sounds much classier than 'very small backyard.' There's a park half a block away, though, so when our kid gets bigger, they can run and run and run."

They had a rickety old dog named Notorious D.O.G. "To be honest, Notorious will probably be waiting at the rainbow bridge by the time we bring home a baby," Sanjay said, petting the dog's graying head.

Monica snorted and said, "Now we're gonna have to do this over." She looked right at the camera. "Notorious here may go to a nice farm in the near future."

I snort-laughed.

Most videos showed couples carefully interacting with kids to show how responsible a parent they'd be, but theirs showed Sanjay going into his parents' house and being swarmed by nieces and nephews, then letting them drag him to the floor as he called out for help. In another clip, Monica held her newborn niece on her shoulder, looking blissful and natural while she stirred something on the stove. I could practically smell the deliciousness.

Monica had grown up in Idaho on a small farm, which

looked beautiful and well-kept. Sanjay's family had immigrated from Mumbai, and they went back every few years to visit relatives.

"My parents gave us everything. They worked so hard so we could have the life we do." His eyes got shiny at that. "Family is everything to us."

Another clip showed Sanjay at school, dancing hip-hop with the kids at recess. Monica had a nice big office and flexible hours, and both she and Sanjay would take long parental leaves. No plans for daycare; Sanjay's parents were four blocks away and eager to babysit if needed.

I put my hand on my stomach. "What do you think, baby?" I whispered.

There was a flutter, like a butterfly, and I bolted up in my chair. "Rosie!" I yelped. "He moved!"

It felt like a sign.

SIXTEEN

HARLOW

I've got your back," Rosie said as we got out of the car at Addie and Nicole's. "Unless I'm flirting with your grandfather or your brother, of course. Otherwise, totally here for you."

It was the night of the dreaded Family Dinner, and I already felt queasy. It felt like years had passed since Matthew had walked into the store just days earlier. I grabbed the two bottles of wine I was bringing (and might drink solo), and we walked up the steps to the front door.

"Oh. Hello," said Addison. "You're not even late." She scanned Rosie's outfit (leopard skirt, yellow cropped shirt, pink sweater and ankle boots). "Rosie. Hi." She sounded as if she were greeting a virus. Addie hated people who dressed better than she did.

"Addison. Hi," Rosie responded with equal enthusiasm. Then she saw my parents and started working her magic. "Ellie! Gerald!" she said. "It's wonderful to see you again. How are you?" She gave my father a big hug. "Still so handsome, Gerald."

Mom accepted a kiss on the cheek. "I understand you've known about my grandson since the beginning."

Someone with a fainter heart might've flinched, but Rosie just smiled and sat down next to her. "I did indeed."

"Lark can't come," Addie announced. "She says she's sorry, but she has to stay at the hospital. I *hate* that she's becoming a doctor. We never see each other anymore."

"I know," I said. "Oncology, too. She's so selfish."

"We're twins, okay? We have a special bond."

There was Grandpop. Imogen and I headed for him at the same time. "Goppy!" said Imogen, burying her face against Grandpop's leg. I sat next to him.

"Hello, little one!" he said, scooping her up. "Aren't you *adorable!*" She beamed at him, a cascade of drool hitting him on the chest. "She's a cutie, isn't she, Harlow?"

My poor little niece. I'd never really given her any special attention. "She is," I said, stroking her hand with the tip of my forefinger. "You are, Imogen."

Winnie came in, dropped her bag, looked around, nodded at Rosie and poured two glasses of wine, handed me one and sat next to me on the vast couch. My guard dog, but with thumbs.

"Why don't I settle the kids in front of a movie?" Mom suggested. "Then we can talk. And after that, if we're all still speaking to each other, we can eat."

"I'm wicked hungry," Robbie said. "Can we eat first?"

"You'll have to wait."

"Yes, Mommy Dearest," he said.

Nicole ushered the girls into the den to be babysat by the television.

Rosie scurried over to sit next to Winnie, a full wineglass in her hand. Grandpop, Rosie, Winnie and I on one side of the room; Mom, Dad, Addison, Nicole and Robbie (a mama's boy if ever there was one) on the other. The battle lines were drawn. If Lark were here, she'd lie down in the middle and probably fall asleep.

"All right!" said Mom in a loud voice. "We all know Harlow

has been keeping a secret from us, and his name is Matthew. Harlow, why don't you tell us what's been going on in your life for the past eighteen years? We're dying to know. Do we get to meet this boy or will we stay in the closet?"

It was better that she was mad at me. If she'd been kind, hugging me and murmuring gentle words, I'd probably dissolve. "Right," I said. "As I told you last week, I got pregnant in college and placed the baby with a couple named Sanjay and Monica Patel."

"Without telling us," Mom said.

"Very good, Mrs. Smith," said Rosie. "Go on, Harlow."

"It was a closed adoption," I said. "That was my choice. They live in California. I did say he could contact me if he wanted to after he turned eighteen. His birthday is July twenty-fifth, so he came a little early. Obviously, I didn't expect him to just appear in the store." I took a slug of wine.

"She *fainted*, she was so surprised," said Grandpop, patting my knee. "Poor little bunny rabbit."

"Thanks, Grandpop. So . . . I've met with the Patels, and we discussed how to proceed. In a nutshell, they're okay with Matthew spending time with me this summer. And meeting you all. Eventually. I want to get to know him a little bit first."

"Understandable," Winnie murmured.

"Are we allowed to ask questions yet?" Mom asked.

"Now honey," Dad said, putting a hand on her shoulder.

She shrugged it off. "Don't shush me, Gerald. My child has been avoiding me after she made this shattering announcement, and I am deeply hurt by it. Deeply, Harlow."

"Yeah, I'm picking up on that," I said. "And, Mom, I'm sorry you're hurt. But I was seventeen, and I handled this the way I thought was best."

"Well?" Mom continued. "Am I allowed to ask a question?"

"Sure, Mom. Fire away," I said. Rosie took my hand and squeezed it.

"Thank you. How *nice* to be able to share my feelings about my *grandson* and my *daughter*. I thought we had a close relationship, Harlow. To say your father and I are betrayed by this . . . well. I would like to know some details about this hugely important event you cut me out of."

"I just can't believe Esme isn't the oldest anymore," Addison said.

"Yeah, that's definitely the most important thing in this conversation," said Robbie. "Esme's fragile psyche because there's another Smith in the world."

"Fine. I'll tell you everything. I mean, there's nothing to hide anymore." Grandpop, my hero, put his arm around me. "I got pregnant about three weeks after I lost my virginity." Grandpop winced, and my brother made a slight gagging sound. "Sorry," I said. "I knew right away. I told Rosie, I told the . . . guy—"

"Who is he, by the way?" Dad interrupted. "I'd like to have a word."

"You're not going to," I said. "Aside from being the biological father, he's not important to this story, okay? I thought about my options. Keeping the baby, ending the pregnancy, putting him up for adoption. And I decided adoption was the way to go."

I stopped for breath, then took another sip of wine. "You're doing great," Rosie whispered.

"I didn't tell you, Mom and Dad, because you would have been crushed and disappointed in me."

"And loving and kind," Mom snapped. Robbie gave a snort. "Why *didn't* you keep him?" she went on. "Were we such awful parents that you didn't want us to help raise your son?"

"No," I said. "You were not awful parents. You were wonderful." My father wiped his eyes, and I had to look away for a second. "I didn't want to be a teenage mother living with her parents, completely reliant on you for the next ten or fifteen years while I tried to scrape an education together. I wanted my baby to have two parents, to be . . ." I waved my hand, looking for the word.

"Special," Rosie supplied. "Not just Smith Child Number Six."

I winced, remembering using those exact words when talking with Rosie in our bunk beds.

"That's ridiculous," my mother said. "You're *all* special. You're hardly lumped in together, are you? You're all unique and wonderful and loved. Fix your face, Windsor. You are."

"And then there was my own life," I said loudly. "I didn't think I was ready to raise a child, even with help. I was seventeen, Mom. I wanted to stay in college. I wanted to do something with my life."

"And how's that worked out?" Nicole said. Rosie gave her the finger.

"Were you always such a bitch, Nicole, or has motherhood brought that out in you?" Winnie asked, making Nicole literally clutch her pearl necklace. "Great for you that you sit on a pile of family money, but maybe try to act a little more human toward my sister."

"Just because I work for my family's foundation doesn't mean I'm coasting, Windsor."

"Who is Windsor again?" asked Grandpop.

"Me, Grandpop," said my sister. "Winnie."

I clapped my hands. "Focus, people! I chose adoption, had the baby, gave him to Monica and Sanjay, the end. Now, before a knife fight breaks out, can we talk about this summer?" I said.

From the den, the song "Let It Go" was blaring, a good message. "I would like you to meet Matthew and his parents this summer. If you behave, that is."

"Well, thank you," said Dad. "Nice to hear we might make the cut. What is this, *Project Runway*?"

"I love that show," Robbie said.

"Is there a lottery?" Mom said. "Who gets to go first?"

"So much snark in this room," said Rosie. She held up her empty wineglass, and Robbie leaped to refill it.

I tried again. "Mom. Dad. I did what I thought was right for my baby. If you can't respect that, well, maybe you're not who I thought you were. Addison and Nicole, if all you care about is Esme being the oldest, you won't lay eyes on my boy. Grandpop, Robbie and Winnie . . . you've been great."

"Maybe you're not who we thought you were, either, Harlow," Dad said.

"And who did you think I was, Dad? Huh?" My voice was loud, and I felt hot all over. "Mom? Who was I in this family? Your unpaid nanny? Aside from me being the helpful one, I was . . . nothing. I was barely there. Only Grammy and Grandpop seemed to really know me. You think I was going to give you my *child*?"

"This is getting so good," Robbie whispered.

"You have an interesting memory," Mom said, not looking at me. "You were hardly Jane Eyre, Harlow."

"What's my favorite color, Mom? My favorite author, Dad? TV show? Stuffed animal? Did my room have wallpaper or paint on the walls? What was my favorite subject in school?"

"English?" Dad guessed.

"History," Grandpop said.

"This is a setup," Mom said, standing up. "We're leaving."

"I made barbecued tofu," Nicole said. "You can't leave."

"You guys stay," I said to my parents. "Rosie and I will go."

"Don't you dare leave me here," Winnie said, standing up. "I'm going with you."

"Me too," said Robbie.

"Oh, wonderful!" Mom said, tossing her hands in the air. "Now all my children have turned against me."

"Well, Addie hasn't," Winnie said. "And Lark hasn't weighed in yet, so you still have the twins."

"What does that mean?" Dad asked.

"It means we're going out to dinner," I said. "You have not been loving or supportive since you learned about Matthew. You've tried to shame me for my choices and guilt-trip me because I didn't trust you enough to tell you about him, and you know what? I was right not to. I love you both, and I'm furious with you both, and we're going out without you."

"Can I come, too?" asked Grandpop. "I'd love a night out with my grandchildren."

"Of course, Grandpop," I said.

"How wonderful!"

"Wait, wait," Addison said. "One more question, Harlow. After you gave him away, was . . . was that the end of it?" Her face was unusually gentle. Maybe it was because she was a mother herself, but she knew there was more.

"No," I said quietly. "I had a . . . a mental health crisis about seven years later. That's why I dropped out of law school."

"With twelve weeks to go," said my dad, then jerked as the words registered. "Wait, what? A mental health crisis?"

"I had a nervous breakdown. I just . . . yeah, those words work. I broke down. Couldn't get out of bed, couldn't shower, just slept and cried."

"And watched *Dexter*," added Rosie. It had become an inside joke with us, code for *I need a vacation.*

"Oh, my God!" said my mother. "Harlow! Another secret? Why couldn't you have told us? We would have done anything for you."

I hesitated before answering. "I was in a bad way," I said. "At the time, I didn't know what I needed, so I went to a treatment facility, and when I was thinking more clearly, I came home. To all of you. And I've stayed home, because this is where I needed and wanted to be."

My mother was crying; my father's face looked broken.

"Look, guys," I said. "I'd like to focus on the present situation, which is that I have a chance to get to know my son. And you do, too. I know you believe you'd do anything for me. But you also have to admit that I've always had a certain role in this family, and it's to be the calm, responsible, cheerful one. I didn't think I could tell you any of this without . . . well, without this exact kind of reaction."

Grandpop stood up, his knees popping. "Harlow is a wonderful person," he said. "She did her best under very difficult circumstances. If she chose not to take her problems to us, well, maybe we need to do some soul-searching. Now. My grandchildren are taking me out. Addison, you should come, too. Your wife can take care of the little ones. Now, kids, get me some food before I collapse like the fragile old man I am."

"I love you, Mr. Smith," Rosie said. "Seriously. I want to marry you."

"I'll take it under advisement, my dear. Robbie, I don't suppose you have a gummy, do you?" he said.

"Meet you at the Ice House, guys," Robbie said. "I just texted

Beth, and she's holding a big table for us. Grandpop, we can swing by the Piping Plover and hook you up."

"Oh, goody, Lark just got out of work," Addie said, looking at her phone. "She'll meet us there."

And so it was that my siblings, grandfather, best friend and I had a rather fantastic evening, and I felt lighter than I had in more than eighteen years. Seemed like speaking your mind could do that.

SEVENTEEN

CYNTHIA

Cynthia had a Facebook page for the simple purpose of spying. Wasn't that why everyone had one? Wasn't that the point of all social media, to encourage people to envy your life? She wanted to know what her so-called friends back home were doing and keep tabs on the Smiths, so she could judge them. Oh, please. Everyone judged everyone else. Cynthia was simply honest about it.

She rarely posted herself. Her cover page was a photo of a vivid Wellfleet sunset from when she'd first moved here three years ago. That had been to show her Kansas City friends where she was, oh, yes, not to mention Henry and his Venezuelan family. *Loving life here on Cape Cod! So blessed to have this view every night!*

Cynthia's house had a small patio in the front (if you could call a slab of cement a patio). She had adorned it with various-sized flowerpots to disguise its crumbling edges and stains. Sometimes, like tonight, Cynthia took a small glass of wine and sat there while she read or scrolled through her computer.

Occasionally, Cynthia would post a picture of her garden, the one improvement she'd made to her property. Gardening was her passion, as it had been Mother's. It was ladylike and genteel and bespoke a certain intelligence and class. Lavender, pink roses, Russian sage and Montauk daisies now flourished here. In the early spring, creeping phlox, witch hazel, daffodils and heather burst forth, hardy enough to withstand the Cape winds and dry summers.

She obviously didn't post photos of her tiny home. Who could call six hundred and twenty-four square feet an actual house? Thank heavens she'd bought before the last housing boom, because she could never have afforded it now. Ridiculous. Her house in Kansas City wasn't worth this much.

Home gave her no pleasure now. The décor in the shack was much as it had been when she bought it, because really, what was the point? You can't put lipstick on a pig, Mother used to say. When Cynthia and Henry had moved into his mother's house, she'd spent more than six thousand dollars on a single *chair*. Mother and Daddy's furniture had been antiques (taken by the bank, may they rot in hell). Oh, what was this? Facebook's news feed bleated that Vivian Stein's daughter was getting married, though how that girl had found someone was anyone's guess. Vivian just had to spill all the details so the world could know her horse-faced, nearly forty-year-old child was finally engaged. The ring was one of those halo pavé rings that everyone wore these days. It was enormous, too. Tacky.

Cynthia doubted she'd be invited to the wedding. It was just as well. A plane ticket, a few nights in a hotel and a suitable outfit would cost thousands, and even Harlow would notice that.

The sun was setting now, the sky vivid shades of orange and red. Cynthia couldn't resist taking a picture to post. She'd gotten used to the sharp, rotten-egg smell of low tide and the noises of families with their shrieking children and loud radios. People were so rude. They'd walk along the beach and peer at the houses as if the owners were zoo animals.

One such rude person was walking on the beach right now. He looked like a vagrant. Oh, for heaven's sake, it was Bertie Baines. He looked her way, then did a double take. Wonderful. He was now scrambling over the breakwater to approach her. What on earth gave him the idea she wanted him to trespass?

"Hey, Cynthia," he said. *Cynthier.* "How are you?"

"I'm fine. Is there a problem? Are you having a medical emergency, Albert?"

He laughed, showing a missing incisor. "Funny, how you call me Albert. Only my mother called me that, and only when I was bothering her." *Only my muthah called me thet, and only when I was bawtherin' heur.* "No, I wanted to thank you for that book. *Where the Crawdads Sing.* I loved it. Beautiful story."

"Yes. It is."

"So this is your place, or are you renting?" he asked.

Was it any of his business? "It's mine," she said.

"This area's got quite the history to it," Bertie said, putting his hands in his pockets. "A Bavarian immigrant named Henry Hiller bought all this land way back when. He was a doctor who made his fortune selling Dr. Hiller's Elixir, which was supposed to cure anything from a brain tumor to a bad mood." Bertie smiled. "He married a woman named France, also a doctor, and they made so much money, they couldn't give it away. One thing they couldn't have, though, was kids. Wicked sad."

"Yes." She wished he would go.

"Then Henry died in a carriage accident, and France, she was eccentric, all right. She had a coffin made for herself, too, and would dress up in her burial clothes, five hundred yards of lace, if you can believe it. Then she'd practice layin' in it with mirrors on the ceiling so she could see how she'd look."

"My goodness, how morbid!" Cynthia said, fascinated against her will.

"Get this, though. A few years later, all her friends get an invitation to her wedding. France Hiller will be marrying Henry Hiller."

"You said he died."

"He did. She'd found another man and made him change his name to Henry Hiller. He was twenty-five years younger than she was, but apparently it was a love match."

"Really?" Cynthia rather liked this woman.

Bertie nodded and scratched his scruffy beard. "Yep. Seven years later, though, she died of liver failure. Seemed she liked the drink a little too much."

"Goodness. What a colorful story," Cynthia said. She wondered how he knew all those details. Clearly a student of local history.

"So your land here, it's got some real history to it." He looked at her cottage. "Cute place."

"Not really my style," she said. "I'm not a fan of dank knotty pine."

He grunted. "Could be quite nice. You could shade this patio with an arbor." To her horror, he cupped his hands around his eyes and peered into her house. "Put in hardwood floors, new cabinets, maybe bigger windows in front here. What's your septic situation?"

"I have no idea," she said, reclaiming her frosty tone. She didn't need advice from Bertie Baines, who didn't seem to know what a barbershop was for.

"Well, if you ever want an opinion, let me know. I restored a few houses and cottages in my day." He sat down next to her, uninvited, causing her to lean back away from his sweaty, sharp smell. "Anyway, that book. Man, it touched my heart. That poor little girl, all alone there, teachin' herself, finding food . . . I didn't like the grown-up girl as much as the little one. That's what stayed with me, her survivin' on her own there, sad but happy at the same time."

"Me too," Cynthia said, again surprising herself. "The writing was achingly beautiful."

"That's the word for it, innit?" he said. "Aching."

Cynthia's summer neighbors—renters—emerged from the large house next door, laughing, heading for the car, all six of them. They waved to her, and Bertie waved back. Oh no. What if they thought she was with Bertie?

"Well. Thank you for the history lesson, Albert," she said. "I'm sorry, I need to go in now."

"Got it. Nice talkin' to you, Cynthia."

She started to say something sharp, something like *please don't come by unannounced.* Instead, she said, "Nice talking to you as well." Mother hadn't raised her to be rude.

Bertie heaved himself off the chair, then shuffled his way back to the beach, the now-pink-and-tangerine sky behind him. She went inside, stayed away from the windows for a few minutes, then looked out to make sure he was gone. The history lesson was fascinating, but that didn't mean she wanted to associate with him socially. Not when bathing didn't seem to be in his repertoire.

However, it had been . . . well, pleasant, having someone to talk to. She hadn't made any friends in this town during the past three years, which she attributed to New England rudeness (in the Midwest, people actually spoke to each other and answered with sentences instead of grunts). Also, she was sure Harlow and

Addison and the other Smith children resented her. Gerald had implied that his mother's "offer" to give her part of the bookstore had been more of a whim than an intended business transaction. Rude, even though there had been no offer at all. And that Elsbeth, so infatuated with herself, the *artist*, the beloved wife, the fertile mother of too many children. Only Uncle Robert was tolerable.

Cynthia put a Lean Cuisine Baked Chicken meal in the microwave for dinner. No point in trying to cook in the minuscule kitchen, though she made soup once a week to take to work for lunch. As she waited for the meal to finish warming, she opened her laptop again.

She had a message on Facebook in the "New message requests" folder. Cynthia didn't even know such a thing existed. She didn't often get Facebook messages (except from men with unfamiliar names). The message request was from a Nancy Barbieri Lawless. Probably spam. The name didn't ring any bells. Fine. She'd click on it. It had been sent four months ago. Why she had just seen it now was anyone's guess.

The letter was broken up in little message balloons. The first one simply said, Hello.

The second balloon made her blood run cold.

This note may come as a surprise. For the past four years since our mother died, my two younger sisters and I have been looking for our older sister, who was adopted through St. Joseph's Catholic Orphanage in Missouri. Her birthday is April 14, and she would be 61 years old. Her adoptive parents may have been Miriam and Carl Smith of Kansas City, Missouri.

The microwave dinged. Cynthia didn't move.

We hired a private investigator who thought you might possibly be her. We are hoping to talk with you if you are willing, and if you are not the person we think, we're sorry to bother you.

The world seemed to tilt, but Cynthia stayed frozen at the table for a good long time.

It honestly had never occurred to Cynthia that she might have half-siblings who'd want to meet her. Why? What did they have in common other than genetics? All those people who loved airing the family's dirty laundry on Ancestry or 23andMe . . . ugh.

Well. The note had been sent four months ago. There was no rule that said Cynthia had to answer. Hopefully, Nancy Barbieri Lawless had moved on.

But now that the can of worms had burst open, she knew she had three half sisters. At least three.

She did not appreciate this one bit.

EIGHTEEN

HARLOW

Matthew and I were going paddleboarding at Nauset Light Beach. On Monday, Robbie and Rosie drove me there in his battered pickup. The plan was for Matthew and me to bond for three hours, at which point Monica or Sanjay would pick him up. Rosie and Robbie would be down the beach a bit, but knew to stay out of sight.

Robbie found a spot in the parking lot, and we unloaded my board and paddle. Matthew and I were going to meet at the top of the path that led to the beach, but we were a bit early. I got out of the car and pulled on my wet suit.

"This will be a great day, Harlow," Rosie said.

"Especially for me," said Robbie. "Since I'm on sunscreen duty." He winked at Rosie.

"She's too old for you," I said. "And way, way out of your league."

"I really am," Rosie said. "But you *are* adorable, Robbie."

"Ten years isn't too much for me," my brother said.

"Rosie, did I ever tell you how Robbie went to the bathroom in church when he was three? He ran up the aisle and yelled, 'I poop! I poop on potty!' It was Easter Sunday."

"God, I was delightful," Robbie said. "The entire church burst into applause. It shaped me, all that adoration."

"You Smiths. I do adore you, all of you. I'm gonna change. Back in a second." She headed over to the bathrooms, newly constructed and not yet taken out to sea by a nor'easter, as happened every ten years or so. I checked the Sharktivity app on my phone, which told us when sharks were near shore and how they'd been identified—buoy ding or sighting or seal blood in the water. There was nothing from today, but four buoy dings from yesterday. Chances were something like one in a billion that we'd be killed by a shark, but I always checked.

The sun was hot; the beach plums were blooming, pink and cheery; and seagulls wheeled and dove in the sky.

"How you doing, Harlow?" my brother asked.

"Good. Why?"

He made a face. "Um . . . because you had a kid no one knew about, and he found you, and our parents are insane with despair and Addison is jealous her child isn't the firstborn anymore and Winnie and Lark are shocked you never said anything?"

"Oh, that." I looked out at the ocean. "Um . . . I don't know. How about you? How do you feel about . . . my son?"

He leaned against the split rail fence, nodded at a pretty young woman who was checking him out, then turned back at me. "I guess I feel a little sad," he said. "I mean, you must've felt pretty alone. I know I'm just your irritating little brother, but I'm also actually an adult now. You can talk to me."

My eyes filled. "Thank you, honey. I just didn't want to drop this bomb, I guess."

"You get to drop a bomb once in a while, Harlot. Everyone else in this family is a drama queen. Why not you?"

"Winnie's not a drama queen," I said.

"Her lack of being a drama queen is her own brand of drama queening. Seriously, though. Why didn't you tell us? Even one of us?"

I sighed. "I guess because being the responsible one . . . that's kind of my job."

"I think what you're actually saying is that being *perfect* is your job, and the one time you weren't, you thought it would destroy the family, so you went through all this alone. I think that's called a martyr complex."

I looked at him closely. "Have you actually read a book? Who are you and where is my brother?"

"Shut up," he said. "I'm not four anymore. Oh, God, here comes Rosie, and sweet baby Jesus, I can't feel my legs."

"Once more with feeling . . . you're too young and she's out of your league. She likes older men."

"So you keep saying. Rosie, let's hit the sand, okay? We don't want to be discovered by her kid and have him like us best."

"Good luck, sweetie," she said, hugging me. "See you in a while. Robbie, if there's a shark in that water, you'll kill it for me, right?"

"Obviously," he said, and off they went. Just in time, too, because a young man was walking toward me with a paddleboard under his arm. Matthew. My heart seemed to lift out of my chest, and he grinned and waved.

"Hey," I said, leaning in for a hug. He didn't, but just as I drew back, he leaned in, so we did that little move in, move out dance until we finally made awkward contact. "This will be fun."

"Yeah, I'm psyched. Dad said to text him around four and he'll pick me up." He shifted his board on his hip.

"Great. Um, this way. Have you ever been paddleboarding on the Atlantic?" I asked as we headed down the path.

"Nope. Just the Pacific near San Fran and some lakes. Kind of tame."

"Okay, a few notes, then. The water is pretty cold, about sixty degrees. The thing to know is that there *are* great white sharks out there, because the seals are one of their main food sources."

"Yeah. So it says everywhere." Ooh. A little teenage attitude. Then again, he had a point. Every beach had a terrifying picture of a great white and a warning.

"The seals are pretty big," I went on, "but they mostly leave people alone, though they'll pop up to look at us from time to time. If you see them charging along, jumping out of the water, they're being chased, which means get to shore immediately. And listen to the lifeguards. Purple flag means a shark's been sighted. Whatever the reason, if the lifeguards say get out of the water, it's no questions asked."

"Can we get going now?" he asked.

"In a minute. Safety first." I checked his life vest to make sure it fit right. "This stays on," I said, "and so does this." I strapped the leash around his ankle. "Since you're new to the Atlantic, let's stay away from surfers and other paddleboarders. If I tell you to paddle in one direction, listen, okay? There's a good undertow here most of the time, and riptides can pop up anytime. Understood?"

"Yep. Let's get out there." He smiled, and God, he was so beautiful. My heart squeezed.

The water was clear and gorgeous today. We lay on our boards and got past the waves. The ocean was gentle, the waves at the shore small and great for kids. A few hundred yards out, a sandbar created some bigger waves, and that was where most of the surfers were at the moment.

"Okay, we can stand up," I said. "Take a minute to acclimate."

"I've done this before, okay?" he said.

"Not here, and not with me."

"God. You sound like my mother." He cracked a grin, and I smiled back.

We paddled out a bit. I kept one eye on Matthew, the other on the blue Atlantic. Soon, we were out over our heads, looking down in the water.

While I had done this hundreds of times, it suddenly occurred to me that taking my newly found child out into the ocean was maybe a bad idea. There *were* sharks here. And riptides. Undertows. Seals with sharp teeth. The Gulf Stream. Was there a reason I thought this was smart? Why hadn't I picked mini-golf? "The water's really clear," Matthew said. "Not much in the way of fish, though."

"They're here," I said, snapping out of it. "But they're not as colorful as what you might have seen in the Pacific." Was that a fin? No, that was a seagull, and I damn well knew it. "If you see a big school of fish, move away from it. It's another sign that a shark might be hunting." What else did I know about sharks? That they were fast and lethal? Shit.

"We went to St. John's one time over Christmas?" Matthew said. "The fish there were unbelievable. Like, you just put your face in the water, and it's *Finding Nemo*. And the Great Barrier Reef, you know? We went to Australia two years ago, and that was amazing."

"I've never been to either place."

"Really?" he asked, as if most people had.

"Someday, maybe," I said.

"Me and my family, we travel all the time. At least twice a year."

"You're really lucky, then." As soon as I'd said it, I knew it was the wrong thing to say. His face shut down immediately.

"Yeah. So lucky. Is that why you gave me away? So a rich couple could take me on nice vacations?"

Wow. That was . . . harsh. A bigger wave tipped me, and I had to shift my weight and use my paddle to stay on the board. Matthew, less experienced, fell in. Kind of served him right. He hopped right back on the board in an instant, curly hair now wet, and looked at me, waiting for the answer to his question.

"Vacations had nothing to do with it." I scanned the ocean. "I just meant you're lucky to have traveled a lot."

He said nothing.

"Hey," I said gently, "we're just getting to know each other. Let's have fun, okay?"

He gave a nod. "Sure. We should go out further," he said.

"I think this is far enough," I said, but he was already gliding away, his strokes even and confident. I heard a lifeguard's whistle and glanced back. No shark flag. Probably just some kid going out too far.

"Matthew," I called. "Wait up, okay?"

He did not. He was a nearly eighteen-year-old male, fit and strong, but I was more experienced, and these were my waters. I didn't like the look of the ocean up ahead—the color was darker blue with some green beneath.

I caught up to him, panting. "Hey, that water there? See how it's green underneath? That's a sign of a current, maybe a rip-tide." Was it? I suddenly couldn't remember. "We don't want to mess with that."

"But there are bigger waves out there," he said. "I want to catch a few."

"No," I said. "Seriously, listen to me. We don't want to get sucked out there and have the Coast Guard have to rescue us."

"Why not? It'd be a good story." And he was off again, gliding through the water toward the bigger waves, which were white-crested, breaking hard and fast.

I followed. Definitely mini-golf next time. This was a test, I got that. What I was supposed to do was another question. I drew up next to him, breathing hard. "We're not going out any farther."

"Okay. But can we surf a little? Please, First Mama?"

I caved. "Only if you do exactly what I say."

"I will."

"Good. So let's get parallel to the waves. Shift your feet a little, like this." The waves were already lifting and dropping us. "When one gets closer, we turn to shore, give a few strong strokes, and when you've got the wave, shift your feet to full surf stance. Like this." He nodded. "Use your paddle to steer."

A wave was rising up, foaming at the top. "This one's ours, kid. Turn to shore, that's it. You ready? Okay, paddle hard!"

We did, and the wave grabbed us and whooshed us along. Matthew was doing great; for a few seconds, it was just him and me and the exhilarating ocean. Then we popped over the crest, the end of our first surf together.

"That was amazing! Let's do it again!" he said.

"You got it." We repeated our setup and caught another, then another. Then, as we waited for the next wave, I saw it. A flash of the gray-and-white body, fucking huge, hidden in the wave. Then it was gone. Adrenaline flooded me so fast, I practically levitated off the board.

"Matthew, stay calm and quiet. There's a shark." If it bumped his board and he fell in the water, what would I do? Would I have time to pull him up?

"Holy shit! Where?" His head whipped around.

"Quiet," I hissed. "I don't see it right now. Just start paddling for shore, nice and slow and calm." I waved my arms at the shore, then put my hand up to my forehead, simulating a fin, the sign of a shark sighting. *Please, let the lifeguard see me.*

"I wanna see it," Matthew said. "Where was it, Harlow?"

"Get going," I said. Thank God, a lifeguard did see me. The whistle blew and the purple flag went up.

My child was not moving. "Matthew! Now." My heart rate must've been 200 beats per minute. I paddled close to him and said, "We are not fucking around. Dip your paddle in the water and get going."

"I just wanna—"

"If you don't get your ass in gear, I'm going to jump in the water so it eats me instead of you. Or we can both get to shore. Your choice."

"I wish I brought my GoPro," Matthew said, but he *finally* started paddling toward the shore. The wind was at our backs, and we sailed along, the waves speeding us up. I kept glancing over my shoulder. No sign of the shark. My shoulders burned as I paddled, and every wave could be hiding the mighty predator. Was that a seal? Please, let that be a seal so the shark would go after it instead of us.

After what seemed like a lifetime, we hit the shallow water of the shore (but sharks could attack in less than three feet). We got off our boards, and I grabbed Matthew's arm and practically dragged him onto the beach.

Why had Monica and Sanjay said yes to this? Sending their

kid out in the ocean with someone they barely knew? Why had I thought this would be a nice way to bond? Was I an idiot? I was.

A lifeguard ran up to us. "Did you see it for sure?" she asked.

My heart was thudding so hard, I thought I might vomit, and I was still clutching my son's arm. "I . . . I think so. There was a flash of white in a wave."

"Did you see a fin?" she asked.

"Um . . . no. Just that white belly."

She looked out at the ocean. "Okay, well, when you signaled, we whipped out the binocs and all we saw was a driftwood log. Could that have been what you saw?"

"Uh . . . maybe." Now that I thought of it, yeah, it could've been a big old tree trunk bleached white by the salt and sun. They washed up on the beach all the time. And it had been kind of floating, not moving with any purpose . . . like many other chunks of driftwood I'd seen while paddleboarding. I mean, if I saw a great white, wouldn't I know it?

"It was a log?" Matthew said, disappointment in his voice. I heard the sound of a drone overhead, which meant someone was looking for the shape of a shark out in the water.

"Sharktivity doesn't have anything," the lifeguard said. "So yeah, I'm guessing it was a log. Shark Conservancy is sending a spotter plane just in case. But it's best to stay in until we get the all clear." She headed back to her post.

"That was awesome," Matthew said. "Even if it wasn't a shark."

"You need to work on your listening skills."

"You were really scared."

"Yes, you little shit!" I said, smacking his arm. "Seeing you eaten by a shark was not how I thought our first playdate would go." I swallowed. "I don't want to lose you the same week you found me."

He smiled at that, then bumped his shoulder against mine. "You swore at me."

"You deserved it." But I smiled back.

We sat there for a few minutes, the wind drying us, the sounds of kids shrieking as they ran along the shore.

"You guys okay?" came a familiar voice. It was Robbie, Rosie behind him. "We saw the shark flag go up."

Matthew jolted to his feet, and I stood up, too, brushing the sand from my ass. "Um, Robbie, this is Matthew Patel. Your nephew. Matthew, this is my little brother, Robbie."

Robbie and he were practically mirror twins, though Robbie had a healthy amount of razor stubble and more muscle. "Nephew," he said, and reached out a hand. They did that handshake-hug thing that guys do.

"Uncle," Matthew said. "Great to meet you." They stared at each other, grinning. This was, I realized, the second time in his life Matthew was meeting someone related to him, not counting Grandpop in the store.

"Man," Robbie said, shaking his head. "You are definitely a Smith. Lucky for you, you take after me."

"This is Rosie Wolfe," I said. "My best friend from college."

"Hi, honey," she said, her eyes shining with tears. "Let's just say I've heard a lot about you from conception on."

"Nice to meet you," he said, accepting her hug.

"Did you guys see the shark?" Robbie asked.

"I might have," I said. "Or I might have seen a log, but I figured it was better not to hang around and find out."

"Crikey," Rosie said. "I almost wet myself when they started blowing the whistles and put up the flag."

"Yeah, Harlow freaked out, too," Matthew said. "She said she'd jump in the water so the shark would eat her and not me. I also heard at least one f-bomb. She swore in front of me. Her child." He smiled.

"Not funny," I said, but something loosened in my chest. "I can't wait to tell your parents what a disobedient teen you are."

"Mm. Might be best if we didn't mention this," he said.

Yeah. I wasn't sure Monica would let me see him again if she knew I'd taken her son into shark-infested waters. To be honest, I'd wanted to show off a little for him, being athletic and cool and showing him this beautiful place. But I'd have to tell them. *No, no, it was a great day! I might have risked your—our—son being eaten alive, but otherwise, so much fun.*

But Matthew was safe, and I told myself that was all that mattered. I was getting to know him, and he had surprised me, but that was to be expected. It would get better, I told myself. And for the rest of our allotted time, my son, brother, best friend and I jumped in the waves and picked up rocks, swam in the cold Atlantic, sat on the blanket and talked . . . like a regular family.

NINETEEN

HARLOW

At the end of our freshman year, Rosie and I parted tearfully. She offered to pay for a ticket so I could visit, but I didn't take her up on it. Plus, third trimester and all that. We swore we'd stay best friends, but my heart was heavy. I'd be transferring to CU Colorado Springs in August. I couldn't stay here. My parents wanted to visit for Parents Weekend, and someone was sure to say "Weren't you pregnant last year?" or "Did you keep that baby?"

The campus emptied, and while quite a few students stayed for the summer, there was only one other girl on my hall. My dorm room took on the feel of a nun's cell (a pregnant nun's cell). Living in hot, dry Colorado felt punitive, a brutal contrast to summertime on the Cape.

My baby was a boy. I'd known it all along, but the ultrasound, with the Patels Skyping in, had confirmed it. My little pal. Jen and I talked about my birth plan. I wanted Sanjay and Monica in the room with me when he was born, and I wanted them to take the baby right away, because by now I loved him so much, it was the only way I could do it. Some birth mothers kept their baby for a day or two, Jen the adoption counselor had told me.

That sounded beyond cruel for both the baby and me. And yet . . . *My son, my son, my son.* The words felt like a heartbeat.

To keep my resolve, I Skyped with Sanjay and Monica a few times a week and reminded myself of what his home would be like. Their sweet little town that looked like a movie set— gorgeous main street with shops, restaurants and a bookstore. Monica reported that her parents had already bought a crib for when they visited Idaho.

Whereas my parents wouldn't even know they had a grand-child.

"Should I not have said that?" Monica had asked.

"No, it's lovely. It's really nice."

She had leaned forward, face serious, her eyes so blue even on the slightly blurry Skype connection. "Harlow," she said. "I . . . I just want to say that I know you're losing a lot. I know— well, I *can't* know, but I can imagine how devastating this is going to be for you. And while we absolutely believe you're a hero, I just wanted to say . . . I'm sorry. I'm so sorry for all your heartache."

For a minute or two, I couldn't speak, and my chest bucked with a sob. "Thanks," I finally whispered, my eyes filling. "Um . . . I have to go, okay?"

I told Monica everything, trying to make myself feel less like the mother, to share my pregnancy with her. How it felt when he rolled, his hiccups, his elbow jutting out against my skin. I re-ported every doctor's visit, my weight gain, his projected size. I told her how hard it was to shave my legs these days. How I couldn't sleep for more than a few hours at a time. The constant, evil heartburn that allegedly meant a good head of hair on the baby. How fast my own hair and nails were growing.

They made plans to fly out ten days before my due date and

stay at a rented house until the baby came. We hadn't yet met in person, but when the day came and I saw them standing in front of the restaurant we'd picked, we hugged and cried and hugged some more.

They were real after all. It was like meeting someone from a previous life. I knew them, and I didn't.

"It's weird, finally seeing you in the flesh," I said after we'd been seated.

"You too," Sanjay answered. "You're enormous."

"Sanjay!" Monica said, but I laughed.

"I meant to say glowing. Radiant. I may need sunglasses."

We perused the menu and fidgeted, smiling at each other, looking away. The server took our order and left again.

"This is incredibly awkward, isn't it?" Sanjay said. "Somebody, tell a joke."

I laughed. "I actually know one," I said. "How do you get a pregnant woman to stop eating?"

"How?" they asked in unison.

"Put the food on the floor."

It did the trick. We all relaxed.

"Are you sure you want us in the delivery room with you?" Monica asked after our food had arrived.

"Definitely," I said. "This is your baby. Um . . . I'm planning to . . . Sanjay, cover your ears." He did. I lowered my voice, not wanting to talk about my boobs in front of him. "I'm going to express some colostrum because the doctor said it would be good for the baby, but otherwise, I'll be . . . um . . . pretty much done after that." I swallowed hard.

Monica's eyes were wet. "Thank you," she whispered, reaching for my hand.

My little pal kicked, and I rubbed his foot, letting him know

I was still here. Then I took Monica's hand and put it on my stomach.

"Oh," she whispered, and her tears fell then. "Hi, baby. Hi."

This is your mother, little pal. She'll take such good care of you. I had to work not to sob. After a minute, Monica took her hand away and wiped her eyes.

"What names are you thinking?" I asked, hoping it wouldn't be too hip or freaky—Hamlet or Thorin or Talon.

They exchanged a glance, clearly having discussed this. "Did *you* have any names in mind?" Monica asked.

I didn't answer right away. I couldn't. I took a slow, steady breath. "I do, actually," I said, clearing my throat. "It's not a super unique name, but . . . um . . . I like Matthew." Then my face contorted, and I couldn't help the sobs that started before I could get myself together. "I'm sorry," I squeaked. "It's just . . . I do love him, even if I'm giv—placing him with you. I love him, and I'll miss him so much."

Monica wrapped her arms around me, and I buried my head in her shoulder. She smelled so nice. Of course she did.

Sanjay came around the table to sit next to me on the other side, making me a Patel sandwich. "Of course you will," he said. "You're a wonderful person and a great first mother, and we'll make sure he knows that."

For the next few days, we three (four) were a family. Though they were not allowed to give me gifts, Monica took me to a spa for an absolutely delicious facial and then to afternoon tea at the incredible Dushanbe Teahouse, where she purred over the tea menu and ordered four desserts for the two of us. We went to the Boulder Museum of Contemporary Art but found only about a quarter of the exhibits interesting, so we left to have nachos instead. I showed them the CU campus. We took a gentle walk at the reservoir, but it was too hot to stay out for long. We ended up at the movies instead.

They were so generous and lovely to me.

Five days after they'd arrived, I felt a little funny. I wasn't hungry, and when I looked in the mirror, I saw that my stomach had lowered. My arms and legs felt loose and strange.

It was happening. As uncomfortable as I'd been for the last month and a half, all of a sudden I didn't want my pregnancy to end.

But my baby would have to be born, of course. My back squeezed, hard, then let go.

"Are you ready, little pal?" I asked. My voice echoed in my nearly empty dorm room. Ten minutes later, another squeeze. I texted Jen to tell her I thought labor had started.

Then I called Monica. "Is it okay if Jen and I come over?" I asked, and my back clenched so hard, I lost my breath. "I think I might be going into labor."

"Yes, yes, of course!" she said. "Sanjay! She's maybe in labor!" I heard a clatter, then his voice.

"Holy shit," he said. "Um . . . breathe? Yes. Breathe." I wasn't sure if he was talking to me or himself. "Breathe in, breathe out."

Monica's voice came back. "Want us to come get you? Sanjay's halfway out the door."

"No," I said as the contraction faded. "Jen will drive me over."

Thirty minutes later, I was in a beautiful Craftsman house, sitting on their couch, breathing in, breathing out, just like Sanjay instructed (as if there were another way). I walked the floor, ate some toast, threw up that toast. Jen and the Patels talked. A few hours passed. The contractions got stronger and stronger, and when they were six minutes apart and I could no longer speak, the four of us headed for the hospital, Jen and me in her car, the Patels right behind us.

We all know how natural childbirth works—the pain of labor, the effort it takes to get that baby through the birth canal. The exhaustion. But in my case, it was something more, too. It was the start of the dreaded goodbye. A fog descended on me, and the only thing in the world was my body, my baby. The contractions rolled through me, awesome in their strength, dazzling, agonizing. I took a shower. I walked. I sat on a big round ball. I tried to sleep.

The labor went through the night, Sanjay on one side of me, Monica on the other, Jen down the hall in the waiting room, popping in once an hour to check on me. The nurses were kind and quiet, aware of the situation, telling me how well I was doing.

I couldn't talk as my son moved closer and closer to the world. The nurses were nearby, a doctor came in and left, and I was pushing, gripping Monica's hand as she counted for me. Sanjay wiped my forehead and said words, but I wasn't really there.

And then, at 10:17 on the morning of July twenty-fifth, in one burning, massive push, we separated, my son and I. He came out on my sob, and the midwife slid him from my body onto my chest. There was only silence in the room.

Time stopped in that second, and the only thing that existed was my baby. He was warm and pink and so little. His arms and legs moved against me, and his back rose with his first breath. I saw the swirls of dark hair on his head, his little nose, perfect pink mouth. Then he opened his eyes, and for a long second, we looked into each other's souls.

"I love you," I breathed. "Oh, I love you."

He was perfect. His face was so round, his eyes so big, his

little ears, his flailing hand. I caught it, and he gripped my fore-finger. I kissed his forehead . . . his skin was impossibly soft. Some-one put a blanket over him and rubbed his back, and he gave a little squawk, and everything in me answered.

"I love you," I whispered again. Every cell in my body loved him.

The midwife cut the cord, and a nurse was packing my groin.

My job was over. If I didn't do it now, I couldn't do it ever. It was time. Time to give my son to his parents. I kissed his wet, bloody head, felt the pulse in his soft spot and looked at him one more time.

"I love you, little pal," I whispered again.

And then, in what was the worst, hardest, most agonizing and wrenching moment of my life, I handed my son to his mother. She said something to me, but I was already gone.

Four weeks after giving birth, I left the campus I had come to so happily one year before. A lifetime ago. I trudged to my new dorm in Colorado Springs, the taxi driver helping me with my stuff. I had a double, but my roommate wasn't there yet. I was nearly completely recovered, already back in my regular clothes. I doubted anyone would be able to tell I had given birth a month before.

There was a sharp knock on the door. "Hey, roomie," said a voice, and there she was.

"Rosie?" We were hugging and sobbing before I realized ei-ther of us had moved. "What are you doing here?"

"Well, shit. I wasn't going to stay at Boulder without you."

"You didn't tell me."

"You would've told me not to." It was true. I didn't want her changing schools just because I'd messed up my life. But now that she was here . . .

"We're gonna have so much fun," she said, same as she had last year at this time. And for the first time in my new post-baby life, I felt a flicker of hope.

TWENTY

HARLOW

After a record-setting seven days off in a row, I went downstairs to the bookstore. Rosie said she'd entertain herself and maybe visit one of my siblings, since they all loved her.

"Oh, do you still work here?" Cynthia said when Ollie and I came in fifteen minutes before we opened. "I was wondering if you'd quit." She bobbed her tea bag in her mug, making the action look somehow violent.

"No, Cynthia, I didn't quit and am happy to say I'm still half owner." Her face pinched. Good.

"Coffee?" Destiny asked, dropping a gentle hand on my shoulder. She more than made up for Sour Cynthia.

"Thank you." A second later, she handed me a cup of steaming Colombian in a mug that said, *This may or may not contain vodka.* Cynthia's mug was beige. Did that not say it all? We sold mugs in the gift section of the shop, including the one I now held. We also had *Coffee—Because Stabbing People Is Frowned Upon; Let the Fuckery Begin;* and a personal favorite around Cynthia: *Never Trust Someone Who Doesn't Swear.*

"Cheers, ladies," I said, raising my mug.

Cynthia muttered something.

"What's that, Cynthia? You were wondering how I'm doing after meeting my son? You're so nice to ask. I'm great. Thank you."

She set down her mug hard, making Ollie twitch. "You know, I'm adopted," she snapped. "It's not always such a big deal."

My mouth fell open. "You are?" I glanced at Destiny to see if she knew, but she looked just as shocked.

"Yes, Harlow," she said with exaggerated patience. "And no, I've never met my birth mother, because I never wanted to. My *real* mother was the woman who changed my diapers, taught me to read, fed me, cared for me and loved me. That other woman was just a . . . a carrier."

"Wow. How vicious you can be, Cynthia." My face felt hot.

"I never knew you were adopted, Cynthia," Destiny said.

"Because I never told you. Because it's not an important part of my life."

"Did you always—"

"No. My parents didn't feel the need to tell me because, as I *said*, they were my real parents. This other woman, let alone the man who impregnated her, were completely irrelevant." She cocked an eyebrow at me, the implication clear. "She was a carrier. That's all."

"Don't push it, Cynthia." I brushed past her and went into the office. We'd had a delivery of new books over the weekend, but God forbid Cynthia did any physical labor around here. She just did the accounting, tapping away at the computer.

"Good morning, my dear Cynthia!" Grandpop boomed. "Don't you look fresh and lovely today!"

I sighed. Grandpop loved Cynthia. Grammy had, too. The reason was unclear.

A carrier. A *carrier*. I took a deep breath and told myself to be careful with the box cutter or I was going to need stitches. Or go to jail, depending on who got hurt.

Today was Story Time with Grandpop, meaning that kids from a few months to six years old could come in and be read to. Children viewed him as a cross between Dumbledore and Santa.

"What will you be reading today, Grandpop?" I asked.

"Oh, is that today? Drat. I have an appointment, I'm afraid. Bertie Baines and I are going fishing! I haven't been deepwater fishing in years and years! I'm quite excited about it. I hope I can keep up with Bertie, though! He's twenty years younger than I am!"

I smiled. "I'm sure you'll do just fine. Oh, here he is now. Hi, Bertie." I looked for my other two employees. "Destiny? Can you cover story time?" I asked.

She looked up from unboxing books. "I have a doctor's appointment, remember?"

"Oh, right. Okay, I'll do it."

Obviously, we couldn't let Cynthia near children, or she'd eat them. I went into the sunroom, where the kids were gathering. Pierce DeJonge was sitting front and center, as he always did, silently commanding me to start, since it was now 10:01. A sweet, serious kid and a great reader.

"Want to pick the book today, Pierce?" I asked, getting a smile from his mom, Alissa.

"Yes, I do," he said, taking the responsibility seriously. He got up and began perusing the shelves.

"How are you?" his mother asked. "Big news."

"I'm doing great."

"You look *wonderful*."

"Thanks, Alissa," I said. "I appreciate that."

I knew most of the other local kids—Melissa Spencer had brought her baby and her niece, Ophelia, of whom Melissa had custody. Remembering my promise to Matthew's sister, I went over to them. "Hi, ladies!" I said. Ophelia was a great kid and an avid reader. The baby, Orion or Orpheus or something, wasn't really old enough to be here, but I wasn't in the habit of kicking children out of the store. "How are you?"

"Oh, we're wonderful, Hayden," Melissa said.

Ophelia rolled her eyes. "It's *Harlow*, Missy," she said.

"So sorry! I'm absolutely terrible with names. Harlow, of course. Orialis, say hello," Melissa said, waving the baby's pudgy hand at me. The baby drooled in response, her giant head wobbling.

"Ophelia," I said, "there's a girl on the Cape for the summer, and she's about your age. Meena Patel. She's dying for a friend, especially one who reads. What do you think? Can I introduce you?"

"Sure," Ophelia said. "I could meet her here sometime."

"Thanks, kiddo," I said. Teenagers were so underappreciated.

Speaking of babies, my sister and her wife pushed through the crowd, each bearing a daughter.

"Gog!" said Imogen. "Gocky gog boo!"

"That's right!" Nicole said. "There *is* a dog here! My God, her verbal skills are so advanced."

"Well, gotta get to work," I said. Those little girls were my son's cousins. Amazing.

The store had filled with over twenty kids and parents, moms outnumbering dads. I saw Grady, sitting cross-legged on the floor with Luna on his lap. He gave me a nod and an almost-smile, and I looked at him a beat too long. How did he do it, raising his child alone? Well, of course he had a nanny. And he hadn't been seventeen when Luna was born.

"Mr. Grandpop isn't here today," I said, "so I guess you're stuck with me, kiddies. Pierce, what did you pick out for us?"

"*Pete the Cat Saves Christmas*," he said solemnly, handing me the book.

"Great," I said.

"It's not Christmas!" called Bramwell Zeblinski.

"I hate cats!" said Uriah. "No Pete the Cat!"

I felt sweat break out on my back. "Well," I said, "we're going to read this book and then something else."

"It's a *stupid* book!" said a kid I didn't know.

"Where's Owiver Twist?" asked Callie. "I want him to sit on my wap! I want him! Mommy! Can I have Owiver Twist?"

"He's on *me*," said Thomas. "He's way better than Pete the Cat. Because he's a *dog*."

"I love Pete the Cat!" said Esme, and I was proud of her for taking Pierce's side.

"It's not Christmas!" said Maeve, starting to sob.

Ophelia went to her and knelt down. "Get over it," she said, not unkindly. "Pierce got to pick the book this time."

Maeve did not appreciate this. "Why is a Christmas book even *here*?" she wailed. "It's *summer*!"

You'd be surprised how early we start pushing Christmas books, kid, I wanted to say. "Okay, okay," I said. "Pierce, maybe we can read another Pete the Cat book?"

"Miss Harlow," said Pierce tearfully, "you said I could pick the book, and I did."

"Fair point."

"No!" Maeve yelled. "No Christmas!"

My younger niece, confused and scared by all the wailing,

also started to cry, her screams quickly becoming so high-pitched that Ollie leaped off Thomas and ran under the coffee table. Thomas began to wail. I couldn't hear myself think. "Nicole, maybe take Imogen outside?"

"This is a horrible story hour," Nicole said, glaring at me over her shoulder.

Tell me about it.

"I'll find a better book!" announced Liam, racing to the back.

"Me too!" said Bryleigh.

Half the kids stampeded past me, and Pierce started to sob.

Suddenly, a voice boomed out. "'Twas the day before Christmas, and Santa was ill. In the cold winter wind, he had caught a bad chill.'" It was Grady, reading from his phone.

Pierce looked up and started reciting along with him. Other kids joined in. I fumbled the book to keep up with them, but on page five or so, they started singing. I held up the book so the kids could see the illustrations.

The miscreant kids came back in, hypnotized by the music. Apparently, the song was as embedded in their heads as "Let It Go."

"'Give it your all, give it your all!'" they sang.

And so, thanks to Grady, *Pete the Cat Saves Christmas* was read and sung, and even Maeve sang through her tears, lower lip trembling. Destiny handed me *Pete the Cat: I Love My White Shoes*, another sing-along, for our next read.

"'I love my white shoes! I love my white shoes!'" the kids bellowed, Grady right there with them. Luna was a Pete the Cat fan, apparently.

I had to say, the tune was pretty catchy, and by the time Pete stepped in blueberries, I was singing, "'I love my blue shoes! I love my blue shoes!'" as loud as everyone else. The cult of Pete was strong. Even Addison looked happy as Esme danced.

When we'd finished four Pete the Cat books, I read the first few pages of *The Wind in the Willows*, partly because I loved that book, and partly because it cost $25 and I had six copies of it. Sure enough, we sold out to the wee bairns who didn't already have the book, and I put in orders for five more. Mercenary bookseller at work, folks.

"Hey, Gray," I said when most of the mob had left. He was watching Luna pet Ollie. "Thanks for saving me. I didn't realize you were in the Pete the Cat fan club."

"Luna's obsessed. And, um, my pleasure," he said.

"That tome you ordered is in, by the way. Let me grab it."

I went behind the counter and found his book on the shelf, tucked in a store bookmark, and handed it to him. "Thanks for shopping with Open Book," I said with a smile.

He looked at me a minute, started to speak, then stopped.

I cocked my head. "Did you want to say something?"

His gaze dropped back to his kid. "I was wondering if you wanted to have lunch or a drink sometime." His face was somber.

An uneasy feeling settled over me. "Why?"

"It's just . . . well, you have a lot going on, and I thought it might be . . . good to talk about it. Your boy. Your family. His family. I thought maybe you could use an impartial party." He frowned a little at that last phrase, and my heart . . . well, it didn't melt, but it bent a little. Grady Byrne had always been an incredibly nice guy.

He wasn't asking me on a date, was he? No. He knew me. We were at that singles thing together when I flat out told him I wasn't looking. This was him just being him. "Sure," I said. "I have a lot this week, but yeah, that would be really nice. Maybe next week?"

"Great." He seemed relieved. "See you Friday at the Ice House?"

"You bet."

"Excellent," he said, looking back at me with a slight smile. He took the book, reached out for Luna's hand and left the store, and for some reason, I remembered prom night, when we'd gone together and he'd come out of his shell a little, dancing surprisingly well, making me laugh. That moment when I thought he might kiss me.

I may have imagined that, and it was a long time ago. But still.

TWENTY-ONE

CYNTHIA

Hello.

   This note may come as a surprise. For the past four years since our mother died, my two younger sisters and I have been looking for our older sister, who was adopted through St. Joseph's Catholic Orphanage in Missouri. Her birthday is April 14, and she would be 61 years old. Her adoptive parents may have been Miriam and Carl Smith of Kansas City, Missouri.

   We hired a private investigator who thought you might possibly be her. We are hoping to talk with you if you are willing, and if you are not the person we think, we're sorry to bother you.

Cynthia had reread that message at least a dozen times since receiving it. She had looked at Nancy Barbieri Lawless's Facebook profile, but it was private, and all she could see was a picture of two people, a young man and a young woman. A Google search had found no results for "nancy barbieri lawless" but had found quite a few women with the name Nancy Lawless. One was a florist. Several were physicians. One had many tattoos and piercings (please, don't let that be her). None of their pictures leaped out as resembling Cynthia.

Initially, she hadn't wanted to answer. Two days later, she decided she would, but changed her mind again. If only Mother were still alive. She would know what to do.

Why *hadn't* Mother ever told her she was adopted? Should Cynthia try to learn about her birth mother and meet her half sisters? What would be gained? Had Mother just gone away for six months and then come back, pretending she'd been pregnant? Or had they relocated afterward? Had anyone ever made a comment?

She didn't think so.

There was only one person she could ask. Uncle Robert. Whether or not he knew she'd been adopted was a mystery, but he *was* her godfather and the only person alive who'd known her as a child. If anyone had information, it was he.

She asked if she could make him dinner at his house on her day off, because her kitchen was too tiny for real cooking. In the past three years, she'd made him dinner several times, because Uncle Robert was truly a kind man. There was also the hope he might leave her something in his will, even though he had too many heirs as it was.

Thankfully, Harlow had plans on the intended night, so she wouldn't be snooping around. Granted, Harlow did have reason to be suspicious, but she didn't *know* she had reason. If only Harlow moved somewhere off-Cape, Cynthia would be much happier. She could move into Harlow's sunny apartment and earn more without Harlow's salary. She could get rid of the irritating gifts Harlow insisted on selling. She wouldn't have to embezzle anymore. Her status in the community would rise, and she could sell the shack to a summer person and have a little money for the nicer things in life.

She took the DART bus to Main Street, since her car was making an unpleasant noise, and picked up the dinner ingredients at the Wellfleet Marketplace, then walked to Uncle Robert's. It was lovely to be in a proper kitchen again. At 5:30 p.m., her godfather walked through the door from the bookstore.

"Doesn't this look *beautiful*!" Uncle Robert exclaimed as she placed the dishes on the table. "And a pretty lady to share it with! I'm a lucky man."

Cynthia smiled. "I'm happy to have some time alone with you, Uncle Robert. Sometimes the entire family can become a little overwhelming."

"An embarrassment of riches, as my Louisa used to say. Only one child, but five wonderful grandchildren, and now three great-grandchildren! How I wish she knew Harlow had a son. She had a soft spot for Harlow, of course. Our first grandchild, and such a sweet girl. So smart and so bighearted, isn't she?"

"Mm. Well, let's dig in, shall we?"

As they ate, Uncle Robert detailed his nap under a rhododendron in Preservation Hall's garden today, waking only when a cranky staffer told him to leave. How he'd given away four books to a scruffy high school student who'd been browsing but not buying. His interest in finding a "lady friend."

"Make sure she's not after your money," Cynthia said, taking a bite of fish. She chewed and swallowed before speaking again. "Sometimes, women will go after a man who's of a certain age so they can inherit everything when he dies."

Uncle Robert laughed as if she'd told a joke. "Well, I'm not worried about *that*. My will is airtight."

Am I in it? she wanted to ask. "I can't imagine life without you, Uncle Robert. I'll be bereft when you pass away. You're the only family I have." Hint, hint.

"Oh, don't be silly, dear! You have all of us! Gerald, Ellie, the kids . . . don't worry."

"You're the one I feel closest to. The best godfather in the world, and my father's closest friend." Hopefully that would remind him that he had a certain obligation to her.

"You're very special to me, dear Cynthia."

And now for the reason she was here. "Uncle Robert," she began, "did you know I was adopted?"

Uncle Robert jerked. "Is that right? No, I didn't realize that! How interesting!"

"I suppose." She put her fork down. "My parents never told me. I found out on my own. It was never discussed, and I wondered how they just appeared with a baby one day."

"Ah, I understand. Let me rack this ancient memory and see if I can remember anything." He leaned back and studied the ceiling. "Well, now, I remember Carl and Miriam asking me to be godfather." He glanced back at her with a smile. "Which was a great honor! All right, I *do* recall the first time I met you. It was at the house in Kansas City. Yes! They'd just moved there, saying their old place hadn't been right for a baby. I remember your mother gave me a tour of the place, and there you were, dressed all in pink. A *beautiful* baby."

Moving when she was an infant would certainly have made it easier to hide her adoption. She cleared her throat. "Uncle Robert, I recently received a message from an alleged half sister, and she wants to meet. But I'm not sure I do."

"Why wouldn't you? Look how happy Harlow's handsome boy has made us."

"Well, it's hardly the same thing. I'm sixty-one years old. My parents didn't want me to know, so it feels . . ." She didn't have the words to finish the sentence.

"Hmm," said Robert. "Well. Think on it, my dear."

She served him the peach cobbler she'd made, which he ate with an expression of pure joy on his face. She allowed herself a tiny portion, and it *was* delicious, she had to admit. When he'd finished two helpings, she loaded his dishwasher, wiped down the counters and wrapped up the leftovers.

"What a wonderful evening," he said happily as she got out a fresh dishcloth. "Ellie, you are a wonder."

"I'm Cynthia, not your daughter-in-law. But thank you."

"Of course! Goodness, I've been getting you girls confused for decades now. Anyway, I thank you very much, my dear. I had a wonderful time catching up with you."

She hugged him, and he chuckled fondly.

"You're my favorite person, Uncle Robert," she said. "I'd be lost without you." Another hint, but it was also true. He *was* her favorite person. There was simply no one else in the running. "Thank you for tonight."

"Thank *you*," he said. "Now, I'm going to sit on the porch and count my blessings with a glass of whiskey. Enjoy the rest of your evening, sweetheart."

The night was just falling, the sky a lonely shade of blue. She'd walk back, rather than spend money on an Uber. They were so expensive here. When she passed Preservation Hall, she saw there was an event going on, a wedding from the looks of it. Very loud. At Winslow's, a heavy woman with a red face stumbled down the stairs and practically crashed into her. "Sorry!" she bellowed, clearly *not* sorry and clearly very drunk. Also, her dress was as big as a tent and just as ugly.

The same type of mood came from the Fox and Crow, everyone laughing and drinking. *Look at ME, I'm having so much FUN, let me shout even more loudly so everyone KNOWS.* She couldn't wait for winter, when all these wretched people went home.

"Evenin', Cynthier. How are you?"

She glanced across the street. "Oh. Hello, Albert." Bertie Baines, resident drifter, was shuffling along.

"Heading home?" he asked.

"Yes."

"I take it you're going by way of Uncle Tim's Bridge."

"Yes." One of the few things Cynthia liked about the Cape was the many secret dirt roads and private drives the tourists didn't know about. Since she didn't give a whit about trespassing, Cynthia could walk from Open Book all the way home so long as the tide was out. On a night like this, soft and gentle with a fat crescent moon just now cresting the pines, she could see just fine. Besides, she had a flashlight with her for the darker paths.

"Okay if I walk with you for a bit?" Bertie asked.

There was no polite way to decline that. "That would be fine." He crossed the street and walked alongside her.

"You look like you're lost in thought."

"Well, I was, Albert, but you interrupted, so I suppose I'm found."

"What a nice thing to say," Bertie said. She'd meant it as an insult. "I like that you're walkin' as the crow flies. You're like a real local."

What could be more insulting, she thought. They walked across Uncle Tim's Bridge. As they got to the island, where there were only paths cutting through the trees, she clicked on the flashlight. They walked without speaking for a bit, until Albert had to break the silence.

"What's on your mind, Cynthia?" he asked.

She glanced at him and sighed. Why not? "I have recently been contacted by my half sister, the daughter of my birth mother, who died several years ago. She wants to meet me. Apparently, I have three half sisters."

"And you didn't know that before?"

"No."

They were through Hamblen now, onto the shore, the smell of low tide sharp in the air. A bird called, and another answered, underscoring the absolute loneliness Cynthia felt. How much longer could Uncle Robert live? She all but hated the rest of the family (except for Lark, but really, they didn't have a true connection—Lark was simply more polite than the others). If Cynthia dropped dead, she doubted anyone would even notice.

"You gonna meet 'em?" Albert asked.

Their feet crunched on the sand, but suddenly, the ground gave as Cynthia's foot sank into the soft, wet muck of a tidal pool. She tried to pull free and stumbled. Albert grabbed her elbow, keeping her from falling flat on her face in the mud.

"Oh, my goodness!" she said. "Thank you, Bertie."

"My pleasure." *My pleazhah.* "Y'okay?"

"I'm fine." She sighed. Her tennis shoes were ruined now, and her foot squelched as they continued walking.

"Anyways. Your sisters? What do you think you'll do?"

"I don't know," she said. "My parents didn't want me to know I was adopted. I found out by accident when I was a teenager and never told them I knew."

"Why not?"

She huffed. "Because it didn't matter, Albert! They loved me, I was well cared for, and why would I care about my genetics? I know it's all the rage now, but honestly, I think those DNA sites should be banned. People finding out their father isn't their fa-

ther, long-lost sisters coming out of the woodwork, adopted children springing themselves on their mothers . . . It's very messy."

Bertie nodded. "Yep, I see your point. A lot of happy stories
in the mess, though, wouldn't you say?"

"Maybe," she admitted. The moon was brighter now, its reflection on the water like a path home. She turned off the flashlight, since they didn't need it.

"So why not meet them? You've got nothing to lose," Albert
said.

"I . . . I don't think that's correct. I have my dignity to lose.
What if they're toothless backwater people who want money?"
Too late, she remembered that Albert was missing a tooth or two,
and the word *backwater* could definitely be applied to him.

"What if they're toothless backwater people who just want to
know you? Might be nice to have a little more family. I understand you're not too close to the Smiths."

"Only Uncle Robert. He's my godfather, and he visited every
year or so when I was growing up. He and my father were best
friends."

The memory of those times—beautiful Louisa telling Cynthia
to sit on her lap for a cuddle, delightful Uncle Robert, Mother
and Daddy sitting around the big table in the dining room, a fire
burning, Mother's wonderful cooking, Cynthia in a fancy dress,
Kimberly serving and clearing . . .

Suddenly, she was . . . well, something was happening to her.
Her chest was hitching, and tears were spilling out of her eyes.
Embarrassing squeaks she couldn't stop slipped out of her mouth,
and she clamped her hand over it to stop the wretched sound.

"Aw," said Albert. "There, there, Cindy. Don't cry." He put an
arm around her, and she didn't even mind, pathetic, lonely creature that she was. He dug in his pocket and pulled out a bandanna

and offered it to her. Heaven knew how clean it was, but when she put it up to her face, it smelled like detergent and sunshine.

"No one calls me Cindy," she managed, blowing her nose.

"Well, no one calls me Albert," he said.

He didn't smell as unwashed as he often looked, and, leaning against his shoulder, she realized he was strong and firm. She stayed a second or two longer, his arm oddly comforting, his scruffy, unshaven chin against her forehead. Then she pulled back, wiped her eyes and tucked the bandanna in her pocket. "I'll wash and press this and get it back to you."

"Ah. You keep it."

They were at the big house now, and she paused. "This is where I cut across," she said.

"Let me help you." He offered his hand, and she took it, finding it calloused and warm. Rather pleasant, really.

The big house was dark, its shades pulled, a sure sign that the owners weren't in residence. "What a waste," Albert said. "To have a house like this and not live in it. Or share it. It shouldn't stand empty most of the year."

"I agree completely."

They came out onto Cove Road. The moon was so bright, it cast shadows.

"The thing about your sisters . . . well, it's kinda nice, innit? That they want to meet you?"

"I suppose." Her foot must be filthy. She'd have to hose off before she went in.

"Aren't you curious?"

"I am," she acknowledged. "I suppose it can't hurt."

"Nope. Can't hurt." *Cahnt heurt.*

"Then I suppose I'll send them a message."

"Atta girl." They came to King Phillip Road, which would lead to Hiawatha.

"How far do you think this walk is, Albert?" she asked.

"Oh, about three miles, give or take," he answered.

That made her feel proud, having ambled that far. They turned down Hiawatha, another dirt road, and without thinking, she took Albert's arm. It was darker here under the leafy oaks and pitch pines, harder to see, but she didn't want to turn on the flashlight.

There was her car, parked at the back of her house, as she had no garage. They walked onto the patio, Albert looking at her garden.

"You sure made this yard pretty," he said. "Used to be just sand and weeds."

"Yes. Thank you," she said.

"One of the prettiest views in Wellfleet. You know, you could shine this place up quite a bit. Maybe even put on a tiny addition."

"The homeowners' association is very strict," she said. Also, she couldn't afford it.

"You just need to woo 'em a bit. Everyone's improvin' their places these days, puttin' in new kitchens, knockin' down walls. Half my business is fixin' up places like this. I could come around, make a few suggestions, if you want."

He had a *business*? She'd thought he was unemployed! "Oh. Well, that's very . . . kind. But I doubt I'm ready to think about that just yet."

"Well, let me know when you are. If you are, that is. Didn't mean to presume anything."

They stood there, the sounds of the small waves whispering against the sand. The birds were silent now, but a few crickets trilled, and an early cicada called out three times, then three more, then three more.

"Thank you for walking me home," she said.

"No worries."

And then, shockingly, she threw her arms around him and pressed her mouth against his. It had been years—years!—since she'd kissed a man, and certainly she had *never* made the first move. But an electric buzzing feeling shot through her. Albert! Of all people! Without taking her mouth off his, she fumbled with the doorknob and practically dragged him inside.

Bertie Baines did not resist.

The next morning, Bertie was gone . . . she vaguely remembered him slipping out of bed while it was still dark and murmuring about work, pressing a kiss on her temple.

She had slept naked. Again, a first. With Henry, she'd always gotten dressed afterward, because she didn't like the feeling of her naked legs pressed together, her breasts sliding around any which way. Yes, she was one of those women who wore a bra to bed, as Mother had. It kept her bosom from premature sagging.

Contrary to what she'd thought, Albert's personal hygiene was satisfactory. Yes, he smelled salty and tangy, and there was the faint smell of wood about him, but to her shock, she found it appealing. His hands were strong, and while they were both in their sixties, somehow he had made her feel . . . amazing. It was strange, those little squeaks that came out of her, the sighing, the . . . the unfamiliar pleasure of it all, not just the, er, culmination, but the way he'd unbuttoned her blouse, slowly and with great appreciation for what was underneath. His hairy arm around her afterward. The appealing creases in his face as he smiled at her. She almost didn't mind his missing tooth.

She took a shower, got dressed and went into the kitchen, noting the muddy footprints from her ruined tennis shoe. She didn't even mind.

Albert had left a note! *Thanks for a lovely evening, Cindy. Hope to see you again soon. Here's my number if you want to call.*

Cindy. Cindy sounded rather cute, didn't it? Cindy. Someone young and energetic. Definitely someone with a beautiful garden, someone who liked taking long walks rather than driving. Someone who might be interested in having a beau.

But Bertie Baines? She thought a moment, stirring her coffee. Bertie Baines. Everyone seemed to think well of him (except Cynthia herself, until last night). Now that she mulled it over, he had been interested in her for some time, hadn't he? Dropping into the bookstore, asking her for recommendations, trying to make conversation. He'd been checking her out!

What a flattering thought.

She glanced at the clock. Plenty of time before going to work. And so, she went to Facebook and composed her message, even before she cleaned the floor.

> Dear Nancy,
>
> I'm sorry it took a while for me to see this message. Yes, I believe I'm the person you're looking for. I was adopted but didn't find that out until my teenage years. Hearing from you did indeed come as a surprise, as I am not the type to register my DNA or do any other type of searching for biological relations. I have always thought of my birth mother as . . .

Here Cynthia paused. A carrier. A rented womb. In hindsight, that was not a very compassionate view. In fact, quite a harsh view. Look at Harlow. She had obviously thought of her child with a great deal of love and anguish.

> I have always thought of my birth mother as generous and wise to know she could not raise me. I had a wonderful childhood and was very devoted to my parents, who have been gone now for many years.
>
> I would be willing to communicate more. Please let me know how you would like to proceed, and I'll see what I can do.

She hit send. Toothless backwater people who might just want to meet her. Maybe they hoped she was rich and wanted money. Maybe not. In fact, maybe *they* were rich. Maybe . . . maybe her mother had left her something. An inheritance. Or maybe these half sisters were just curious.

For the first time, she realized Bertie was right. She had nothing to lose.

TWENTY-TWO

MONICA

When they had left the hospital with Matthew, two days old, and taken the flight home, all he had done was cry and cry and cry. So had Monica. It was impossible not to be heartbroken for Harlow, and the image of her holding Matthew, her face so full of love and pain, was seared into Monica's brain. Was Matthew crying because he missed his birth mother? Sure seemed like it.

It was supposed to be the happiest time of her life, but it wasn't. She loved the tiny, red-faced infant, but God, he did not seem to love her. It was as if he knew she wasn't Harlow.

"Ridiculous," Sanjay said. "He can't even see, Moni. She didn't even hold him for ten minutes! You are his mother."

But they'd read the books that claimed adopted babies would never get over being adopted. It was a horrible thought—should babies all stay with their birth mothers, regardless of their ability to care for them? Should adoption be eradicated? Of course not. Babies needed love and safety and comfort, and Monica and Sanjay could give all of that. The child psychologist they'd seen had said that the idea that a moments-old infant could miss someone was not possible. Their brains were simply not developed enough. The truth was, no one knew.

Matthew cried so much, though. The pediatrician said it was

colic. Of course, the baby slept, too, but it was as if he knew when she herself might doze off or relax, and then the crying began again. Sanjay could soothe him more easily than she could, which stung.

She was the one staying home for this phase of Matthew's life, and God, the days could last for years. He didn't seem to sleep for more than ten minutes at a stretch. He hated baths, being changed, being dressed, being put down in his bassinet, and being held only comforted him so much. But she held him. Oh, yes. This was her son, biological or not. She hummed and patted his back, rocked him in her arms, wrapped him tightly in a swaddle. "It's okay," she'd murmur. "I've got you. Mommy's here."

Her arms ached from carrying him as she walked through their small house. The neighbors gave sympathetic looks and told her horror stories of their own kids. She pushed him in the pram, took him for car rides, set his car seat on the dryer and dragged a kitchen chair in front of it in case the vibrations moved him too close to the edge. She had never understood true exhaustion before now.

And then, when he was about three months old and her hair had a gray streak in it, he smiled at her. A toothless little grin, his eyes on her face. Suddenly, nothing else mattered, and the world slipped away.

"Hi, baby," she whispered cautiously. "Hi, Matthew."

He cooed at her, the first sound she'd heard that wasn't a cry or a burp, and her heart doubled in size.

"I love you, honey," she said, and he cooed again.

Things were better after that.

As a toddler, he was full of energy, bouts of sunny happiness contrasting with rages that had him banging his feet and fists against the floor. The pediatrician said it was normal. Not all babies had tantrums, but most did, at least a few times.

"A few times a day?" Monica had asked.

"That's . . . well, it's notable. But my best guess is, he'll grow out of it."

Some of the other adoptive moms in her online group commiserated. Did their children *know*? Had the babies felt wrenched away? When would it fade? Other mothers were blissful and smug, talking about how their infant had stopped fussing the moment she was placed in their arms. One mother had started breastfeeding (apparently it was possible). And one woman gave her baby back to the agency and abruptly left the group.

Around three and a half, Matthew seemed to come into himself, a reliably happy, affectionate child. He was her darling boy, her treasure. He wasn't perfect, but God, that smile, those eyes, the feeling of his sticky little hand in hers. There was that saccharine but true saying—he hadn't grown in her belly, but he had grown in her heart from the day she first saw Harlow on Skype, all wide eyes and tangled curly hair, mouth trembling with emotion. She had loved Harlow, and she loved Harlow's baby.

When Matthew was five years old, her period was late by two, then three weeks. She got a test, and sure enough, she was pregnant, the first and last time such a miracle would occur. She was stunned and scared . . . would her uterus be able to keep this baby? Not only did she have endometriosis and a half-strangled ovary, she was now classified as a "geriatric pregnancy." (Well done, medical world. Way to make mothers feel great about themselves.) What if she miscarried? There was a fair chance she would. Would Matthew be better or worse for having a sibling? If she did lose the pregnancy, how would Matthew feel then? What if she didn't love the baby as much as she loved Matthew? What if she loved it more?

Sanjay was copacetic, which irritated her. "We just do our best, sweetheart," he said, his arms around her, which should have been comforting. "That's all we can do. Take things as they come."

Not if you were a mother. Mothers researched the *shit* out of things. She read hundreds of articles, talked to child psychologists, consulted obstetricians who specialized in high-risk pregnancies, went on Reddit to post questions in the hope that a stranger would have an answer.

From the moment she found out she was pregnant, she made sure she did something special with Matthew every day—read him an extra story, or lay on his bed making animal noises as he said, "Elephant! Horse! Chicken!" She made sure Sanjay, too, spent special time with him.

When she was six months along, they sat him down.

"Honey," Monica said. "Maybe you noticed Mommy's getting a little bit fat."

"Yes," he said. "But you're still pretty, Mama."

See? He was an angel! "Aw, thank you, sweetie. But I'm actually *not* fat. There's a baby in my tummy, and it's your little brother or sister." Sanjay's younger sister had just had her third child, so the idea of pregnancy was familiar to him.

Matthew didn't say anything.

"How do you feel about that, buddy?" Sanjay asked.

He looked at Monica oddly. "A baby? In your tummy?" he asked.

"Yes, honey."

"But I didn't come from your tummy," he said solemnly.

"No," she said. "You didn't. Babies come from a lot of different places, but they all start off in their mother's tummies."

"Where's my mother? The one who grew me in her tummy?"

She and Sanjay exchanged a look. "She's not too far away," Sanjay said. "She lives in Colorado."

What they couldn't tell him was that they didn't know where she was. That she'd chosen not to have contact with them. That she didn't want updates about him.

"But she loved me?" Matthew asked, fear in those beautiful brown eyes. They had told him his birth story over and over, emphasizing that his birth mother had *absolutely* loved him but wasn't grown up enough to take care of him and had wanted him to have two parents.

"Yes," Monica said. "She loved you very much, but she wasn't able to take care of you."

"But you can still take care of me? Even though you're having another baby?"

She felt her heart crack in half. She pulled him onto her lap and held his sweet head against her shoulder, fingers in his beautiful, shiny curls. "You're my first baby," she said. "Of course we can take care of you. We are already, and we'll never stop. You'll always be our son, and we'll never—" She started to say *give you away*, but she didn't want to put the thought in his head. "We'll never stop loving you," she finished.

"You're our little guy," Sanjay said. He smiled and put his hand on Matthew's back. "We'll love you forever and ever and ever."

Matthew stayed on her, his little arms around her neck, cheek warm against her. Monica breathed in his smell. "How about if you pick out the baby's middle name?" she suggested.

"That will make the baby very special, having a big brother who picked out their middle name." She and Sanjay had already decided that, like Matthew, this baby would have an Indian name and a Western name. Since they'd kept Matthew for his first name to honor Harlow's suggestion, they wanted this baby to have an Indian first name with a Western middle name.

"Really? Okay!" he said, happy again. He sat up and looked at her small baby bump. "Am I squishing the baby?"

"No," she said. "I think the baby likes feeling his or her big brother there." Just then the baby rolled, and Matthew's big brown eyes widened. "The baby is saying hi to you, Matthew!"

"I felt him! Or her! Is it a boy or a girl?"

"We don't know yet," she said.

"I hope it's . . . a girl. Or a boy." Then, too soon, he scrambled off her. "Daddy, can we ride bikes?"

It had gone well, Monica thought. Meanwhile, she loved being pregnant, this experience she had never expected, a baby growing inside her. Monica thought of Harlow going through all of this with the knowledge that she wouldn't keep the baby, and the thought made her knees weak and her heart ache. But she didn't want to dwell on Matthew's first mother. She wanted to focus on her unborn child and her son.

Meena Jane Patel was born on her due date. Labor and delivery were not nearly as bad as billed—Monica didn't need pain medications, and while the pain was huge, it was awesome in the truest sense of the word. She would never have this experience again, she knew, and she tried to savor every moment.

But the best part, even better than seeing her daughter for the first time, was seeing Matthew meet her, his face reverent.

"Hi, Meena," he said. "I'm your big brother." Then tears flooded his eyes and he said, "Oh, Mommy, I love her so much."

Meena was the best thing they could have done for Matthew. He was not just a son and grandson and nephew and cousin. He was a big brother, and he took the job seriously, presenting Meena with stuffed animals if she cried, playing peekaboo with her as Monica changed her diaper. Sometimes Monica wondered if he was so devoted to Meena to prove something . . . to make himself indispensable. But they loved each other, it was clear.

And Meena was an angel. She was an incredibly easy baby, sleeping long hours at a stretch, nursing like a champ. She rarely cried and smiled all the time, especially at Matthew. Matthew made blanket forts for Meena and decorated a large box to become her spaceship. He pushed her on the swing and played Candyland with her.

For eight years, their family was everything Monica had ever dreamed it could be. Her kind and happy husband adored her. Her beautiful children were friends. Her in-laws were warm and helpful, and while her own parents weren't quite as involved, they loved the kids, too. When the summer vacations began, it was icing on the already wonderful cake. Six or eight weeks somewhere lovely, Sanjay teaching the kids about the local history and cultures, animals and geology. She, on the other hand, had to work. A lot. But her income provided financial security and a lot of the material things that brought them comfort and safety—their house, their sturdy cars, good health care, college funds for the kids, retirement savings. She had the job that would earn those things much more easily than Sanjay ever could. It was what it was, and Sanjay made sure she felt appreciated. Foot rubs and little notes, a delicious lunch packed each morning, flowers for no reason.

There was a tiny part of her that resented the arrangement. It would be nice, she thought, to switch places with him, have a spouse who brought home a huge salary and stunning bonuses. She would have liked to have been the parent who got two months off with the kids in some beautiful place, not the one flying back and forth and fielding phone calls from work during their vacations.

But she knew they were lucky. Their children were healthy and loved them and each other. She and Sanjay had built a strong marriage, paying close attention perhaps because they were from different cultures, always checking in with each other, making time to listen and nurture and appreciate. It was a very good life.

And then came puberty, and Matthew changed.

It did not happen overnight. Not the physical parts, anyway. It made her cry the day his voice became a little froggy. He passed her in height when he was thirteen and crowed about it. But then, one morning he came downstairs for breakfast and in his body was a sullen, disrespectful teenager who would throw his homemade lunch away before he even got into the school building and buy hot lunch instead. Who said he wasn't going to his grandparents' house because it was "boring." He started slacking off in school, and Sanjay had many intense talks with him about the future, his opportunities, the hope that Matthew would always do his best.

But even Sanjay couldn't get through to him. Matthew would sit slumped at the table, staring with dead eyes as his father lectured.

"You've been given everything, son," Sanjay would say. "Your responsibility is to make the most of that. Not to be half asleep in class or bringing home mediocre grades when you're as smart as you are. Okay? Are we clear?"

"Sure," Matthew would say in a voice that dripped with boredom and contempt.

His bedroom door was always closed. He didn't want to come down for family movie night, and if Monica or Sanjay insisted, he'd sigh frequently with thinly veiled impatience. He didn't want to play with Meena (though he was never unkind to her), but seeing the hurt in her little girl's eyes tore at Monica's heart.

Then came skipping school and hanging out with the kids who were notorious for trouble. He simply shrugged when busted and answered their questions in grunts. One day, she left work early to see a cross-country meet, and was stunned to see him kissing a girl. A girl whose name she didn't know. Were they dating? Having sex? When she asked about it, he said, "It's no big deal, Mom. Jesus. Relax."

That little boy she had loved was gone, and in his place was a pain in the ass she sometimes wanted to smack. Oh, it was all normal teenage stuff (though not in the Patel family, where parents were honored and respected in a way that was completely un-American). And God, she missed her little boy. She had worked so hard to win his love, to ensure he felt like he belonged and was safe and important, all those things adopted kids worried about. And now, it seemed like all that work was for nothing, because she had a sulky, irritable teenager who made it very clear he'd rather be anywhere but home.

When Matthew brought home a report card full of B's and C's in eighth grade, they took away his phone for the rest of the school year. The grades immediately improved, though not the attitude. Matthew was better with Sanjay, perhaps afraid to go too far with his Indian father, who was such a good son to his own parents. But with her . . . sometimes Monica thought that if a bus ran her over in front of him, he wouldn't so much as flinch.

Her friends and online community commiserated. Teenage boys were not renowned for being wonderful companions to their parents, especially their mothers. This was normal. Horrible, but normal.

She had thought he was growing out of it this past year. He'd become a little friendlier, offering a few details of school and friends. Not a lot, but some. He started hanging out with Meena again, sitting on her bed some afternoons, or goofing around as they played video games. Monica felt herself relax a little. He even hugged her spontaneously one morning and told her to have a great day.

Two weeks later, he met Harlow. So all the time when Monica thought he was maturing, he'd been keeping secrets, making plans to get close to his birth mother, choosing Cape Cod as their vacation spot, finding his birth mother online, looking at her family's social media accounts, googling her name. He'd been lying to the three of them, making plans to find his other family, greasing the skids at home by being nice again.

Her son was manipulative. It was undeniable. And why? They had always told him he could meet Harlow if she was willing; always understood his sadness that his first mother hadn't been able to keep him; always encouraged him to speak about her, acknowledge her on Mother's Day and his birthday. They told him he got his curly hair from her and said how pretty she was, how smart. They had never once implied that they would be hurt by him looking her up and meeting her, having a relationship with her.

And then he'd gone behind their backs anyway.

Now, this summer, Monica was not the mother closer to her son. She had to be in California or on a plane. She had to hope that Sanjay, the "nice" parent, would be as vigilant as she would be, picking up on subtleties that should be addressed. Did Matthew feel rejected? Angry? Were he and Harlow in that "honey-moon" period when the birth mother and child were infatuated with each other? Would that ever end?

And selfishly, Monica wondered if Matthew was thinking of *her* at all. Her feelings, her shock, her generosity in encouraging him to spend time with his birth mother. Did it even occur to him that this was terrifying for her? Harlow was so young, so pretty, so . . . so cool with her bookstore and her kayak and paddleboard, her cute dog, her siblings and grandfather. How did Monica measure up? She saw herself as the slightly anxious, always-working mother whose job was dull as hell to anyone outside the industry; who'd had shadows under her eyes for the past ten years; who was the boring, irritating parent who made sure teeth were brushed and vegetables were eaten; who nagged about the dirty laundry and cleaning the cat's litter box.

This summer—the last summer of normalcy, since next summer they'd be getting ready to send Matthew to college—had been turned completely upside down, and Monica's heart was being chipped away with a chisel, it seemed. Every time Matthew Face-Timed, he was so happy . . . because he'd seen Harlow. Because he'd be meeting her family. Because he and his uncle looked so much alike. Monica would fly out again on Thursday for a few days, and she'd been texting with Harlow about times she could see Matthew, and this was not the summer she had wanted.

Thank *God* she had another child. Oh, that was a horrible thought, but truly, thank God that Meena had been born. She was everyone's heart, her daddy's girl, her mommy's shadow, her brother's biggest fan. With Meena, Monica never had to wonder if her child loved her and felt connected to her. She never had to worry if her daughter would find someone to replace her. Sure, that day could come—a mother-in-law who swooped in to claim her, a professor or boss who took her under their wing. But Meena had only one mother.

At least she had that, Monica thought, because Harlow and Matthew were just about killing her.

TWENTY-THREE

HARLOW

Matthew and I were spending just about every other day together. It had been painfully wonderful, hearing about all the things I'd missed, looking at him in wonder, this human I had grown inside me.

We talked mostly about him—his early years, becoming a big brother, how his parents let him pick her middle name. His hobbies, his friends, his favorite subjects, the color of his room, where he might want to go to college. He talked about his grandparents—all four still alive; aunts; uncles; cousins who ranged in age from twenty-eight to six.

Monica had warned me—elegantly and in person when they picked him up after the beach day—that I should always be thinking of Matthew's feelings, with mine being a distant second. I was not to bring up any painful subjects—like me, for example—and only discuss that if Matthew asked. The first few times were mostly information swaps. But on the fourth visit, he started asking the hard questions.

We'd gone to Herring Pond with Ollie sitting on Matthew's lap the whole ride over, gazing worshipfully into his eyes. Herring was one of the beautiful kettle ponds formed by the glaciers deep in the woods on the ocean side of town. Lillie Silva had offered us the use of her house for the day, as well as her private dock and canoe (and her big goofy dog, Zeus, who assumed Ollie was his puppy).

We swam with the dogs, who fetched sticks. (Well, Ollie did. Zeus may have eaten a frog.) A little while later, we took the canoe out and dropped some fishing lines in the water. We caught nothing other than a sunfish, which I unhooked and tossed back, but we did see a shockingly large bass, an osprey and a skunk family trundling along the shore. Matthew swam again, flipping on his back to look at the sky as I tied up the canoe. It was a perfect day, hot and sunny, the leaves rustling in a slight breeze.

When Matthew came out of the water, we sat on Lillie's screened-in porch, looking at the pond. She'd left us homemade cookies, and I'd brought bottles of iced tea. Zeus and Ollie lay panting and damp beside us.

"It's so beautiful here," Matthew said. "So different from California."

"Your town looks so pretty in the pictures," I said.

"Oh, yeah, it is. But, you know, it's a city. The nature isn't like this. All wild and stuff." He gestured to the pond.

"It is a special place, the Cape in general, and this house in particular."

"Yeah, it's wicked cool."

I smiled at the Cape Cod phrase. That hadn't taken long. "Do you go to San Francisco a lot?"

"Sometimes," he said. "I'd go more, but Mom and Dad are pretty strict."

"So what's fun to do in Pleasanton?" I asked.

"Nothing, really. I mean, it was great when I was little. I don't know. It's not for me." He ate his fifth cookie. "I think this place is part of my DNA."

I smiled, but a faint alarm bell sounded. I doubt Monica would've liked hearing that. "Do you feel that way about India?" I asked, trying to honor Sanjay's role and culture. Matthew was raised as a half-Indian child, after all.

"No. Hey, you wanna hear something funny? No one ever asks if I'm adopted, and when I tell them I am, they say, 'But you look just like your father!' Stupid. I mean, we both have brown eyes and black hair. That's it, though. I mean, I look at you and I can see how much we look alike, except for the hair color. Right?"

"Sure," I said. "And you and Robbie . . ."

"Totally. When I was little, I was kind of jealous of my friends who were obviously adopted, like the interracial families, because they got so much attention. At least it was out there. Me, I always had to announce it, and then I'd get that condescending smile and people would say, 'Oh, you're *chosen*, how lucky you are!' and it made me want to puke."

"Why?" I asked.

"Because! I mean, it's not like my parents chose me. *You* chose them. They got what they got."

"And they're the lucky ones," I said.

Understandably, he made a face. "Not really. Maybe. Some adopted kids are shitheads. Some are great. Some adoptive parents are shitty. Some are great. Some are mediocre."

"Where do your parents fall on that list?"

He shrugged. "They do their best. I mean, Dad's okay. He's more casual and relaxed. Mom's pretty uptight, though. She wants everything to be perfect all the time."

I hesitated before answering. "My guess is every parent wants that."

"Whatever. She works it way too hard. You know, she's never yelled at me? Never."

"Isn't that a good thing?"

"Not really. I know she wants to sometimes." He looked at me and smiled, flashing Lark's dimple. "You yelled at me the first time we hung out."

I rolled my eyes and smiled, but I felt guilty, letting him compare me to Monica. But he was being honest. We sat in silence for a minute, listening to the birds and wind.

"Can you tell me about my bio-dad?" Matthew asked, and while the question was inevitable, it still felt like a throat punch.

"Um . . . sure." This was one of those topics that was fraught, and yet I didn't want to spin a happier picture than the truth had been. All the articles I'd read said to be honest but tread carefully and be kind. The kid might not want to hear your feelings on the matter. "He was really good-looking," I said, and Matthew smiled.

"Do I look like him?"

I hadn't wanted to acknowledge that, but . . . "A little bit. You got his black hair and olive skin. He had green eyes and was six feet tall. My guess is you'll grow at least another inch or so."

"Yeah, that's all in my non-identifying information. Anything else?"

"He was great at golf."

"Really? Because I'm *great* at mini-golf," said my son. "That's kind of cool, right?"

"Mm-hm."

"But what was he *like*?"

I took a deep breath as my internal organs seemed to shiver. "He was . . . fun. Outgoing, kind of casual about studying because he thought he'd become a golf pro." *He was selfish and unkind. He wanted me to get an abortion. He abandoned me. I hated him.*

"What else?"

"We . . . we really didn't know each other that well. We only dated a couple months."

"How did he feel when you told him you were knocked up?" Matthew asked.

"He . . . well, he kind of panicked. As would most eighteen-year-old boys."

"Yeah, a *hundred* percent." He grinned. "So what else?"

I hesitated. "He wasn't great, to be honest. I mean, he was immature. We both were." The memory of him accusing me of getting pregnant *on purpose* made my teeth clench. "I asked him to sign away his paternal rights before you were born so I could have you adopted, and he did."

"Bet he was glad to."

He couldn't grab that pen fast enough. "He was." Honesty but also kindness. "I know he was happy that you'd be well taken care of." He had never said anything like that. My first parental lie. I glanced at my phone for a time check. "I should get you back home, okay? I know you guys have dinner plans."

"We're going to Winslow's," he said, naming the restaurant just down the street from Open Book. "You should come, too."

"Oh, thanks, sweetie, but—"

"Mom's in California. It's just the three of us. Come on, it'd be nice. Meena would love it. Dad, too. He's totally chill with this."

"Why don't you text him and see if that's okay. He might want it to be just his kids."

Matthew's thumbs flew across his phone. A second later, he smiled. "Dad says it's cool."

I drove Matthew back to Eastham, then went home. Rosie was lying on the couch, cheeks flushed.

"You okay?" I asked, pressing the backs of my fingers against her forehead. "You're warm."

"I'm fine, hon. How was your day?" She sat up, and her eyes were a little glassy.

"You sure you feel okay, hon?" I asked.

"I'm completely fine."

"I'm having dinner with the Patels, minus Monica. You want to come? They're going to come to the store first, maybe pop up here to see where I live."

"I'll pass. You should have this time alone together. That sounded weird. Alone together. Hey, remember that movie with Hugh Grant? Single Parents Alone Together? SPAT?" She laughed. "So funny."

"Rosie, are you stoned?"

"In the middle of the day? No. Give me a break, Harlow. I'm fine. Maybe I'll call Winnie and see if she wants to hang out. She's so awesome."

"Okay, I have to shower and wash this beautiful and elegant dog here, so I'm gonna get going."

"Sounds like a plan," she said, getting up and heading for the stairs. "I'll tidy up."

The Patels admired the bookstore (which, of course, they'd all seen before), and my apartment, which Meena thought was "the coolest." I watched Matthew's face as he looked at the paintings I'd hung up, the family photos, the view from the windows. This was where his birth mother lived, and clues about me were everywhere. The color yellow, the jam-packed bookcases, the wooden giraffes that stood on a shelf, the houseplants, a little bronze statue of a mustang that reminded me of Colorado in a nonpainful way.

"Nice place" was all he said. He seemed to be looking for something . . . possibly signs that I'd had a son once upon a time. Obviously, there were none. I had nothing. Not a lock of his baby hair, not a photo of me pregnant, not his hospital bracelet. I felt abruptly guilty that I'd tried to erase his memory.

We walked down to Winslow's, and I acted as tour guide, telling them about the shopkeepers, Preservation Hall, the garden. Then we went up the stairs to the restaurant, which seated us inside, since the patio was full. I was glad, in case one of my family members walked past.

"Here we go," said Kim, the maître d'. "Enjoy your dinner."

"I'm so glad you could come," Sanjay said, pulling out my chair.

"Me too!" said Meena. "Did I tell you that Ophelia and I are friends already? I went to the bookstore on Sunday and met her and we totally hit it off. Thanks for that. Because HRH here is ignoring me so far this summer." She elbowed him.

"Because you're so boring," he said. "Reading all the time. Yawn."

"Hey, I resent that," I said. "Don't forget what I do for a living."

"Right, sorry. Books are so cool." He made a face, looking very much like Sanjay.

"You're such a Neanderthal," Meena said.

"I love your kids," I said to Sanjay.

"I love yours," he said with a lovely smile. His words caught me off guard, and I had to swallow hard. "So tell us what we must do this summer in order to have the full Cape Cod experience."

It was kind of him, giving me something to talk about. I went into full-on tourist guide mode, recommending everything from the Oceanair Himalayan Salt Cave in Orleans to the Coast Guard Heritage Museum in Barnstable, the summer theater, the beautiful cemeteries. I told them they should go on a whale watch and a shark cruise, to brave the crowds in Provincetown for the Blessing of the Fleet and the Portuguese Festival.

"Harlow. Hi." I turned, and for a second, I didn't recognize the man speaking to me.

"James! Oh. Hi, how are you?"

How does one introduce one's fuck buddy to one's long-lost son? "Guys, this is my . . . friend. James." Oh, my God. I had forgotten his last name. "James, these are the Patels, Sanjay, Matthew and Meena."

"Hello," he said. Apparently, he was alone. It went with the deep and moody musician image he cultivated. Was he gorgeous? Yes, his dark hair was long and wavy, his blue eyes tormented as the cliché dictated, his jeans loose and low-slung, his T-shirt a David Bowie concert tour from the '70s. Original, he had told me in the past. Not one of those mass-produced knockoffs. "We haven't gotten together in a while," James said.

Sanjay raised a knowing eyebrow.

"Right," I said. "Yeah. Um . . . well, the summer turned out to be a little busier than I thought."

"I'm her son," Matthew said. "She's my birth mother."

"You have a *kid*?" James asked.

"I do. He was adopted by this lovely man and his wife, who couldn't be here tonight." My God, that sentence sounded freakishly normal.

"And I'm the sister, who's boring by comparison," said Meena.

"No, you're not, Meena Jane the Hurricane," Sanjay said. He stood and shook James's hand. "Sanjay Patel. Nice to meet you."

"Same," said James. "Well. Harlow, I'll text you sometime."

"Okay," I said. We looked at each other. "Have a good night."

"You too." He trudged away.

The Patels looked at me. "He's a cello teacher," I said.

"Do you take cello lessons?" Matthew asked.

"No. But he's played in Wellfleet a few times. He's really good. Do you play any musical instruments, Meena?"

She told me she was taking flute in school, and I congratulated myself on diverting the subject of James. The truth was, I had barely thought of him for weeks.

"I don't play anything," Matthew said, "but I'm really good in art. Dad, did you know Harlow's mom is a painter? Kind of a big deal around here."

"Really. So that's where you get it, huh?" Sanjay looked at me. "The rest of us are talentless when it comes to art. You should see Meena's little pinch pot from kindergarten. We only kept it because we felt sorry for her."

"Daddy!" She laughed. "You're so mean."

"Oh, were you listening?" he said playfully. "Listen. I love that pinch pot. Even if it's really lumpy and brown. It's very, very special." God, he was a good father. I had been right about him.

Dinner was wonderful, as it always was here, and when the check came, I tried to grab it. Sanjay was faster. "Oh, no, you don't," he said. "You're our guest."

We went out to the patio to say our goodbyes. "My family is dying to meet all of you," I said. "Maybe when Monica's in town next?"

"Absolutely," said Sanjay. "We're eager to meet them as well."

I glanced at the patio and did a double take. There was Grady Byrne, sitting at a table by himself. "Gray," I said. "Come say hi."

"Hey," he said, standing and coming over. "How are you?"

"Great. Grady, this is . . ." My throat tightened. "This is my son, Matthew, and his father, Sanjay, and his sister, Meena. Guys, this is Grady Byrne, our resident marine biologist."

"Nice to meet you," he said, shaking hands with everyone rather formally.

"We went to high school together," I said. "And we play on the same trivia team."

"How dorktastic," Matthew said.

Gray smiled. "You nailed it."

"We should head home before the mosquitoes eat us," Sanjay said, slapping his arm. "Harlow, lovely to see you, and Grady, very nice meeting you."

"Same here," Gray said.

Then the Patels left, laughing about something as they went down the stairs and headed for the parking lot next door. Soon they'd be tucked in for the night at that fabulous house, watching TV maybe, or playing a game. Sanjay would tell them to brush their teeth. Maybe they'd call Monica. Such a normal picture of an ordinary night. But to me, it felt like an exotic vacation, dreamy and soft.

"Want to sit down?" Grady asked.

"Sure," I said. "That'd be nice. Oh, are you with someone?"

"I was, but she left." Yes. There were two dessert plates on the table, an empty wineglass.

"Were you on a *date*?" I asked.

"Not exactly."

Hm. That wasn't a no, was it? He sat down across from me. He wore a white button-down and jeans, but he looked . . . I don't know. Dead sexy. That stubbly, neat beard; his intelligent eyes.

"How was dinner?" he asked.

"It was . . . it was great," I said, but my voice turned to a whisper, because I was crying a little. Gray handed me a napkin, and I used it, wiping my eyes and blowing my nose. He didn't comment, just tilted his head a little. "We spent the afternoon together, and it was so . . . easy. And kind of agonizing, too." I felt my face scrunch, and Gray put his hand over mine. His was warm and big and it felt wicked nice.

"I get it," he said.

"I've actually never been that close to anyone outside my family and Rosie. I've never even had a real boyfriend," I blurted out, then cringed. "I never thought I could handle anything . . . deep."

"Why?" he asked.

I pulled my hand back and wiped my eyes again. "Because I gave my beautiful baby to someone else," I whispered, "and something broke in me. And maybe I don't feel like I deserve a family after . . . Matthew."

He didn't answer for a few seconds, then said, "Would you say that to a teenage girl who'd just chosen adoption for her baby? That she wouldn't ever deserve a family?"

"God, no! But in my case . . . Gray, I could have kept him."

He nodded. That was it. He didn't contradict me or tell me how noble I was to have gone the adoption route. He just nodded and looked at me with those kind green eyes, and somehow, that said more than most people said in a week.

I sighed hugely, and Grady smiled a little. "Let's talk about you," I said. "You weren't exactly on a date. So what was it?"

He took a measured breath. Honestly, Grady Byrne was the most measured person I'd ever met, never upset, never drunk, never angry. At least, not that I'd seen. "That was my former sister-in-law, trying to convince me to get back together with my ex-wife."

"Wow! Okay, go on. Unless this is deeply painful and you don't want to talk about it, even though I just spilled my guts to you."

"Fair point." He waved to the server, who came over. "I'll have another glass of wine," he said. "How about you, Harlow?"

"Whatever he's having. Thanks."

"Be right back," said the server.

"In answer to your question," Gray said, "my former sister-in-law is a very nice person. And an attorney, so she's very convincing." He straightened his fork so it was at an exact right angle to his side of the table. "She said her sister regrets leaving Luna and me and is very sorry for cheating on me. She would like to get back together, now that she understands how hurtful infidelity is."

"She was unaware of that before?"

"Exactly." His attention once again turned to the fork, making a forty-five degree angle now. "The thing is, it wasn't just once. Or one guy."

"Oh, Gray. I'm so sorry." My turn to reach across the table and touch his hand.

"Yeah. So I'm a little dubious. Some things can't be changed. Or fixed."

"Who would cheat on you, the world's nicest guy?" I asked.

"Bentley Blakefield Byrne, that's who."

"Is . . . is that her real name?" I tried not to smile, since Grady's heart was pulsating on the table—but really? "Triple B?"

He looked at me, the tiniest smile at the corner of his mouth. "Bentley Canyon Rose Blakefield Byrne."

I had to cover my mouth with the napkin.

"No, it's okay," he said.

The waiter brought our glasses of wine, smiled and left.

"You married a woman named Bentley Canyon Rose?" I was suddenly giggling. "I'm sorry. It's just . . ." Oh, inappropriate laughter! Why are you so hard to stop?

"Yeah, it's funny *now*," Gray said, smiling a little and shaking his head. "I may not have been thinking too clearly when I proposed."

"She's from Texas, right?" I asked.

"Yep. And her daddy owns half the state."

I took a sip of wine, tried not to think of the words *Bentley Canyon Rose*, sputtered, then calmed down again. "I'm sorry. This must be horribly painful for you."

"Not really. No."

"Really? How'd you manage that?"

He leaned back in his seat. "We were married for four years. The minute the wedding was over—this ridiculous four-day extravaganza with thirteen bridesmaids and a thousand guests—"

"A thousand? I would've loved to have seen that."

"Yes. I would've invited you, but we hadn't spoken since high school."

Ouch.

"Anyway, she got pregnant right away. Which was great. I wanted kids. But she wasn't that excited. I think she just wanted to go back to being the bride. She thought she looked ugly—I assure you, she did not—and she hated being pregnant and said how much she wished she'd waited."

"That must've been hard to hear." I knew how much Grady loved his daughter, after all.

Another nod. "It was." He studied my face a second or two.

"The only thing she seemed excited about was picking out a name. Want to hear her choices?"

"God, yes. Wait, let me prepare for this." I sat back, took another sip of wine, lay my hands on the table. "Hit me."

"For a boy, Ranger Coyote Byrne."

I let out a whistle. "That's got some legs."

"And for a girl . . . Falcon Skye."

A shout of laughter escaped my lips. "Falcon. Like the bird."

"No," he said, smiling. "She wanted to spell it creatively. F-A-L-K-Y-N-N-E."

"Grady!" I dissolved into laughter again. "Well, it's good you have custody, because she clearly hates children. Luna sounds so normal now."

He smiled. "I wanted a name from nature. Something that had to do with oceans because, obviously, I love oceans."

"That's pretty romantic, Luna's dad. Well, I can't make fun of anyone's name. I'm named after a gravestone my mom saw in Boston. It means 'rock hill.' Very unromantic."

"I always liked it," Gray said.

"Thanks, pal." I paused. "Does Triple B have visitation rights or anything?"

He looked down again. "Luna is supposed to spend a month in the summer with her, but something came up last year and the year before that. A man, I'm guessing. And now she regrets it and wants to come live here and be a happy family." His eyes flickered. "I'm not sure Luna would even recognize her at this point. But Mercedes, Bentley's sister, she's decent. She comes to visit a few times a year. The only good one in the family."

"What is it with these people and cars? Do they have a brother named Ferrari?"

He laughed. "Beemer. But that's just his nickname. I don't actually know his name. He's Something Blakefield the Third."

"How do the grandparents feel about Luna?" I asked.

"Luna has a trust fund. Otherwise, they haven't been up to see her. They have a bunch of other grandchildren."

It sounded horribly lonely for sweet little Luna. "And your parents?" I asked, vaguely remembering them from high school.

"They live in Plymouth now and drive up a few times a month. Sometimes they take her for the weekend. They worship her."

"As they should. She's a great kid. Very smart and charming."

"Thank you. So while it was good to see Mercedes, you can see why I'm not interested in getting back together with my ex-wife."

"Yes. I can. You deserve much better, Gray."

His eyes were steady on mine. "Walk you home?" he asked.

"I'm just up the street."

"Yes. I know where you live."

"That makes you sound creepy, Gray."

"Harlow. Everyone knows where you live."

"Fine, fine. Walk me home. Protect me from the little fox I saw in my yard this morning."

He paid for our wine, and we went down the street, shoulders bumping here and there. I suddenly wished I lived farther away so the walk would take longer.

When we got to my door, I turned to him and said, "Thanks, Gray. Thanks for the wine and listening and for being . . . you know. A prince."

"Right back at you. But a princess."

I laughed. We looked at each other a minute, and for the second time in my life, I thought Grady Byrne might want to kiss me.

For the second time in my life, I was wrong. "Good night," he said, and off he went.

"See you soon," I called, watching him silhouetted by the streetlight, all that intensity and goodness and those broad shoulders. And despite everything else I had going on at the moment, I kind of wished he *had* kissed me. Just to know what it was like.

TWENTY-FOUR

HARLOW

After ten years of a social life that was based around trivia night and family but otherwise consisted of reading at home alone, I was suddenly swamped with things to do. There was Matthew, of course, first and foremost. We'd gone bike riding the other day, then swum on the bay side at high tide. Rosie, he and I had watched *Game of Thrones* on a rainy afternoon, me covering Matthew's eyes whenever I thought something was too violent or sexual, making him laugh.

"I've already watched the whole series," he said.

"Not with us, youngster," Rosie said.

Rosie had rearranged her work schedule to stay for at least two more weeks, so every night, I had someone to come home to. We hadn't spent this much time together since Los Angeles, and then she'd been so busy and I'd been in law school. This was wonderful. She was such a social creature and loved going out to the many restaurants and bars our fair peninsula offered. But some nights, we'd make dinner for us and Grandpop. Winnie or Lark joined us if they were free, and Robbie did, too, a couple of times.

The date for the big family picnic had been set. I'd talked with Monica a few days ago—she was back on the Cape—then texted my family members to let them know. Mom and Dad were still licking their wounds, and for the first time in my life, I didn't care that I was disappointing them. I had more important things on my mind.

The night before the family picnic, which would be held at my parents' house (a concession to them), Rosie and I were making potato salad—rather, I was making it, and she was nursing a glass of wine, telling me about her run-in with Cynthia that morning at Open Book.

"I mean, I know she doesn't like me, but today it was a full body slam."

"Where was I?"

"In the back, doing your mysterious yet romantic bookstore stuff. But you saw it, right, Ollie?" she asked. She was holding Ollie like a baby, and he didn't mind one bit.

"Ah. Breaking down boxes. Very romantic. Yeah, she's been weird lately," I said. "She's an odd one, but even for her, she's been pretty shut down."

"Make sure she doesn't bite a customer," Rosie said, and I snorted. "How exactly is she related to you?"

I sliced up another scallion. "No one knows," I said. "Grandpop is her godfather. He and her dad were third cousins or something like that, but they were close friends, too." I put down the knife. "She just told me the other day that she's adopted, too."

"Really?"

"Yeah. But she made sure to tell me that she views birth mothers as essentially incubators, keeping the fetus alive until it can be adopted by superior people."

"I love hating her," said Rosie, getting up to refill her glass.

Just then, my door opened, and Grandpop came in. Ollie leaped neatly out of Rosie's arms and ran to him, lacing around his legs with joy. "Why, hello, Oliver!" Grandpop said. "Who's a good boy?"

I put down my knife and kissed my grandfather's cheek. "Where've you been all day, Grandpop?" I asked. "I feel like I've hardly seen you."

"I've been on a mission. Hello, Rosie dear," he said.

"Hello, handsome Mr. Smith. Want a glass of wine?"

"No, no, thank you. In answer to your question, Winnie—"

"Harlow," I corrected.

"Harlow, of course. Well, I was down in Orleans at the senior center, screening potential wives, and then I went to Rock Harbor and someone invited me out for a fishing trip, and I accepted! What a treat! I can't remember the last time I went out on the water!"

I remembered he'd gone recently with his friend Bertie, but just asked, "Did you catch anything?"

"At either fishing expedition?" Rosie added.

"I caught something, Rosie dear, but I gave it to the captain, whose name escapes me now. Oh, Harlow, unfortunately he needs three hundred and fifty dollars for the trip. Would you write the check, dear?"

"Got it." Grandpop did have the habit of not differentiating between paid services and actual invitations. "You didn't have to pay any potential wives, did you?"

"No, of course not! But I'm here to ask you girls if you'd come out with me tonight! I have a date, and I think I need some *help*. I did make a list of questions to ask, but I've misplaced it."

"I'm totally in," Rosie said. "Let me go change. Harlow . . ." She eyed my T-shirt du jour, which said *Dinosaurs didn't read, and look what happened to them* with a picture of a T-rex skeleton. "You also need to change."

"I absolutely do not," I said. "I'm clean, and that's enough."

"I'm meeting the young lady in half an hour," Grandpop said. "At the Land Ho! I love that place. So cheery!"

It would also be crammed to the gills on a Saturday night in July, but I knew the owner, and I'd bet I could get us a table. I called, and indeed, John said he'd save a spot for us.

Exactly a half hour later, we were standing in the crowded foyer of the Ho, which had the best clam chowder and brownie sundaes on God's green earth. Grandpop waved to a woman in the back near the jukebox. Unlike his choice on Winnie's singles night, this lady was in the realm of age-appropriate. She had the classic Older Cape Cod Woman look—thick white hair cut in a bob, her figure slim and ropey from gardening or clamming, tanned skin creased from the sun. She wore cropped white pants and a white shirt with large red poppies splotched all over it . . . in other words, she had a better sense of style than I did. Then again, so did everyone. At least I had good hair.

"Hello, hello," Grandpop said. "Oh, I'm sorry, I've forgotten your name, madam."

She stood up. "Frances," she said. "Frances Black."

"Of course!" Grandpop said. "This is my beautiful grand-daughter, Lark—"

"Harlow," I said.

"Harlow," he echoed, "and her lovely friend, Rosie."

"He never messes up *my* name," Rosie murmured as we sat down.

"Frances," I said, "it's very nice to meet you. Grandpop invited us to tag along because we're two single women with no plans on a Saturday night, and he feels sorry for us."

"She's being very diplomatic," Grandpop said. "They're my wingmen."

"I see," Frances said. "I think that's sweet." Her face creased into a smile, crow's feet and a hundred other wrinkles fanning out. So far, so good.

"I did remember my list of questions," Grandpop said. "I found it in my pocket, of all places!"

"Let's order first, Grandpop," I said, because the server was right there, and the place was jumping. We Smiths came here often, so the menu wasn't exactly a mystery. Fried seafood in eight or ten varieties, chowder, Portuguese kale soup, and your basic pub food. All of it delicious and comforting.

We chatted about the weather and tourism, and how long Frances had lived on the Cape (thirty-nine years), and did she have any children (four, with eleven grandchildren), and what she liked to do (garden, golf, fish, power-walk every morning with her gals, as she called them). She'd been widowed for a decade and was hoping for someone to share her twilight years with.

"You don't mind if I run a quick background check, do you?" Rosie asked impishly. "I have very deep feelings for Mr. Smith, and I want to make sure you're not wanted by the Feds."

Frances laughed. "Go right ahead. I have to say, Robert, their loyalty speaks well of you."

"Don't I know it," Grandpop said. "I thought you might be more interested in marriage if you met the good part of the family first."

He was flirting! My heart flooded with love. When Grammy had died three years ago, he'd been so sad, and so noble, too. He would pat our hands when we tried to comfort him and say he was fine. But he'd stare into the middle distance, and for a long time, his days consisted of walking to the cemetery and back. He'd come into the bookstore, try to be chipper for the clients, but his heart was with Grammy. Only in the past six months or so had he come back to his old self.

So if Grandpop wanted a wife for the last few years of his life, I had no problem with that. As long as she was perfect.

"So I'm curious, Robert, what's on this list of questions?" Frances asked when we were mostly done with our meals and Rosie and I were debating whether or not to share a dessert like civilized people or follow our hearts and get our own.

"Oh, yes!" Grandpop said. He took out the piece of paper with great aplomb. "Frances, may I ask what your feelings are on the issue of teeth?"

Rosie choked on her drink.

"They're very useful," Frances said.

"Good answer," I said.

"I have dentures," Grandpop said, "but they're the good kind. Very high quality. My late wife insisted."

"A sound investment," Frances said.

"Incontinence?" Grandpop asked. "I'm hoping to avoid that, but I'll just say that if *you* became incontinent, I could handle that. I was very involved with my wife's care in her last few years. I'm sorry to say she died of cancer."

"That's touching, Robert. It truly is. I believe in the sickness and health bit in marriage vows, so I think I'd be fine."

"Good! Let's hope the incontinent bridge is one we never have to cross." Grandpop winked at her and looked at his list again. "Bedtime preference? I like to be in bed before nine, and I love a good nap."

"Well, I'm more of a night owl," said Frances, "being that I hit the hay around nine thirty, but I don't mind if you go to bed first."

"I don't know," said Rosie. "This could be a deal breaker. It's nice to go to bed at the same time."

"Shall we compromise and say nine fifteen?" asked Grandpop.

Rosie clutched my hand under the table, and we exchanged a smile. "This is the best date I've been on in my entire life," I said.

"Same," said Rosie. "Keep going, you two."

As the two senior citizens moved on to which foods caused intestinal problems, Rosie and I demolished our desserts.

"I got food poisoning the last time I had Vietnamese," Frances said. "One of my daughters was adopted from Vietnam, so it's not like I'm unfamiliar with the cuisine. It was just that one time, but it was horribly memorable. Biblical diarrhea."

Rosie laugh-coughed into a napkin.

"You adopted a daughter?" Grandpop exclaimed. "How wonderful! Harlow here put up her son for adoption, but guess what? He's visiting this summer! We're all terribly excited to meet him."

"Oh, how wonderful!" Frances said.

All these years of secrecy and repression, and now we were talking about Matthew in the Land Ho! as if he were just another fact of life.

"How old is he?" Frances asked me.

"Almost eighteen."

She beamed, and I kind of loved her for being so delighted for me.

"All right, back to my list. If we go to a Vietnamese restaurant, I promise to ask the owners if anyone's had food poisoning recently," Grandpop said gallantly. "How do you feel about recreational marijuana?"

"Yes, Frances, do tell," said Rosie, finishing her martini.

"I'm not opposed," she said. "It's legal here, supposedly less harmful than alcohol, so whatever floats your boat, as long as you're not driving."

"Excellent answer," I said. "Grandpop occasionally has a gummy for back pain."

"I'll admit I've taken one or two when I've had trouble sleeping," she said. "No regrets."

"Well, I think we've made some great strides, Frances, don't you?" Grandpop asked.

"I do, Robert, and I've had a real nice time."

I waved to our server for the check. "Just promise me if you do get married, I can be your flower girl, Grandpop."

"Of course!" he said. "And you, too, Rosie."

"Guess I'm not gonna be your step-grandmother, Harlow," Rosie said, pretending to sulk. "Frances, I hate to say it, but you've got me beat."

Frances smiled and blew Rosie a kiss. Oh, yes. She was lovely.

"If you were fifty years older, Rosie," Grandpop said.

"You'd be amazed at how many men have said that to me," she answered.

"Now, we just have to find someone for you girls, and I can die a happy man."

"Don't forget Lark. And Winnie. And Robbie," I said, slipping my credit card to the waitress.

"Well, I don't want to live past a hundred, Harlow," Grandpop said. "Frances, I will absolutely call you again! What a pleasure tonight was!"

We walked her to her car, and I got in behind the wheel of Rosie's little rented Tesla, which was much sportier and sexier than my poor little Subaru (as was everything). Monica and Sanjay had each rented one as well. Very popular, not paying for gas.

Tomorrow, the Patels would meet the Smiths en masse. I hoped they liked us. Well, I hoped Monica liked us. I was pretty confident my son, his sister and their dad would like us just fine.

But first, I needed to run an errand. "I'm going to drop you two off and pop by Mom and Dad's, okay?" I said as I pulled into my driveway.

"Lovely," said Grandpop. "Rosie and I can have a little chat before bed." I smiled—it was 8:35.

"Love you both," I said, then headed for my childhood home.

I'd loved being the oldest Smith kid when I was little. All the way till college, I supposed. It was only with some distance that I saw my early years a little more clearly—the benign neglect, the invisibility, the responsibilities my parents just assumed I would cover. *I never have to spare you a thought, Harlow.* It was both a compliment and utterly heartbreaking, because it had been so true.

I went in and called out a hello. There was Mom, reading in the family room.

"Oh, hello," she said. Her face was wary, but she didn't say anything hostile.

"Hi. Where's Dad?"

"He took a shift at the hospital."

Dad still did a few per diem shifts a month. He'd always loved his job. "Got a minute?" I asked.

"Of course."

My mom and I had never had a fight before. I'd never been mad at her except in some passive-aggressive way, resenting her for not seeing me more clearly, sensing my heartache or how much I'd changed.

"I'd like us to be friends again," I said, and she burst into tears. "Oh, Mommy," I murmured, sitting next to her and pulling her close. Her curly hair, just like mine but streaked with gray, tickled my face. "I'm sorry."

"No, baby, I am." She straightened up and grabbed a tissue, and I noted there were several balled-up Kleenexes on the side table. "I . . . I just can't wrap my head around the idea that you went through so much alone. For *years*. What kind of mother am I?"

"You're a good mom," I said. "We all had a happy childhood."

"But everything you said is true," she said, tears streaming down her cheeks. "You were right. I look back now and can't believe what we asked of you. You used to give the Littles their baths when you were *eight*. No one would ask a kid to do that now. What were we thinking? And you took care of them after school. No wonder you didn't want us to raise your son." Her shoulders shook with sobs.

"Mom, listen. I was very, very close to asking you to do just that. It wouldn't have been the worst thing, not by a long shot. It just wasn't . . . it wasn't the best thing."

She nodded, her face misery incarnate. "But never to tell me, Harlow. My heart is broken, thinking that you had to do this without support, except for Rosie . . ." She was sobbing again. "And now everyone knows what a shitty mother I am. I can't pretend that doesn't hurt. The Littles, your grandfather, my sister, the entire town. You must have *hated* me all these years for not being the kind of mother you could turn to at the saddest time of your life."

I leaned back against the worn couch, taking in the familiar comfort of the room. My parents had never renovated, so it was just as it had always been. So many happy times in this room, watching movies, playing games, making forts, Christmas morning.

"You know what?" I said. "I think not telling you was some kind of self-preservation. I was already so messed up, so sad and lost that I couldn't take seeing you and Dad being sad, too. And I didn't *want* you to see me as anything other than the good kid. I didn't know how to be anything other than that."

"You're still the good kid, honey," she said. "That will never change."

"Yeah, but . . . I didn't want you to see me as a stupid teenage girl who got pregnant three weeks into her first relationship. I didn't want to be that girl. So it wasn't just disappointing you and Dad. It was keeping myself the way I was. I was too young to become something else, especially someone's mother."

Mom blew her nose again, and Buster, her elderly cat, jumped on her lap. He meowed at me, and I bopped him on the nose with my forefinger.

"I want tomorrow to be a happy day," I said. "I want you to be glad to meet your grandson." Tears flooded my own eyes. "I want you to be proud of me for what I did, giving him to Monica and Sanjay. It was the hardest thing I'll ever do in my life, and I have to believe it was the right thing."

Mom nodded, not looking at me. "When I think of the day you were born . . . the love I felt, like nothing else in my entire life, that fierceness . . ." She gripped my hand. "The fact that you did what you did, Harlow . . . you were so strong to do that. I want to go back in time and wrap you in my arms and take care of you and tell you how much I love you, my brave, good girl."

Well, that was it. I put my head in her lap and sobbed, and she stroked my hair and murmured, and at long, long last, my mother was there for me, easing my heartache just a little, finally understanding all that I'd lost and how far I'd come since that day.

TWENTY-FIVE

CYNTHIA

Cynthia hadn't expected to be invited to the family picnic, so when she was, she was rather disconcerted. Granted, it was one of those lazy email invitations, but when she read it—*Please come to a family picnic to meet Matthew, Meena, Monica and Sanjay Patel!*—she felt an odd lift in her mood. Yes, Gerald and Elsbeth invited her to the big holidays, and Cynthia accepted, only because staying home in the shack was worse. But this was new, and she was interested for just that reason.

She asked what she could bring, and Elsbeth told her nothing. Cynthia sighed. She didn't like showing up empty-handed, but she didn't like bringing liquor, either. She'd pick some flowers. Mother had always said flowers were a thoughtful and personal hostess gift.

Social invitations were nonexistent up here. Uncle Robert didn't mind if she popped in from time to time, but he was too old to host a party. Harlow had invited her up to her apartment all of twice before crossing her off the guest list. When she'd first moved here and begun work at the store, several people had asked her to have coffee or to join the Wellfleet Gardeners, having met her at Ponderosa in Eastham or Agway in Orleans. But they were so nosy! *Are you married, Cynthia? Do you have any children? What did you do before you came here? What did you study in college? Kansas City? No, I've never been. Flyover state, ha ha.*

Now, however, she had three half sister strangers she was going to meet in the near future. She kept that fact to herself. And now, Albert was her . . . friend, another secret. She was still a bit unsure if she wanted him as a suitor, but he was the first man on Cape Cod to show some interest. Not a single man had asked for her number at that wretched singles event, which she attributed to her old-fashioned values. She'd gone on CapeCodSeniorMatch .com, which seemed to specialize in men holding dead fish. They all also favored wraparound sunglasses, which made them seem hostile and secretive.

As for female friends, who knew with these Cape women. They made Cynthia feel . . . outdated. They did things like yoga and meditation. They took care of their grandchildren, were in cycling clubs and went out in their boats, did competitive swims or gave lectures at libraries. They raised money for food pantries and held protests.

Initially, Cynthia had tried to edge into the wealthier Cape Cod crowd, making conversation with the bookstore customers who projected wealth through their lean bodies and Vineyard Vines clothing, their little straw Coach bags and Chanel sunglasses. But she was of no interest to them—she was just an older woman behind the counter. They'd ask for Harlow or Destiny, practically fall on Uncle Robert, their faces lighting up when the *preferred* Open Book staff appeared.

Fine. She read for hours on her days off. Every evening, she watered and weeded her garden. She watched television, mostly BBC crime shows. She took long walks on the Cape Cod Rail Trail to maintain her trim figure (*fat* was a curse word, her mother used to say). She arranged flowers in little vases, placing them throughout the tiny house. It reminded her of Mother, who said a house without flowers could never be a home.

Thus far, her . . . encounters . . . with Bertie Baines had been surprisingly pleasant. They had seen each other twice since she . . . kissed him. (Mother would turn in her grave at Cynthia making the first move.) She liked talking to him. He was one of the few people who didn't seem to judge her. He and Uncle Robert.

Well, now she had a picnic to attend, and while it was sure to be loud and disorganized, she had to admit, she was somewhat pleased to be acknowledged as part of the family. Perhaps someday, she'd tell the Smiths about her half sisters, so long as they didn't turn out to be riffraff. It would be so nice to have a family that actually embraced her, rather than tacked her on as an afterthought.

She arrived at Gerald and Elsbeth's house at 1 p.m. on the dot, holding a large bouquet of flowers.

"Oh," said Elsbeth, who answered the door with Imogen on her hip. "Let me find a vase."

Cynthia gritted her teeth. Not so much as a thank-you.

"Come in," said Elsbeth. "We're out in back. The Patels aren't here yet."

Cynthia went through the rather shabby and unkempt house to the backyard, which wasn't in the best shape, either. Elsbeth was probably too busy being *artistic* to garden. Sure enough, there were five easels set up with blank canvases on each one. Were they doing crafts? For heaven's sake, this wasn't a children's party.

Addison and Nicole's girls ran around, chasing each other as their mothers photographed them, then stepped back to post to Instagram. (Cynthia followed them just to see if Addie could get any more annoying and was never disappointed.) Uncle Robert pretended to chase them, which entailed him holding up his hands and roaring, causing them to shriek with joy. Winnie, Rosie (not family but somehow included) and Harlow were in a huddle, Robbie was sleeping in the hammock, and Gerald and Elsbeth were at the grill, predictably joined at the hip.

Lark came over to kiss Cynthia's cheek. "Hello, Cynthia, how are you? I love that color on you."

She was Cynthia's favorite for a reason. "Thank you, Lark. I'm well. And you?"

"Great!" She wore a long, flowy peasant-style dress, and her hair was loose. She would be so much prettier if she dressed and styled herself with a bit more care.

"How are things at the hospital?" Cynthia asked.

Lark's eyes filled with tears. "Oh . . . they're okay. We had a sad case this week. The sweetest old man. He reminded me of Grandpop, but he was dying. His grandkids were all there, and one of them started singing to him, and . . ."

Cynthia let her talk, though death was hardly a pleasant topic. While many people confused Lark and Addison, Cynthia never did. Lark could cry at the drop of a hat and was always sweet and eager to please. Addison looked at the world as if it were a disappointing birthday present.

"Oh, my gosh, here I am talking your ear off, and you don't have anything to drink," said Lark now. "There's lemonade, iced tea, some sparkling water, wine . . . We're all so nervous, to be honest, Cynthia. We're meeting our nephew!"

As if on cue, the front doorbell rang.

"I'll get it!" said Harlow. "Stay here, guys!" She charged inside.

Everyone else took what seemed to be their assigned positions—Lark scuttering over to Addison and Uncle Robert. Nicole hoisted the younger girl to her hip, Addison positioning the older one in front of her. Winnie kicked Robbie to wake him up, and he scrambled out of the hammock and joined her and Rosie, saying something that made them laugh.

Cynthia went over to Uncle Robert. Addie gave her an irritable look—*don't mess up our aesthetic*—but Cynthia ignored her. She imagined Addison had been one of those brides who chose her attendants based on hair color and height.

"God, I'm so nervous," said Gerald, who had left the grill with his wife to join everyone else.

"He'll love you," said Elsbeth, wrapping her arm around his waist. "Just like everyone."

I don't love you, Gerald, thought Cynthia.

"He'll love you more," he said, kissing her on the lips. *Please.*

Then there they were. Harlow and the Patels came through the sliding glass door and out onto the deck. Harlow had her arm through her child's.

"Everyone," she said, and her voice was shaking, "this is my son, Matthew Rohan Patel." Her face spasmed with emotion, but she held it together, more or less. "These are his parents, Monica and Sanjay, and this is his beautiful sister, Meena." She turned to the Patels. "Meet my family—Mom and Dad, there, and Grandpop—Robert, that is. My twin sisters, Addison and Lark; Addie's wife, Nicole; their daughters, Imogen and Esme. That's my sister Winnie and my brother, Robbie. In the red dress is my best friend, Rosie. Don't worry, everyone has a name tag. Oh, and our cousin, Cynthia."

Oh, and our cousin, Cynthia. Typical.

"Hi, Smith family," Matthew said, and suddenly, there was a big cheer. Cynthia clapped a few times, too. It was expected, and . . . well, she supposed it was a big day for everyone else here. Harlow, Lark and Elsbeth were crying already. So was the adoptive mother. Was she like Cynthia's beloved mother, the best in the world? Maybe Cynthia would engage her in conversation.

They were all hugging and mingling, and the boy was calling people "Auntie Addison" and "Uncle Robbie." Gerald and Elsbeth told him to call them "Poppy" and "Gran," the way the little girls did. Matthew also reached down and touched their feet when he was introduced . . . was he just showing off, or was he more Indian than American? The Smiths were quite busy sucking up to the Patels, pressing their hands together in prayer position and bowing, saying "Namaste." Good Lord. Had they all sent out a group text with hints for meeting families from India?

Addison and Nicole acted as dueling photographers, posing everyone (except a certain cousin) talking with the Patels. The air rang with voices—*You're so handsome! We're so glad to meet you! These are your cousins! I'm your aunt! Oh, we love you already! Monica, Sanjay, welcome! Meena, we're so happy you're here!* Rosie called herself his honorary godmother, trying to make herself more important.

Cynthia didn't have a godchild. It might have been nice, being able to buy pretty clothes and send gifts. She'd have wanted a girl. It dawned on her that she might have a biological niece or nephew out there in the world. In fact, chances were high that Cynthia *did* have quite a few relatives. Well. It didn't matter. Those people were nothing to her, even if they turned out to be pleasant and clean. They had nothing in common. They hadn't grown up together. Her *real* relatives, Mother and Daddy, were dead. All she had left was Uncle Robert.

"Nice to see you again," Matthew said, finally approaching her. He started to reach for her foot, but Cynthia jerked back, startled. The boy glanced at her chest. "I'm sorry, I don't re-member your name." Ah. Her name tag must've fallen off. "I'm Matthew."

"Yes, hello. I'm Cynthia Smith Millstone," she said. "A cousin."

"Oh, you have another cousin, Matthew, how wonderful!" said his adoptive mother. "Hello, I'm Monica, Matthew's mother. So lovely to meet you."

"And you as well." She wore a pretty blue-and-white dress, espadrille sandals and diamond stud earrings (real, Cynthia could tell). Mother would approve.

"Hello again," said Sanjay, offering his hand. "Thank you for coming."

"Of course. This is a very . . . unusual situation, isn't it?"

Monica smiled. "Definitely. And I'm sorry, how are you re-lated to Harlow?"

"We're distant cousins."

"And coworkers, if I recall," Sanjay said.

"Yes. We own the bookstore together." There was an awk-ward pause. "You know," Cynthia said, "I'm adopted, too. My parents were everything to me. My adoptive parents, that is. The *real* parents, since they were there for me every day of their lives. They were wonderful. *I* certainly never felt the need to find my birth mother."

Though she'd just given them a compliment, their faces froze.

"Everyone's story is different," Monica said after a moment. "We've always known Matthew wanted to meet Harlow some-day, and we're very happy for him. And for us. We were very close to Harlow when she was pregnant, and so grateful she chose us to raise Matthew."

"I was adopted out of an orphanage."

"Really."

"Yes. My mother said I was the prettiest baby there."

"Is that so," said Sanjay. "What a nice story."

"Excuse us a moment," Monica said. "I think Elsbeth wants us, Sanjay."

Rude. Cynthia was throwing them a bone, trying to validate them. She just didn't understand people these days.

The Patels had brought gifts for the entire family. They started with brilliant patterned scarves for each adult woman. Monica presented Cynthia with one in yellow, a color Cynthia never wore. She accepted politely, of course. There were sparkly bracelets for the little girls, long embroidered shirts for each of the Smith men, a huge box of cookies in bright colors. Everyone was exclaiming and kissing and thanking everyone else. Elsbeth gave each one of the Patels a painting of her own work (of course). She'd never given *Cynthia* a painting, and from what Cynthia had heard, they were worth a fair bit. She would've sold hers and banked the proceeds.

Winnie, Robbie, Lark and Elsbeth brought food out from the kitchen—skewers of chicken and little fried pockets of something or other, a few steaming bowls of lumpy stew that made Cynthia's nose tingle. What it would do to her digestive tract, she was not willing to discover. At least there was American food, too—hamburgers and hot dogs, chicken wings, green salad and lobster rolls with butter, raw oysters that Robbie was shucking, demonstrating how it was done to his newfound nephew. There was enough here to feed half of Wellfleet.

She took her plate to a chair under a locust tree in the corner of the yard, where she could watch the unruly mob. Rosie served as bartender, loudly shaking a cocktail mixer, handing out martini glasses or pouring wine. The Indian girl, Meena, chased Addison's children, making them shriek even more loudly. Gerald and Elsbeth couldn't seem to stop hugging Matthew and crying joyfully. (*Some people just love drawing attention to themselves*, she could hear Mother saying.) Sanjay was laughing with Winnie and Nicole. Harlow kept putting her arm around her son and looked at him like he was Prince Harry. Cynthia supposed he was, in a way.

Would her sisters be this happy to meet her? And if so, why?

She ate her food. Eventually, Meena, came over to her and said, "Hi. I'm the boring biological daughter. My name's Meena."

"I'm the boring cousin," Cynthia said.

"I've seen you at the bookstore."

"Have you?" Cynthia didn't pay much attention to the children who came in.

"Mm-hm. I've been there twice with Ophelia Finch. Do you know her?"

Ophelia was the niece of the wealthiest woman in town, Melissa Spencer, a rival for Addison and Nicole. "I do. Are you enjoying your summer?"

"Oh, yeah! I love it here. The ocean is so cold, though! I almost died when I went in. Have you lived here your whole life?"

"No, I recently moved from the Midwest."

"Where in the Midwest?"

Heavens. A tween who actually asked questions. "Kansas City."

"Cool! Aren't there a few Frank Lloyd Wright buildings out there?"

Knock her over with a feather. "There are. I take it you're interested in architecture?"

"I am. My grandfather's an architect. Well, nice talking to

you!" She bounded away. Above-average manners, Cynthia decided, and smarter than most children her age.

Elsbeth announced that the children, including Matthew, should have a go at painting, and soon enough, Addison's daughters were scribbling on the canvas, getting themselves filthy with pastel crayons. Meena drew Pilgrim Monument in Provincetown rather well. Elsbeth lectured her new grandson on "underpainting" and "blending."

"Look at mine, Matthew's Daddy!" said Esme, and so Sanjay admired her work, then Imogen's.

Then there was the taking of the pictures. Harlow and Matthew. Harlow and Matthew and his parents. Harlow and Matthew, Meena and his parents. Matthew and Harlow, Gerald and Elsbeth and Uncle Robert. The entire Smith family with Matthew. Robbie and Matthew. Matthew and Robbie and the Smith girls.

Finally, someone said, "Cynthia, over here, we're getting a picture of everyone!" and she went over, forced a smile until Addison's camera timer went off, then went back to her seat in the corner of the yard.

Matthew was another star in a family laden with stars . . . Elsbeth and her paintings, Addison and her money, Lark with medical school and her sweetness, Robbie with his good looks and so-called charm. Uncle Robert was, of course, the patriarch. Gerald was more of a secondary character, as his only job seemed to be to agree with his wife. Neither Winnie nor Harlow had ever been headliners, though Harlow had certainly drawn attention to herself this summer. And somewhere trailing far, far behind in the rankings was Cynthia herself.

She wished everyone here could've seen her gracious home in Kansas City. Both of her gracious homes. She wished she could show them pictures of Henry and her at galas and dinners, black tie, her Givenchy dress and emerald earrings, now sold to ensure she wasn't homeless. She'd never invited Gerald and Elsbeth or their children to visit her and Henry, but now she wished she had, just so they could've seen her in her element and respected her a bit more.

Here she was, a woman in late middle age, scratching out a living at a bookstore, going home to an embarrassing little shack, sleeping with a vagrant man, watching from the distant border of the Smith family, included only for Uncle Robert's sake.

Suddenly, she couldn't wait to meet her half sisters. She would write to Nancy tonight.

TWENTY-SIX

HARLOW

After I had the baby and moved to Colorado Springs for the rest of my college days, I made some decisions.

I would not think about the baby. That chapter was over. When he did cross my mind (at first, every ten seconds, then twenty, then every two minutes, then every five, then every ten), I'd repeat a mantra. *You did the right thing. He's not yours anymore. You did the right thing. He's not yours anymore.*

Matthew . . . well, whatever they named him . . . he probably had a great life. I'd done my best to give him to a family who'd love him. My work was done.

I refused postpartum counseling and didn't return Jen's calls once I'd moved. When I went home for Christmas that December, I was less patient with the Littles, who weren't so little anymore. I spent more and more time with Grammy and Grandpop, less with my parents. Mom and Dad grated on me . . . all that affection with each other, their little inside jokes. It was my parents' world, and we were just evidence of it. They didn't even notice I was giving them the cold shoulder, and that irked me even more.

In my junior year of college, I had a boyfriend who could best be described as "nice." Eventually, we slept together, me on the pill *and* with an IUD, him wearing a condom that I watched him put on, every time. After a couple months of mediocre sex, we agreed to break up. Senior year, I had an excellent flirtation going on with a guy in my building. We had some very hot make-out sessions, but no sex.

Sometimes at night, I'd jolt awake, gasping, confused, wisps of a dream melting away. I swore I could smell that newborn scent, the tiny eyebrows, the warmth of his soft, soft skin, that little squawk, the incredible rush of love when my son had been in my arms, skin against skin, heart against heart, for that one perfect minute.

You did the right thing. He's not yours anymore. Memories were a monster bursting out of a closet, and like Hodor in *Game of Thrones*, I had to guard the door, lean against the door, bolster the fucking door so the monster would stay in and I wouldn't be eaten alive.

I kept up my grades, because studying all the time didn't leave a lot of room for thinking about other things. When I got my LSAT score, I found I was in the top 2 percent nationwide. Rosie had said outright that she hoped we could live together after college, so without telling her, I applied to UCLA Law, since they gave out full scholarships to people who'd overcome "personal, educational or socioeconomic hardships." Almost as if I were writing about someone else, I dashed off an essay about being pregnant my freshman year and graduating summa cum laude. They gave me the money.

When I told Rosie, she burst into tears. "Thank you, Lolo. This means the world to me. Hand to God, you're my only real friend."

She had moved for me; this time, I'd move for her. Her dad found us a lovely apartment near the law school, telling me I was a good influence on Rosie.

By the time I started law school, she was a full-time location scout. She traveled a lot, was always cajoling and charming permit people or homeowners on the phone when she was home. "Come on," she might say. "It's only six weeks. For the rest of your life, you can say that Michael B. Jordan was naked in your house. Right? Okay, fantastic! A picture with him? Let me see what I can do."

Law school was all about reading and absorbing long, random facts, boiling down those ridiculous run-on sentences into something that actually made sense. It kept me occupied, and my grades were good. My real goal was to stay away from the black hole of grief. I'd be fine. I already was. Hell, I was killing it.

"Can you see Reese Witherspoon stabbing someone here?" Rosie might yell over the music of the most recent celebrity DJ when she dragged me out. "I don't know about the lighting, though. Let's go to the Warwick. I can't hear myself think here, and they have the best cocktails ever. Thank you, DreamWorks!"

At the end of my first year, Mr. Wolfe offered me a summer internship at his firm, which I accepted. Interns there had a helluva salary, too, more than my father made in a *year*, since everything in LA was about excess. My bank account swelled.

Only my love for Rosie seemed genuine. She said she felt more confident around me, so I'd go out with her whenever I could manage it. If she hit a snafu or got yelled at, I'd comfort and encourage her. If she drank too much, I'd make her drink a glass of water and take Motrin before tucking her in. Because I always got up first, I set up the coffeepot for her and made sure there was an easy breakfast option so she'd eat. In return, she accepted this new version of me and loved me anyway.

My parents came to visit with Robbie, and we did all the touristy stuff, the studio tours, Disneyland. Robbie was now as tall as I was, the little bastard. We had fun. We did.

There was just one thing I couldn't bear, and that was a

baby. Any baby. If I saw a stroller coming my way, I'd cross the street. If one of my classmates brought in their baby, I wouldn't go over to coo. When Mom mentioned that one of my former classmates had given birth, I'd murmured, "Nice," and let it slide right out of my head.

Don't go there. You did the right thing. He's not yours anymore.

In February of my third year of law school, just three months until graduation, an office waiting for me at Wolfe-Greenberg, my carefully built world imploded. No particular reason, no trigger. It was just time, I guess.

Rosie went on an extended scouting trip to Normandy for a World War II film. Her mom was flying out to take her to Paris afterward, so she'd be gone two full weeks. It would be the longest time I'd been alone since the summer I had the baby in that sad, echoing dorm.

On the first morning without her, I met with my adviser on a securities regulation project and sat there, nodding, tapping away at my laptop, not processing a thing she said. Finally, she gently touched my arm and asked, "Harlow, are you feeling okay? You seem a little off."

I was about to say, *Yes, of course*, but instead, I said, "I think I'm coming down with something."

"Go home, then. We can pick this up on Friday."

"Thanks," I said.

A day off in the middle of the week. That *never* happened. I got home, stripped out of my dress and cropped cardigan ("power casual," Rosie called it), and went to bed. Maybe I *was* sick, because I slept the rest of the day. Around 8 p.m., I woke up, ordered a pizza and ate the entire thing while channel surfing, then went back to bed.

When my alarm went off in the morning, I turned it off,

switched my phone to Do Not Disturb and fell back asleep. There was nothing different about that day. Nothing remarkable, nothing noteworthy. Just . . . nah. Didn't feel like it. I wasn't sick. I was just . . . here. I ordered Chinese food that night and ate it while watching *Dexter*, then fell asleep on the couch.

By the third day, I had a few texts from my law school friends and my adviser. I didn't bother responding. That night, I ordered delivery from a Cuban restaurant, inspired by Dexter's food choices in Miami. That was the deepest thought I'd had in days.

By the seventh day, my phone was irritatingly full of unanswered calls and texts. None from my parents, I noted, but three from Winnie and two from Lark.

Really busy with school, I texted Winnie, knowing she'd tell anyone else not to worry. I'll call soon. The effort of that text was exhausting, and as soon as I hit send, the phone dropped out of my hand and thunked to the floor.

By the time the two weeks had passed, I hadn't been out of the apartment in six days, and that had only been so I could get food from the taco truck down the block. My hair was matted at this point, and I felt bloated and weak, but didn't have the energy to do anything about it. Take-out containers and pizza boxes littered the apartment, and I was rewatching all of *Dexter*. Dexter and I would get along just fine. Both of us were just pretending to be human.

Rosie banged into the apartment with her pale blue suitcase, kicked off her shoes. She said some words to me in what seemed like a cheery tone, but I couldn't quite make them out. When she came into the living room, I didn't have the energy to lift my head and look at her.

"Harlow?" Rosie asked. "You okay? You look like death. Are you sick?"

I heard her from a distant place.

"Lolo?" she asked. "Harlow? Hey. Snap out of it."

I managed to turn my head. "Hi." I'd forgotten about her blue highlights. "You look cute."

"What's going on?" she asked. "You smell *horrible*."

"Oh. Sorry."

"Are you drunk?" she asked.

I thought about it. No, I was pretty sure alcohol and I had not been mingling recently. "I don't think so."

"Did you take something? What's wrong with you, hon? You're scaring me!"

I just looked at her, slightly confused. On the TV, Dexter Saran-wrapped another victim. So tidy.

Rosie turned off the TV and knelt in front of me, taking my hands. "Harlow? Talk to me."

"I . . . I don't know what's wrong."

"Is this about the baby?"

"What baby?" I asked, confused. We didn't know a baby.

"Oh, God. Something's wrong. I'm taking you to the hospital." She stood up and pulled out her phone.

"Oh, *my* baby," I said. "No. Nope. No. It's not. I mean . . . he's not really mine, though, is he?" The way it had felt when he hiccupped inside me. My hand on my bump, as if I could soothe him when he rolled and kicked. That incredible slide when he came out of me on the last superhuman push, miraculously whole and healthy. Oh, his soft, soft skin. His little limbs moving against me. His tiny eyebrows. The smell of him, fresh from my body, fresh from God. The way he'd opened his eyes and all the secrets in the universe shone forth. We'd stared into each other's eyes . . . and then, and then . . .

I had given him away.

A wail of anguish came out of my mouth, emanating from every cell in my body. I didn't know why now, but it was *brutal*, this pain. If there was any mercy in the world, I'd burst into flames and be done with it. Rosie dropped her phone and clutched me tight, but I couldn't stop the sounds, the wrenching of my lungs, my hands fisting in my hair, pulling hard. I slid to the floor, huddling, howling like a wolf caught in a trap.

Rosie called 911 and I was taken to the ER. By then, I had cried so hard, a blood vessel had burst in my eye. Rosie talked to them in a whisper, glancing my way, wiping away tears of her own. Her father came and made paternal noises, touched my head, asked if they could call my parents. I said no. Absolutely not. They gave me a sedative and I fell into sleep, still shaking with sobs even as the world slipped away.

The next morning, a psychiatrist assessed me, prescribed meds, said a lot of words. I spent a few more days there on the psych ward, sleeping a black, deep sleep when the little pills came, staring into nothingness until they came again.

Then Mr. Wolfe—Victor, I was supposed to call him, though I didn't—came to the hospital with Rosie. "I'm sorry you're going through this, sweetheart," he said, and the endearment made my eyes fill. He patted my hand. "This happens to my clients all the time. Rosie told me what happened your freshman year, and given all that, it's completely understandable. You're going to have a nice little vacation of sorts, get some counseling, figure this out. Okay? Don't worry, after all you've done for Rosie, it's on me. You're going to be fine."

I wasn't sure what I'd done for Rosie, but *vacation* wasn't exactly a euphemism. The Willows in Santa Monica was a treatment facility for people like me . . . people having a nervous breakdown, or *mental health crisis*, as it was now called. *Your mind, body and soul will heal*, the mosaic in the lobby promised. Sounded good to me.

It was the nicest place I'd ever stayed. Beautiful grounds, a room overlooking the ocean, the most comfortable bed in the world. We patients (clients) were fed by a Michelin-starred chef three times a day, all organic food, as much as we wanted, plus healthy, organic, sugar-free, gluten-free cookies before bed (shockingly delicious). We started the day with yoga and meditation, followed by talks with a psychiatrist and various therapists. We were offered acupuncture, daily massage, hypnosis, hyperbaric therapy, group therapy, vitamin infusions, cleanses, Reiki, motivational exercises, somatic experiencing therapy, sound therapy, art therapy. We could go for runs or take a swim in the Pacific (supervised, of course).

My shrink said I had experienced acute loss and trauma caused by placing my baby for adoption, resulting in post-traumatic stress disorder. Because I had never fully processed the pregnancy, birth, adoption and grief, those feelings had waited for me. The monster in the closet had finally burst through. She said that stuffing those memories down just didn't work, and not sharing the burden of grief had intensified it. In a nutshell, what happened to me was a normal reaction to what I had been through. I was a person who had suffered a trauma by giving up my baby, and this recovery process was necessary.

The other Willows clients were like me. There was a woman there who had found her husband hanging in the garage one Thursday evening just before they were supposed to have dinner with their friends. A middle-aged man had lost a child to cancer. Another man had alienated every person he'd loved because of his addiction to Oxycontin. A young actor with bipolar disorder had just lost a huge acting job because he wouldn't stay on script and talked nonstop for four days until he collapsed from exhaustion.

It was comforting to be around other broken people. We could carry these scars, and we would, as long as we did the work to let the wound heal, as it were. It was hard to picture myself as anything but that sad teenager, that failed mother who'd handed her baby over to someone else. But day by day, I was given a different message. I could be healthy and happy and strong. I could grow from that broken place and be better for it. A flower growing through a crack in the pavement, as it were.

I was at the Willows for just over a month, and it helped. More than I expected, really. Rosie and her dad visited. The healthy food and exercise cleansed and strengthened my body. The therapy let me grieve and find ways to cope. The young actor went on to become a pretty big star, and I always felt a little thrill when I saw him in a movie, happy for his success and the way he advocated for mental health.

At the end of my stay, my therapist asked what my next step was going to be. "I'm going home," I said. "Back east." I needed to be back on the Cape, with its mighty ocean and glorious bays and inlets. I ached for my family, another thing I'd suppressed for the past seven years—how much I loved them. I missed my siblings, my grandparents, Mom and Dad like crazy. I didn't want to be a lawyer. I didn't know *what* I wanted, except to be near my family again, to get back to being my old self . . . the responsible one, the one who was never any trouble.

My therapist said she didn't think I should keep my experience a secret, but she also understood how difficult it would be for my family to hear it seven years after the fact. My parents were disappointed and confused by my decision to leave law school.

"It's certainly a surprise," Dad said, "but if this is where you need to be, then this is where you should be."

I found a therapist and stayed with her for the next three years. I poured myself into Open Book. I took long walks and bought a kayak. Helped Addie plan her wedding, drove down to Boston to see Lark in med school, advocated for Robbie when he told our parents he didn't want to go to college. When Grammy's cancer came back, I was there. Mr. Silva helped me put a kitchen into the second floor, and my apartment became IKEA-chic. I discovered, bit by bit, that I was . . . okay. I was doing fine, and that was enough for now.

I didn't feel lonely. I had my family, and there was always something going on at the bookstore. Addie got married and had the kids. Robbie became a boat mechanic. Winnie and I took a vacation together to England. After Grammy died, Grandpop leaned on me, and I was there for him. We discovered we liked those Russian car crash videos on YouTube, as well as animal rescue clips. Grandpop and I sometimes held hands as we watched TV, the two of us alone together.

On my son's thirteenth birthday, I went to Nauset Beach in Orleans. I always took this day off, and always disappeared from my family. This particular day was unsympathetically beautiful, and I figured I'd take my kayak out and see if I could find some seals and maybe glimpse a shark.

As I was unloading my kayak, I heard a little sound from an SUV with New Jersey plates. Cupping my hands around my eyes, I peered in the window. At first, I didn't see anything and thought I must've imagined the noise. It might've been a seagull or some other bird, or just a kid squeaking on the beach. Just as I turned away, I heard it again. I looked more closely. "Hello?" I said, and there it was, a little movement. A tail.

Some asshole had left their dog in a closed car on a day when it was at least 85 degrees.

I had one of those little devices on my key chain—a window breaker, the kind with a blade to cut a seat belt in case someone was stuck in a car. Those car crash / animals-in-need videos had taught me well. I pressed the blunt end against the front passenger window, so the dog wouldn't be hit with exploding glass, and bam! The window broke. I pressed the unlock button, opened the back door and saw a black-and-tan puppy with longish fur. He was panting dryly, too exhausted to lift his head.

But his tail moved the slightest bit.

"I've got you, sweetheart," I said, and I scooped him up and ran across the hot sand to the ocean, laying him in the cool, wet sand and yelling for people to bring drinking water.

Long story short, the family had lost interest in the puppy (monsters). I offered to take him and renamed him Oliver Twist on the spot. Obviously, I didn't have to pay for the broken window. The *Cape Cod Times* did a story on me with a photo of me kissing a now energetic and happy dog. I became locally famous and didn't pay for a single drink for a month. Sales at Open Book spiked for a week or so.

But better than any of that . . . I had a dog who loved me more than anyone else, even Grandpop, and I guess I had needed that. Technically, I had saved him, but we all knew he really saved me. It seemed like a sign that it had happened on my son's thirteenth birthday.

Life was good. It was fine.

That's what I thought, anyway, until my son came back to me.

TWENTY-SEVEN

MONICA

So far, the summer had been exhausting, and it was only halfway over. Emotionally exhausting, physically, spiritually, mentally, everything. Flying across the country every week or ten days was too much. Monica hadn't known she'd have to; the original plan had been to fly out with Meena for a few days, come back for a week in July and two more in August. That plan went down the toilet when Matthew found Harlow.

And speaking of Matthew, he'd informed Monica via text that Harlow would be baking his birthday cake. That was it. The whole message. Harlow's gonna make my birthday cake this year. The little fucker.

Monica had always baked the kids' cakes and decorated them elaborately—the cake that had been shaped like a dump truck, spilling Oreo cookie crumbs from the back. The castle cake for Meena's fifth, four turrets and a drawbridge over a hot chocolate moat. The *Death Star* cake. The mermaid cake. The Pikachu cake. The one she'd made for Matthew last year, showing him in his bed, under the covers, clothes strewn around his room. He had loved it. Laughed so hard when he saw it.

But now *Harlow* was baking her son's birthday cake, and really, fuck that. He could have at least asked her if she minded. He had taken a huge step away from her this past year, and this summer, taken a huge step toward Harlow. She understood his need to know Harlow. She didn't blame him. But God, it hurt, his casual comments about spending time with her, how much fun he'd had with his uncle and great-grandfather, how he was learning to paint from his grandmother. How cool and young and athletic Harlow was, kayaking and swimming. The two of them had gone for a six-mile run yesterday. Matthew had never asked her to go for a run with him. Ever.

So far, she'd been to the Cape four times in six weeks. Yes, she flew first class. Yes, she had a car service to take her to and from each airport. Yes, her boss had begrudgingly given her the time, though she was expected to work from home (and on the plane). "Even though we pride ourselves on flexibility for mothers," Peter had begun.

"Parents," she said. "Flexibility for parents."

"Whatever. Even so, don't get too comfortable, Monica. We need you here or with our clients." He paused. "Don't forget promotions are coming at the end of August."

It was a veiled threat. Produce or lose. And Monica wanted that promotion, because it would give her more visibility in the industry, more recognition and more money. Enough money, she'd calculated, to let her retire four years earlier than she planned (unless stress killed her first, of course). It would've been easier to stay home and put in the hours at the office or flying to whichever client's security system had been breached.

But Matthew needed a close eye, and Sanjay was the mellow parent. The nice parent. The fun parent. Monica was the one who noticed the subtleties in his behavior, the lack of eye contact, for example, that said he was up to something. "You're reading into things too much," Sanjay had said the night before she left the Cape this last time. He'd been massaging her shoulders, even though it would take hours before her knots would loosen up. "We need to make love more often," he'd whispered, and while she loved her husband very much, she'd wanted to stab him right then. "Relax you."

"This massage is relaxing," she said.

"I can relax you in many ways, my queen," he said, and she was glad her back was to him, because she rolled her eyes.

It wasn't that she wanted him to be or do anything different. But sometimes, it felt like Sanjay got to live on a much nicer planet than she did. He was so . . . happy. It was something she loved about him, the thing that had attracted her to him the first day they met in college. He'd been leaning in a doorway, so relaxed, and he simply smiled at her, a smile so beautiful and warm, she literally stopped in her tracks. She knew she tended to be anxious and overachieving, and he got her to slow down. And she was good for him, too, something his mother often told her, focusing him, helping him find a field he loved after several misfires, making him stop acting quite so much like the baby of the family and more of a family man.

But God, she was tired. Sanjay simply told her she needed to step back a bit. "Don't worry about everything," he said, as if he'd never met her. "Make time for yourself when you're home." Sure. Like that happened. She hadn't been to yoga in three months. She hadn't seen her closest friend, Michelle, since her birthday in April. Self-care felt like another chore.

She wanted to go back in time to when her son had held her hand and begged her to tuck him in. She wanted to hold her infant girl in her arms and rock her to sleep. She wanted to quit her job and become a florist.

But she needed to figure out how Matthew could be at peace,

because now that he'd met Harlow, the inevitable insecurity would come. *Why didn't you keep me? What would I be like if you had?* She needed to make sure Meena didn't feel lost this summer. She needed to spend more time with her husband, having fun. She needed to return Sita's call and assure her all was well on Cape Cod. She needed to be gracious and welcoming to Harlow. She needed to visit her parents and sister, and she needed to be a star at work while not creating any resentment among her colleagues.

The weight of it all pressed down on her like a lead blanket.

Sanjay was going to fix that with . . . sex?

She said yes. After all, she also needed to make sure Sanjay didn't feel neglected. Oh, the sex was lovely. It always was. He took his time to make sure she was satisfied, and if she could shut off her brain—or conversely, force her brain to focus on him—sex was great. But afterward, she had to get up and shower so she wouldn't smell like sex in the morning when the kids woke up. When she got into bed, she wished he'd rub her shoulders again, but he was already asleep.

It was almost a relief to come back to California and not be around her family; at the same time, she constantly felt on the verge of tears because she was away from her family.

Tonight, she was working from home. The house was quiet and clean, thanks to Sheryl, their housekeeper. It was nine o'clock. Monica hadn't eaten but felt too brain-weary to go through the process of ordering something. Popcorn and wine would be fine.

For three days, she'd been putting out a fire for one of their biggest clients, working twelve or fourteen hours each day. Now she had to write another best practices protocol, one that might sink in this time. The client was a chemical company filled with scientists, engineers, PhDs and physicians. The CEO, CFO and

COO and more than half the staff had graduated from Ivy League or better schools—Stanford, Georgetown, Cal Poly, Notre Dame, Tulane. One would assume the employees would be smart. One would be wrong.

At least, they were not smart when it came to common sense. In her analysis, she learned that the CFO had answered phishing emails telling him he'd just won a $500 gift card from Costco. The man made $13 million a year before bonuses. A senior chemical engineer had accepted fifty-four invitations on social media from people she didn't know. The head of patents had been sexting with someone he met online, clicked on what was promised to be a dick pick, and unleashed a virus. All of this had been done on company computers and the corporate server. Data breaches galore. Proprietary information insecure. Financial records out there for all the world to see.

More than 90% of our data breaches come from human error, she wrote. We cannot fight cybercrime without you, our employees. You, each of you, carry the responsibility of making Santé Chemical secure. Stop watching porn, you idiots, stop taking personality quizzes that ask for your birthday, and read the fucking manual.

She deleted the last sentence with a sigh.

Sometimes, having it all felt a lot like punishment.

TWENTY-EIGHT

HARLOW

After the picnic, my family battled for time with my son, and he was more than willing to hang out with all of them. Mom invited the Patels to Long Pond Arts and proudly showed them Matthew's painting from the picnic, hung in a place of honor. It was quite pretty . . . the sky and sea with a little seagull in the corner. Very Cape Cod–ish. Mom had printed up a little card—*The Harbor at Dusk, pastels, Matthew R. Patel. NFS.*

"What does NFS mean?" Meena asked.

"Not for sale," Mom answered. "Because I'm keeping it forever."

Winnie took Matthew and Meena to one of her events, a five-year-old's birthday party. She texted me a picture of him and Meena and a mass of tiny kids inside a huge bounce house, and I smiled to see my son with little kids. He and Lark rode their bikes down the rail trail, stopping for ice cream twice. Addison and Nicole had him over for lunch so he could get to know his cousins. Robbie took him and Dad out on his boat, and Matthew got a little seasick but proclaimed it a great day just the same.

However, the next time he and I got together, things felt weird between us.

It was a cloudy day, chillier than usual with highs only in the low sixties, despite the fact that it was July. (New England didn't care much about the calendar when it came to weather.) The sky was gloomy with occasional spits of rain and mist, but Matthew said no to the movies or wandering around P-town. We settled on hiking the Great Island Trail, which was about eight miles and showed the Cape's best features—pitch pine forest, sandy dunes, views of Cape Cod Bay and Wellfleet Harbor, Great Island Beach.

He met me at the trailhead on Chequessett Neck Road, and we started off. The trail was a big loop or a small loop, depending on how much hiking you wanted. I figured we'd take the long route, giving us more time together, and headed inland through the pitch pines.

"Where's Ollie?" he asked.

"At the store. He hates the rain. He swims, goes out on the kayak almost every day, but if water falls from the sky, he's terrified." I waited for a response. None came. "Also, dogs aren't allowed on the trail. Too many nesting birds."

Matthew grunted. Our feet crunched on the path. At first, I pointed out various birds and plants, a horseshoe crab shell, but got very little response. Okay, then. We'd just walk in silence.

"Everything okay?" I asked after a half hour of this.

"Yeah."

"Seems like there's something you want to say."

He side-eyed me. "Nope." A chipmunk darted across the path.

"Okay. But if there is, you can tell me anything, you know." God. It sounded so trite.

He said nothing, just increased his pace a little. Message received. It was inevitable that I'd see the grumpy side of Matthew. Teenager on the cusp of adulthood with all this change, all these new people . . . it was normal, I hoped.

"I'm glad you never had another kid," he said abruptly, stopping at the top of a hill. "I always pictured you with other kids, kids you wanted, and it . . . it sucked."

"Matthew, I did want you. You know that." The wind gusted hard, making the seagrass ripple.

"Yeah. But you also *didn't* want me. Even though you have this awesome family who could've helped out. I mean, I figured you were from seriously dysfunctional shit, but here you are, like, the most normal family in the world, and you all get along. I lost out on all that."

I took a slow breath of the heavy salt air, wanting to get my next words right. "There was always something that would've been lost no matter what route I took. If I got an abortion, obviously that was a loss. If I kept you, you would've been one of a mob of kids, raised by a teenage mother and your grandparents. It wouldn't have been hell, but I wanted better than that for you. And if I'd kept you, you wouldn't have had your parents and Meena."

"Yeah, Harlow, I *know.* I'm just saying. Can we go now?"

"Sure. Whatever you want, honey."

"Can you not call me that? It feels weird."

"Of course." It stung. We kept going, rounding Jeremy Point and coming to the beach section of the hike. It was low tide, so the sand was firm and wet. Given the weather, we hardly saw anyone else.

I knew I didn't have the right to weigh in on his mood. He had good reason to feel conflicted and upset. But I was beginning to get a fuller picture of my son. He was smart, funny, loving, irritable, sulky, a bit spoiled. I knew I wasn't his mother in the traditional sense, and I wasn't his friend, either.

His moodiness sent a trickle of fear through me. Would this summer deteriorate into blame and accusations? I didn't want our time together to be about the road not taken, as much as I'd fantasized about the past. Maybe Matthew needed to do that, though—picture himself in the heart of my family—but honestly, I didn't know how to handle it. It felt more like an issue for a therapist. I'd talk to Monica about it, but while she'd been completely gracious so far, I sensed her . . . distrust. Or her protectiveness. She was waiting for something to go wrong. I could feel it.

When we'd finished the loop, Matthew went to his car. "By the way," he said, "my parents want to have dinner tonight with you and Gran and Poppy."

"Oh! Great! I'll let my parents know."

That night, we met for dinner at C-Shore, a cool, rather hip place across from the Audubon Sanctuary. I thought Meena and Matthew might like it.

It seemed my son's mood had not improved. He acted impatient and bored, only lighting up when my parents spoke to him.

"Sanjay and Monica, you have so much to be proud of," Dad said as we looked at our menus. "What wonderful people you've raised!"

"You sure did a great job," Mom said, reaching for Matthew's hand.

"Yes. Thank you," I said, then cringed inwardly. What an awkward thing for me to say.

Monica looked at me with a weird expression. "Well. Thank *you*, Harlow. But yes, we worked very hard raising both our children."

"How would you know? You're always working," Matthew said. Wow. Full-on sulky teenager.

"Matt! Totally unfair, buddy," Sanjay said.

"Seriously, Matt, what bug is up your butt?" Meena said.

"Apologize to your mother," Sanjay said.

"Sorry," he muttered. Monica's cheeks flushed, but she said nothing.

"It's so hard to find a balance," Mom said. "I worked, too, and with five kids, it wasn't easy."

I suddenly felt like saying something similar to what Matthew had just said.

"Child-rearing was *grueling*," Sanjay said, breaking the awkward vibe. "Matthew used to poop behind the couch every morning. He'd take off his diaper first, of course. How old were you then, son? Fifteen?"

"Funny, Dad," he said.

"What about me, Daddy?" Meena asked. "What did I do that was gross?"

Sanjay looked stumped.

"You used to hide dishes in your room rather than take them downstairs," Monica said. "Remember when I found the ice cream bowl in your sock drawer? The smell of rancid milk? I almost threw up."

Meena beamed proudly and rested her head against her mom's. "Gross," she said.

"Yes, you are," Matthew shot back, and suddenly, he was the charming, impish boy again who loved his sister. He shoulder-bumped Monica, and she gave him a faint smile and patted his hand. "Love you, Ma," he said.

"Love you, too," she said, and this time her face flushed with love.

This is what a parent is, I thought. This was what I had missed. The daily currents and undercurrents of moods, sibling dynamics, inside jokes, teenage irritability. The instant forgiveness of a parent.

"By the way," Sanjay said, "July twenty-fifth is fast approaching, and of course, we'd love to have you all come to Matthew's birthday party. The whole crew."

My parents exclaimed with joy and asked what they could bring. I looked at Monica and gave her a slight nod of thanks.

July twenty-fifth. I'd be with my son on his birthday as he became a legal adult. For the first time ever, I'd get to celebrate his birthday. I was even baking his cake.

So I ran into our trivia hottie this morning," Rosie said later that night when we were watching *Game of Thrones*, Season Three, Episode Five, in which Jon Snow shags Ygritte, thus breaking his vow of celibacy. "Oh, rewind that part. Can you slo-mo it? He asked about you."

I obeyed. "Who asked about me? Jon Snow or Grady or Lillie or my grandfather?"

She threw a piece of popcorn at me. "Grady. He likes you."

My cheeks felt hot. "Well, we've known each other since third grade, I think."

"Don't be obtuse," she said. "He's a unicorn. Hot, dorky, smart, nice, and my God, his arms, Harlow! I bet he can do five hundred pull-ups." She ate another fistful of popcorn. "It's time you got back on the horse and started dating, and not just that fuckboy cellist you bang once in a while."

"'That fuckboy cellist I bang once in a while.' Hallmark, are you listening?" I said. "About Grady . . . he has a four-year-old and he's still getting over his divorce. Besides, I can't see myself with someone who has a kid."

"Everyone else can. I personally think you'd be a great stepmother. Marry my father and be mine."

I snorted. But then I hit pause and looked at my pal. "Theoretically, how could I raise someone else's child when I didn't do that for my own?"

"You move in," Rosie said, "and you start making peanut butter and jelly sandwiches. It goes from there."

"Teeny bit more complicated than that, I'm pretty sure." I did like Gray, of course. And found him attractive. But he'd been shafted by one woman who had abandoned her kid. I didn't see myself on the list of appropriate women. Besides, his daughter was so young. What if it didn't work out? How would that affect her? What would Matthew think?

Rosie shoved the popcorn bowl at me. "I never accepted Ygritte," she said. "Kind of loved the idea of Jon Snow being pure." She leaned back against the couch pillows and sighed happily.

"Rosie . . ." I began, not wanting to kill the mood.

"Go ahead. I sense a lecture coming."

"Well, I was just wondering if everything's okay at work. You've been here for a month now."

"Getting sick of me?"

"No. But you're not on your phone all the time, or looking up housing codes in Spain or Patagonia."

"Did I tell you we got Clooney to agree to let us use his Lake Como house? I may actually meet him."

"So you're still working?"

"Sort of. I'm on a break. Much deserved, I should add." She refilled her glass of wine. "More for you?"

"I'm good," I said. "I'm a mother now. I have to be responsible and shit."

"Guess I'll be childless for life, then." She tossed a piece of popcorn at me, then rewound once again. "If I can't have Jon Snow's baby, I'm not having anyone's."

Friday night and, once again, trivia night. Last time, the King-slayers had won by 340 points, getting every single answer right, smiting our foes.

Matthew was away for the weekend. Monica had taken him back to California for five days to have a doctor's appointment before school started. Seemed like a long time to be gone for a doctor's appointment, but I guessed Monica probably wanted some time alone with him. She'd had eighteen years, of course. I wasn't happy he'd be gone so long.

But I had to admit, I felt a little more normal back at trivia night without him. It had been so new, being a parent this month, always afraid I'd say the wrong thing. Tonight, though, I was on sure footing. I wore my lucky *GoT* T-shirt—*I drink and I know things.* Rosie, on the other hand, wore a long, loose-fitting dress, red eye shadow and black lipstick, and it all looked amazing together.

We knocked on Grandpop's door, then went in.

"Oh!" he said. "I forgot! Well, I'm so sorry, girls, but I have a date with that lovely . . . now, what was her name? The one you met."

"Frances?" I said.

"Yes! She's coming here for dinner, and after we eat, she said she'd cut my toenails."

"So romantic," Rosie said.

"*I* usually cut your toenails, Grandpop," I said. "Have I been fired?"

"No, no, of course not, honey. I just thought she should know what she's getting into before we're married."

"Well, if she still wants to see you again after tonight," I said, "you have a winner. Good night!" I smooched his cheek.

Rosie did the same. "I'm not gonna lie. I'm a little jealous, Mr. Smith."

"Is that right!" Grandpop said proudly. "Maybe you can trim my ear hair, if that would make you feel better."

We snort-laughed our way to the sidewalk. I noticed that Rosie was a little unsteady. "You okay?" I asked.

"Yeah, yeah. I had a glass of wine on an empty tummy," she said.

"I'll run up and make you a sandwich. It'll take five minutes."

"Nah. The Ice House has so many carbs to choose from. It's wicked pissah," she said.

"Very good Massachusetts speak!"

"That's the thing. Californians don't have an accent," she said, slowing down her speech and relaxing her jaw. "Like, Killa-fornia? We don't have *inny* accent. We just let our jaws hang so our mouths don't close all the way? So our vowels can go on, like, waaayy too long. And we sound like we're asking a question? But we're not? And like, we loovve street names. You gonna take the 405? Ew. I'm taking Se*puul*veda. Man! Anyone got weed? Thanks, compadre! I'm, like, totally stressed."

I countered with, "Hon, theah's a dispensry on every othah cawnah heah. Just don't make a left on Six, cuz the traffic's backed up to the Prawvincetown. Some asshole sawr a shahk at Mah-coni, and the turrists ah outta control, bro, mahk my weurds."

"I have no idea what you just said," she laughed, and we giggled all the way to the restaurant.

The Ice House bar was packed, as it was now high season on the Cape. We went to the Kingslayers' table. Lillie was already at the bar, getting our customary beers and ordering our nachos.

I went up to her to help carry the glasses, ordering seltzer for Rosie.

"I heard things are going great with your son," Lillie said. "Saw him at the Fairway. He was with his sister and dad. Looks just like you."

She saw the resemblance! After eighteen years of trying not to think about him, this kind of statement was a shot of pure adrenaline.

We made our way to the table with the drinks and some napkins. Grady came over with the trivia sheets and pencils and sat next to me.

"Hey," he said. "How are you?"

"Harlow, tell me about Gray when he was in high school," Rosie commanded, putting me on the spot. I widened my eyes at her a fraction, hoping she'd get the *knock it off* vibe I was trying to send.

"Grady Byrne was the nicest boy at Nauset," I said. "Smartest, too."

"And you guys were friends?"

"Absolutely."

"Best friends?" she asked.

Grady cocked his head and gave a half smile.

"Well, one of my best friends," I said.

"Really?" Gray said. "I don't remember that part."

"Are you about to disillusion me, Grady Byrne?" Was I flirting? I think I was.

Gray looked at me, that slow, *here it comes, wait for it . . . bam!* smile. My stomach curled in on itself, a warm, squishy, tingling feeling spreading through me.

"You're very cute, Gray," Rosie pronounced. "I like your beard. Long enough not to be sandpaper, short enough so you don't look like a Confederate soldier in a POW camp. Well done, sir. Well done."

"Thanks for the vote of confidence," he said, smiling at me. *She's a hoot,* his expression said. I had seen it a thousand times.

"Heard you're divorced," she said. "Was it awful?"

"Rosie needs food," I said. "Where are our nachos?"

Just then, the server set down a monstrous platter. "Nachos, no beans, extra salsa, extra guacamole, extra jalapeños, extra cheese. Enjoy!"

"I love nutrition," I said.

"So eat some broccoli tomorrow," Lillie said, taking a slab.

"Oh, miss? Can I have a vodka martini, straight up, stirred, no fruit? Thanks."

Lillie glanced at me. "We're walking home," I told her.

"Rosie," said Grady, "you need to stay sober enough to answer all the TV and movie questions."

"And pop music," Lillie added. "Remember when we picked Adele instead of Olivia Rodrigo? Even my father knew the answer."

"*That's* embarrassing," Rosie said.

Robbie tapped the mic. "Welcome to the Outer Cape trivia tournament. The winners tonight will go to the All-Cape semifinals!"

Everyone cheered.

"I love these people!" Rosie yelled.

"Maybe keep an eye on her," Lillie whispered. I nodded. Rosie always seemed to have three livers. Sloppy wasn't in her repertoire. I should've made her that sandwich before we left.

"Tonight," Robbie said, "our teams are the Beach Bums; Blood, Sweat and Beers; Sherlock Homies; and in the bloodthirsty battle for first place in the Outer Cape Division and with it all on the line, we have I See Dumb People and the King-slayers!"

"I love our name," Rosie said.

"How can we be tied?" I asked.

"They won two games in May," Lillie said. "Ben lorded it over me for weeks."

At the sound of his name, Ben got up, picked Lillie up right out of her chair and smooched her. A real kiss. I hadn't had a kiss like that . . . well, maybe ever. James and I kissed, of course, but there was no love in it. Besides, I couldn't remember the last time I'd seen him. Romantically, that is.

Lillie was flushed and smiling when he set her back down. "This means nothing," she told Ben. "We're still gonna kick your ass tonight."

"Try," Ben said.

"Robbie!" barked Mr. Silva. "Let's get it going in here!"

"Yes, sir! Question number one," Robbie said. "What is the highest-grossing Broadway show of all time? Is it (A) *Phantom of the Opera*, (B) *Hamilton*, (C) *A Chorus Line*, or (D) *The Lion King*?"

Our heads came together in our huddle. "*Hamilton*?" Grady suggested.

"Gotta be," said Rosie. "It's been on tour all over the world. I've seen it six times."

"I think it's *The Lion King*," I said.

"I don't know," Lillie whispered. "*Phantom* was on Broadway for eons."

"Think about the power of Disney," I whispered.

"But everyone's seen *Hamilton*," Rosie said. "Seriously. Even a few Republicans. Second thoughts, Lillie?"

She took a nacho. "Okay. *Hamilton*."

It was *Lion King*, answered correctly by I See Dumb People and, improbably, Blood, Sweat and Beers. Robbie played the Zulu part of "Circle of Life" as DJ.

"You should all be ashamed," I told my teammates. "I'm disappointed in all of you."

"Okay, okay, moving on," Lillie muttered. "Where's your grandfather tonight, Harlow?"

"He's having his toenails trimmed by a nice woman from Brewster. Their second date."

Grady choked on his beer.

"Relationship goals," I said, smiling at him. There was that warm tug again. Quite nice, that tug.

"Next question," said Robbie, reading from his screen. It was an easy one, and everyone got it right. (What is deer meat called in a restaurant?)

No one contradicted me on the third question when I whisper-announced that Jane Austen's first novel was *Sense and Sensibility*. Four teams, including ours, got the correct answer to how many suns the planet Tatooine had (Grady was a total *Star Wars* geek). Dumb People and Kingslayers answered correctly to the real-life couple who starred in *Who's Afraid of Virginia Woolf?* Rosie knew the answer to Alan Rickman's first film credit (*Die Hard*).

The last question in the first round was cause for debate. "In what state is Area 51?" Robbie asked. "(A) New Mexico, (B) Idaho, (C) Nevada, or (D) Utah?"

"New Mexico?" I suggested, fairly confident.

"Yeah," said Rosie. "I'm with my roomie on this one. I think I scouted a location near there. I remember the food very fondly. Green chili sauce on everything."

"I'm pretty sure it's Nevada," said Grady.

"My vote is also Nevada," Lillie said. "I think they mentioned it on *The X-Files*. Dylan's whole dorm binge-watched it last semester."

"You have a son in college?" Rosie asked.

"Yes. Thank you. I'm Portuguese. We age beautifully. Also, I was twenty-three when Dylan was born. Started young."

"Not as young as some of us," I said. She fist-bumped me. "Two for the Land of Enchantment, two for the land of gambling and legalized sex work. Who's gonna break?"

"You have to trust me on this one," Grady said, looking at me. "Do you really think I wouldn't know where Area 51 is?"

"Oh. There are pheromones in the air!" Rosie exclaimed.

"And no more alcohol for you, missy," I said. Still, my face was hot. "Okay, Gray. I trust you."

"Are we having a *Titanic* moment or what?" Rosie said. "'Trust me, Kate Winslet. Do you trust me?' 'I trust you, Leonardo DiCaprio.' God! So romantic."

Grady gave her a look, then took our answer up to Robbie. I leaned in to Rosie. "Hey. You're being pretty loud, and you seem smashed. Are you?"

"Little bit. Should've eaten something today."

"I'll get you some bread."

"And water," Lillie said.

Rosie was never like this. Well, not since college party days. I found Tanner and asked him to get some bread, then went to the bar and asked for a pitcher of water.

"Let me help." I turned, and Grady's green eyes looked right into mine.

"Hi," I said.

"Hi."

Did anyone make eye contact like this anymore? I mean,

Gray had no trouble in that area, and it was . . . it was . . . I felt very . . . tugged. He had long eyelashes, which I'd never noticed before. And he smelled good. I could feel my heartbeat in my eyeballs, and I suddenly felt . . . warm.

"Here you go," Tanner said, thrusting a bread basket into my hands.

"Thanks, Tan. Um, Grady, do you like bread?" I asked. "I . . . I love bread. I mean, I love the bread *here*, at the Ice House. It's so good. Also, Rosie needs to soak up some of that alcohol in her system."

Grady took the bread from me and grabbed the pitcher of water. His hands were very big. Neatly trimmed nails, a cut on his right thumb. Very . . . masculine hands. Well, of course. They did man stuff all day, in the water, handling crustaceans or . . . whatever. Maybe he'd cut himself on a shell. Maybe a fish had bitten him. "How'd you get that cut on your hand?" I asked.

He glanced down. "Not sure."

"Okay, we finally got the Beach Bums' answer," said Robbie, "and right at the wire. The correct answer to where Area 51 is . . . Nevada!" The theme song from *The X-Files* came on.

"Told you," said Grady, still looking at me.

"Yes, you did."

The subtext was thick enough to cut with a knife.

I think I had a crush.

We went back to our table. Rosie had her head on her arms, but smiled when we came up. "Eat," I said, and she took a roll like an obedient child.

We breezed through the next few questions, as did I See Dumb People. But Gray knew where the Tim Tam Slam originated, having honeymooned in Sydney, and Dumb People thought it was England.

"Slam that," I called over to Mr. Silva.

"She seems so nice at the bookstore," he said. "It takes trivia night for her to show her fangs."

"Damn straight," I said. We were only down by ten.

Honeymoon in Australia, huh? Expensive. Beautiful. Lots of ocean to see. I bet Bentley Blakefield Byrne rocked a tiny little bikini. Bet they held hands as they glided over the Great Barrier—

"Okay, kids," said Robbie. "Listen up. If you get it right, you get twenty points. If you don't answer, you don't lose anything, but if you give a wrong answer, you lose twenty points, and this is a nail-biter. I See Dumb People, you're only ahead by ten, so bet wisely. Kingslayers, this could be your moment. Ready? What does Billy Mack do on Christmas Eve?"

Rosie immediately scribbled down the answer and held it up for us to see. *Gets pissed and watches porn with his fat manager.*

"And we have the winning answer," I said, because I loved that movie, too.

Sherlock Homies also knew the answer, but they were 140 points behind. And Dumb People had gone big and taken a chance, thinking Billy Mack was the dad in *A Christmas Story*, poor fools, and had written *Goes out for Chinese food with his family.*

"You are so, so off," Lillie said. "You could've just sat there and kept your dignity, but no."

"You're a horrible woman," Ben said. "I can't believe I'm stuck with you."

In the end, we won by forty points. Our team high-fived each other and graciously spoke with the losers. "I'm sure you'll find something else to live for," I told Watty, Ronnie, Mikey and Pete of Blood, Sweat and Beers.

"There's always alcohol," said Watty.

"It's the Massachusetts way," said Ronnie.

Mrs. Silva congratulated us on our "disturbingly deep knowledge of trashy pop culture," for which we thanked her effusively.

Rosie was leaning against the wall. "Can we go? I'm whipped."

"Sure," I said.

"I'm walking you two home," said Gray.

"It's okay," I said. "It's only a few blocks."

"That was a statement, not a question," he said.

"Chivalrous," Rosie attempted to say.

Out on the street, Gray took Rosie's hand and tucked it against his arm. "Hold on, miss," he said. "No falling down drunk in the streets."

"As if," she said. "Harlow, have I ever fallen down drunk? In the street?"

"Not to my knowledge," I said, but I was worried. She'd obviously had more to drink than a glass of wine and one martini.

"So you guys roomed together in college?" Gray asked.

"And after, too. We lived together in LA when I was in law school," I said.

"She speaketh the truth," Rosie said. "We had so much fun, didn't we, Lolo?"

"We did. And we had too much fun tonight, didn't we, Rosebud?"

"I'm a little drunk," she admitted.

"No shit."

Grady steered her up Main Street to Open Book. The picture window was lit up, and the beach books display looked lovely. Grandpop's floor was dark, and Frances's car was gone. I hoped Grandpop's toenails hadn't scared her off.

Gray, Rosie and I made our way upstairs, and I was glad he was here, because Rosie was, in a word, shit-faced.

Ollie greeted us as if we were veterans returning after a long deployment, weaving between our legs, whining for love. I picked him up in my arms, felt his joyful wriggles and let him lick my face, then kissed his silken head. "I missed you, too," I said with another smooch, then set him down. "We'll cuddle in five minutes, okay?"

Grady negotiated Rosie up the stairs to her room, me trailing behind. She flopped down on the bed. "I'm just gonna rest before I wash up," she said, but her eyes were already closed. I took off her shoes and put a blanket over her. Oliver Twist leaped neatly on her bed, the traitor, then gazed at me with his liquid eyes, chastising me for the delay in cuddling. I'd let Rosie have him for a few minutes before I called him back downstairs.

Grady and I went back down the creaky stairs. "Thanks for walking us home," I said. "You want some water or anything?"

"No, I'm good," he said. "Listen, Harlow." He paused a second. "My wife had a drinking problem. I wonder if your friend does, too."

"Oh, no," I said. "She does love wine and cocktails, but she's hardly ever drunk."

He didn't answer. Just looked at me, and for one incredibly hot second, I pictured him scooping me up and sitting me on the counter, then kissing me hard and hot, my legs wrapped around his waist, and his hands—"What?" I said too loudly.

He cocked his head a little. "I asked when we could have that dinner."

"Dinner?"

"I asked you out for dinner a couple of weeks ago."

"Oh! Um . . . shoot, let me look at my calendar." I pulled out my phone. "Okay, I have inventory tomorrow, and it's Lark and Addie's birthday on Sunday, and Monday Matthew will be back home."

"I see," he said.

"So how's Tuesday?" I asked, looking up.

He smiled, and I felt that delicious . . . tug. "Tuesday works."

"Do you need to check with your nanny or anything?"

"Nope."

"Great. Tuesday it is."

He didn't look away. "Good night, then."

The tug became a lovely pull. "Night, Gray."

For the third time in my life, I thought that Grady Byrne was about to kiss me. For the third time in my life, I was wrong. He left me standing in the middle of my kitchen, wondering what the *heck* was going on there.

TWENTY-NINE

CYNTHIA

Just a few weeks after she'd read the message from Nancy Barbieri Lawless, Cynthia found herself driving to Connecticut to meet her . . . relations. Nancy, the eldest of the three, was fifty-seven and lived in Queens, New York. Donna, fifty-six, lived on Long Island, and Michelle, also from Long Island, was fifty-four. Three children in four years. She couldn't imagine the chaos.

From their correspondence, Cynthia knew all three of the Barbieri sisters were married and had thirteen children between them. Thirteen! Clearly, they had no qualms about the earth's population issues. Nancy was a middle school teacher; Donna was a nurse; and Michelle was a stay-at-home mother. It all sounded very middle-class and, to be honest, not that interesting. She'd clicked on their Facebook pages and seen a lot of family photos, but nothing that made her "recognize" anyone. Picnics, the beach, lots of average-looking children and spouses, lots of food. All three sisters were overweight, Cynthia had observed. All that cheese and pasta. Hard to believe Cynthia was Italian. She didn't even like the food.

They were meeting in New Haven at a restaurant Nancy had chosen. An Italian restaurant. Cynthia would have to order a salad.

"Keep an open mind," Albert had said over dinner last night

when she admitted she didn't expect much from either the sisters or the food.

"Good advice," she said. It was not the first time Albert had come for dinner (and more), but she didn't want to think about their budding relationship too much, or else she'd talk herself out of it. Bertie Baines was so different from Henry, with absolutely no sense of style or finesse. No, Albert had worked hard all his life, and whatever he had, he'd earned. Not like that idiot Henry. But Albert, with his questionable hygiene, missing tooth, sparse hair and weathered face, was not the type of man Cynthia had ever considered. The problem was, she . . . well, she liked him. Very much. She hadn't been listened to in a very long time, or touched, or sought out. Albert did all those things.

An open mind. That was something Cynthia had never mastered or, to be frank, wanted to master. She hadn't been raised that way . . . she had learned judgment and a delicious sense of superiority at her mother's knee.

She drove through the traffic of Providence and the gentle green farmland of Rhode Island, then through the hills of Connecticut, past signs announcing towns with pretty names. In New Haven, she exited the highway and went down a warren of one-way streets, following the signs to Wooster Square, where Nancy had told her to park. Apparently, Wooster Square was quite an attraction, but it was just a small, flat park, nothing to write home about. She failed to see why it warranted *signs*, as if it were—

Open mind. Open mind.

The restaurant was within walking distance. Cynthia parked the car, flipped down the visor and reapplied her lipstick. Then she took a deep breath and got out of her car. The air smelled like pizza, and the houses around the square were all historic and genteel-looking. Reminding herself that she had nothing to lose at this luncheon, Cynthia started walking. After all, *they* had been looking for *her*. This was a simple curiosity, good manners and something different to do.

Unexpectedly, her stomach cramped with nervousness. She glanced at herself in the reflection of a car window and saw a trim woman dressed well enough in a navy cotton shirtdress and Easy Spirit flats. Her wavy hair was as it always was, an unremarkable shade of light brown sprinkled with gray. An ordinary-looking middle-aged woman, even though she'd taken her time with makeup this morning. Nothing special.

Albert didn't think so. He made her feel . . . well . . . beautiful. The thought brought a pleasant warmth to her face and a tingle to her belly. At least she'd had some decent sex, she thought. She wouldn't have to die without experiencing a proper orgasm.

There was the restaurant, and it was 12:05. Now or never.

"*Buongiorno*," said a waiter. "How can I help you today?" He had a strong Italian accent.

"Hello. I'm joining—"

"Oh, my God, there she is! Cynthia? Look at you! Hello!"

A gaggle of heavyset women descended on her, hugging her, crying, sobbing even. They were all talking at once, and Cynthia couldn't distinguish a word.

"We're overwhelming her," said one of them. She had brown-and-blond hair, colored in what could only be described as stripes and too long for someone her age. "Sorry, Cynthia, we are just so . . ." Her voice choked off.

"Come, sit down," said another. "I'm Nancy. It's so wonderful to meet you!"

"It's very nice to meet you as well," Cynthia said.

"Oh, my Gawd, listen to the accent," said another. "I'm

Donna." She was not in a place to comment on accents, Cynthia thought, with her nasal voice and strange vowels.

"And I'm Michelle. We love you already."

They led her to the table, which was in a corner by the window. People walking past would see four women. Would they know they were sisters? Certainly, the three of them looked alike.

"Givver a second to breathe, girls," Nancy said. "Want some wine, hon? Cawffee?"

They all sounded like the Long Island Medium. Not one of them had natural hair, and all of them had hard artificial nails in various shades of neon.

"I'll have a glass of wine, thank you," Cynthia said. They'd already ordered a bottle of pinot grigio, and Michelle poured her a generous glass.

"You. Are. Beautiful," said Donna. "I would kill for your figure! She sure didn't take after us in that department, am I right, girls?"

"Okay, so you have to tell us everything," Nancy said. "Tell us where you grew up and what your life was like."

"Well. As you say, it's a little overwhelming to meet all of you."

"Oh, here's the food!" Donna announced. "Cynthia, we ordered without you, but hopefully there's something you like here. You're not a vegetarian, are you? Or gluten-free? God strike me down if I ever have to give up bread."

"No, I'll . . . I'll eat anything." This was terribly uncomfortable, but at least the interruption gave her time to study these women. As noted, they were all overweight, their shoulders solid and strong-looking, their upper arms plump. Two of them wore animal print blouses, giraffe and leopard. All wore a gold crucifix and at least one other gold necklace, gold earrings, gold bracelets. Cynthia was the only one wearing a dress.

Her sisters shoveled food onto her plate—pasta, sausages, lasagna, salad, bread, chicken parmesan—enough for three meals at least.

"How was the drive down?" Nancy asked, and it was a relief to answer a normal question.

"It was fine. A little traffic, but I enjoy driving." Did she? It didn't matter. She took a bite of the cheesy chicken. Not bad.

"So you live on Cape Cawd. Didja grow up there?" Nancy asked.

"I moved there about three years ago after I inherited a share in a bookstore," she said. "My aunt died and left it to me, and I thought it would be a nice change." Now there was a spin if ever there was one.

"Oh, my God," said Michelle, stretching the word *God* into two syllables. "That sounds like a movie or a novel, am I right, girls?"

"We took the kids there about six, seven years ago," Donna said. "It was beautiful. Just beautiful."

Nancy, as the oldest, clearly was the one in control. She gave Cynthia a wry smile. "This is crazy, I know. But we want to know about you."

"May I ask a question?" Cynthia said.

"The manners! Sure, of course, hon."

"What made you look for me?"

The Barbieri sisters quieted. "Michelle, you're the family historian. You go ahead," Nancy said.

"Okay." She swallowed her mouthful and took a sip of wine. "Okay, Cynthia . . . do you go by Cindy?"

"Sometimes," she said. Cindy who had three sisters. Cindy who had a boyfriend. She'd never once responded to Cindy before Albert had called her that. *It's Cynthia*, her mother always told someone when they shortened her name. *If I wanted her to be called Cindy, I would have named her that.*

Now, however, Cindy sounded like someone she might like to be.

"So Cindy," Michelle said, "here's the thing. We always knew about you. We did. When we were, I don't know, about twelve, median age–wise, Mommy and Daddy sat us down and said they had something to tell us. Mommy was already crying. We thought she had cancer!"

"Oh, my God, that's right!" Donna said. "We were sure they were either gonna get a divorce or drop dead."

"I'm talking, Donna," Michelle said. "Eat and keep your mouth busy."

Donna laughed and obeyed, and Michelle continued. "So they said that before they got married, Mommy had gotten pregnant. She was sixteen. Young, obviously. Her parents said she had to give the baby up for adoption. She was heartbroken, but she wasn't a full adult, right? And back then, the parents could force you to do that kind of thing."

"I don't think Mommy ever forgave Noni and Papa for making her give you away," Nancy murmured.

"She didn't," Michelle went on. "She said she never loved them the same after that." She ripped off a hunk of garlic bread and took a huge bite. "So, okay, they sent Mommy to Uncle Patsy in St. Louis so no one would know she got knocked up. Then she had you, Noni and Papa went out there, they put you in a Catholic orphanage and took Mommy back home."

That was more or less the scenario Cynthia had always pictured. Teen mother, too young to raise a child, deadbeat father, orphanage.

"I see," Cynthia said. "And when did she meet your father?"

The sisters exchanged a glance. "Our father is your father, too, Cindy. They never broke up."

Cynthia felt the floor drop away. Her eyes fluttered. "I . . . so my birth parents . . . stayed together?"

"They did, Cindy, they did," said Nancy. "In fact, they got married on Mommy's eighteenth birthday."

"They loved each other so much," Donna said. "May they rest in peace." She crossed herself.

"So we're . . . full sisters?"

"We are," said Nancy. "And we found you at last. Mommy would be so glad." She turned her face to the ceiling. "I hope you're looking down on us, Mommy. You too, Daddy." Nancy returned her gaze to Cynthia. "She and Daddy had done Ancestry and 23andMe, but they could never find anything. She wrote to Catholic Family Services, but the records were sealed tight."

"Like a vault," Donna said, taking more pasta. "Have some more, Cindy. This sauce is delicious."

Cynthia took a bite automatically, tasting nothing. Her parents had gotten *married*. These three women had grown up with the same parents who'd relinquished her. Who'd been *forced* to relinquish her.

Now *that* was not something she'd ever considered.

"Every couple of years," Michelle said, "they'd try again. They even went to St. Louis once. But then the grandbabies started coming, and life got busier, and I think Mommy just thought it was hopeless. Daddy died six years ago, in his sleep, God bless him, and Mommy tried to find you one more time. And still, they wouldn't or couldn't help her."

"I stopped going to church for seven months, I was so mad," said Donna.

"Then Mommy got sick," Nancy said. "She'd had a serious heart attack, and things went downhill from there. She knew she didn't have a lot of time, and all she could talk about was you, Cindy. She made us swear that we'd find you." Her voice choked up.

"She died three weeks later," Michelle said, her eyes full of tears. "All of us were there, us three and our husbands and all the grandkids, except my Tony, who's in the Air Force. It was very peaceful."

Donna wiped her eyes with her napkin. "She always said—"

"Give her a minute," Nancy said, putting her hand over Cynthia's. "This is all new information for her, and it's a lot."

That was an understatement. Cynthia took a long sip of wine. She never turned to alcohol to feel better, but today demanded an exception. Then she downed her glass of water.

The waiter came over to refill her glass. "How is everything?" he asked.

"Wonderful," Donna said. "And we're Italian, so we know. This bread? Incredible."

"So glad to hear it, *signore, grazie.*" He walked away.

"You're white as a ghost, Cindy," said Michelle. "Talk to us."

Her birth parents had loved her. Wanted her. Had *searched* for her. Had Mother and Daddy known this?

She took a shaky breath. "The idea that they would stay together never even crossed my mind."

Her childhood flashed in front of her—they'd been so insulated, so cloistered in that lovely house. So . . . smug. So united. A very close family, just the three of them, while all that time, her other parents, who had *wanted her*, had been mourning her. Searching for her. They had kept her memory alive. Her mother's dying wish was for her sisters to find her.

All the horrible things she'd thought about birth mothers and reunions while her parents had looked for her for more than fifty years, and Cynthia had barely spared them a thought.

She burst into tears.

"Oh, honey!" a sister exclaimed, and then they were there, kneeling next to her, standing behind her, hugging her, murmuring comfort and love. Cynthia covered her face and sobbed.

"It's very emotional," Nancy said. "You go ahead and cry, hon."

She couldn't seem to stop, and it was rather mortifying. But her sisters were very kind, patting her, saying nice things. Finally, she dug in her purse for a tissue and blew her nose. "I'm fine. Thank you."

"Sit back down, girls," Nancy instructed. "Gianni? Could we get some cawfee? And a tray of desserts, okay, hon?"

Gianni obeyed, bringing a silver pot of coffee, cups and a platter of various cookies and bite-sized desserts.

"So now you know, Cindy," Donna said, taking a slurp of creamy coffee. "Tell us about you. How old were you when you learned you were adopted? Did you ever ask your parents where you came from?"

Cynthia shifted in her seat. "Yes. Well, I only found out I was adopted when I read my mother's diary. I was sixteen and snooping, and in it, she said . . . she had written that she was so happy to be a mother at last, and that I . . . I was the prettiest baby in the orphanage. That I smiled when I saw her. I don't even know how old I was when that happened."

"Babies start smiling around eight, nine weeks," Donna said. "I work in pediatrics, plus I have four grandchildren."

"Were they good to you?" Nancy asked. "Your other parents?"

"Oh, yes," Cynthia answered. "They were . . . they were wonderful. Very traditional, upper middle class. Daddy was a banker, and Mother was a housewife. My childhood was very happy and safe."

"Thank God for that. It would've killed Mommy and Daddy if you'd been miserable."

"I was the opposite. Spoiled and . . . very happy." *Superior*, she'd been thinking. At least she'd thought she was.

"So once you found out you were adopted, what did you think?" Nancy asked.

Cynthia paused. A *carrier*, she'd called her birth mother, and to Harlow of all people. "I assumed she was a teenager," she admitted. "And simply that she'd gotten pregnant too young to raise a child."

"All true," Nancy said. "But they would've given it their best shot. We turned out okay, didn't we, girls?" The Barbieri sisters exchanged warm glances.

Cynthia broke a cookie in half. "I pictured her being relieved to give me up. I even wondered if she'd been . . . assaulted. I tried to put my adoption out of my head, as if it didn't matter, because I thought it might hurt Mother and Daddy if I told them I knew. So I just . . . pretended she didn't exist."

Her sisters were silent, exchanging looks. "We all do what we have to to get by," Donna said kindly.

"I'm so sorry," Cynthia said, tears flowing again. "I'm so

sorry I never looked for her. For any of you. I just wanted to stay . . . to have things stay the way I wanted them to be. I didn't want any . . . sadness or unpleasantness to be part of my story."

"Listen," said Nancy firmly. "You were a kid. Don't beat yourself up."

Cynthia wiped her eyes yet again. "What were their names? Our parents?"

Our parents. Amazing.

"Their names were Luigi Antonio Barbieri and Anna-Maria Priscilla Ricci Barbieri," Donna announced. "They were in love for sixty-three years."

"That's . . . remarkable," Cynthia said.

"It was a love story for the ages, Cindy," Michelle said.

"And they were happy, don't get me wrong. They had each other, and they had us," Donna said. "But you were always in their hearts."

Her birth parents had loved each other. She wasn't the child of rape or a one-night stand. She would have been the eldest of four girls. She would have grown up on Long Island and had an accent of dubious appeal. She would know how to make chicken parmesan. She would've been Catholic and had saints to pray to.

She would've been in the heart of a very close family.

"Tell me everything," she said. "Your childhood. Your kids. Aunts, uncles, your husbands. I want to know all about you."

It was well after dark when the three Barbieri sisters walked Cynthia back to her car. They hugged for a long time, all four of them teary. The Barbieri sisters promised to visit her on the Cape this fall, wanted her to come to Long Island and see their childhood home, now owned by Michelle, and meet their many children.

They'd call her tomorrow, made her promise to text when she got home.

Cynthia was a different person from the one who'd driven down here this morning. Something had started with that walk home with Albert, like a foundation beginning to crack. But today, it had burst open.

If her life was a building, it had been a prison, and she'd been the one to lock herself in. Even as a child, she'd had impossible standards, judging children, allowing them to be her friends only if they passed certain criteria in clothing and manners and address. She'd had no goals in life other than to keep it the same. Henry had been convenient, but clearly, she'd only used him, her best bet at being like her mother.

Now, that metaphoric prison was rubble. Construction would have to begin on something new.

It was *remarkable*. All her life, she had been loved by her birth parents. They had been young, yes, but not irresponsible or flighty. She had been conceived in love. She had been *remembered*. The fact of her existence had been shared with her sisters, who had honored their mother's dying wish by finding her.

She had never been alone at all.

THIRTY

HARLOW

On Tuesday, Grady texted to ask if I could come to his house, rather than him picking me up, because we were finally having that dinner. He and Luna had gone to the beach and he was running late.

You got it, I texted back. Then I realized I didn't know where he lived. What's your address?

"So what are we wearing?" Rosie asked. "And should I make arrangements to sleep elsewhere? You know what? I retract the question. Harlow, I'm having a sleepover with one of your sisters tonight. I'll be back tomorrow morning." She grinned, and my face flushed and knees tingled.

As if in approval, my dog barked once.

"Don't drink too much," I said in passing, sitting next to Ollie, who flopped on his back for a tummy scratch. The day after our magnificent trivia win, however, I had asked her about her alcohol intake.

She had apologized immediately. "I am so sorry about that. I really overdid it. Honestly, I don't think I had a single thing to eat that day until we were there, and I was surprised how wasted I got, and how fast."

"Yeah. That predinner glass of wine . . . you sure that was the only thing you drank?"

"It was a generous pour, as they say. But come on, Harlow, you know that's not like me. Something was off that night."

"Yeah. It scared me," I said. "It's one thing to enjoy a drink, and another to need someone to drag you up the stairs."

"At least I chose a very cute guy to drag me, right? And gave him an opportunity to walk us home like the old-fashioned sweetheart he is."

But I'd been watching her more closely, and all weekend long, the only thing I saw her drink was a glass of wine on Saturday night, when we went to Pepe's in Provincetown for dinner.

But when she was out the other day, I'd gone upstairs, something I hadn't had reason to do. The bottle of vodka I kept in my freezer and the gin in the cupboard over the stove remained untouched, and a quick and guilty search of the guest room showed me nothing more than her clothes and a few books. No empty bottles under the bed. Rosie *did* drink more than the average person—she'd grown up in an industry that wined and dined and drank—but I had hardly ever seen her *drunk*.

Now Rosie was riffling through my closet. "No, no, no, no, maybe but probably not, no, no."

"What about that dress?" I asked, nodding to a denim calf-length thing I'd had for a few years.

"Too chaste," she said.

"Chaste is okay. Grady and I are just friends." My face warmed again.

"Just friends so far," she murmured.

"Yes, but this summer is probably not the best time to start a relationship." Ollie whined from the bed.

"Ollie disagrees," Rosie said. "Ollie thinks you've been single for too long."

"Jeans and a T-shirt, no logo. That's my final offer."

"He's taking you out to dinner. You dress up to show him you appreciate it. God, I wish we were the same size. Okay, here." She pulled out a pair of white jeans I hadn't worn in a couple of years and the blue striped oxford I wore to professional events, added my trusty Levi's denim jacket and dug around for some shoes, sighed, went upstairs and returned with an utterly adorable pair of bright pink suede mules.

"Okay, those are amazing," I said, pulling off my *I love books more than most people* T-shirt. I got dressed, let Rosie stuff the tails of my shirt into my jeans.

"Is French tuck a real thing, or did you just make it up?" I asked.

"Could be slang for something very dirty," she said. "Use your imagination. Unbutton the top three and let him have a little peek at your cami." I obeyed. "Harlow, no socks! Come on."

"But the mosquitoes . . ."

"No socks."

I put my socks back, then scooped my hair into a messy bun, put on some earrings and said, "Do I pass?"

"You're gorgeous. Take your hair down and show it off. If I could kill you and have that hair, I would. Just warning you."

"It's the curse of womankind. I hate my hair and would kill *you* for yours. So shiny, never tangled. A squirrel could jump out of mine at any moment." I grabbed my purse, which was a battered leather bag big enough to hold a hardcover book or three. "Can I go now?"

She smiled. "Have fun, my darling friend."

I kissed her cheek. "You too."

I drove to Grady's house, which was on Bound Brook Island Road . . . the boonies of Wellfleet, at least on this side of town. We had more boonies over near the kettle ponds where Lillie lived.

His house was a white Cape, built in the 1800s from the looks of it, but with new windows and at least one addition. Rhododendrons in the front, the required Cape Cod rambling roses climbing up the chimney. In the back, I spotted a swing set.

The door opened. "Bonjour, 'Arlow," said a *very* pretty young woman. She had a beautiful French accent. "I am Vivienne. We have seen each other at the store, yes? But I do not think we have exchanged names yet."

"Nice to officially meet you," I said. Her skin didn't seem to have a single pore.

"Gray said to come right in. He is in the shower, but he is never long. Please, sit down, be comfort. Luna, here is a guest! Come say hello!" Vivienne looked at me and smiled. "Oh, *zut alors*, I forget she is painting with the fingers. I will be sure her hands are clean. One moment, please."

"Sure," I said, feeling awkward. Her ass was tiny yet still a perfect booty. How? I noted she also called him Gray. I thought only his old high school friends did that. Also, how could he live in a house with such a beautiful woman and not be crazy in love with her? Then again, maybe he was. Grady hadn't specifically asked me out on a date, after all. He had offered to listen to me talk about my chaotic summer.

I took a look around as Vivienne and Luna chatted (in French) in the kitchen. Gray's house was really nice. There was a great balance of old pieces—an old sideboard, an intricate Victorian side table, a faded Persian rug—and contemporary stuff. The couch was dark blue and sleek, and a wicked cool starburst light hung overhead. Built-in shelves flanked the fireplace, and they were laden with tomes about the ocean. There was the one I'd sold him a few weeks ago. Colored sticky notes peeked out of the pages of many of the books, and it made me glad. Books should be used for what was inside them, not as décor. Or not *just* as décor.

There were dozens of children's books, too—the all-popular Pete the Cat series, *Where the Wild Things Are*, *Cloudy with a Chance of Meatballs*, *Guess How Much I Love You*, a whole row of Dr. Seuss, and oh! The Old Mother West Wind series! In the original hardback! My favorite. I touched their spines gently, smiling at the image of Grady reading to his daughter, cuddled up on the couch.

I had never read to my son. I doubted I'd ever have another child. I'd never wanted another kid. Today, for the first time, the thought of it made my heart fold in on itself. I'd missed my chance, not knowing Matthew would be my only one.

Snap out of it, I told myself. I was lucky. Damn lucky. My boy had found me, and that was so much right there. And I had two beautiful nieces I could definitely spend more time with, and someday, I was sure my siblings would have more.

But the image of reading to a little boy with curly black hair, nestled against my side, was hard to shake.

To change my train of thought, I peeked into the dining room, which adjoined the living room. Giant table, windows with the original glass, a fireplace with an incredible skyscape hanging over it. I wondered if my mom would recognize the artist, because it did have that Cape Cod feeling. There was a piano tucked in the back, and even from here, I could see the familiar red music book for kids. Nice, that Luna was taking lessons.

"Hello," said a little voice. "Oh, it's you! Hi, Miss Harlow!"

I laughed. "Hello, Luna. It's nice to see you again."

"You're out of the bookstore again," she said.

I quashed a smile. "Yes. I am allowed to go out and see friends."

"Am I your friend?" she asked, a finger twisting in her hair.

Her eyes were just as green as her father's, and her words poked at my heart. "I hope so."

"Vivienne is my *best* friend," Luna said. "But you can be my friend, too."

"Thank you," I said. "I appreciate that."

Grady came in. "Hey! Sorry about making you wait."

"No problem," I said.

He scooped up his daughter, making her shriek and giggle. "Give Daddy a kiss, okay? I'm having dinner with Miss Harlow tonight."

"I want to come."

"Another time, pumpkin. Vivi, can I bring you anything?"

"No, no, thank you, I am fine. We are all set, *n'est-ce pas, ma petite?*"

"*Oui*," said Luna. "That's French for yes, Miss Harlow."

"Oh," I said. "Very cool."

Grady kissed her head and set her down, then turned to me. "Ready?"

"Sure. Nice seeing you, Luna. You too, Vivienne."

"And you," she said, picking Luna up with practiced ease. "Luna, shall we go on the swing? I will push you so high!"

We got into Grady's car, which was electric (because he was always saving the earth in one way or another). "First question," I said as I buckled myself in. "Are you madly in love with your nanny? Because there are dozens of novels about that, and I wouldn't blame you if you were."

He laughed and pulled out into the street. "No. I'm not. Which is a good thing, since she's fifteen years younger than I am, and I'm not her preferred gender."

"Oh, so it's a one-sided, longing kind of a thing? Got it."

He cut me a glance. "You've gotten very sassy recently."

"It's Rosie's bad influence."

"No. I think it's been there all along. Dormant, brought forth by the happiness of finding your son. How is he, by the way?"

"Great. It was so nice to see him yesterday. I missed him. Almost eighteen years without seeing his face, but when he was gone for five days, all I could think about was him."

"How's the rest of his family?" Grady asked.

"Good. Meena comes to the bookstore almost every day to hang out with Ophelia Finch. Do you know her?"

"The blond kid with the attitude?"

"That's the one."

"Yeah. She's great."

"Sanjay drops Meena off, and the girls hang out in the store or walk around Wellfleet."

"How are Matthew's parents doing with your son spending all this time with you?"

I thought about that. "They're being very generous," I said. "I think Sanjay has an easier time of it. Monica . . . well, she's protective. Of course. She's coming back here on Thursday, and they invited us for Matthew's birthday party on Saturday."

"Nice."

"Where are we going?" I asked as we turned onto 6A. "Provincetown, obviously, since there's no other destination this way except the ocean, but specifically?"

"The Mews," he said.

"Oh, fancy!" I said. The Mews was one of the best (and most

expensive) restaurants in P-town. I looked out the window at the passing condos, the sky over the sandy dunes. It was cloudy this afternoon; the mainland was getting hit with big thunderstorms, but they usually broke up before hitting the Outer Cape. But the Mews had beautiful views of the water, so if there was lightning, we'd be in for a show. We went past the Days Cottages, all named for flowers. "My mom does paintings of these every year," I told Grady. "They sell like hotcakes."

We turned onto Commercial Street by the sign I so loved— the fishermen pulling up their nets, MacMillan's Wharf behind them—and squeezed down the street, passing the prettiest gardens and sweetest houses in the world, if you asked me. "What's this?" I said. "A free parking space? Jesus must be in town, because this is a miracle. Keep an eye out for Lazarus walking down the street, heading for a tea dance."

Grady laughed, and I realized that I really liked that sound. His resting expression was so serious—*the oceans are rising, the reefs are dying, and life as we know it is not sustainable*—but when he was with Luna, or when he laughed at trivia night, his whole face changed. He had a great smile, I realized. A really, really nice smile.

There was that tug again.

Over drinks and dinner, we talked easily—updates on my siblings, Rosie, Grandpop's new girlfriend, Cynthia's suspiciously improved mood. I told him about how I thought I saw a great white shark that time paddleboarding with Matthew.

"You may well have," he said. "And I know it's hard to believe, but they really hardly ever bite anyone."

"It's just that when they do, you lose a limb and bleed to death."

"There is that, yes." His grin went straight to my girl parts.

Sex with James was physically fine but emotionally nonexistent. My human vibrator.

To distract myself from these thoughts, I said, "How are the oceans of the world, Gray? Are you terrified about the future?"

"Actually there's a little good news," he said. "Some parts of the Great Barrier Reef are growing better than they have in decades. And last year, they found two species of fish we thought went extinct. Oh, and get this. You may have seen a great white, which, you know, is really exciting." The server came and asked if he could take away our plates, because look at that, we were done.

"Dessert menu?" he asked.

"Yes, please," we answered in unison, then smiled at each other.

"So you were saying . . ." I said.

"Yeah. Great whites, beautiful creatures. But last week, I was in Florida for a couple days at NOAA down there. And we were using the deepwater cameras in the Gulf of Mexico, just tooling around, seeing the sights—"

"You were swimming?"

"No. The camera is operated by remote control, and it was about seventy-five hundred feet down."

"Holy heck."

He raised an eyebrow. "I know. It's so beautiful, Harlow. It's just as beautiful as outer space, but with living things. So there we were, sitting in front of these screens, mapping the area, and suddenly, we see this very thin tentacle in front of the camera. I said, 'What the heck is that?' and Grace turns the controls so the camera catches it." He sat back in his chair, completely in his element. "And there it is. A bigfin squid. Incredibly rare. It was so . . . otherworldly, so beautiful and . . . languid."

"Good word," I said, completely caught up in the picture he was painting.

"The fin itself looked like a flower opening, which is how it swims, and the tentacles were waving and undulating behind it. The body is completely transparent, but also pale pink and white, like a beautiful ghost or alien. Hang on, I have a clip of the video here."

He pulled out his phone and came around the table to kneel at my side so I could see, and I couldn't help noticing how good he smelled . . . Dove soap, I was pretty sure. "Here," he said, and on the screen was the squid, so strange and beautiful that I forgot to be lustful.

"Wow," I breathed. "It's so . . . hypnotic."

"Good word," he said with a quick smile at me.

"How long are those tentacles?"

"About twenty feet."

"Wow. Really." We stared at the screen, heads touching. "You're right, it looks like it's in outer space," I said, "and all those things are stars. There's a whole mysterious world down there. The deep ocean, I mean."

"Yeah." He grinned up at me, pleased with my reaction.

How had it taken me so long to realize that Grady Byrne was not only a nice guy, but smoking hot at that?

He went back to his seat, taking that good smell with him, and our server came back with the dessert menu.

"I'll have the key lime pie with toasted meringue and mango coulis," Grady said, reading from the menu.

"I was gonna get that, but I just made mango coulis yesterday," I said.

"You did?" the waiter asked.

"No," I said. "I don't even know what it is. I'll have the . . ."

I glanced at the menu and read off my choice. "The dark chocolate mousse cake with hazelnut praline crémeux, Drambuie whip and nutty pistachio gelato, and then, Gray, you should kill me, because I don't think my life will ever be any better once I've had that."

"Consider it done," Grady said, handing our menus back to the server.

"You two are cute," he said before he walked off.

"We *are* really cute," I said. "*Cape Cod Life* just voted us the cutest people in Wellfleet." Grady smiled again, and my girl parts smiled right back. "Gray?"

"Yes?"

"I'm having a really nice time."

The smile widened. "Me too."

"Hey, I was wondering . . . what's happening with your wife?"

The second I said the words, I regretted it. The smile fell right off Grady's face, and without otherwise moving a muscle, his entire demeanor changed.

"Never mind," I said. "I'm sorry. None of my business."

"No, it's fine. Her sister left after making her case. I thought about letting Bentley see Luna . . . you know, just a visit, because I have full custody."

"You do?"

"Yeah. Because of her alcohol use disorder. So I called her and got her voice mail. She hasn't called back. Mercedes said she's found a new guy and is drinking again." He shrugged. "Same old, same old. So until she's been sober for a year with AA attendance to prove it, I told Mercedes there would be no visitation. But Bentley doesn't seem to be motivated, even so."

"How could she do that?" I asked. "Walk out on her chi—"

God. *I* had done that. Different circumstances, but shit.

Grady's horrible ex-wife and I had one basic thing in common. We didn't want to raise our kid. "Hang on one second, okay?" I said, then headed for the restroom. *Well done, hypocrite. Way to ruin an evening. Any more open wounds you can stick your finger in? His or yours?*

I ran my hands under the cold water in the tiny sink, staring at myself in the mirror. We'd been having *such* a great time. Now my eyes looked sad. I tried to smile, but I looked like Joaquin Phoenix as the Joker, and let my face fall back.

When I came back to the table, Grady stood up. "You okay?" he asked.

"Absolutely. These look great," I said, since our desserts had come. We both sat down.

"Listen," he said, reaching across the table to take my hand. "If you just hid in the bathroom because you think that acknowledging you were too young to raise a kid and picking out his parents and ripping your own heart out is *anything* like what my ex-wife did, you're wrong."

The tears were immediate. I pulled my hand away from under his so I could wipe my eyes with my napkin. "She must have had terrible postpartum depression," I said.

"No. She had boredom and selfishness and an addiction. She said she hated that Luna was more important to me than she was, and that's why she was drinking and having one-night stands. Because I loved our daughter too much. The fact is, she was never a good person, and I was too smitten to notice."

"I always wonder why the nicest guys are drawn to the meanest girls."

He was quiet at that, and looked down at the table for a minute. "She's incredibly beautiful, and we only dated for four months before I proposed. Not my smartest move. Now. Eat your dessert."

"Yes, sir," I said. I had to admit I wondered where that impulsivity had come from, since he was otherwise such a measured guy. But I took a bite of my chocolate mousse cake, reached over to grip Gray's hand and said, "I was right. This is the happiest I'll ever be."

"I'm . . . I'm honored to witness it."

I laughed and held out a forkful for him to try, and as courtship rituals went, I think we crossed a hurdle. *Shared food, same fork, check.*

"I see what you mean," he said after he'd swallowed. "I'm a believer."

The drive home seemed a lot shorter than the drive up. When he made the turn toward his house, I blurted out, "Hey. Want to come up for some coffee? And you could see Ollie. Rosie's at one of my sister's houses. Everyone in my family loves her. And, um, yeah, I have good coffee."

"Is all that babbling code for something else?" he asked, glancing at me.

Busted. My face was on fire. "Wanna make out?"

He laughed and my ovaries frothed with eggs. "Yes. I do."

I did a quick check on Grandpop, saw that he was still alive and sound asleep, then ran back to the stairs. "Welcome. I mean, you've been here before, but welcome again," I said over my shoulder as we went up the stairs. My heart thudded erratically, but in a good way.

I opened the door, and Oliver Twist danced around my legs. "Yes! I'm home, Ollie! You've met Grady. Say hello." God, I sounded like an idiot. "Anyway, here we are. Um, have a seat and I'll make the coffee."

"None for me," he said, those calm green eyes on me.

"Okay. Pet my dog before he dies from neglect." He crouched

down and scratched Ollie behind the ears, and I turned to the coffeepot.

You don't have to be so nervous, I told myself. *It's Gray.*

That was the problem. It was Grady. It was not nothing, like it was with James. I sucked in a breath and let it out slowly, filled the coffeepot to three cups (who was I kidding, I wouldn't be drinking coffee), put a few scoops of Beanstock Deep Sea Blend in the filter and hit brew and jumped when Gray came up be-hind me.

"Nervous?" he asked, trapping me by putting his hands on the counter.

"I certainly am."

"Turn around."

I did. We were touching, our torsos against each other, and he was warm and delicious. I looked into his eyes, which were faintly crinkled in a smile.

"Would it help if I mentioned I've wanted to kiss you for the past twenty years?" he whispered, and that was it. I slid my hands up his deliciously muscled arms and pressed my lips against his. His mouth was warm and perfect, and my knees weakened in a delicious rush. Oh, he knew how to kiss, his mouth moving gen-tly, his lips firm and soft at the same time. Then his tongue brushed mine, and ladies and gentlemen, he did lift me up on the counter, just as I'd fantasized he would, and I did wrap my legs around him.

"Well done," I muttered.

He laughed and carried me to the couch, where he unceremo-niously dumped me. I reached out and grabbed the waist of his jeans and pulled him down on top of me. Ollie jumped up, too.

"No, Ollie," I said. "Go on your mat. Sorry. I'll make it up to you." My dog looked at me, hung his head and obeyed.

"Wow. Really effective guilt trip," Gray said.

"I know. Um, Gray . . ." My hand ran up his arm, feeling the solid muscles there. "For the record, we won't be having sex tonight," I said.

"Understood." His eyes crinkled, and I fell a little deeper.

His weight pressed me into the couch, and he kissed me again. My hands wandered over his shoulders, and his mouth moved to my jaw, his beard scraping gently against my skin, making goose bumps break out all over my left side. Then he kissed just below my ear and I sighed with the heavenliness of it all.

"Where did you get these muscles?" I whispered. "Are you a gym rat, or do you hurl sharks out of the water?"

"It's the sharks," he said, and I could hear the smile in his voice. His mouth moved to my neck, and I felt limp with lust. He kissed the skin just below my collarbone, and I was so glad Rosie had made me unbutton my shirt. Then his hand slid up my rib cage to my breast, and I nearly came right then and there.

Grady stopped for a second and looked at me, face serious. "I really like you, Harlow," he said, his voice quiet. "I always have."

I touched his face. "I really like you, too."

After another hour of world-class kissing, he drove me back to his place so I could get my car. The drive was silent, but my own smile warmed me through and through, and I thought I saw a similar expression on his face. Once we'd arrived, we just stood in his driveway a minute, looking at each other.

Then he kissed my forehead and tucked a tendril of hair behind my ear, and somehow, that was the most romantic thing of all. "See you again soon?" he asked.

"Yes, please."

Then he stepped away to open my car door, and on pleasantly weak legs, I got in, fastened the seat belt, took one more look at that gentle, kind face and put my car in drive, hit the gas, jolted forward and then slammed on the brake an inch before I crashed through his garage door.

"Sorry!" I yelped, putting the car in reverse.

"It would've been worth it," he said.

Those words were almost as good as the kissing. "Bye," I said, and finally backed out without endangering anything or anyone.

The moon was hidden, and the sky was inky.

Grady Byrne. It was always the quiet ones you had to watch out for.

THIRTY-ONE

MONICA

Sanjay had done everything on her list for Matthew's birthday, bless him. Oh, God, it was good to be back with him and Meena and, yes, Matthew, even though her boy was edgy and irritable again. When she asked if everything was okay an hour after she got in on Friday, he gave her an incredibly bored and pained expression and said, "Why wouldn't it be?"

"You have a lot going on this summer, emotionally speaking. I just wanted to check in."

"I'm *fine*," he said. It never ceased to amaze her how maternal love was so easily rejected. Well. Her maternal love, at least.

Today was his birthday, though, and he'd eaten his birthday pancakes cheerfully enough. Because of their vacations, his birthday was always somewhere fabulous. Some years, her in-laws flew in to celebrate with them, but it had often just been the four of them. Today, the entire Smith clan would be here.

The first time Harlow would celebrate Matthew's birthday with him. That had to feel huge.

Monica did a quick check of everything. They'd rented a tent, tables and chairs, and Monica had brought Indian tablecloths from home—gifts from Sita over the years. They were all different colors, making the interior of the tent very cheerful.

Red, green and yellow balloons were bouncing in the wind, tied to the tent poles. She had set up the aarti, a tray on which there were several candles representing different deities. A bowl of turmeric, ghee and uncooked rice waited for the parental blessing, a tradition Monica loved.

It looked beautiful. Sanjay had been cooking for the past three days, so the food would be plentiful and delicious. Hopefully, it would be a wonderful, happy day for their son.

She went inside to change into a sari. She loved wearing them as a sign of respect to Sanjay's family, but also because they reminded Matthew that, while he was not genetically Indian, it was still his family's culture.

"You are the most beautiful woman in the world," Sanjay said.

She smiled. "And you're the most handsome man," she replied. He was. She still loved looking at him, his big dark eyes, that easy, genuine smile, the silver sprinkled in his hair.

"Have I told you how incredible you've been this summer, Moni?" he asked, and her eyes filled with tears.

"Um . . . maybe," she said. Had he? Mostly, they talked about the kids and Harlow.

"Then shame on me," he said, taking her hands and kissing each of them. "Thank you for everything, the traveling back and forth, the kindness, the patience. You are the strongest, most amazing woman I've ever met."

"Thank you," she whispered. The summer would end. There were only a few weeks to go, and then her kids and husband would come back, and they could settle into their routine again, a routine that had worked beautifully, more or less, for eighteen years.

The Smiths seemed to arrive all at once, and Sanjay and

Monica went outside to greet them. There was Harlow with a towering cake covered in chocolate.

"Hi!" she said. "Matthew said this was his favorite. Vanilla cake with chocolate frosting? I hope I got it right." She bit her lip.

"It's absolutely *gorgeous*, Harlow," Monica said. She was reluctantly impressed, and tamped down her feelings of jealousy. "Wow! Thank you so much for doing this. I'd take that from you, but I'm afraid to. Come on in." She followed the younger woman up the stairs to the kitchen.

Harlow set the cake down on the counter and looked around. "Where's Matthew?"

"He's in his room. It's our tradition to have the birthday boy or girl come in last so we can announce them."

"That's really nice. Is it an Indian custom?"

"I don't think so. I think it's just . . . ours." They looked at each other for a minute. "The cake is really special," she said. It was at least three layers, with swirls and whorls of thick chocolate icing.

Harlow's eyes grew shiny. "Thank you for letting me do this," she said, gesturing to the cake. "First time." Her voice squeaked, and she put her hand to her eyes.

Monica was suddenly glad she hadn't made the cake this year. She stepped closer and put her hands on Harlow's shoulders. "I'm so glad our son has gotten to know you this summer," she said firmly, and to her surprise, her words were true. Yes, it had been chaotic and surprising, but . . . "He's needed this." She hugged Harlow carefully, felt her hiccup with a sob. "Now. I think Matthew's two mothers need something to drink, don't you? A glass of wine or an Aperol Spritz sounds perfect right now."

Harlow wiped her eyes and gave Monica a wobbly smile. "I

knew I picked a winner when I picked you," she said. "You're incredibly generous, Monica."

Suddenly, all the wariness Monica had felt for the past six weeks melted away. She squeezed Harlow's hands, gave a watery smile. "This is an emotional day," she said. "For all of us. Now come. Let's go outside and join the party."

The crowd seemed bigger than the actual number of people invited, but there were a lot of them. Ophelia Finch, Meena's friend, had come so Meena would have someone her age. Rosie, Harlow's roommate from long ago, was also present. Cynthia, the rather reserved cousin, was on one side of the older Mr. Smith, as well as a woman Monica hadn't met.

She greeted all of them in order of age, hands in prayer position, bowing slightly. Sita and Ishan would be proud. The littlest girl, Imogen, hugged her.

"Pitty bayoons," she said, pointing to the balloons.

"Thank you, sweetheart. You can have one later."

The Smith women exclaimed over her sari and Meena's salwar kameez and the beautiful yard and decorations. There were presents galore, which Meena and Ophelia were taking to the gift table.

Then she found Sanjay and took his hand, and led him to the front of the group. There was Harlow, standing next to her own mother.

"Harlow, please join us," she said. Harlow came up, hesitant, and Monica took her hand. The crowd quieted in anticipation.

"Will you do the honors?" she asked Sanjay.

"Of course," he said, his eyes so beautiful and warm. "Everyone, welcome to this very happy and important day. Smith family, we are so glad to have you share this turning point in Matthew's life. Harlow, as we have always done on Matthew's birthday, we thank you for the gift of our son."

Monica turned to Harlow and gave her hand a squeeze. Tears were pouring out of her eyes, so Monica slipped her a tissue.

"And now," Sanjay said, mimicking the MC of a quiz show, "the guest of honor, Matthew . . . Rohan . . . Patel!"

"Matthew, Matthew, Matthew," Meena started chanting, clapping Imogen's hands together to the rhythm, and everyone joined in. Then Monica's utterly beautiful son came into the yard, grinning, and everyone cheered. He held up his arms and jumped up and down, Rocky-style, and everyone laughed. Oh, her boy. Her beautiful son.

Then he came over to Sanjay and reached down to touch his foot, the traditional way to greet an elder. He did the same with her, then gave her a quick hug.

"Happy birthday, honey," she whispered. Had he grown taller this summer? He had.

"Thanks, Ma," he said.

He moved on to Harlow, touching her foot as well, then hugged her. A long time. Longer than Monica's. *Don't compare, don't compare.* Harlow whispered something, and he responded, hugged her a little more. There was a collective hum from the Smiths, and Monica heard someone crying . . . Harlow's mother.

Monica couldn't remember the last time she'd gotten a hug like that from her son.

Matthew's eyes were wet when he pulled back. He wiped them, then went on to touch the feet of his Smith grandparents, great-grandfather and aunts and uncles. Robbie, Harlow's brother, laughed and they did a complicated hand-grasp hug.

"What about your sister, dummy?" Meena asked. *Yeah, Matthew. What about the girl who's worshipped you since birth?*

"Oh, you. I forgot about you," he said, and picked her up under the arms and swung her around, making her laugh.

"Indian birthday parties have some traditions you might not have seen before," Sanjay said. "Because, I'm sorry to tell you, Americans, no one throws a party like an Indian family. Right, Moni?"

"One thousand percent," she said.

"We'll do our best to explain them as we go, but suffice it to say, we started the day with Matthew doing an act of service, which in this case meant cleaning the kitchen." Sanjay smiled. "Which was quite a mess, since we have been cooking for days. Then we said prayers for Matthew's life, health and prosperity. Unfortunately, there is no Buddhist temple here, so we went to the beach instead."

It had been lovely down there. Both kids took their heritage seriously and had prayed in silence for a few minutes as the waves came and receded.

"Another tradition is to give to the poor and less fortunate. This year, a donation was made in Matthew's name to UNICEF, and you can thank your mother for that one, son."

"Thanks, Mom," Matthew called from where he was standing next to Robbie.

"What a wonderful tradition! How thoughtful!" the grandfather exclaimed.

"And now comes the aarti. Come over here, son." Matthew came and Sanjay explained that it was tradition for the women of Matthew's family to hold the tray of candles in front of him, moving it in a circle as they asked for blessings in the year to come.

It was Monica's favorite tradition in her husband's culture, this acknowledgment of motherhood and sisterhood. She took the silver tray, stood in front of Matthew and looked into his eyes.

He raised his eyebrows, and she smiled, then moved the tray slowly in a circle.

Please, God, let him find closure and peace with Harlow. Keep him healthy. Help him be happy. Help him be kind and responsible.

She reached into the bowl of rice and turmeric and pinched a few grains, then sprinkled them on her son's head. She couldn't help it; a few tears leaked out of her eyes.

"Oh, Mom," he grumbled, but there was affection in his voice.

Then it was Meena's turn, and she took her time, grinning impishly.

"You better be saying nice prayers, Meenie," he said.

"*You'll* never know," she answered, getting a laugh. She took far too much rice and rubbed it in his hair. "Blessings upon you, older brother," she said. Monica knew her husband loved when she spoke so formally, and sure enough, he was laughing.

Harlow was watching, her heart in her eyes.

"Your turn, Harlow," Monica said.

"Really? Are you sure?"

"Of course," Monica said. She handed her the tray with the flickering candles, and everyone watched as Harlow said her prayers. She was crying. Matthew, too, pinching his eyes as men did. After Harlow had sprinkled the rice on his head, she took his face in her hands and said, "I love you, little pal." They hugged again, and Monica felt tears running down her own cheeks. She smiled at one of the sisters—the doctor—who was also crying. Her twin sister handed her a tissue and wiped her own eyes.

Then Harlow came over to Monica and hugged her, hard and long. Monica hugged her back, fiercely, suddenly protective of Harlow, wanting to be able to erase all the sadness of her life.

"Okay, all right, I think we have had enough sobbing for the day," Sanjay said, coming over to her. "Let's have some food, shall we?"

They all went to the buffet table, exclaiming over everything and filling up their plates, and then everyone sat down. Immediately, there were moans and coos at how good everything was—the crowd favorite, chicken tikka masala, as well as the curried vegetables, saag paneer, lamb vindaloo (the Patels were not vegetarians, thank heavens, because Monica loved red meat). There was meen moilee made from fresh sea bass and three kinds of naan. In addition to his many other qualities, Sanjay was an amazing cook.

"Honey, this is so wonderful," Monica said, standing on tiptoe to kiss his cheek. "Thank you."

"It was my pleasure. Thank you for our wonderful son."

He said that every year on the kids' birthdays, and on Mother's Day as well. "Thank *you*," she whispered, her throat suddenly tight.

She and Sanjay, Matthew and Harlow sat at the same table, along with Harlow's parents. Everyone ate and ate, professing to be too full before taking a few more spoonfuls, another piece of naan. Harlow's siblings laughed and bickered amicably, all of them at one table.

Everyone was happy, especially Matthew. It was truly lovely. Maybe today, all the insecurities and worries Matthew had would be put to rest.

When everyone had had thirds, and the kids were playing cornhole and running around, and everyone had had time to digest a little, Monica stood up and said in a loud voice, "Now for the pièce de résistance. Harlow made Matthew's cake this year, and it's beautiful. The birthday boy feeds a bite to each guest, and then we all get our own piece."

"I'll go get it," Harlow said.

"Absolutely not," Sanjay said. "You are our guest. Stay exactly where you are." He winked at Monica and went inside.

Matthew, who had been playing cornhole with his great-grandfather and twin aunts, came over and flopped into the chair next to her and his grandmother. So strange, that her son had all these relatives, actually related to him. Frances—who was apparently dating Harlow's grandfather, Monica had learned—joined them.

"Not a fan of cornhole?" Gerald asked.

"My bursitis," she said. "I had a flare the other day. Monica, thank you for including me. That food was incredible."

"My husband is a wonderful cook," Monica said.

Frances then turned to Harlow. "This must be a very special day for you, dear."

"It is," she said, pushing a strand of her wild, beautiful hair away from her face. "I mean, it is for everyone, Matthew especially, and his parents, but . . ." Her voice grew husky. "Yes. I'm very grateful."

Matthew gave her an odd look.

Uh-oh. Monica knew that face. It was the transition face between his Jekyll and Hyde moods the past two years. She tried to catch his eye and failed.

"Matthew, did you ever think about Harlow on your birthday?" Elsbeth asked. Shit. The worst question she could have asked, though her expression seemed innocent.

"Mom," Harlow said, the warning clear in her voice.

"Well, Sanjay said they always thanked you, honey. I'm just curious how my grandson felt. I've read that adopted children can be very . . . conflicted on their birthdays."

Monica leaned forward. "Matthew, you don't have to—"

"No, I'll answer," Matthew said, and his voice was a little hard and loud. "Yeah, of course I thought of you, Harlow. How could I not?"

She nodded, her eyes shiny once again. "I thought of you, too. Every year."

"Yeah. Sure. It made the day always kind of . . . shitty, to be honest. All this fake happiness."

"What?" Monica said. "There was nothing fake."

"Well, *Mom*," he said with exaggerated patience, once again a condescending teenager. "It *was* the day my mother gave me away. Handed me over to you guys. Being all psyched because I managed to stay alive another year . . . it felt stupid. Plus my parties were always so over-the-top, like if we had enough balloons and presents, I'd forget I was adopted."

Monica closed her mouth. "We *never* tried to make you forget, Matthew. Never. And to say she just handed you over . . . that's incredibly reductive, and you should apologize immediately. Harlow sacrificed a lot for you, and you know it."

"Yeah, well, Gran asked how it felt. I wished I *didn't* have to think of you, Harlow, but of course I did. So I'd pretend to be happy for the sake of everyone else, but a lot of the time, I just wanted to go to my room and cry. Yeah, you picked out these nice people to raise me, so thanks for that. But birthdays were also a reminder that you didn't want me."

Harlow's face was white.

"Stop it, Matthew," Monica said. "You're being cruel. Harlow, I'm so sorry."

"I'm being honest, okay? Am I allowed to do that?"

"Please excuse yourself," Monica said.

"Fine." He got up and went around the tent toward the water.

Harlow looked like she'd been clubbed, just as she had on this very day eighteen years ago. Everyone else sat in silence.

"Do you want to come inside?" Monica asked her quietly. "We can talk."

"No. No, like he said, he's being . . . honest. It's okay. He should be." Harlow took a shaky breath. "I'll just . . . just walk around a little. This yard is so beautiful." Her parents went with her.

And here was Sanjay, carrying the cake and setting it carefully on the table. "Time for this glorious cake! Matt? Cake time, son." He looked at Monica, finally noting the tension. "What did I miss?"

"A lot," she said. She pulled him a few feet away. "Matthew just informed us that his birthdays are all sad, he fakes happiness and he resents being given up for adoption."

"Oh, dear."

"Yes, Sanjay! Oh, dear! Can you speak to him? He was horrible to Harlow. And to me."

"What did he say?"

Too many people were watching, having seen or overheard Matthew's rudeness. "I'll tell you later," she whispered. "Just tell him to apologize to Harlow and let's get this party finished."

"On it," he said, looking around. "Meena, where's your brother?"

"He and Robbie went out in the kayak," Meena said, pointing. Sure enough, there they were, out in the salt marsh, paddling away.

"Matt!" Sanjay yelled in his schoolteacher voice. "Matt, get back here, son."

The little *shit*, leaving his own party, dumping that emotional vomit on both her and Harlow and just walking away. Monica's face was hot with fury.

He wasn't being fair. Yes, he sometimes got sad on his birthdays, and when he was small, he did cry. He forgot to mention who had held him during his tears, though. *She* had. She had told him it was normal to miss his first mother, and that Harlow was thinking of him, too, and it was okay that he was crying. Sometimes she'd cried with him, goddamn it, because she'd never forgotten how ruined Harlow had looked when she'd handed her baby to Monica. It had to have been the worst and most difficult moment of her life.

Fake-happy for her sake. Bullshit. He'd been legitimately happy, and he'd been sad sometimes, too. The two were not mutually exclusive. He had not faked happiness. She knew her son too well for him to claim that.

Sanjay called Matthew again. They were ridiculously far away, and neither Robbie nor he responded, because the wind was gusting. Finally, Sanjay whistled, something she hated—"Our children are not dogs," she would say—but she had to admit, it worked now. Robbie waved, and they turned around and began paddling back. The wind was against them, and their progress was not quick.

Finally, they came ashore, laughing, dragging the kayak up on the lawn. Laughing. How dare he? Her son studiously did not look at her.

"Cake time, Matthew," Monica said, her voice hard. "Harlow made you a beautiful cake."

Except it wasn't. In the time between when Sanjay had brought it down and when the two guys had come back, the cake's swoops and swirls had slowly and inexorably melted in the heat, sliding down the side of the cake. Harlow's face, not great at hiding emotions, spasmed as she tried not to cry.

"This is what happens when you leave your own party, Matthew," Monica hissed as he came near. She tried to use a butter knife to push the frosting back, but it was futile. "It was rude and unkind." Where was Sanjay? He was supposed to be saying this, but no, he was talking to Grandpop. "You need to apologize to Harlow immediately."

"I'll do it later," he said. "I'm eighteen, Mom. You can't tell me when to talk to my other mother."

She couldn't reprimand him without making a scene, and he knew it. She gave him a look, then cut the cake in hard, angry moves. She chopped up a slice into enough pieces for Matthew to feed his guests, but the happy, united feeling was dead in the water.

There'd be a stern conversation later this afternoon, but Monica already knew it wouldn't do a damn thing.

THIRTY-TWO

HARLOW

After his birthday, Matthew didn't seem to have a lot of time for me. As we slid into August, I heard that he and Robbie had gone fishing again. He and Winnie had gone out for lunch at the Ho. He'd stopped by the gallery for a painting lesson with my mom. My mom, who'd inadvertently ruined his birthday by asking if he'd missed me.

He didn't drop in at Open Book, and he let my texts sit for hours before answering them in a few words. His time on the Cape was running out, a thought that made my heart bang erratically in my chest.

Grady and I met for dinner, but it fell flat. The magic from that first night was missing, and we both noticed it as we ran out of things to talk about.

"What's going on?" he asked. "You seem down."

"I just . . . I'm getting sad about Matthew leaving."

"You'll see him again, won't you?"

"I hope so. He's been avoiding me. Let's talk about something else. Tell me about your conference." But my heart was elsewhere.

I reminded myself that Grady was a father. If he and I got serious—and Grady was a pretty serious guy—there was Luna, and she was a terrifying prospect. Without her, being with Grady was a no-brainer. But look at the damage I'd done to Matthew. How would he feel if I had another kid in my life? As sweet as Luna was—and I winced thinking the next thought—she might be a deal breaker. What if I messed up with her? She was only four.

Today, the weather was clear and hot with low humidity, a perfect beach day, and Open Book was relatively quiet. I tried to busy myself by looking through the winter catalog online to see what I'd order.

"Hey," Destiny said, making me jump. "Sorry," she added. "A little tense?"

I sighed. "Yeah. What's up?"

"I just wanted to share the happy news that Kate and I are officially dating, thanks to you."

"Kate, the hot bartender from singles night?" I asked.

"The very one." Destiny blushed.

"Honey, that's great!"

"It is," she said. "I've been looking for a while. Tons of horrible online dates. It's hard to hope when you're"—she gestured to herself—"complicated."

"There's nothing complicated about you, Des. You're a lovely, smart, kindhearted person. Kate is a lucky woman."

She smiled. "You'll be my maid of honor if we get married."

"Damn straight I will. Aw, Destiny, I'm so happy for you."

"Thanks. I've been single a long time. I'll admit I've been lonely."

I have, too. I was surprised by the thought. I didn't think I had ever really admitted that to myself before.

My phone chimed, and I jumped as if electrocuted. It was Grady.

Going out to take some seabed samples this afternoon. Want to
come?

Sorry, I'm at work, I responded. Another time, I hope.

As long as I had my phone out, I checked my most recent
exchanges with Matthew. Four bland, hi-how-are-you texts over
the past two days. No responses.

This was stupid. I felt suddenly angry. The kid had manipu-
lated his entire family into coming to the Cape so he could be
with me. My thumbs moved across the screen.

Matthew, you're leaving in a couple of weeks. I'm sorry for every
negative feeling you have about being adopted, but do you think we
could talk in person like adults? Because this silence is childish and
irritating.

Before I could talk myself out of it, I hit send.

I think, for the first time, I'd spoken to him like a mother.

The three dots waved immediately. okay. when did you have
in mind?

I'd taken a ton of time off this summer already, but I had a
ton banked, too. The store was quiet, Grandpop taking his afternoon nap on the couch with Ollie.

Now works, I typed.

Can you come here?

Sure.

I knocked on the office door, then opened it.

"What?" Cynthia said, slapping her laptop shut.

"Watching clown porn again, Cynthia?"

"No! Of course not! Oh. That was a joke."

"It was." I hadn't had a conversation with Cynthia in a long time, for the simple reason that she liked to lecture me about failures as a business owner. Still, I always felt a little guilty for not liking her more, since Grandpop loved her.

"How have you been?" I asked.

"Oh, fine. Actually . . ." She paused. "I'm actually doing very well."

Wow. Surprising. "That's good to hear."

"Thank you." Was that . . . was that a smile on her face?

"Thanks for coming to Matthew's birthday party," I said.

"I was happy to be invited." Another pause. "He's a nice young man."

Had she been drinking? This was the most pleasant conversation we'd ever had. "Cynthia, I hate to do this to you again, but I need to take a few hours off this afternoon."

"Go ahead," she said. "Things are slow today."

She *had* been drinking, then. "I'll make it up to you."

"I would appreciate that, actually, because I'm planning a trip to Long Island in the near future, and I'll need a good week off."

She looked at me expectantly, so I bit. "Visiting friends, or just being a tourist?"

She sat up a little straighter. "Family, actually. I've recently met my biological sisters. Apparently, they've been looking for me for a long time. There are three of them."

"Oh, my gosh! How was it?"

"It was . . . unexpectedly wonderful," she said. She smiled again, looking ten years younger.

"I'm really happy for you. Pretty big development, am I right?"

"Well, let's not make a Hallmark movie just yet, Harlow," she said. "You said you had somewhere to go?"

"I do. Thanks, Cynthia."

"I'm going by Cindy these days."

"Okay. Thanks, Cindy."

Was it possible that my sour-faced, judgmental cousin was becoming . . . I hesitated at the word *human*, but now that I thought of it, she *had* been a little nicer to the customers, complimenting Pierce DeJonge on reading above his grade level, telling our resident erotica lover, Karen Henderson, to have a nice day. She'd even had an entire conversation with Bertie Baines that lasted at least twenty minutes.

I scooped up Ollie from my grandfather's chest, because Ollie was the ultimate icebreaker, and Matthew loved him. Checked to make sure Grandpop was still breathing, then drove down to Eastham. The house the Patels had rented never failed to take my breath away. I could only imagine how much it cost to rent for the entire season.

Matthew was standing in the yard. "Hi," he said as I got out of the car. "Ollie! How are you, buddy?" Oliver leaped and danced around him. *Well done, doggy.*

"Thanks for meeting me," I said. "Are your parents home?"

"Mom's back in California, but Dad and Meena are inside doing a science project. Meena's probably a genius, in case you haven't noticed."

"I have. She's helping Ophelia with math, and she's a year behind her in school."

Matthew looked toward the water. "Want to go kayaking?"

I wanted to talk, but he obviously had to be receptive and open. "Sure."

"I'll just tell my dad." He went to the front door, opened it and yelled, "Dad, Harlow's here and we're going kayaking. Okay. Yep. Bye."

We walked down the yard to the edge of the water. It was full-on high tide, and it would be easy to kayak down the twisty little river. It was a perfect day, the sun hot, the air dry. We made our way past the muddy hummocks of grass that, at low tide, you could stand on but now were evident only by the sharp tips of grass peeking out of the brackish water. Horseshoe crabs trundled along on the sandy bottom, and an osprey flew overhead, a fish in its talons still wriggling.

Matthew stopped paddling, withdrew his phone and took a few pictures. Would he show them to his friends back home, saying, "My birth mother and I went kayaking here," or would he delete them in anger someday?

"Want to pull up here so we can talk?" I said, pointing to a stretch of sand up ahead.

"Sure," Matthew said.

We paddled up, then got out to pull our kayaks up on land. Ollie leaped off and rolled in the sand, then flipped over and sneezed, making Matthew laugh.

On the other side of the little beach was the ocean, the salt marsh we'd just paddled through behind us. We sat down side by side, watching the ocean, calm today, lapping at the shore.

"Someday, this little beach will be gone," I said. "The Cape changes every year."

"Yeah, we saw the movie at the Visitor Center," he said, and his voice was neither hostile nor friendly.

"*The Sands of Time*," I said. "A classic."

A seagull flew overhead, dropping a crab to crack its shell, and Ollie raced over to eat it first.

"Oliver, drop!" I said, and my genius dog did, looking at me with disappointed eyes. The seagull dove in, cackling, and re-trieved its catch, then flew away. Ollie came over and lay down next to Matthew, panting, and Matthew petted him idly.

"So do you want to talk?" I asked.

He sighed. "As good a time as any, I guess." He picked up a stone he apparently found fascinating and turned it in his fingers.

"Why have you been avoiding me, honey?"

He cut me a look. "See, that's just it. You're awesome, Har-low. We've had a blast this summer, and you call me 'honey' and introduce me to your whole family, and *they're* awesome, and like . . . why didn't you let me have this?" He threw the pebble into the water. "It's not like we would've been living in a shelter or under a bridge."

I watched the ocean for a long minute. "There's no good an-swer to that, Matthew. We've talked about this. Every choice was wrong in some way, and every choice could've also been right."

"But you didn't even try," he said.

I turned to look at him. He was so tan, so handsome. "Should I have kept you for a month or two, then figured out that I couldn't raise you? Would that have been better?"

"No. But you could've brought me here. Your parents are great. They would've helped, right? And your sisters and Robbie?"

"Robbie was eight when you were born, honey. The twins were sophomores, and Winnie was eleven."

"Still. I guess I feel robbed of all this. Of being a Cape Cod kid in this big, happy family. You gave me away, and I can't not feel mad about it."

Suddenly, I'd had enough of that idea. The *agony* of that en-tire experience had brought me to my fucking knees, and I was sick and tired of people telling me I'd done the wrong thing.

"Matthew," I snapped, surprising us both, "I didn't give you *away.* I gave you *to* your parents. I didn't throw you in a garbage can or pass you off to a stranger on the bus or leave you in a cardboard box in front of a firehouse."

"Yeah, but—"

"Listen to me. I chose your parents out of more than a hundred couples, because I thought they would be best for *you.* I put you in their arms, literally. And it *killed* me. Part of me died that day. But if I could travel back in time, I'd do it again. They did a better job than I *ever* could have because they were *adults.* They *wanted* a child. They had jobs, a house, savings. I was seventeen. Seventeen! Not even old enough to vote! Do *you* feel ready to raise a child? Take care of an infant? Even if your parents would help? Do you?"

He started to say something, then changed his mind. After a second, he shook his head. "No."

"You have that letter from me. I wrote it at the most vulnerable time in my life. I was terrified to keep you and terrified to give you away. Read it again. Then go look into your mother's eyes and tell me I did the wrong thing."

He covered his eyes with one hand, and it took me a second to realize he was crying.

"Hey," I said. "Come here. Ollie, not you." I wrapped my arms around my son, and my eyes filled, too. "It's okay," I whispered. "It's okay to feel both ways. I know exactly what that's like."

"It's never gonna be over, is it? Thinking about the life we might have had."

"No. It'll never be over," I said, pulling back to look in his eyes, those beautiful dark eyes, the same shape and color as mine. I wiped a tear from under his thick lashes. "Matthew, sometimes we just have to hope that things work out, because being absolutely sure of something . . . it doesn't happen a lot." I ran my hand over his wet hair. "But I'm absolutely sure that having you was right. I've never been sorry about that. Not for a second."

He dropped his forehead to my shoulder. We stayed there a moment, me holding my boy. Then, inevitably, he straightened up. Ollie, who'd been watching us morosely, leaped onto Matthew and started licking his face, making him smile.

"Okay," he said. "Let's do something tomorrow, maybe. But right now, I want to go home and just be with my . . . my family."

My brain felt soggy with emotions and exhaustion by the time I got home. It was past six already. The sky was darkening with the promise of thunder, big clouds rolling in from the west, matching my mood. I could wax the boat tomorrow.

I checked my phone—Grandpop had texted, Hello, my dear Hharlow!!! I am fine, and how are you? Don't worry about dinner tonight, because I am going to the lovely Frances's house to meet her son, who is forty-nine. If you can believe frances has a son that old, that is!!! Ssee you tomorrow and sleep well, honey.. Also, this text took me twenty minutes to type. Technology is perhaps beyond your old Grandpop.

The world's most perfect man. I smiled, typed a quick response and sighed.

I was wicked tired. It would be great to shower, get some takeout and watch a movie with Rosie. I went inside, heard a noise in Rosie's room and went up to chat. Gave a quick knock and opened the door, and found my best friend in bed with my little brother.

THIRTY-THREE

HARLOW

I shrieked. Rosie also shrieked.

"What are you doing here, Harlow?" she asked, clutching the sheet to her throat.

"I *live* here. This is my house!"

"Right, right. Shit, Robbie, we're in trouble."

"Yeah," Robbie said. He started to get out of bed.

"Stop!" I barked. "I don't want to see you naked. Just . . . just get dressed and come downstairs. Jesus, you guys."

I went down to the kitchen, fed my dog, got the bag of frozen peas out of the freezer and pressed it against my head, since I had an abrupt headache.

Rosie and Robbie? She was eleven years older than he was. *Eleven.* He'd met her when he was, what . . . eight? Ew! Also, my brother was a whore, more or less.

I heard him coming down the stairs, and there he stood, looking suitably embarrassed. "Harlot—"

"Call me that again and I'll kick you till you're dead." I glared at him. "How much did you two drink or smoke, by the way?"

"Not that much."

"Not that much *what*, Robbie?"

He looked guilty as sin. "We had a couple drinks at the Ice House, just kind of flirting, and decided to walk back here."

"How many drinks is a couple?" I demanded.

"Two beers."

"How many did *she* have?"

"Um . . . three maybe?"

"Three what? She hates beer."

"Three martinis."

"So you slept with a drunk woman. You know what we call that, Robbie? Sexual assault."

"Jesus, Harlow! It wasn't like that." He paused as my dog put his front legs on his knee, begging for a pat. "I've been in love with her my whole life."

"What? No, you haven't. You've slept with half of the female population of Cape Cod."

"Yeah, well, I don't get to see her very often." He looked at me, his face serious for once. "But when I do, I love her. I'd love her all the time if she was around more."

"You sound like an idiot. You know what? Get out. I'll talk to Rosie alone. Go. Out with you." I grabbed him by his shirt and dragged him to the door, Ollie leaping and barking excitedly at our new game—Evict the Brother.

"Don't be mad," he said.

"Too late." I closed the door in his face.

I could hear the water running upstairs. Rosie was taking a shower. Good.

Three martinis before 6 p.m.? That was problem drinking. No doubt about that.

Finally the water shut off, and a minute later, Rosie came down in blue-and-white-striped pajamas, looking about twelve years old. She sat on the couch and didn't look at me.

"How drunk are you right now?" I asked sternly.

"Not very. A little buzzed." She sat on the edge of the couch, looking appropriately chastened. Without makeup on, she had clearly visible shadows under her eyes.

Images from the past month reshuffled in my mind. How my recycling bin was always empty. How often Rosie disappeared to "do some work" allegedly at the library or a café, even though she said she was taking a break from work. She always came home looser and more carefree than when she left. Last week, we'd gone into the packie, and Joe behind the counter had said, "You again, gorgeous!" The night Grady had walked us home.

"Rosie," I said, my voice abruptly soft. "Forget about Robbie. I'm worried about you."

She nodded.

"You have a drinking problem."

"I know," she said, her voice cracking. "I'm sorry."

"Oh, honey," I said, and I went over to her and put my arms around her. She was shaking. "Talk to me."

"I don't know when it went from a couple of drinks a night to a few to five or six," she said, tears falling. "I've been drinking in secret for two years now. At work. At my father's. Here." She glanced at me. "I go to the landfill every day so you won't see the empties."

"Oh, Rosie." Tears slid down my face, too.

"Every morning, I wake up and tell myself this is Day One without alcohol, and by noon, my hands are shaking and all I can think about is having a drink. So I have what I tell myself is just one little glass of wine, which is more like a huge glass of wine, and I feel better. Then an hour later, I need another, and then it's three, and then you're around and I have a cocktail." She blew her nose. "I got fired, in case you couldn't tell. No one in LA gets a month off."

"Why didn't you say something? I'm your best friend."

"Because who wants to admit that they're a drunk? And now you walked in on Robbie and me, and I'm so sorry, Harlow."

"Okay, okay," I said. "Eventually I'm going to skin him alive, though. He should know better than to have sex with a drunk person."

"Well, I made the first move. And really, I've been wanting to for a while."

I winced. "It was probably a dream come true for him." I got up to get her a glass of water from the kitchen, one for myself as well, and sat back down in my chair.

"I didn't want to lie to you," she said. "But I didn't want to shit on your parade, either. You were so happy about Matthew, and I didn't want you to worry about me. Harlow . . . you're my best friend. Please don't tell me I just ruined that."

"Of course not! God, you've gotten me through the worst days of my life. I'm not gonna dump you because you have a drinking problem."

"Substance use disorder," she sniffled.

"Right." I looked at her a minute. "Listen, honey. I'm gonna call your dad and we can figure out what to do, okay?"

"He'll be so disappointed in me."

"He'll be glad you're being honest and asking for help." I paused. "You are asking, right?"

"Definitely. I knew it was getting out of hand. I was just waiting till . . . well, I'm lying. I was seeing how long I could get away with it. I knew it had to a stop, but I wasn't gonna do anything until I got caught. But yeah, I don't want to be like this, Harlow. I'm such a fucking mess."

"Well, you're my fucking mess."

She sob-laughed, then blew her nose again. "I'll call my father. It's time."

When she had spent twenty minutes on the phone with her father, she handed the phone to me. "He wants to say hi," she said, her eyes red.

"Hi, Mr. Wolfe," I said.

"You're supposed to call me Victor," he said. "Hi, Harlow. How are you? It's been quite a summer, from what I understand."

"That's an understatement," I said. "What can we do for Rosie?"

"I'm going to get her on a plane and fly her back here as soon as possible," he said. "I'm really sorry you had to deal with this."

"No, it's okay. She's my best friend in the world." I pointed at Rosie as I said this, and she smiled.

"I'm making a reservation at a rehab place I know."

"In Los Angeles?"

He hesitated. "Do you have another place in mind?"

I glanced at Rosie. "Do you want to be up here, or back in California?"

"Near you," she answered immediately.

"Mr. Wolfe, can you find a place closer to me?"

"That's not necessary," he said. "I'll always have time for my daughter. You know how much I love her."

"I do," I said. "But I love her, too. She saved my life, Mr. Wolfe. You both did. I wouldn't mind repaying the favor. At all." I looked at Rosie, who looked achingly hopeful. "In fact, I insist on it."

"Well, okay. I'll take a look around and find a program. Residential, though. Once she's through that, we can talk again."

"That sounds good."

"You give my girl a hug, okay? She's the most important thing in the world to me."

"I will. Thanks, Mr. Wolfe."

"Victor." I could hear the smile in his voice as he hung up.

"Your dad said he loves you," I said, hugging her. "And I love you. You'll be okay. You'll get sober, and we'll take it from there."

Once Rosie was fed, we went through her room and gathered her stash. A vodka bottle under the bathroom sink. Gin in her suitcase. A few little bottles in her makeup kit, and a bottle of wine on the windowsill. I got rid of them, and my stuff, too, dumped it all down the drain. Then I tucked her in, assured her she'd be okay.

"Will you tell Robbie? About rehab?" she asked.

"You bet." I sat on her bed until she fell asleep, then went downstairs and summoned my brother, filling him in about her plans.

"Yeah. Okay," he said, sitting at the kitchen table looking utterly wretched. "That sounds smart. I mean, I knew she overindulged. I didn't realize it was this bad."

"It is."

"Can I see her before she goes?" he asked.

"That's not up to me. You can ask her tomorrow when she's awake."

He looked up at me. "I've loved her since I was twelve, Harlow."

"Robbie, you're such a pain in my ass."

He grinned at that, and just like always, his adorableness made it impossible to be mad at him. If what he said was true, it was kind of . . . well . . . as much as I hated to admit it, it was kind of sweet.

He got up, gave me a hug and said, "Love you, sis."

"I love you, too, idiot." I gave him a smack on the head.

"Hey, totally meaning to change the subject," he said, "you good with Matt?"

I softened. My brother had noticed and cared to ask. "Yes," I said. "Thank you for asking."

"I really like him."

"Me too."

"I'm glad you got knocked up, Harlot."

That stopped me for a second. No one had ever said that to me before.

"Me too," I said. "Now get out. Don't text me for at least a day." But this time, I was smiling as I closed the door.

THIRTY-FOUR

CYNTHIA

In the weeks that had passed since she'd met her sisters—and had been seeing Albert a few times a week—Cynthia felt unmoored.

But not in a bad way. In a freeing way, like a sailboat that had been stuck on a sandbar, waiting for the tide to come in. She had told Albert about her lunch, and the subsequent warm flurry of messages and phone calls she and her sisters had exchanged.

"I don't think my mother—Miriam—knew my birth mother was looking," she said now, as they sat on the patio. He'd surprised her with two wooden Adirondack chairs he'd made himself. "If she had, there would've been a sign, some indication."

"Then you're probably right." He put his warm, calloused hand over hers.

"When I picture my birth parents, missing me, going to the orphanage . . . it's heartbreaking."

"It sure is," he said calmly. "Those poor people, losing their little girl."

"I'm glad they had other daughters. I hoped it helped ease the pain a bit."

"Mm. Doubt it. I lost my older boy when he was ten. My wife and I had another a couple years later, but Rudy didn't take Jeb's place. We loved Rudy, of course, but we still had a hole in our hearts."

"Oh, Albert! I'm so sorry."

"He was a good boy. A sweetheart."

Albert had never mentioned that tragedy. Cynthia supposed that with all her talking and fretting, she hadn't given him much room to. "What was he like?" she asked.

Albert glanced at her with a little smile, his eyes gleaming with tears. "Big heart. Loved to fish. Not book smart, but common sense, you know? Looked out for his little sisters, taught Lizzie to tie her shoes. That kind of thing. Real steady."

"How did he die?"

"Appendicitis that took a bad turn. It was an awful shock. When they told us, my wife, God, the sound that came outta her. I hope to God never to hear somethin' like that again."

Cynthia squeezed his hand with both of hers. "I'm so sorry. How devastating, Albert."

He gave a gruff laugh. "Look at you with your soft heart. Sweet of you to be sad for me over somethin' that happened decades ago. But I've made my peace with it. I hope to see him in heaven someday."

"I'm sure you will," she said, though she didn't quite know what to believe about all that. It was a nice thought, that all four of her parents would be there, happy to see her, holding her in their arms again. And certainly, she wanted Albert to reunite with his son.

"You got a lot to be happy about, Cindy. You have three sisters you didn't have a couple months ago. And all those nieces and nephews, and their babies, too. That's a real blessing, innit?"

How was this crusty old man so positive? He'd lost his wife and his young son, he wandered the streets like a vagrant. But he was liked by everyone, always helping out a neighbor . . . and somehow, he'd seen something positive in her.

The sunset was beginning, a ray peeking from under the clouds, suddenly lighting up the western sky. A flock of terns winged past, chattering, and out on the mudflats, the little piping plovers darted back and forth, dipping their beaks in the shallow water. The tide had rippled the sand, and the remaining water reflected the sky.

She was so glad to be here, in this moment, with Bertie Baines.

"Bertie, I have to ask you . . . why did you try so hard to be my friend when I gave you absolutely nothing in return?"

He cocked his head and looked at her, then took a sip of his Narragansett beer, which she now kept on hand for him. "Guess I saw how lonely you were."

That sentence went straight to her heart. All her judgment and hardness, all that pretense that she was better than everyone else . . . and this raggedy, weathered man had seen right through her.

"You're also pretty easy on the eyes," he added. "I said to myself, 'Play your cards right, Bertie boy, and you might have a chance with that one there.'"

She laughed and her heart lightened. "I'm glad you took it," she said.

"So am I. I hope I get to meet these sisters of yours," he said.

"I've already told them about you," she answered. "They're

coming to visit in October, so watch out. You'll have all four of us to contend with."

It was his turn to laugh. Then they just sat, watching the brilliant sunset gentle until the sliver of a moon, as sweet and delicate as a baby's fingernail, appeared in the sky.

There was no place she'd rather be.

THIRTY-FIVE

HARLOW

Two days after Rosie had admitted her problem, she and I headed off-Cape to a rehab facility in Mattapoisett, just fifteen minutes over the bridge.

We had talked more honestly about her life in the past two days than we had in years. How she'd take clients out to dinner, send them off and go back into the restaurant to keep drinking. On business trips, she'd order room service from whatever posh hotel she was staying at so she could drink to a blackout state. She told me how alcohol began creeping into her workdays. How she vomited on the owner of a house she was scouting and lied about eating bad fish as she staggered to the bathroom. The lies she told her father, so he wouldn't know how much she drank. She was less careful with her mother, who finally told her not to visit if she was just going to get wasted.

I was devastated to hear it all. How had I missed it? What kind of friend was I not to realize Rosie was sinking? But she assured me she'd been working very hard to hide it, and we hadn't spent any real time together for years. Not like we had this summer. Matthew finding me was what brought Rosie and me back together and, in doing so, gave me this chance to help my friend.

"I guess what I'll find out in rehab is why I'm such a mess," she said, looking out the car window. Her voice was sad and sincere.

I glanced at her, then took her hand. "I'm so proud of you for what you're doing. You know, a lot of people are so sunk in denial, they can't agree to get help. You're already a step ahead."

"Well, the truth is, I kind of hit bottom. I mean, even though it looked like I came here to be a great pal, it was also the perfect place to hide."

"But you're not hiding now."

"I guess."

"Rosie, even I can see that you were a little girl essentially abandoned by your parents. They loved you, but they were too busy for you. So you pretended to be happy, to be the life of the party so they wouldn't forget about you, and you haven't stopped since. You're afraid no one will like the real you."

She wiped her eyes. "Shit, Harlow. I think you just saved me thousands in therapy."

"You're wrong, you know. I know the real you, and I love you with all my heart."

"That's what your brother said."

I turned my signal on (a quaint skill no longer taught in Massachusetts) and changed lanes. "He says he's been in love with you for a long time."

"Yeah, he told me. But I don't know if he really knows who I am, or if I'm just this hot fantasy . . . his big sister's best friend. There are hundreds of pornos about that." She grew more serious. "He has a big heart, but I need to get my head straight before I think about that."

"Just keep in mind that I'm very protective of him. *And* you." I paused. "That being said, he's been an amazing brother this summer."

"Yeah, I noticed that. One of the reasons I . . . never mind. So this place, Meadowbrook," she said, changing the subject. "You were at what, the Willows? Mom's second husband went to Mustang Creek. Dad's law partner is currently at Blue River, and I'm going to Meadowbrook. Why all the nature names? Why not Liver-Rest or Napping House?"

"Because no one would ever leave Napping House," I said. "Which is also a very fine children's book."

"Oh, and Dad's partner? An actor they represent yelled at him, and he just broke down. Turns out he's exhausted because . . . yes . . . he has two families, one in LA, one in Thousand Oaks."

"Are you kidding?" We spent the rest of the drive speculating about how a person would pull that off.

We took the exit and found Meadowbrook, which had once been a boarding school for boys. It was lovely. Lots of trees and flower beds and paths. We parked, and I hauled Rosie's suitcase to the reception area, where they started the check-in process. Name, date of birth, insurance, emergency contact.

"Harlow? she asked. "Would you do me the honor of being my emergency contact?"

"I will," I said, my throat tightening. She had been mine when I was pregnant. We'd come full circle.

"We'll have to go through that suitcase and make sure you don't have any drugs or alcohol or other contraband," the staffer told Rosie with a kind smile. "And your friend has to leave, too."

"Can't she come in and see my room?" Rosie asked, suddenly sounding like a little kid.

"Afraid not. No visitors until you're approved. Same with phone calls and texts. You should say your goodbyes now."

We started to go outside for some privacy. "Sorry," called the staffer, whose name was Liara, according to her name tag. "Rose, you have to stay inside now that you're checked in."

I faced her and put my hands on her shoulders. "You can do this, Rosie. You *will* do this."

"I'm scared," she whispered. "What if I can't?"

"You can and you will."

"How do you know?"

"Because I've known you for half your life, and you're the best, kindest, funniest person I've ever met. You love being alive, more than anyone I know, and there's just too much great stuff you don't want to miss because you're drunk. You came through for me when I was pregnant. You came through when I needed you this summer. Now you're going to come through for yourself."

She wiped her eyes. "That was a great speech."

"I mean it."

"That's why it was great." She hugged me, and I kissed her temple.

"I love you," I whispered, because my throat was so tight.

"I love you, too." She squeezed me a little harder, then let go. "Thanks, bestie," she said. "I don't know what I'd do without you. Now get out of here. I have sobriety to find."

Thank goodness I had a date with Grady that night. It was a big day, and I still felt very emotional about leaving Rosie at Meadowbrook. So much had happened that I wanted to tell him about. He picked me up at seven on the dot.

"You want to walk?" he said. "We have reservations at the Wicked Oyster."

"Sure," I said. "Let me say goodbye to Grandpop, okay?"

We went down the stairs and into my grandfather's place. He was sitting in front of the TV, watching *The Crown* and eating goldfish crackers. He paused it when we came in, but didn't get up. I knew his knees were hurting in this weather—you could predict a storm based on Grandpop's knees.

"How did you like that chowder?" I asked him. I'd brought him supper at five o'clock.

"Delicious!" Grandpop said. "And the bread, Harlow! I loved it."

I smiled. "I got it warm at the market," I said. "Are you going to stay in tonight?"

"I am. Who's this handsome young man?"

"This is Grady Byrne, Grandpop. You know him. He's a Kingslayer."

"Of course! You're out of context, that's all. And you're Luna's father, am I right?"

"Yes, sir."

"Such a sweet little girl!"

"Thank you," Grady said. "I agree."

"Well, take care of *my* little girl. Don't tell anyone, but she's my favorite," he said.

"You say that about Lark, too," I said.

"I'm an old man. I can do what I want," he said.

I laughed. "I'll check on you when I get back, okay?"

"I'll be asleep, but you do you, as the kids say these days." He took another fistful of crackers and turned back to Queen Elizabeth.

As we walked, Grady took my hand. It felt both wonderful and strange. Everyone who saw us holding hands would know we were a thing. The thought made me giddy.

The hostess seated us outside. "Rain's not supposed to start till after midnight," she said, giving us our menu and a list of cocktails.

"I could use a drink," I said, feeling guilty at the thought of Rosie. "A glass of sauvignon blanc, and a big glass of water," I added.

"Make it two," Gray said, and she smiled and went off.

"So what's new, Grady Byrne?" I asked.

"Not much. Being a dad. Working."

I waited for more, but he didn't say anything. Instead, he just looked at me, a faint smile flirting with his mouth. And it was a nice mouth, I had to say. "When did you get so hot?" I asked, then clapped my hand over my own mouth.

He gave a big laugh. "I think the bigger question is, when did you finally notice?"

"Well, *someone* has an ego."

"No, trust me. Being in the friend zone since I was fifteen has kept any ego in check."

"What? You've loved me for twenty years? Except for that brief decade away when you were married to a Texas billionaire beauty queen?"

He tilted his head and raised an eyebrow. "No comment."

"Let's get back to our conversation. How are you, Gray?"

"I'm good," he said, chuckling. "Luna starts preschool in September, and she's really excited and I'm . . . not."

"Your little girl is growing up."

"Exactly. Also, Vivienne has given notice that she wants to start college in January, so I'm looking for another nanny. And my parents are coming for a week in October, so that'll be nice." He paused. "You'll have to come for dinner."

"Okay." Wow. He wanted me to meet his parents. It felt very . . . relationship-serious. And while that was great, it was also terrifying. That whole family thing. Maybe Gray and I could just date forever. That felt a lot more comfortable. A nonresidential partner with frequent visitation rights. How much harm could I do to Luna that way?

"I also just got a grant from the Gates Foundation for coastal conservation."

"Whoa! Congratulations! Very big deal, Gray! Here's to you." I raised my water glass.

There was that crooked smile. "Yeah. Thanks."

"So this grant, does it say you get a congratulatory kiss?" I was flirting. Not badly, either.

"I think that's part of the fine print, yes."

"Let me do it right, then," I said. "In case Bill is watching." I got up, tugged my dress (yes, a dress), fluffed my hair and leaned over him, my face four inches from his. Those green eyes . . . unfair. "You ready, Dr. Byrne?"

"I am."

I kissed him, his lips soft and firm, just long enough to let him know I liked him, short enough so as not to horrify any parents with kids here tonight. Then I waved to Karen Henderson, who was holding hands with a man at least twenty years younger than she was, then to Reverend White, who also appeared to be on a date. Seemed like everyone was smiling.

We ordered dinner and ate; flirted; talked about Matthew, Luna, my family. Then, about halfway through dinner, I heard one of my favorite songs of all time, an instrumental version of "Heroes" by David Bowie (may he be reincarnated, and fast).

"I love this song," I said.

"Yeah, he's pretty good."

"David Bowie? He's more than pretty good, Gray. He's a *god*."

Grady smiled, doing that thing to my sensitive parts. "I meant the guy playing the cello."

The music was live? My head whipped around like the little girl in *The Exorcist*.

It was James. My human vibrator.

"Um . . . Gray, so I . . . I kind of know that guy."

"You know David Bowie?" he teased.

"The cellist. James? His name is James. He and I had a little . . . uh . . . arrangement? Nothing serious. We didn't date or anything."

Grady gave a nod. "Got it. You were fuck buddies."

I cringed. "Yeah."

"When was the last time you saw him?"

"May? April? It's been a while."

He thought a minute, which was the problem with smart people. The thinking. "Do you want to say something to him?" he asked.

"No. I do not."

"Well, he'll probably see you. I mean, we're twenty feet away." He smiled suddenly. "You wanna hide?"

I sagged with relief. "You're not . . . upset or anything?"

"If you were sleeping with him right now, I would certainly be upset."

"I'm not." I let out a breath. "Thanks."

The smile was back. In that moment, I wanted to climb him like a black bear climbs a tree.

The song ended.

"Brace yourself," Grady said. "Here he comes."

Sure enough, James approached us.

"James!" I said. "That was just . . . lovely. Can't go wrong with Bowie."

"Hi." His broody musical thing, complete with long unkempt hair and a tattoo of the first bars of Bach's first cello concerto on his neck, now seemed really . . . dumb.

"This is Grady Byrne."

"Hi," Grady said.

James looked between us. "I guess I won't be seeing you anymore?"

"You're correct," I said.

"Well. Have a good night."

"You too," I said.

He went back to his stool in the corner of the courtyard and started playing again. "Here Comes the Sun," by George Harrison.

"Can't fault his taste in music," Grady said.

"You could probably sense the deep and meaningful bond we had," I said, and I started giggling in the most wonderful, unstoppable way until tears ran down my face. And all the while, Grady Byrne looked at me with those warm green eyes as if I was the most wonderful woman on earth.

Our server came and cleared our plates, then asked if we wanted to see a dessert menu.

I didn't. I wanted to bring Gray back to my place and take off his clothes. His eyebrow rose as if he'd read my mind. That was one eloquent eyebrow, that was for sure.

"I'm fine," I said. "We'll take the check."

This time when we walked down the street, Grady's grip was a little tighter, and our steps were a bit faster. When we got to my doorstep, he turned me to him and, without preamble, kissed me, hungry and solid, and my God, he *was* incredibly hot. His mouth was gorgeous on mine, and when our tongues met, my legs practically gave out. He gripped my hair, gently, and pulled my head back so he could kiss my throat, and I had never felt anything so electrifying and molten in my life.

There was something different this time than our other make-out session, I could feel it. A tension . . . an awareness. I thought I knew what it meant.

So this was what it would be like to make love with someone who really cared about me. Someone I knew. Someone I trusted. Someone I was already in love with. I slid my hands to his waist and pulled him closer and got a delicious groan as thanks.

Just then, a car screeched around the corner and right into my driveway, its tires throwing bits of crushed clam. Grady stepped in front of me, shielding me, and for a second, I thought the car might crash into the house. Instead, it jerked to a stop.

"Monica?" I said.

She practically threw herself out of the car, incandescent with . . . fury? "I *knew* this would happen! I knew it! How dare you?" She was a foot from my face, shouting, and it seemed so . . . so surreal that I looked around to see the reason for her rage.

"What happened?" I asked. "Is Matthew okay?" I gripped Grady's arm, terror like a flash flood, drenching everything.

"Is he okay? Okay? No, he's out of his mind." She was shaking from head to foot.

"Monica, what happened?" I asked.

"He wants to *stay* here, with you! For his entire senior year, with his 'other mother,' he says!" She made violent air quotes. "To spend more time with your side of his family!"

"Mrs. Patel?" Grady said. "Maybe you could lower your voice. Her grandfather is sleeping."

Her hissing was worse. "Matthew wants to live *here* with the fun, beautiful young mother who has never so much as made him a meal or nursed him through a cold! He wants to *abandon* his family the last year of school. The last year we'd have him home. What did you say to him, Harlow?"

My mouth was hanging open. "I don't . . . I didn't . . . Monica, I didn't know about this."

"Well, you planted some kind of seed, didn't you? He told me about your conversation the other day."

"I don't think I planted anything, Monica. I . . . I . . ."

At that moment, Sanjay pulled up in his car, the headlights flashing against the house. "Monica," he called as he got out. "Calm down." Even I knew that was a mistake. He strode over to us. "Hello. So sorry about this."

"Do *not* apologize for me, Sanjay." Her tone was steely and sharp. "And don't you *dare* be the nice one right now."

"Okay, let's just . . ." I was about to say *calm down.* "Gray, I think you should probably go."

"Yes. Please," said Monica. "This is a family matter."

Grady looked at me. "I'll stay if you want."

"No, thanks. Um . . . I'll talk to you soon."

After a second, he gave my arm a squeeze and went to his car and pulled out of the driveway.

"I'm confused," I said. "This is the first I've heard of this. I didn't tell him to stay with me. I wouldn't do that."

"I told you, Monica," Sanjay said. "I knew she wouldn't have done this."

"Can you please stop being Switzerland?" Monica snapped. "Can you please take my side for once?" She turned to me, her blue eyes on fire. "My son—*my* son, Harlow—tells me he's now an *adult*. He just informed us that he wants to do his senior year *here*. And he also informed us there wasn't a thing we could do about it. So you had better walk back whatever you said to him that made him think this was even in the realm of okay. Tell him he cannot stay with you. You owe us that."

She was a bit terrifying. I'd never imagined she could be so angry. "I . . . I . . . I'll talk to him."

"Yes. Talk to him," Monica said. "And think of this, Harlow. You're not only breaking my heart and Sanjay's. You're breaking Meena's as well. Not to mention his grandparents and aunts and uncles and cousins. His entire family will be gutted if this happens."

"Moni—" Sanjay attempted.

"So take *that* to bed with you and think about it. Think about a little girl who worships her older brother and is about to lose him a year early because he wants to discover his *roots*. We bent over backward this summer to accommodate him. We were more than generous about welcoming you into our family. Don't you dare say yes." Sanjay reached out for her arm, but she jerked away, got into her car and tore out of the driveway, taking off Sanjay's side-view mirror in the process.

The cicadas were the only sound all of a sudden. It started to rain.

"Sanjay, I . . . I'm sorry."

"Yes," he said. "So are we all." And with that, he went to his damaged car and drove off.

THIRTY-SIX

MONICA

Something was torn inside her. She could picture it, feel it, the raw, bloody, helpless flesh hanging there, dying.

It was 2 a.m. and she was sitting on the screened-in porch of their rented house, listening to the sounds of the night marsh. Sanjay, whom she currently hated, was sleeping. Sleeping! Oh, sure, he'd asked if she wanted him to stay up with her. She did not. He could have shut this down in an instant if he'd acted, just once, like the heavy. The strict parent. Matthew would never have been so bold if his perfect dad had raised his voice and said, "Absolutely not. Discussion over."

But that was not Sanjay's way, was it?

Yesterday, she'd taken a late-night flight from San Francisco to Boston, landing at 8:30 a.m., then gotten her rental car and driven to the Cape, fighting the traffic, eager to be with the kids and Sanjay. Finally, it was time for her to have a real vacation. The fires had been put out at work, Isamu, her last hire, was up to speed, and she had actually set up an automatic response on her emails and temporarily blocked all her contacts at work. If there was a crisis, they'd have to handle it without her. She wanted to show Peter Bidwell just how valuable she was so he'd give her that damn promotion.

Sanjay had been waiting with a gorgeous lunch spread, and Meena and Matthew had hugged her and said how glad they were to see her. Well, Meena had shrieked, "Mommy's home!" and catapulted herself into Monica's arms. Matthew had said, "Hey, Mom. How was the flight?" Good enough for her.

She'd taken a long nap, completely exhausted from the flight and work and the entire summer, if she was being honest. Sanjay had followed up lunch with a gorgeous dinner, after which they sat around the living room, talking about what they wanted to do this week—a whale watch for sure, an afternoon of strolling through Provincetown, a bike ride on the rail trail. She and Sanjay were cuddled together, Meena and Matthew sitting kitty-corner to each other, occasionally reaching out a foot to kick the other.

"Let's all pick a day for our activity," she said, "and then leave three days to be spontaneous."

"Even on vacation, Mom, you have to schedule spontaneity," Matthew said.

"I'll work on that," she answered, smiling at him.

"Someone has to keep us organized," Sanjay said. "Your mother is gifted in that area."

"I think my day should happen tomorrow," Meena said, "because it's the most fun."

"I'm not going parasailing," Matthew said. "It's dumb."

"No, it's not," Meena said. "You're dumb." This earned her a gentle kick from her brother.

It was a perfect moment, Monica thought, taking a sip of wine. This house, the darkening sky, the kids fondly bickering, her husband's arm around her. This was what a family vacation was all about. On the last week of their summer, a summer in which she'd flown across the country six times in eight weeks, it was just the four of them.

She could feel the tension from the past two months draining out of her. In eight days, they'd all be home. Sanjay and the kids would start school, and life would return to normal.

"I should talk to you guys about something," Matthew said. "Maybe not with Meena-Beana in the room."

"I'm not going anywhere. Is it about sex? Drugs? Are you gay?"

"All of those things," Matthew said.

"I knew it!" She jumped off her chair and tackled her brother, who gently pushed her to the floor.

"Easy, kids," Sanjay said, though they were all laughing.

"I'm old enough to stay, right, Daddy? Mommy?"

"Is she?" Monica asked Matthew. "You're eighteen. You make the call."

He shifted. "Um . . . yeah, sure, Meena."

"Hooray." She got back into her chair and curled up, looking at her brother attentively.

"So . . . okay," Matthew began. "I've obviously had a pretty big summer this year. Lots of emotions and stuff. It's been kind of a roller coaster, you know?"

"Of course," Sanjay said. "A time long in coming, meeting Harlow."

"Yeah. That's just it, Dad." He leaned forward, elbows on his knees. "So I've made a decision. I'm gonna spend my senior year here. With Harlow. I feel like I need more time with her and the rest of the fam."

There was a moment of silence.

Had she heard him correctly, or was she still buzzed with fatigue?

"You can't *stay*," said Meena. "You have to come home with us."

"It's just . . . I don't know. I feel, like, a real connection with her. I mean, you guys did, too, right? You said how much you cared about her back when she was pregnant with me. And I want to get to know my aunts and uncle and grandparents. And Grandpop. He's the coolest one in the family. So I know you won't be psyched, but I'll totally visit at Thanksgiving and Christmas and stuff."

"You're not *staying*," Monica heard herself say. "You're coming home with us. Your family."

He turned to her. "I have two families now."

"Matthew." Her voice was hard. "You haven't thought this through."

"See? I knew you'd say that. You think I'm stupid."

"No, I don't. But this is your senior year. All your friends, your sports, your last year in Pleasanton . . . you can't want to skip that."

Meena started to cry, and Monica held out her arms. Her daughter came to her and buried her face against Monica's shoulder. Monica looked at her son and gestured to Meena. "Not to mention your sister."

"Here comes the guilt trip," Matthew said. He flopped back and stared at the ceiling. Monica wanted to kick him. She elbowed Sanjay so he'd chime in.

"Son," he said. "Listen, we understand that you have a connection with Harlow, and that's great. And the Smiths are very nice people. But how about visiting *them* at Thanksgiving and Christmas?"

"Yeah, I thought about that, but I want to know what it's like to live here. With my biological family."

Meena jolted up. "*We're* your family! If you don't know that, you're an asshole!"

"Meena," Sanjay said, and really? He was upset with her swearing?

"I have two families, Meena-Beana," Matthew said patiently. "And it's time for me to spend some time with the other one."

"I hate you!" she screamed and ran down the stairs to her bedroom. The door slammed. It was an extreme reaction, but Meena was acting out exactly how she herself felt.

"Well done, Matthew," Monica said. "You've just gutted your sister."

"Again, Mom. Easy on the guilt-tripping, okay?"

"I'm stating a fact, Matthew."

"Matt, buddy," Sanjay said. "This is a big decision, and as your mother said, you'll be missing out on so much back home."

"I've already missed out on an entire fucking life here!" he said. "I'm eighteen now. I can do what I want. I don't need your permission."

"Don't you dare pull that bullshit with us," Monica said, jolting to her feet. "You are still completely dependent on us. You're an adult? Really? Where's your job? Who pays for your health care? Your car? Your phone? Your clothes and food and shelter? Who's going to pay for college? You're not an adult. You're a teenager."

"It's not your decision," he said. "I'm just stating a fact." How dare he throw her words back at her?

"What about a gap year?" Sanjay said, and Monica could hear the desperation in his voice. "Do it next year. Don't miss out on your last year of high school with friends you've had since kindergarten."

"Dad," he said, "I've given this a lot of thought. I'm sorry it hurts you guys, but like I said, I'll come home. I need to do this, and the discussion is over." He stood up.

"No, it's not!" Monica said. "Sit back down, young man!"

He didn't listen. Instead, he went down the stairs to his room. HRH indeed.

"My God, I did not see that coming," Sanjay said. "Wow. I mean, I understand his need to—"

That was the last thing Monica heard. She grabbed her purse, ran down the stairs, out the door, into her car.

What kind of *fuckery* had Harlow put in her son's head?

THIRTY-SEVEN

HARLOW

I didn't sleep that night. Monica's rage echoed in my head, and my heart thumped erratically. I had not anticipated this at all. Not for a second. I didn't want Matthew to hurt his family this way; of course I didn't. His senior year should be spent in California. His home.

And yet . . . in the small, honest hours before dawn, I let myself picture what it would be like to have my son live under my roof. To make him meals and hear about school, watch his games, talk to his teachers, have him go upstairs to bed, remind him to brush his teeth. To simply be able to look at him, touch his shoulder as I passed him, maybe ruffle his curls and see those beautiful dark eyes. To have him smile at me, and say, "See you later, Mom," as he went out with friends.

Not that he would call me *Mom*, of course. But for the first time since I'd given birth to him, I could be his *mother*. Not just his birth mother. His actual, taking-care-of-him mother. Yes, it was selfish to want this. But he *was* eighteen. I wasn't stealing him. I was simply here.

And I loved him, my little pal who had grown so perfectly inside me, who had looked into my soul seconds after he was born. Don't tell me babies can't see. We had stared into each other's eyes and *known* each other. I loved the teenager he was, moods and all. I loved his smile, his laugh, his thoughts.

I wished I could call Rosie, but she didn't have phone privileges yet. I'd texted Grady last night, but his answer had been cryptic. I'm sure you'll figure it out.

At 6:42 a.m., my phone dinged. Matthew. Can we meet somewhere private?

Of course. Is here okay?

Be there in half an hour.

I tumbled out of bed, startling Ollie, pulled on jean shorts and a T-shirt, then threw together a batch of cranberry scones, manically zipping through the motions, shoving the cookie sheet in the oven, then quickly cleaning up.

At 7:27, Matthew pulled in the driveway. I went downstairs to open the door.

It was clear he'd been crying. His eyes were red and his lashes were clumped together.

"Hi," I said, and he hugged me. He smelled like sleep and soap and Cape Cod.

He ate a scone in silence as I poured him coffee, adding a teaspoon of sugar and plenty of half-and-half, the way he liked it. Poured myself some, minus the sugar. "Here, I said. "Have another." I put a scone on his plate, gave him a napkin.

He swallowed half the scone without visible chewing, took a slug of coffee, set his cup on the table and clasped his hands. Man hands. "Listen, I know my parents were here last night and told you I want to stay," he said.

"Yeah. They were here."

"Harlow, I don't want to go home. I want to spend senior year here. With you. Can I?"

I'd braced for that question. "Before I answer, I think we need to talk and make sure you've thought this out."

"I did. I totally did. You know how you said sometimes a decision is right and wrong at the same time? Like your choice to have me adopted . . . it was right, but it was also wrong for you." He swallowed. "That's what I think right now. Going back home would be right. But it's also wrong because I . . . I want to stay here and see what life might've been like if you hadn't, you know, relinquished me. I want to really get to know the family. And I won't get the chance again. It's now or never. I'll be going to college next year." He stroked Ollie's head and gave him a bite of scone, which Ollie inhaled.

My hands were shaking as I broke my own scone in half, my stomach jumpy and tight. "Matthew, this will break your parents' hearts. What if you finished high school back home, then came out for the summer? Or you could put college off for a year and come then?"

"I want to see what it would've been like to be a kid here. Go to school here. Have a routine. Be a normal mother and son with you."

The kid's aim was impressive. "I get it. Believe me, I do."

"Grandpop could be dead next year. And I'm here now. I want to stay. So can I?"

Slow breaths, slow breaths. "I'm not going to answer before I say this. I understand what you want. I hear you. But the consequences of doing that . . . Matthew, they won't just last for a week or two. You'll hurt your parents, your sister, your extended family. Maybe in a way that can't be erased."

"So I have to do exactly what they want because I'm adopted, or they'll stop loving me?"

I cut him a look. "I think we both know that's complete bullshit."

He shrugged. "Maybe. Look, it's not like I wouldn't talk to them. I'd FaceTime and text and call and go home for the holidays and still be their son. And brother. Mom's fucking furious right now, and Dad's sad, and Meena's crying nonstop, but they should understand why this is so important. It's not like I'm disappearing off the face of the earth. I just wanna be here with you, First Mama."

Oh, the kid was good, I had to give him that. I said nothing, weighing his words.

"And I *can* do that," he added. "I'm eighteen. So if you say yes, it's a done deal. And if you say no, I'll ask Robbie if I can live with him."

"Have you seen where he lives? Or more accurately, have you smelled where he lives?"

"Okay, well, I bet Gran and Poppy would take me in." He paused. Gave another chunk of scone to Ollie. "But I'm hoping to live with *you*, Harlow. I mean, you said you've loved me every day of my life. Since before I was born. Don't you wanna see what it would be like? Just a regular mom and her son?"

He had me there. I lowered my eyes. "I do want to see that, Matthew. I'm just not sure this is the right way to do it."

"It's the right thing, and it's the wrong thing, and sometimes we just have to make a decision and hope it's the right one. You said all those things. Were they true?"

I nodded.

"I'm staying on the Cape, Harlow. Can I live with you? Yes or no?"

I raised my eyes to look at him a long minute, this child of mine, this living, breathing, beautiful aching question I'd had since the minute I'd put him in Monica's arms.

What if I had kept him?

He was giving me the chance to find out, and it felt like a little ray of sunshine suddenly burst out of my heart, cracking open all the dark places. My son had always been that light. Now, I'd get to see it up close.

"Yes, Matthew. Absolutely yes."

Monica would not take my phone calls. Sanjay said he was stunned that I would support such an impulsive decision. Ophelia told me Meena wouldn't be coming to the store anymore.

I told Matthew he could not move in until his parents went back to California, and he should be compassionate and sensitive to their feelings. He agreed, and the only text I got was, they're still not on board yet but they're getting there.

I wasn't fooled. The Patels were devastated.

My family, on the other hand, was overjoyed. Grandpop was the only family member who was somber. "Very hard for his parents," he said. "And a very abrupt move as well."

"I know, Grandpop. I know."

I told Destiny and Cindy the situation, and Destiny suggested a drink after work. "You too, Cindy," she added. Later that day, we sat at Winslow's on the patio, the first time we'd ever gone out just us three, occasionally waving to people we knew who walked past.

"Destiny, where did you get that skirt?" Cynthia asked.

"eBay. Carolina Herrera. Forty dollars."

Cynthia frowned, ever jealous of Destiny's wardrobe.

"About Matthew," Destiny said. "Family is complicated. Damned if you do, damned if you don't. My son was so upset when I told him I was transitioning that I almost didn't do it. But I had to, you know? It was that, or suicide."

"Oh, Des," I said, my heart twisting. "But you guys are close now, right? You got past it?"

She smiled. "Yeah. He got over it. Or rather, he decided to understand. He still calls me Dad, but I can't fault him there." She took a sip of her cosmo. "From what I've seen, the Patels are excellent parents. They'll forgive their son."

"What do you think, Cindy?" I asked. "You were adopted."

She looked a little startled that I'd asked for her opinion, then frowned. "Well, I . . . I suppose he's trying to have both lives. It's immature of him, shoving this down his parents' throats at the last minute. But Destiny is right. They're kind people." She took a sip of her wine. "That being said, my own mother would've stabbed my birth mother in the heart if she'd done something like this."

Even so, the ray of sunshine in my heart hadn't dimmed. Oh, I was sad for the Patels, of course, especially Meena. But to be given this chance to be Matthew's mother . . . it was a gift I'd never even dreamed of.

That left Grady. Another gift, but one I had to turn down.

My throat tightened like a vise when I thought about it, but it had to be done. There was no way I could be in a relationship while having my son live with me. No way. I had to focus on Matthew, not be in a relationship. I couldn't be distracted or absent when my child, my actual child, was living under my roof. He wasn't doing this so I could have dinner with Grady a few times a week. And what if Matthew saw me bonding with Luna during the one time of his life he'd live with me?

The day after Monica had stormed my house, Gray had left for a conference in San Diego. It was just as well. A little distance would make our breakup that much easier. That's what I told myself, anyway.

The day he got back, I drove over to his house. There he was, pushing Luna on the swing.

"Higher, Daddy!" she shrieked. "Push me *much* higher!" He obliged, and she laughed with delight. Then he saw me standing there in the side yard like a stalker, and he turned his smile on me.

It was *such* a good smile. Tears pricked my eyes, but I blinked them away. No crying. No need to. He'd understand.

He pulled Luna off the swing and said something to her. She ran toward the house and shouted, "Vivi! Vivi! Daddy says it's snack time!" The back door banged shut.

Grady came over to me, and I had to look away.

"Hey," he said in that gentle, gentle voice. "How are you?"

"Good! Great, actually." I didn't feel so great right now. "Gray . . . Matthew *is* actually going to spend his senior year here. Starting in three days."

He didn't say anything for a few seconds, then, "Wow."

"Yeah. Big news. So, Gray, I can't . . . you know. You and me. We can't, um, be dating. I mean, at least until he goes home. But also, I don't want to stand in the way of you finding someone else if you're looking, you know? So if you want to date other women, go for it."

He folded those arms and looked at me, unsmiling. "I don't want to date other women, Harlow. I want to date you."

"That's great. Good. Just . . . we have to go on sabbatical until June or so."

He was still not smiling. "It's August."

"Right. So only ten months." I resisted the urge to pick at my cuticle.

"In ten months, you don't get a night off?"

"Not with a guy," I said. "You, I mean. I can't. I have to concentrate on Matthew's well-being."

"And how would dating me hurt his well-being?"

"Because . . . because I don't want him to feel second-best. Or inconvenient."

"Daddy! Can you push me again?" Luna was back outside, her little dress fluttering in the breeze as she climbed up the slide. "Vivi doesn't push high enough."

"I do my best, Luna," Vivienne said, laughing.

Grady turned. "Be there in a minute, honey," he called. "Vivi can get you started."

"She's so cute," I said, and I could hear the nervousness in my voice. "Your daughter, I mean. Wicked cute. Vivienne is also very cute. Beautiful, really, not cute. Not that Luna isn't—"

"You know what I think, Harlow?" Gray said. "I think you're scared. I think you could talk yourself out of a relationship with *anyone* in about five minutes. You tell yourself you were broken by giving up Matthew, you tell yourself you don't get to be involved in another kid's life, you tell yourself anything to keep yourself safe and tucked away where no one can get close enough to break your heart." His eyes didn't leave mine. "Other people get hurt, you know. And somehow they find a way to get over it."

I swallowed. "Mm-hm. Well. Nothing you said is wrong." I dug my fingernail into my cuticle to keep myself from crying. "But Matthew—"

"Forget Matthew for a second. Tell me the truth. You can't see yourself with me for the long run, can you? Because of Luna."

I didn't answer.

"Okay, then. At least you didn't jerk me around for too long. Take care." He didn't wait for me to say goodbye, just walked back to his daughter.

THIRTY-EIGHT

CYNTHIA

The last half of August was one of Cynthia's favorite times of the year. The beach out front was quieter, since so many children started school early. Sunset came earlier, and there was a chill in the air at night that made sleeping more comfortable.

She and Albert were seeing a good deal of each other. With him around, the shack felt more like home. Cynthia thought she might paint the kitchen cupboards, and possibly wallpaper her bedroom, make it a little cozier, a little more reflective of her good taste.

Her trip to Long Island was set for Columbus Day, and there were already family dinners scheduled, a trip to New York City and tours of Long Island wineries, though how good could Long Island wine be? (*Open mind, open mind.*) Donna had had their server in New Haven take a picture of the four of them, and Cindy had it printed and framed. It hung with the only other photos she had—Mother, Daddy and her on her sweet sixteen, and one of Uncle Robert and her when she was about five years old.

And there was the problem.

Three years ago, she had lied to the one person left on earth who loved her. She had forged a letter from a woman who had been her lifelong friend. And she had stolen from the very store that employed her, adjusting the numbers so she could take a little extra here and there.

Cynthia Millstone had done those things. But Cindy Smith . . . she was someone better than that. Imagine what her sisters would say if she told them she was cheating a sweet old man out of his business's profits! The idea of cheating Harlow wasn't as awful, but that was just semantics.

Albert . . . Albert would drop her like a piece of granite. She had learned a lot about him, and he was a man of integrity, that was certain. She couldn't bear to see the disappointment on his face if he found out.

Harlow had come back from her errand with red eyes and now was in her apartment, getting Matthew's bedroom ready, she said. Today was Destiny's day off, so Harlow said to text her if things got busy, but it was very slow. At four thirty, Cynthia flipped the Open sign to Closed. A half hour wouldn't make a difference.

"Uncle Robert?" she called. "Care to have a cup of tea with me?"

He appeared from the back, where he'd been dusting. A cobweb was stuck in his hair, and it was rather adorable. "What was that, Cynthia dear?" he asked.

"Would you like a cup of tea?" She reached up to clear the cobweb. "There's something I want to talk about."

"Why, I'd *love* that!" he exclaimed, as if no one had ever offered him tea before. He had a unique talent for happiness, Uncle Robert did. He'd been that way ever since she could remember. He radiated kindness.

Cynthia turned on the electric kettle and set out two cups. Nervousness leaped like small flames around her feet. She hadn't planned on what to say . . . she just knew it needed to be said.

When she took the tea to the center of the store, Uncle Robert was sitting in one of the wing chairs with Oliver Twist, reading a book on the history of Cape Cod and the islands, one of at least twenty they carried. He looked up with a smile.

"Thank you, my dear! What a nice idea this is. How are things with you?"

"They're fine." It occurred to her that she could slowly funnel money back into the store and make things right that way with no one the wiser. But that would take years. "I've been keeping in touch with my sisters."

"What a blessing that must be! Another family after all this time! It seems to going be around, doesn't it? How lucky you must feel."

"Yes. I do, actually. And, um . . ." She felt herself blushing. "Well, I appear to have a suitor, Uncle Robert."

"Do you? How *wonderful*! Would I know him?"

"It's Bertie Baines." She felt her cheeks warm.

Uncle Robert looked pleased. "A fine man," he pronounced. "Bertie Baines is good people."

"I'm glad you think so, Uncle Robert." She set her teacup down. "Uncle Robert, there's something I have to tell you. Something unpleasant."

"You're not sick, are you?"

Her heart sank a little lower. His first thought was for her health. "No, I'm hale and hearty." She took a deep breath. "Uncle Robert, remember when I first came here and showed you Aunt Louisa's letter? The one that said that she wanted me to be a part-owner in the store?"

"Of course." He put down his teacup as well, his wrinkled old hand going to pet Ollie's silky coat. "What about it?"

"I . . ." Her eyes prickled with tears, and her nose began to run. She fished a tissue from her dress pocket and blew her nose. "I forged it, Uncle Robert. She never said that. And I've been skimming from our profits. Embezzling."

"Embezzling? From Open Book? How much have you taken?"

"Fourteen thousand, eight hundred and forty-three dollars." The tears spilled over. "I'm so sorry." She forced herself to look him in the eye.

His faded blue eyes regarded her. "Fourteen thousand?"

"And eight hundred and forty-three."

"Yes. That matches my math as well."

"I never thought I'd—excuse me? What did you say?"

"Cynthia, my dear, I'm old, not stupid. I can certainly still do basic mathematics. It's Harlow who never looks at our finances, not me."

She blinked rapidly. Opened her mouth to speak, then closed it.

He smiled. "Cynthia, my dear, when you came here with that letter, my heart went out to you. It made me *terribly* sad that you were so afraid of rejection, you forged a letter from my dear Louisa. I knew your divorce had just occurred, and I added things up." He took a sip of tea. "I would have given you money, had you asked."

"Why didn't you say anything?" she asked. She felt dizzy. "You knew? From the very start?"

"Of *course* I did. Do you think I couldn't tell a forgery from my wife's handwriting? I was trying to save your pride. As for the skimming, I've been keeping track. In fact, it's been a rather engaging project for me, tallying up your sneaky money." He smiled. "I'm not quite as dotty as I seem."

"I'll pay it back," she said. "I don't know how, but I will. I already sold my good jewelry, but I might be able to—"

"Cynthia. Dear. You don't have to. If I ever die," he said, his eyes twinkling, "you'll get a small sum from me. I told my lawyer to deduct whatever you've taken from that amount. Now there's no need to wait. I can transfer that right now. Well, tomorrow. The banks close so early!"

She wiped her eyes. "Why didn't you say anything?"

"I was rather hoping for this day," he said. "For my sweet little godchild to come clean."

"Uncle Robert," she whispered. "I'll pay you back. I don't deserve this kindness."

"Sometimes kindness finds its way to you nonetheless. And you won't pay me back. I've been lucky all my life, with money, with my Louisa, with Gerald and Ellie and the kids. And with you, sweetheart."

"Thank you," she whispered. His kindness was humbling, to say the least.

He offered Ollie the rest of his tea, and the dog lapped it up. Cynthia would be sure to wash that cup in scalding water. "I don't want to speak ill of the dead," Uncle Robert said, "but I always thought your parents were a little too . . . attached to you. They never sent you out in the world to find your own way. They should have *insisted* you get an education. I told your parents I thought so, but, well, they thought you were perfect just the way you were."

This made her cry a little harder, the longing for her father, who had once made her feel so safe but had left her destitute. The mother who'd thought the most useful thing Cynthia could do was become a housewife. They hadn't had a lot of foresight, but they had loved her. She never doubted that.

"Thank you, Uncle Robert," she said when the tears tapered off. "For always being there for me."

"Well, I *love* you! Of course I'm here for you."

"I love you, too, Uncle Robert." She thought a minute, all this new information rolling around in her head. Then she raised her head and looked at him. "How much are you leaving me in your will?"

He tsked at her. "Now that, missy, is none of your business. Not too much, but a little, how's that? Come. You can make me dinner. Did you know, I went out onto the roof today to chase off a squirrel, and it was so *nice* out there, I stayed right through lunch, just looking at the trees and spying on the people who walked past. I felt like a boy again."

She stood up and offered her hand to help him up. "I'd love to make you dinner, Uncle Robert. And then I'm taking you out for ice cream."

THIRTY-NINE

HARLOW

The day before the Patels were supposed to go back to California, I was gardening in front of Open Book, planting some mums and deadheading the daisies, when I heard a voice.

"Do you have a moment, Harlow?"

It was Monica. I jumped to my feet.

"Hi! Yes, of course. Good to see you." Shit. That feeling was probably not mutual. She was dressed impeccably in white linen pants and a sleeveless white top. I, on the other hand, wore jeans that were torn at the knees and a black T-shirt that said, *Books: your best defense against unwanted conversation.*

"Would you like to come upstairs? I can make us coffee."

"No, thank you. How about in the backyard? I see you have a bench."

She didn't want to come into my home. I understood. "Sounds good."

I followed her to the backyard, and we sat, a world of space between us. Then she turned to look at me, her blue eyes telling me I'd stabbed her in the heart. "This is not what we envisioned when we invited you into Matthew's life this summer," she said, her voice calm and measured. "This is the worst outcome we could have imagined. You're taking my son, Harlow."

My eyes stung. "I know," I said, my voice quiet. "I did discourage him. I thought he could maybe visit again in the summer or do a gap year, and—"

"Sanjay and I welcomed you as a friend, included you, never spoke a word against you, not in eighteen years. When Matthew asked why some birth mothers visited their kids but his never did, we told him you loved him but only wanted him to have one mommy and one daddy. We didn't say we had no idea. We didn't say 'she might be trying to forget you.' We just said that you loved him and did what you thought was best for him. Which was true, wasn't it?"

"Yes," I said. "It wasn't easy, but—"

"Then do what's best for him now!" I jumped at her sharp voice. "Do you really think it's in his best interest to be away from his family, his home, his friends, his school this year? Do you, Harlow?"

"Not exactly, no."

"Meena is heartbroken, and Sanjay is beyond sad. And I . . ." Her voice broke. "You've destroyed me. You've destroyed our family. We need Matthew. He's part of us."

"Monica, he said he'd move in with my brother or parents if I told him he couldn't stay with me."

"Then you *all* should say no!" she said. "He's still a boy! He's immature and impulsive. You need to tell him it's not going to work."

"I tried. Really, Monica, I told him all the reasons he shouldn't stay, but his mind was made up. And he *is* eighteen."

"You didn't try hard enough. I can't believe you'd be this . . . this selfish."

Selfish? Something snapped in me. "Well, Monica, maybe now you know how I felt eighteen years ago," I said. "Except *you* get to call him and FaceTime him and visit him and have him at the holidays. He loves you. He *knows* you. You got to raise him. You had eighteen years with him. I got a nervous breakdown and a hole in my heart the size of . . . of Australia."

"You *chose* us," she said. "And you chose a closed adoption. That was *your* decision. No one forced you. You could've changed your mind at any minute, even after he was born, and we reminded you of that again and again. But you *didn't*, Harlow! You didn't change your mind. And now it's pretty goddamn unfair that you suddenly want to play mommy to my son."

"*Our* son," I grated out, "wants to get to know me. I didn't invite him here. I didn't reach out to him on social media. I kept up my end of the bargain. And I told him how much this would hurt you. He didn't change his mind." My voice gentled. "I'm very, very sorry for the pain you're going through. All three of you. But it wasn't my call."

If looks could kill, I'd be a bloody pulp. "Bullshit."

Anger, my least favorite feeling, flared again. "Here's the thing. If you think I'm excited and happy about this, Monica, I am. Of course I am! For eighteen years, I've missed him and loved him and wondered about him and prayed for him. Now I finally get to live in the same house as my son. Not to raise him, because you already did that. Not for a lifetime. Just for one school year."

"The most important year of his life thus far," she replied. "Meanwhile, his *parents*, who have done all the work and made all the sacrifices and poured ourselves into making his life a good one . . . we just got kneecapped."

"You raised him to think independently, and now you're mad because he is. This is Matthew's choice. You cannot blame me."

She stood up. "And yet I do." She shook her head a little, jaw clenched. "Once, you trusted me with your son, and you were right to. This summer, I trusted you with mine, and I shouldn't have."

"Monica . . ." The tears in my eyes spilled over. "I couldn't turn him away. I gave him up once. I couldn't do it again. Of all the people in the world, you should understand that."

She looked at me another minute, then strode across the lawn and disappeared onto West Main, leaving me alone with my conscience.

As soon as Matthew moved in, my conscience shut up. It was done. He'd made his decision, and I wasn't going to pee all over it by feeling guilty. Hadn't I spent most of my adult life feeling that way? I was going to live in this moment and enjoy it. Matthew deserved nothing less.

I'd painted his room navy blue. We drove down to Hyannis, and he picked out new sheets, curtains, a comforter, throw pillows and towels, all in gray or navy or white. We stopped at Earth House in Orleans and Buddha Bobs in Eastham so he could buy some posters, a statue of the Buddha, a singing bowl, and a metal wall hanging of a fish. Mom gave him three of her paintings for his room (she'd never given me a painting, because they sold for thousands of dollars, but grandchildren were different, apparently). Winnie gave us a papasan chair, which Matthew loved.

The guest room was now a teenage boy's bedroom. I framed a photo Robbie had taken with his timer at the welcome picnic— both families, all of us looking so happy, except for Imogen, who'd been in the throes of a tantrum—and set it on his desk. Matthew got a bulletin board and tacked up pictures of his friends, his parents and sister and their cat, Hoosier. Otherwise, he didn't acknowledge his life in California.

Ollie slept on his bed the first night and didn't seem to re-member just who had pulled him out of that hot car, because he was suddenly Matthew's dog now. I didn't mind a bit.

Right from the start, we talked about everything—family life, books, politics, global warming, career choices, each other. I told him about my life after giving him to the Patels, transferring to Colorado Springs, getting into law school, life in Los Angeles. I was honest about burying my feelings and trying to move on, but I didn't mention my stint at the Willows, obviously. Maybe when he was older.

One night over dinner, he said, "I want to ask you a question. Be honest, okay?"

My stomach tensed. "Sure."

"Why did you pick my parents? You said you watched, like, a hundred videos before you chose them."

I thought a minute. This summer had somewhat changed my take on Monica and Sanjay, the heated conversations aside. Monica had been more relaxed back then, but she hadn't been a mother yet. Or such a big deal in her field. I also got the impres-sion that Sanjay was a little *too* laid back. But the young couple I had chosen . . .

"They weren't trying to impress anyone in their video," I said. "They were just themselves, and they really seemed to love each other. And like each other. That's more rare than you think."

The image of Grady laughing at trivia night over something flashed through my head. I really liked Gray. I'd liked him for a couple of decades before that evil little four-letter word had crept into my heart. Love. It messed up everything.

"They do. Like, Dad is home more, but Mom is the . . . well, she's the brains of the family, you know? She calls the shots, and Dad goes along with her, and most of the time . . ." He looked at his now-empty plate and toyed with his fork. "She's kind of a control freak."

I felt the need to put in a good word for Monica. "She's a very impressive person. And she did a great job raising you. Back then, I wanted her to adopt me, too. She was incredibly kind and understanding. So was your dad."

"Yeah. But your own parents are awesome, right?"

I nodded, not wanting to . . . lionize them, as it were. "No parents are perfect," I said. "Mine probably tried to make me an adult too fast, but they were solid."

"Mine want to keep me a little kid forever." He took another taco, loaded it with an impossible amount of ground beef, salsa and guacamole, and took a bite, half of the taco disappearing into his mouth. He got that from me, I thought proudly. The ability to power-eat tacos. "This is great, by the way," he mumbled through his food. "Speaking of fathers, I'm gonna reach out to mine."

"Good. You should call regularly. They all miss you."

"I meant my birth father."

I jerked a little, then recovered. "Wow. Really?" He'd been here less than a week.

"Well, I met you. I should meet him, too. Don't you think so?"

"Um . . ." I scrambled for a wise answer, something Sanjay might say. "I think it's your call."

"You said you'd give me his information."

"I only know his name. I'm sorry."

"What is it?"

"Zachary Baser." I spelled it out for him. Matthew whipped out his phone. "No phones at the table, please," I said.

"Extenuating circumstances. Huh. It's an uncommon name. You don't know where he lives?"

"He was from the Chicago area. Otherwise, no, I don't know anything about him."

Matthew put his phone away. "I just want to see what he looks like. Talk to him a little. It's not like he was the pregnant one, though."

"No. We had essentially no contact after I told him I was placing you for adoption."

"He was probably relieved you weren't keeping me."

Even after all these years, I still felt a flare of rage when I remembered just how relieved he was. "Yes, he was."

Matthew stopped chewing and looked at me. "You mad?"

"No. Do what you want to do on that front. Just . . . manage your expectations, okay?"

"Cool. Thanks, Harlow." He demolished another taco. "Hey, do you think I should call you Mom?"

"No. That's for Monica." I paused. "You call her Mom, right?"

"Yeah. Also Ma, which is more Indian. I could call you BM, for birth mother." He grinned.

"No, you could not," I said, my heart melting at his smile.

"First Mama? FM? Hey, FM!" he said, testing it out. "I'm gonna stay out all night and do drugs, FM. Is that okay? I've been arrested, FM, can you bail me out?"

I laughed. "Let's stick to Harlow."

That night, I got to talk to Rosie while Matthew was upstairs in his room, headphones on. She was still a little shaky, not so much from the physical withdrawal from alcohol, but from realizing how much of her life had been spent drinking or drunk. "I've been pretending I was just a party girl, you know?" she said. "But I had my first drink when I was thirteen, and I didn't stop until a couple weeks ago."

"It'll work," I said firmly. "You're doing great."

"So . . . Robbie sent me a letter," she admitted.

"Oh, God. Are you going to be my sister-in-law?"

"No. I mean, probably not. But that would be awesome, right? You and me, sisters at last? No, he's just being nice. He's sweet."

"You need to focus on yourself for a while," I said.

"You sound just like one of the many therapists here," she said, smiling. "Boring! No, just kidding. I know I'm not ready for anything like that, so don't worry, Lolo. I'm so thrilled for you about Matthew. I hope it goes well."

"Thanks, Rosie. Me too. Talk to you next week."

Matthew and I got into a routine. I woke up early to make him breakfast, then drove him to school for the extra talking time. I'd go to the bookstore, my heart soaring like a red kite in the blue sky. I was Matthew's mother, not just a birth mother, but the kind of mother who went to soccer matches and washed sweaty clothes and made nutritious meals.

At Nauset High School, he fit right in and already had friends. He'd been accepted as a walk-on for the soccer team, which helped, and he was incredibly good-looking and glamorous, this new kid from Northern California. I'd pick him up after practice and listen to him talk about his teammates and coach. Mom and Dad went to his home games, and it was a dream, standing with them, cheering for Matthew, talking to other parents about colleges and the SAT and AP classes.

Matthew told me not to worry about his grades. "I'm Indian and the only son. Only perfection or better is acceptable." He smiled as he said it, but he did take his classes seriously, heading up to his room to do homework until late at night. AP classes in physics, biology, calculus and computer science. I could never fall asleep before his light was out, so I stayed up, reading, our house quiet. So many little, beautiful moments like this that I'd never let myself imagine.

But I missed Grady. I'd given my place on the Kingslayers to Winnie so I wouldn't have to make him uncomfortable. That is, so *I* wouldn't be uncomfortable. Lillie Silva texted me, and I told her about Matthew and left it at that. They won the All-Cape trophy the last weekend in August, and I sent a group text, congratulating them. Gray didn't respond.

As September wore on, Matthew was no longer always the center of attention at family dinners, which we were now having every Sunday afternoon. He laughed with the rest of us as Dad told us about Mom cheating on her new veganism by eating a BLT, made faces at Imogen, played tic-tac-toe with Esme, asked Lark detailed questions about medical school, made inside jokes with Robbie. It was as if he'd always been with us.

I asked if he was calling home regularly, and he said yes, but otherwise we didn't talk about the Patels. Neither Sanjay nor Monica reached out to me, and that was a relief. The truth was, I tried not to think of them. Anything Matthew needed from them, like a copy of his last physical so he could play soccer, he'd handled himself. As he'd said, he was an adult.

Frances was a regular at Grandpop's now, or he at her place. It was a little strange, both Grandpop and me having other people in our lives. Ever since I'd come home, Grandpop and I had been a team. We still were, of course, but it was different now. He also seemed to be spending a lot of time with Cynthia at the store.

"What is up with Cindy?" Destiny asked. "These days, she's actually . . . I'm afraid to say it."

"Pleasant?" I suggested. We were freshening the New Releases area and switching out some of the staff picks, the section from which we sold most of our books.

"That's the word," Destiny said.

"I think finding her sisters has softened her a bit," I said.

"The summer of discovery," Destiny murmured. "For the whole Smith family." Destiny taped Grandpop's shelf talker underneath *The Marriage Portrait* by Maggie O'Farrell. He did love historical fiction. "How is it?" she asked. "Having your boy with you."

My eyes filled with happy tears. "Beyond wonderful. And hopefully speaking of wonderful, how are things going with Kate?"

"They are *absolutely* wonderful." She made a cute, scrunched-up face, then put her choice on the shelf.

"How was that one?" I asked, looking at the cover. *The One That Got Away* by Charlotte Rixon.

"Absolutely riveting."

I held up one of my choices, the latest from Elinor Lipman. "This was great. I love everything she writes. I want to be her best friend."

"Hey, I hope it's okay, but I asked Ophelia to write a few, too."

"No, that's great. We need the youth perspective." The other day, I'd asked Ophelia if she'd heard from Meena, and she said, "Oh, sure. We text all the time."

"How is she?" I asked.

Ophelia gave me a very adolescent look. "Fine." In other words, *none of your business*. Poor Meena. It was awfully hard to think of her back home without her brother.

In a town this size, though, it was impossible for me not to run into Gray, and sure enough, we found ourselves standing in front of the meat section at the Wellfleet Marketplace. He seemed lost in thought, face somber.

"Hey, Gray," I said.

He gave a little start. "Oh, hi. How are you?" No change in expression.

"Good. Good. Really good." I suddenly felt the need to vomit up sentences. "It's so fun having Matthew here, you know? I mean, he's great. And he eats so much! Look at this cart, right? Have you tried this bread? He loves it. So do I. With butter, obviously. Lots of butter. Otherwise, it's basically rope."

Grady just looked at me. His ability to make direct eye contact was making me sweat.

"How's Luna?" I asked.

"She's really good."

I wanted to ask how *he* was doing, if he'd found a new nanny, what was up with his Gates Foundation grant, how his research was going. If he'd forgiven me.

But Gray was not mine to interrogate.

Christopher, who ran the meat department, handed over Gray's order.

"Thanks, Chris," he said.

"You bet. What can I get you, Harlow?"

"A pound of ground turkey, please."

Grady nodded at me, and then walked away. It was best this way, I told myself, trying to ignore the ache in my chest.

One evening in late September, Matthew had an away game that I had to miss, since it was Cynthia's day off. He wouldn't be back till after ten, as the team was going out for dinner after the game. I checked my texts and emails. There was nothing new other than a cheery update from Rosie. Her dad was visiting on

Saturday and maybe Matthew and I could drive down and have lunch with them.

Nothing from Sanjay or Monica, of course. I wished we were all still friends. I wished they weren't so angry and sad.

And nothing from Grady. Again, I didn't know what I expected. With a sigh, I glanced at the pile of books on my coffee table, all of which I wanted to read—Pam Jenoff, Robyn Carr, Stephen King, Jane Austen (again). I just didn't want to read right now.

"Wanna go for a walk?" I asked Ollie, who lifted his head and pricked up his ears as if he couldn't believe the good news. "Let's go, boy."

He did his flying squirrel leap off the couch. I clipped on his leash, grabbed the big flashlight, then went downstairs, knocked on Grandpop's door and went in. "I'm taking a walk, Grandpop," I said, but he didn't appear to be around. At Frances's maybe? His car was in the driveway, though.

He was probably in bed. I tiptoed to his room, knocked softly. No answer. It was impossible not to picture him dead . . . he was past ninety, after all. I cracked the door. Very dark in there, so I pressed the flashlight against my jeans and clicked it on so the light wouldn't wake him, but so I could still see a little bit. All I wanted was proof of life.

There he was, asleep.

And not alone. With Frances. Okay, then. Old people still got it on. Grammy would approve, I supposed. But didn't a lot of old men die this way, after—my brain shuddered away from the thought. Grandpop's bare shoulder, tufted with a clump of sparse white hair, was above the cover. I'd just wait to see or hear him breathe—this looked very *Sophie's Choice* to me, that final scene where Nathan and Sophie are lying on the bed, both dead—but nope, there it was, a slight snore and a twitch.

"What are you doing?" Frances whispered, and I nearly jumped out of my skin.

"Sorry," I whispered back. "Just checking on him."

"He's fine," she whispered.

"Yes. I can see that. More than fine."

"You can go now," she said, smiling a bit. "Creeper."

"Put a sock on the door handle next time," I said.

She laughed softly. "Will do. Bye, Harlow."

"Bye, Frances."

I was smiling as I left. My grandfather had a woman. While I knew no one would ever take Grammy's place, I also knew that Robert J. Smith had a lot of love in his heart. More than just about anyone in the world.

My phone chimed. Ah. My son had texted me.

ETA 11:12. Sorry it's so late.

No worries! Text when you hit Chatham, and I'll be waiting when you get here.

It was only 8:49 now.

I walked down West Main, past the library, Ollie trotting merrily beside me, thrilled to be out in the dark. Usually, we headed for Commercial Street or Uncle Tim's Bridge, but tonight, we were changing it up a bit. It was a beautiful night, the Milky Way spread across the sky in a great wash of stars and planets. I stopped for a minute, looking up. I'd always believed in God, though I didn't like asking for stuff, imagining that God had a lot on His plate. Truth was, the only thing I'd ever prayed for was Matthew. "Thank you," I said. "Thank you for bringing him back to me."

Then I kept walking, past the public works building. At the three-way intersection of West Main, High Toss Bridge Road and Pole Dike Road—we really had the best street names on all of Cape Cod—I headed up Pole Dike. Only then did I realize I was walking to Gray's house.

Pole Dike led me to Bound Brook Island Road, and when I got to Grady's, I looked at my phone again: 9:30. There were a couple of lights on, so I knocked quietly. A second later, he opened the door, wearing a white T-shirt and jeans. He was barefoot, and his hair was rumpled.

"Hi," I said.

"Hi."

He didn't smile. Ollie jumped up, paws on his leg, wagging furiously, and Grady ran his hand over my dog's head.

"Can we talk a second?" I asked.

He looked over my head, face impassive, about to say no. But then his broad shoulders dropped an inch. "Sure. Come in." He led me into the living room, which I'd seen that one other time.

Should I sit? I sat. Grady remained standing.

"I like your choices," I said, gesturing to the bookcases. "I snooped the last time I was here." It had also been the first time, and I had a feeling tonight would be the last.

"Why are you here, Harlow? It's late." By Cape Cod off-season standards, that was true. The entire town tucked in by nine. Even the Cumby's on Route 6 closed at ten.

"I wanted to talk to you. Maybe you could sit down?"

He glanced out the window, sighed, and took the chair across from me. "Have you changed your mind?" he asked.

"About us? Um . . . no."

"Then what's there to say, Harlow?"

"I miss you." It wasn't what I'd planned to say, because I'd planned nothing.

He just looked at me a minute, then gave a slight nod. "I miss you, too."

"I wish things were different."

He drew in a slow breath, his eyes on the floor, not a man to rush with words or thought. "I can't be involved with someone who doesn't want to be a significant part of my daughter's life. I've done that already."

"I know," I whispered.

He looked at me again. Ollie jumped up on his chair and flopped over Gray's lap, rolling so his belly showed. Grady obliged, running his hand on Ollie's silky tummy, making me jealous of my dog. Idiot thought.

"I had the biggest thing for you in high school," he said. "But I was too shy to do anything about it, except ask you to the prom. And we were friends. I didn't want to mess that up right before we went to college. I figured we'd see each other on breaks and maybe we'd both end up back here. I thought we'd stay in touch. I emailed you a few times. Never got back anything more than basic courtesy."

"Right," I whispered, ashamed. That kindhearted boy, my lab partner and prom date, a person who'd never said or done anything that had *ever* made me feel invisible. And as thanks, I'd ignored him.

"Then you just . . . disappeared. Didn't come back much, and when you did, I could tell you were different. Shut down. It seemed like you were going to stay in California, because your mom told me you had a job out there. Then I got married, which was a mistake in every way except for Luna. When I moved back here, I found out I still had a thing for you. And since then, for more than a year now, I've been waiting. There's a reason I joined that trivia team, a reason I order all my books through your store when I could get them a lot cheaper on Amazon, a reason I stop work to bring Luna to story time with your grandfather. The reason is you, Harlow."

I dashed away a tear. Sincerity was awfully hard to hear, especially when someone was essentially saying you'd been breaking his heart.

"But Luna is the best and most important thing in my life, and she always will be. She's already been abandoned by her mother. It can't happen again."

I nodded. "I want it to be different, Gray. I'm just . . . well, as you said, I'm scared. I can't promise anything, but I'd like to try."

"'Do or do not. There is no try.'" He was quoting Yoda, and it made me remember what dorks we'd both been in high school, how much fun we'd had swapping *Lord of the Rings* and *Star Wars* quotes as we dissected frogs and broke covalent bonds. I wiped away another tear.

He continued, "We can't be your experiment on whether or not you're going to rejoin the land of the living. And honestly, I don't think you're ready, Harlow. I wish you were. But you're stuck in the past in a place you've never left."

As usual, nothing he said was wrong. Damn scientists and their observations.

"Well, I really miss kissing you," I said. He almost smiled at that. "I miss everything about you, Gray."

"Thank you." With those words, our conversation was over. We looked at each other another minute, his face resigned and calm.

"I'll drive you home," he said.

"No, thanks. Ollie and I like to walk."

"I'm driving you home. It's wicked dark out there. Give me a minute." He left the room, and I heard his footsteps on the stairs, heard him speak to Vivienne, heard her voice. Ollie's big sad eyes seemed to say I'd fumbled this talk. Then Grady was back, opening the door, waiting for me to leave.

We didn't talk on the ride home. My throat was too tight, and besides, there was nothing left to say.

When he pulled in the driveway, I opened the door. "I hope we'll still be friends," I whispered.

"Me too," he said. "Good night." I watched him drive away.

We weren't going to be friends. I'd ruined that.

I went upstairs to have a good cry before picking up my son.

FORTY

CYNTHIA

At the mandatory staff meeting, Harlow went over the usual things—changing the merchandise; the incoming Christmas books that would be arriving on Tuesday; doing a fresh window display based on mysteries, which Cynthia offered to do, since it was her favorite genre. Harlow said she was asking a teacher friend of hers to get the kindergarteners to cut out leaves with their names on them, which Open Book would hang from the ceiling.

"Use the children to lure the parents in. Sneaky but effective. I like it," said Destiny. She was wearing a boatneck cashmere dress that looked like Chloé. *Where* did she find such wonderful clothes?

Cynthia sighed. It wasn't as if they needed a meeting for all this. There were only four of them, with Uncle Robert basically a part-timer, given his afternoon naps and occasional disappearances.

Destiny then asked if she could work for the Main Street trick-or-treating—Halloween was only four weeks away. Ever since Louisa had opened the store, the staff had dressed up for Halloween, choosing a different theme every year.

"What should we do this year?" Destiny asked.

"There's always *Game of Thrones*," Harlow said.

"I call Khaleesi," said Destiny.

"I see you more as Cersei," said Harlow.

"Oh! I'm flattered and insulted at the same time."

Cynthia pursed her lips. "Can we please do something other than that violent, pornographic show? It's hardly appropriate for children. How about Agatha Christie or something a little more genteel?"

"Agatha is little obscure in this day and age. Plus, I want a dragon," Destiny said, forever on Harlow's side.

"I see your point, Cindy," said Harlow, and Cynthia nearly choked on her tea. "How about something that's kid-related and not *Harry Potter*?"

"Well, then," Cynthia said, rather surprised her opinion was being considered. "What about E. B. White characters?"

"Ooh, I love his books," said Harlow. "Great idea."

"I call Snowball the Cat," Destiny said. "I have a white faux fur dress. All I'll need are cat ears."

"I'll be Stuart Little, then," said Grandpop, suddenly appearing from an alcove, "and Destiny and I can have it out at last." He winked at her. "They become great friends, of course."

"Cindy?" asked Harlow.

"Hm," she said, a little surprised that they were running with her idea for the first time ever. "I think I'll be Templeton the Rat, even though I'm a woman."

"We don't care about assigned genders in this store," Destiny said. Cynthia had to smile.

"Guess I'll be Charlotte," Harlow said. "I have a spider costume from when we did *Lord of the Rings*."

"Ophelia can be Fern," Uncle Robert said. "Such a lovely girl."

"Maybe we can get Matthew to be Wilbur," Harlow said.

"Gotta have a Wilbur. And we can do a table display of E. B. White books to tie in, the kids' books and his essays. Great idea, Cynthia." She made a few notes on her laptop, then glanced up. "Anything else?"

"Yes," Cynthia said. Oh. Oh, dear. Apparently she wanted to *say* something.

"Go ahead," said Harlow.

Cynthia looked at Uncle Robert. He gave her a nod. "I'm afraid I've done something I shouldn't have," she said, steeling herself. But she sat up straight, as Mother would have had her do. *Never be ashamed of admitting a mistake, Cynthia. It builds character.* Whether or not Mother had actually said that didn't matter. She could still hear her voice. "Over the past three years, I've . . . I've taken money from the store. I'm very sorry. The money has been repaid, but . . . well, obviously, it was wrong of me." She swallowed. "Harlow, if you want to fire me, I understand."

Harlow looked stunned. "How much?" she managed to ask.

"Almost fifteen thousand dollars."

"Dear God!" Destiny said.

"Fifteen *thousand*?" Harlow squeaked.

"Yes." Cynthia shifted but didn't break eye contact. "You should pay more attention to our finances, Harlow, since you do own half of this place."

Uncle Robert gave a cough that sounded suspiciously like a laugh, and Harlow cut him a look.

"I can't believe we have fifteen grand extra just lying around," Destiny said.

"Why?" Harlow asked. "Why would you steal from us? You own twenty-five percent of the store!" Her face was flushed in anger.

"Because I was . . . scared about my financial future. When I first came here, I was used to having a lot more. I wasn't sure I'd have enough to live on. So I cooked the books, to borrow an expression. It won't ever happen again, of course."

"No, it won't," Harlow said, her voice hard.

"Am I fired, then?" Her heart sank. Believe it or not, she'd miss working here. And where else would she get a job? At the grocery store?

Destiny was glaring at her, frowning. Harlow . . . she probably couldn't *wait* to tell her siblings and parents. Gerald and Elsbeth would be so *smug* about this. And Uncle Robert couldn't exactly defend her honor, since she'd been so . . . well, dishonorable. She stood up to get her purse.

"Cynthia. I mean, Cindy," Harlow said. "Hang on." She took a deep breath. "You made a mistake, but you came clean. You have a point about me not paying enough attention to the books. You're a hard worker, and . . . well, you work hard. I think you should have another chance." She paused. "I'd do the same for Destiny. You're both family."

"Hear, hear," said Uncle Robert. "Well said, Harlow! Very well said!"

Cynthia looked at Destiny. "What about you?" she asked. "I won't stay if you think it's unfair."

Destiny cocked her head a little, tucking her hair behind her ear. "You're giving *me* the deciding vote?"

"Yes."

"Really? You'll quit if I say so?"

"Yes." She stood up a little straighter.

Destiny crossed her legs (they were very nice legs, Cindy had to admit). "All right, yes. Stay, and close on Friday nights for a month. *And* the day after Thanksgiving. Fair enough?"

Cynthia felt something like affection give a tiny flare in her heart. "Fair enough. Thank you, everyone. I . . . I appreciate you all."

"Let's keep this to ourselves," Harlow said. "This is our business, and ours only."

Cynthia's eyes suddenly filled with tears. Harlow was saving her pride. That was . . . that was very generous.

"My lips are sealed," said Uncle Robert. "I'm very proud of you, Cynthia. That took courage."

Courage. That wasn't a characteristic she thought she possessed. But if Uncle Robert said it, it must be true.

That evening after work, Cynthia and Albert took a walk on Great Island Trail, the shorter version that began on the spit of land called, for some reason, the Gut. The views of the salt marsh and harbor were glorious at this time of year. The wind gusted and blew, and the pine needles in the woods smelled lovely. It was just cool enough for a jacket—autumn seemed to have come overnight.

"Think you'll stay here forevah?" Albert asked.

She didn't answer right away. "I suppose I will," she said. "My family's here. Well, my sisters are from New York, but I can't see myself moving to Long Island. And I'm a part-owner of the bookstore." She hesitated. "Speaking of that, Albert, I should probably tell you something, even if it won't cast me in a very flattering light."

"Uh-oh. You got another fella on the side?"

She laughed. "No. Not that. Something worse, maybe." She grew somber and stopped walking so she could look him in the eye. "I embezzled money from the store. It's been paid back, but I did it."

"Robert Smith's store?"

"Yes. I did."

"Why?" he asked, his face grave.

"I was afraid to be poor," she said, her eyes going to a blue jay squawking from a pitch pine. "And I was angry at my husband for leaving me with nothing, and jealous of the Smith family. I wanted to hurt them on some level, I suppose." She shook her head slightly. "Because I wasn't really one of them." But after today, maybe she was.

Albert said nothing.

"I wanted to tell you," she said, swallowing. "I thought you deserved to know."

"Did you, now?"

"I did. You're a good man, and I know you'd chop off your hand before you'd do something like this."

"I appreciate that, I suppose." He took a breath. "Shall we keep walking? It's gettin' dark."

She didn't move. "Do you still want to . . . date me?"

"You know, now that you bring it up," he said, "I don't think I do."

She pressed her lips together, praying she wouldn't cry. "I understand."

"I'd rather marry you. What do you say?"

"Excuse me?"

"What do you think, Cindy?" he asked, turning toward her. "Marry a smelly old carpenter like myself?"

Her heart stuttered, then raced, practically clacking in her chest. "Really?"

"How many times do I gotta ask?" he said, smiling, showing the gap where his incisor had once been.

"I . . . yes! I will! Thank you, Albert!" She threw herself into his arms, a little unsure of what had just happened, but certain of one thing. Life would be better with this man. And so would she.

She was getting married! Oh, her sisters were going to be absolutely thrilled. She'd be posting about this on Facebook, oh, yes, she would! She couldn't wait to tell Uncle Robert, Harlow and Destiny, too. Maybe Destiny could help her pick out a wedding dress. They'd all get such a kick out of this, and the thought made her heart warm with something that felt suspiciously like love.

FORTY-ONE

HARLOW

Hey, can you meet me at Local Break at 4 today? I'll walk there after school. Kind of important.

That was odd. Surely he hadn't flunked a class. Something with sports? A girl?

Is everything okay? I texted back.

I got the thumbs-up emoji. Sometimes, I really hated texting.

I left the store somewhat reluctantly, as it was busy, as it always was on a rainy day. But since Cindy had come clean, we were all working better together. They could handle it. They'd handled my unpredictable schedule all summer.

I got into my car and headed down Route 6 to Eastham, wipers smacking out a fast rhythm. Local Break was a tidy little bar and restaurant with great food and a wide offering of beers. We used to have trivia night there before it became such a thing.

I missed the Kingslayers and the other teams, missed hearing Robbie pick funny songs that went with the questions. I missed the trash-talking, the camaraderie. I missed being something other than the bookstore owner, or one of the Smith kids. I had *loved* being a fierce competitor and captain of the best team on the Cape.

You know what? I was going to rejoin when the winter season

started in January. If this meant Grady and I felt uncomfortable, well, too bad. We'd have to get over it.

The rain had become downright torrential when I pulled into the parking lot of Local Break. I grabbed my backpack, sloshed through a huge puddle and dashed inside, then smoothed my hands over my head to calm my hair.

"Hey, Thom," I called as I hung up my windbreaker. "Crazy out there, isn't it?"

"Hey, stranger! How you doing?" answered the bartender. "Can I get you a drink?"

"I'm meeting my son. Oh, there he is."

"You have a *kid*, Harlow?"

"Long story." I smiled at him and headed toward the back, where Matthew sat facing me, someone else opposite him, a friend from school, I guessed. Matthew had a huge cheeseburger, fries and a silo of Coke in front of him, since he was eighteen and ate every three hours, like a baby. I guessed Monica and Sanjay were giving him an allowance, or he had some savings, because he never asked me for a dime.

"Hi!" I said as I got to the table. "How are—"

The person he was sitting with was Zach Baser. The floor seemed to drop away, and my vision blurred.

"Harlow. Nice to see you again."

Nice to see me again? Nice? I looked at Matthew, who was biting his lip.

"Matthew? A moment, please?" I grabbed his arm and hauled him a few tables away. "What the hell is he doing here?" I whispered. For the first time in my life, I felt a flash of pure parental fury, and wow, it was formidable.

"You said I could contact him." There was a whiny note in his voice.

"I said *you* should contact him if you wanted to. I never said *I* wanted to see him. You ambushed me, Matthew!"

"Well, I figured you . . . yeah. 'Ambushed' is the right word, I guess. He just got here, like, three minutes ago. We haven't even talked yet."

"First you walk into my store without warning, now you toss me in front of him? Seriously, Matthew?"

"I . . . I'm sorry."

"You have to stop springing humans on me! What's next? Your twin daughters?"

He smiled at that. "No. Not yet, anyway."

I took a shaky breath. God, I did *not* want to see Zach Baser.

"I didn't think it would be such a bad thing," Matthew said. "At least, not for me. I just . . . I wanted to see both of you to-gether." I said nothing. "But I get why you're upset. I'm sorry. If you want to go, that's totally fine, and I'll, like . . . clean the whole house when I get home. Give Ollie a bath. Cut Grandpop's toe-nails."

"Frances does that these days." I inhaled slowly. "Well. I'm here. Let's do this."

I marched back to the booth and slid in across from the man who'd impregnated me. "Zach."

He was still recognizable, though he looked soft, at least fifty pounds heavier than when he was eighteen. His black hair was shot through with silver, and he wore a wedding ring. His face was puffy, his eyes unreadable.

Matthew sat down next to me. "I didn't tell her you were gonna be here."

"Yeah, I picked up on that." He fake-smiled, and his teeth were annoyingly perfect. "How are you?" he asked.

"Fine." *None of your fucking business.*

There was a long silence. Zach looked oily and rich, dressed casually in a white shirt and brown leather jacket that probably cost more than I made in a month. Something told me Zach Baser didn't deserve nice things.

"So, I wanted to see you both, like, at the same time," Matthew said. "Once-in-a-lifetime chance, you know?" He fiddled with a french fry, breaking it in half. "Maybe that wasn't a great idea, but now that we're here . . ." He looked at me, his eyes worried. "I just thought we could talk a little." His leg was jiggling, and I put my hand on his knee without taking my eyes of Zach.

"Why don't I tell you how this has unfolded, Harlow," Zach said. I didn't remember his voice being this deep and smooth. It seemed fake. "I got a message a few days ago at my work email. It was from Matthew here, saying he wanted to meet me. I booked a flight to Boston as soon as I could and drove up here."

"Wow. Father of the year."

Matthew's leg resumed its jiggling.

"I live in Chicago, where I grew up."

"I guess golfing didn't work out?" I asked. I turned to Matthew. "Your sperm donor suggested I got pregnant on purpose so I could tap into his future golf winnings." I looked back at Zach. "But I guess you aren't quite the success you thought you'd be."

Zach gave a fake laugh. "First of all, I doubt I ever said that. I mean, I do love golf, of course, but . . . Anyway, Matthew, what can I do for you? I assume you want money?"

Matthew's head jerked back. "No!" he said. "No, not at all."

"Good, because you're not getting any."

Ooh. My whole body tensed. People didn't change. He'd been a selfish asshole then, and he was exactly the same now.

Matthew looked at me again, then back at Zach. "I . . . just wanted to meet you. I said that in the email. To see you, see if we . . . looked alike and stuff. If we had anything in common."

"And do we?" Zach asked. His eyes were glittering and cold, and my knees tingled with premonition. This was off to a bad start, and I sensed it was about to get uglier.

"Um . . . a little? I see where I got my black hair, I guess."

Zach sat there, staring at Matthew. I was happy to say that, aside from hair color, I didn't see any resemblance. No. Matthew looked like *my* side of the DNA.

"Anything else?" Zach asked.

Matthew glanced at me. "Medical history? Like, anything I should be aware of?"

"No." He said nothing more. Another painful few seconds ticked past.

"Okay, good. Good to know. Um . . . do you have other kids?"

Zach leaned forward, his voice low and mean as a rattle-snake. "That is none of your goddamn business. I signed away my parental rights to you for a reason. You were just an embryo that this stupid twit just *had* to have. You don't exist as far as I'm concerned. If you think you can just pop into my life and fuck with my *real* kids, or blackmail me, you'd better think again, because— Jesus!"

I was on my feet, and Coke was dripping from Zach's face onto his once-pristine shirt and expensive leather jacket. "How dare you speak to my son that way," I snarled, not recognizing my voice for the fury in it. "You are the dog shit I scraped from my shoe, and if you ever threaten my son again, I will *kill* you."

Zach held up his hands. Oopsie. I seemed to have a fork in

my hand, pointed at his smug, stupid face. I didn't put it down. Thom the bartender suddenly got very busy polishing glasses.

My son looked like a twelve-year-old who'd just been punched by the school bus bully, eyes wide, face pale.

"Matthew," I said calmly. "I made a huge mistake when I slept with this reptile. That was my mistake, and mine alone. It has nothing to do with you. Thank God you have the parents you do."

Zach opened his mouth again, and I moved the fork a centimeter closer to his face. He wisely chose to be silent.

Then I threw the fork down on the table, making Zach jump. Taking Matthew's hand, I towed him toward the door. "The burger's on the asshole in the back, Thom," I called.

"You got it," he said. "Take care, both of you."

The rain drenched us the second we stepped outside, the wind blowing so hard, it almost knocked me over. We practically fought our way to the car. My hands were shaking, but I wasn't just going to sit here and watch that lowlife shit-ball walk to his car. I didn't trust myself not to run him over. I started the car and drove up the parking lot to the Friendly Fisherman, afraid to drive any farther while I was this mad. I'd left my windbreaker in the restaurant, but there was no way I was going back.

I turned off the car and looked at Matthew. He was crying, his hand over his face. I put my hand on his shoulder.

"I'm such an idiot," he said, his voice choked. "I just thought he'd want to meet me. I didn't want anything from him. I just wanted to . . . show him I turned out all right. I thought he'd be glad."

I tried to think of something comforting to say and came up empty, so we just sat there, Matthew crying, me handing him a couple of paper napkins I had in the car. The rain pounded on the roof, and we sat there a long while in the near-dark.

"Matthew," I finally said, "he was a selfish, mean-spirited bastard then, and he hasn't changed a bit."

"Why did you sleep with him, then?"

"Because he was cute, and he liked me, and I didn't think past that. I was naïve and irresponsible. But he gave me you, and even when I was seventeen, I knew you'd be amazing and special. And you are, Matthew. You are."

Matthew said nothing.

"I'm sorry he's such a shitty, cruel person, honey, and I'm so, so glad you dodged that bullet."

He wiped his eyes and stuffed the napkin into the side pocket of the door. "Can we go home?" he asked.

"You bet."

He didn't want supper that night, even though his burger had gone to waste at the restaurant. Instead, he went straight upstairs, leaving Ollie and me to sit on the couch and fret. A few minutes later, music drifted down, but even so, I heard him crying.

Karma had better be very accurate in what it had handed out to Zachary Baser. Very painful and accurate. I tiptoed up the stairs and knocked softly on Matthew's door, but he didn't answer.

I looked at my dog. "Sit, Oliver," I whispered. He did. "Stay." I crept down the stairs. "Ollie, speak." My dog barked once.

A second later, I heard Matthew's door open. If I couldn't comfort him, at least my dog could.

FORTY-TWO

HARLOW

Things were more solemn for the next couple of days. Matthew didn't want to talk about the encounter. Fresh hatred for Zach flooded through me. At least I'd threatened him with a fork, and while maybe that was a teeny bit illegal, he deserved it.

On Thursday, Matthew had a soccer game in Falmouth, which I went to. Afterward, since he was going out with the team, I drove over the bridge to see Rosie and told her about the horrible meeting. Rosie had chosen to stay a second month at Meadowbrook to be sure she felt strong enough to face the outside world. That month was over now, and she was leaving in two days, back to the City of Angels.

"I'll miss you," I said.

"Same here," she said. "I never could have done this without you, Harlow. I mean, I was hiding from myself for so long. I think I was only able to do it last summer because I was with someone who truly loved me. And that's you." She wiped her eyes. "So I think I might be visiting you more. It's so beautiful out here, and . . . well, you're here. You never know. Maybe I'll buy a fishing boat and move here." She smiled, looking more beautiful and healthy than she had in . . . well, years. "But I'm not gonna make any big decisions now. I'll just go home, hang out with Dad, visit Mom, and go to AA, see what I want to do for a living."

My eyes stung. "I'm really proud of you, Rosie. Prouder than I've ever been."

"I'm proud of *you*, Harlow. You're a great mom, you know that? God, I would give ten grand to see you with that fork, and Zach the Asshole drenched in soda."

"It *was* one of my finer moments," I said.

And yet, Matthew still hadn't gotten over the harsh rejection. He probably never would. If I were honest with myself, *I'd* clearly never gotten over what a shitty choice I'd made in having anything to do with Zach, and how he'd reacted to my pregnancy.

We said our goodbyes, hugging tightly, crying a good bit, as we always had when we had to leave each other after a visit.

"I'll come visit at Christmas," she said. "Or I could send you a ticket. I know Matthew will be with the Patels then, so you should come to us. And you know Daddy and his miles. You'd fly first class."

"I'll think about it. I love you, Rosie," I said.

"Love you, too. And hey. Tell Robbie I kind of love him."

"Not gonna do that. Bye!"

She was laughing as I got into my car. I'd always known I was damn lucky to have Rosie Wolfe for a friend. It was nice to realize she was also lucky to have me.

FORTY-THREE

MONICA

Monica's family was broken.

Not just her, Sanjay and Meena. Sita and Ishan couldn't understand why they'd "let" Matthew stay. Sanjay's sisters and brother were bewildered. *Their* children wouldn't leave *them*, so surely Sanjay and Monica had done something wrong. Accusation hung heavily in the air.

She ached for Matthew. Her entire body felt wrong without him here, as if her arms and legs had been borrowed from another body and stitched onto her. Her chest hurt all the time, as if a fist was squeezing her heart to pump the blood. Because her heart *was* broken. She'd never known how accurate that term was. Heartbroken. Soulbroken.

She took an extra two weeks off work for Meena's sake, wanting to be there when her daughter got home from school. During the day, Sita came over, wringing her hands over the situation. Monica made dinner, baked, weeded, cleaned out a few closets—the things her regular work schedule didn't allow. She took Meena to the Center for Architecture + Design in San Francisco one Sunday, cuddled her at night, started reading to her again, even though Meena had the reading comprehension of a second-year college student.

Of course, Matthew called and FaceTimed. She asked the usual questions—how are you, how's school, soccer, the weather, friends. He answered, staying very positive but not sharing a lot. He didn't talk about Harlow, though the other Smiths got a mention. He and Grandpop played chess sometimes. Ellie was continuing to teach him to paint. Robbie took him fishing and had him help take apart a boat engine. Winnie took him out to breakfast.

"Sounds nice," she might say, but inside, she was screaming. The ache in her chest didn't cease. Maybe she should see a cardiologist. Maybe there was something wrong, and she'd have a massive heart attack, and then Matthew would *have* to come back, wouldn't he?

Sanjay, of course, was the first to break from the gray pallor that hung in their house. "Listen," he said one night at dinner, "we all miss Matt terribly, but we know he's doing something that's very important to him. I think we should be happy for him, and support his decision and make sure we're getting on with our own lives."

"But I don't," said Meena, her voice flat. "I don't support him, and I can't get on with my own life because I used to have a brother and now I don't. I hate him for doing this. I can't believe he cares more about *Harlow* than us."

Damn right, Meena, Monica thought.

"It's your fault," she said to both of them, and oh, God, here it came. The blame. "You spoiled him rotten. There's a reason I call him HRH, you know. Because whatever he does, whatever he says, you give him a pass because he's adopted."

"Darling, that is not true," Sanjay said.

But maybe it was. Monica didn't know. Her brain throbbed.

On her last day home, she got a company-wide email saying Abdel El Khoury, one of the poker bros, had gotten the promotion Monica had hoped for. She emailed Peter, asking why he'd chosen Abdel, who was four years junior to her and didn't have nearly the amount of experience she did. Peter's answer: *He's a better fit. Extremely devoted to Guardian.* In other words, she shouldn't have taken those extra two weeks. Or any time, really.

The next day, she went into work, dressed in her carefully elegant work wardrobe, saying hello to everyone as she went to her corner office.

"Thank God you're back," said Mitchell, her assistant. "The sky has been falling without you. I just sent you a list of priorities. We've got six open projects, and guess what? They're all time-sensitive and horribly important."

"So same old, same old," she said. "Thanks, Mitchell."

Before she'd even put her purse in the drawer, Peter Bidwell was in her office. "Nice to finally have you back. How was your vacation?"

"It was a family issue, not a vacation, Peter. I told you that."

"Well. Good. We've been foundering without you. Can you put together an analysis for Tetris Oil and Gas? The meeting's Friday. Sorry it's such short notice, but I know you're up for it, especially since you're so well rested. The meeting's in Dallas, so we'll fly out at 6 a.m. Sonia already booked your tickets." He stood up to leave.

"Shouldn't Abdel be on this?" she asked mildly. "As senior vice president? Tetris is a Fortune 100 company."

"Yeah. Well, the client asked for you specifically." He didn't have the grace to look the least bit sheepish. "But Abdel is doing great as SVP. He's going golfing with the president of Amber Medical tomorrow."

Golfing. That fucking boys' club.

"Peter?" she said. He turned back.

"Consider this my two weeks' notice. And no, I won't be going to Dallas. Better tell Abdel to step it up."

She hadn't expected to say that, certainly. But it felt right. It felt . . . amazing.

She observed Peter's meltdown with something like amusement but held her ground. After he'd left her office, Monica went to Shaunee in HR, murmured the words *gender discrimination lawsuit*.

"I have to admit," Shaunee, the HR manager, whispered, "I've kind of been waiting for this day. Cheers, Monica."

The team of lawyers was called. Monica strolled around Guardian, chatted with Caroline and Isamu, had lunch by herself in the executive dining hall, then kicked back in a conference room and played solitaire on her laptop while people (all men) literally ran up and down the halls.

Finally, Peter, Abdel, four lawyers and Shaunee came into the conference room. Peter said he apologized if she had ever felt overlooked, and would she reconsider if he offered her a well-earned promotion?

She would not. "But I will accept a very generous bonus and severance package, payment for comp time for the past year and health care for my family and me for the next, oh, two years."

"Don't be ridiculous," Peter said.

"But you won't sue?" asked one of the lawyers.

"Depends," she said. "Suffice it to say, I'll be watching your hiring and promotion policies very carefully. I wonder how Caroline is feeling these days."

"I think we can come to an agreement," said the lawyer, the only one allowed to speak, apparently. He whispered to Peter, but Monica could hear the words. Of course she could. She was a mother, and bat-like hearing came with the territory. "Give her anything she wants. She sues, you're screwed." Music to her ears.

"Of course, I'll give you a wonderful reference," Peter said after the papers were signed and the money deposited in her account. Technology certainly had its upside. Getting this done in one day meant she'd never have to see Peter and the golf bros again.

"Save it," she told him. "My work speaks for itself. I don't need an aging white male speaking for me." She looked back at Shaunee, the head of HR, who was smiling. "Anything else, Shaunee?"

"Nope. You are all set," she said. "And thank you, Monica. It's been a pleasure working with you."

"Same here. If you need any input on updating Guardian's very nebulous criteria for promotions, let me know."

Shaunee smothered a smile. Then Monica handed over her badge, grabbed her purse and walked out with a huge smile on her face. She had a feeling work was about to become more pleasant for the women at Guardian, but beyond that, she really didn't care about the company. It had taken enough of her life these past ten years.

As she pulled out of the parking lot, she rolled down the windows in her car, switched her Spotify from the parenting podcasts she usually had on and found a pop station that was playing Lizzo's "About Damn Time." Sign. Universe. She headed for the coast, stopped at an In-N-Out and got a huge burger, fries and a milkshake. Then she drove to Eden Landing Ecological Reserve, where she sat in the sunshine, eating her food and watching the birds.

Sanjay was sitting at the kitchen table, laptop open, when she walked into the kitchen around five. "My queen! What are you doing home so early? This is a wonderful surprise." He got up to kiss her. "Everything okay at work?"

"I quit today."

His beautiful brown eyes widened. "Did you, now? Well! Let me make my queen a drink and you can tell me all about it." He reached up for the cocktail shaker.

"I'm sorry I didn't talk to you about it first. It was impulsive. I'll find something else, not to worry."

Sanjay turned back to her and looked into her eyes. Really looked at her. "Take your time, Moni. What you've done for our family is remarkable. Utterly remarkable. We have no mortgage, the kids have plenty for college, we have retirement savings and it's all because of you. Take a hiatus. I know I'm only a lowly teacher, but if I have to get another job, I will. These past few months have been hard on you, my love. Count on me now. We've all been counting on you for far too long."

She burst into tears, and her husband took her in his arms and let her cry.

Being understood was one of the best feelings in the world.

"Now," said Sanjay. "Vodka or gin?"

FORTY-FOUR

HARLOW

The week before Halloween, Cindy invited me to a cocktail party. Not just me, but also Matthew, Grandpop, Frances, Ophelia and Destiny.

"Cindy's hospitality is unexpected," Destiny murmured, holding the ladder as I tried to reach the extra stock stored over the bookshelves. Sonali Dev's Jane Austen series had just been released on one of the big streaming services, and we couldn't keep the books in stock.

"I know," I said. "She's been here three and a half years, and I've never been invited over."

After work, I drove Matthew and Ophelia to Cynthia's. Grandpop and Frances had come together, and Bertie Baines was there, too. I imagined Grandpop had invited him along.

"Hi, Bertie!" I said, kissing his scratchy cheek. "How are you?"

"Never better," he said.

Cindy gave me a glass of wine, looking a bit flustered. "Thank you for coming," she said, accepting the bouquet of flowers I'd bought. "Oh, and thank you for these beautiful flowers. How thoughtful of you."

"Thank you for having us," I said, smiling. She hustled off to put them in a vase.

"I love this place, Cindy," Ophelia exclaimed. "Wicked cute."

"Really? Thanks," she said. She seemed surprised to hear it. But I agreed with Ophelia. Sure, it could use a little updating, but it was a classic. She placed my flowers on the coffee table.

"You have a *fireplace*," Destiny said. "I'm so jealous." She took a tiny quiche from a tray and popped it in her mouth.

"This view," Grandpop said, taking a sip of his drink. "You can't put a price on a view like this!"

Ophelia pulled out her phone. "Hey, Matt, let's take a picture and send it to Meena."

Matthew's eyes flickered, but he stood with Ophelia, arm around her shoulder, and forced a smile.

I needed to talk with my son. I knew that. He hadn't said more than hello and goodbye to me since the scene with Zach, and his sadness was palpable. I knew what he needed, but oh, God, I didn't want to say the words.

Cindy clinked her wineglass with a fork, and Bertie closed the oven, then came to stand next to her. "Well, thank you for coming, everyone," she said.

"Our pleasure," said Destiny, crossing her fabulous legs.

"I have a little news," Cynthia said, blushing. "I wanted you all to come and help us celebrate because . . . Albert and I are getting married."

Bertie? The guy Cindy had once called a hobo? No one said a word for a second, then the room erupted in exclamations.

"Congratulations, my dear!" Grandpop said. "This is wonderful! A wedding!"

"No way!" said Ophelia.

"Huzzah!" said Destiny. "What happy news!"

I got up and hugged them both. "Bertie, you dog, you," I said. "Dating Cindy on the sly! You clever man."

"Lucky man, if you ask me," he said.

"Will you live here?" Frances asked, ever practical. One of the things I loved about her.

"We haven't decided yet," Cindy said.

"She just saw my house the other day. I told her we could live there, or we could do a little overhaul of this place," Bertie said. He lowered his voice. "She thought I was poor. Nice to know she said yes when she thought I was broke."

Destiny and I laughed. Bertie was more than flush, all those years of building houses, decks and additions. To be fair, he did look like he slept on the beach.

"To my dear godchild and her fiancé," Grandpop said, raising his glass. "We wish all the happiness in the world!"

"Hear, hear," we chorused, raising our glasses, and Bertie kissed Cindy, who beamed.

Only Matthew didn't seem utterly delighted. He sat on a kitchen chair just outside the living room. I went over to him. "Everything okay?" I asked, putting my hand on his shoulder.

"Yeah. I'm fine." His eyes met mine for a second before he glanced away. "Everything's fine."

I recognized that answer for the lie it was. After all, I'd given the same lie for years.

When we got home later on, Matthew went right to his room. "I have a lot of homework," he called over his shoulder.

"Okay. I'm gonna take Ollie for a walk." The words caused Oliver to turn madly in a circle, drunk with joy.

No answer. "Matthew?"

"Yep. Heard you."

Oliver and I went down Main Street, our usual nighttime stroll, and then to Uncle Tim's Bridge. I crossed over to Hamblen, took the trail through the woods to the narrow strip of sand that looked out to sea. Then I unclipped Ollie's leash so he could run off and sniff things.

Tears were already falling, because I knew what was coming next.

I had to send Matthew home. He needed his family.

These past ten weeks had been among the happiest of my life . . . but not of his. His decision to stay here had been the wrong one. I had known it then and could see it now. The encounter with that asshole Zach had broken a part of him, and he needed his mom and dad, and I was neither. I was First Mama, and he loved me. But my son needed the people who'd raised him, who knew him from his first hour onward, who understood him better than I ever would.

For the second time in my life, I had to let my son go.

I sat on the sand, knees bent, the dampness creeping through my jeans, buried my head in my arms and cried. Ollie crawled onto my lap, licking my face, but even my sweet dog couldn't help this time. My time with my son was over.

Finally, I stood up, brushed the sand off my jeans and clipped Ollie's leash back on, then headed for home. As we walked down East Commercial Street, I saw a car in the parking lot, a man opening the trunk and putting in a duffel bag which, I knew, would be full of measuring equipment and sand and water samples and an underwater camera because, of course, it was Gray. I could see him clearly by the light from his car, and my heart seemed to fold in on itself with regret.

Ollie began whining, and Grady looked our way.

"Hi, Gray," I said.

"Harlow. How are you?"

I wanted to tell him the truth. I wanted to say I was aching and already mourning the time I'd had with my son. But Grady wasn't my person. Funny, that he'd been the first one I'd told about Matthew, all the way back in June. How kind he'd been in that understated way of his. His first question had been if I was okay. That was Grady Byrne in a nutshell.

"I'm good, Gray. How are you? How's Luna liking preschool?"

He reached down and gave Ollie a pet. "She loves it. She's really good."

"Did you find a new nanny?"

"I did. A nice grandmother type from Fall River."

"That's great." I paused. "And how are you?"

His eyes, so gentle and so . . . so good . . . flickered downward. "I'm okay."

Ollie put his front paws on Grady's leg, tail swishing wildly.

"Well," I said, clearing my throat. "Take good care of yourself, Gray."

"You too."

At home, I took off Ollie's leash and gave him fresh water, then drank a glass myself. Then I headed upstairs, knocked on Matthew's door. He didn't answer. I cracked it anyway, expecting to see him wearing headphones and sitting at his desk. He wasn't. He was lying on his bed, curled on his side. He wiped his eyes at my approach but otherwise didn't move.

I sat down next to him and reached out to touch his inky black curls. "Hey, buddy," I said.

"Hi," he whispered.

"Homesick?" I asked.

He looked at me, startled, then nodded.

I forced my throat to relax so I'd sound normal. "Do you want to go back, honey?"

Matthew started to cry in earnest. "We had a huge fight before they left," he said. "I told them they didn't get to tell me how to live my life, and they were jealous of you, and if they really loved me, they wouldn't be guilt-tripping me, and my mom was so hurt, and Dad was trying not to cry . . ." His voice choked off.

"That sounds awful."

"Yeah. It was. And we haven't really talked since then. Just superficial shit, mostly through text." He rubbed his arm across his eyes. "Meena's still so mad, she won't even FaceTime." He sobbed harder now.

"Oh, sweetie," I said, stroking his hair. "I'm sorry."

"I told them I knew what I was doing. That I belonged with you, that I wanted to know my real mother. I don't know if they'll forgive me. They might make me stay here just to . . . to learn my lesson, but I . . . I miss them so much."

I wiped my own eyes, but when I spoke, my voice was steady. "They absolutely will forgive you. And they'll be overjoyed to have you back."

He wiped his eyes on his sleeve once more, then looked at me, his dark eyes hopeful. "You think so?"

"I know. How about if I call them?" I asked. "Tell them there's been a change of plans."

He sat up and put his hand over mine. "What about you?"

It felt like a knife had just been shoved in my chest. "Matthew, honey," I said, my voice calm. "I'll always want what's best for you. Always have, always will. There's a place here for you for the rest of your life." I took a careful breath. "But I think you need to go home now."

He looked down at our hands, his so much bigger than mine, then looked back at me. "Thanks, Mom," he said.

Mom. My little pal, who'd rolled and kicked and hiccuped inside me. The gripping, rolling contractions. That last, surreal push. His soft, soft skin, those huge dark eyes, his little hand gripping my finger. And now, his big hand holding mine.

"I love you," I said. "Now let me make that phone call."

Three days later, Matthew and I were on a plane, heading to California. First class, thanks to Monica, who may have broken a record for fastest ticket booking. We'd had a goodbye-for-now party at Addison and Nicole's the day before yesterday, and Esme and Imogen had cried and clung to Matthew. Grandpop had hugged him hard and wished him well and told him he was a fine young man. My father had sobbed quietly in the corner. Mom had held Matthew's face in her hands and just gazed into his eyes, tears streaming down her face as she told him she loved him. Robbie promised to come to California and visit, Winnie had made a photo book with pictures from the summer, and Lark couldn't stop crying or kissing him on the cheek.

I had to go in the kitchen at one point for a glass of cold water. My throat felt like it had a shard of glass in it. *It's not the end*, I told myself.

But it sure felt that way.

Grandpop came in and put his arm around me. "I'm so proud of you," he said, his voice quiet for once, not the booming exclamations he usually spoke in. "So proud. You keep it together, sweetheart. There'll be time for crying when you get back. You can do that."

I nodded, and he hugged me. "You're my favorite," he whispered. "Don't tell anyone."

Now, the country sprawling below us, Matthew was sleeping. I sat quietly, not taking advantage of the in-flight entertainment.

We'd see each other again. Of course we would. We'd already talked about it. I'd visit him at college, and he'd visit the Cape. But he'd never live with me again. I'd never get to take care of him, never be his everyday mom, picking him up from school. I'd never be his first call, ever again. Our time, so special and achingly wonderful, was over, and I knew it would never be re-created. As glad as I was to have had the experience at all, for now I could only feel the pain of it ending.

Matthew woke up when we were over the Rockies. He looked out the window, his leg jiggling, and I knew he was counting the minutes till we landed.

When the descent into San Francisco began and the pilot told us we were ten minutes ahead of schedule, Matthew took my hand. "I love you, Harlow," he said.

"I love you, too," I whispered. "So much."

He put his arm around me, but he was already back home in his heart. As it should be.

My gift from God.

We landed with a bump and the rush of the reverse thrust of the engines. His leg jiggled again as we taxied to the gate, and he jumped up the second we stopped. Being in first class meant we got to deplane first, and I towed my carry-on behind me, almost needing to run to keep up with him. Out in the noisy bustle of the airport, Matthew texted his parents, then shoved his phone in his pocket. We were meeting them at baggage claim.

And then, there they were, Sanjay, Monica and Meena.

"Matthew!" Meena yelled, and they ran toward each other, meeting in a hug so big, he picked her up off her feet. Then his father hugged him, clapping him hard on the back. When he let go, Matthew stood in front of Monica.

"I missed you, Mom," he said. "I really, really missed you." And they hugged for a long, long time.

Everyone was crying, including me. But I stood back and let them have this moment.

Then Monica broke away and came over to me and grabbed both my hands. We looked at each other, tears streaming down our cheeks. "Thank you, Harlow," she said. "From one mother to another, thank you."

FORTY-FIVE

HARLOW

I stayed at the Patels' home, which was as I had remembered in that first video, snug and beautiful, rich with character, pictures of Matthew and Meena everywhere. I met their cat, Hoosier. That night was a welcome home dinner, and I met Matthew's grandparents, aunts, uncle and cousins. No one said anything unkind; no one accused me of trying to steal Matthew back. It was absolutely wonderful to see how much they all adored him, how much a part of this family he was and had always been.

Already, Matthew's time on the Cape was part of his life's mythology, that time he'd lived with his "other" family, a vacation of sorts. He told them about the family, showed pictures on his phone, held a cousin on his lap.

I hadn't told Sanjay or Monica about Zach Baser. That was Matthew's story to share. Through his cruelty, Zach had shown Matthew what a parent shouldn't be . . . and what they should be. A parent was the person who'd walk the floor with you when you had colic, who could go for two days straight without sleep when you were sick. The person who was proud of every little milestone you hit, from sleeping through the night to getting an A. The people who forgave you, over and over, every time you hurt them. Every time you sliced off a piece of their heart, they grew it back so you could do it again.

Monica and Sanjay were the best parents I'd ever met in my life.

Whatever connection Matthew and I had had on the Cape was fading. He was polite and friendly to a fault, but he kept a distance of sorts, devoting himself to the Patels. Meena and Sanjay, too, were only polite.

Oddly enough, it was Monica I felt closer to. Now that I'd walked the walk of motherhood, and now that she'd felt the terrible ache of loss, we understood a little of what the other had sacrificed.

I slept in the guest room of the house where my son had grown up, and Hoosier the cat slept at the foot of my bed. The next day, we had breakfast together, the four Patels and me—a huge spread of rotis, idlis and spicy potatoes as well as scrambled eggs, bacon and bagels.

I had to leave for the airport at eleven. Sanjay said he'd drive me, but I said no. "I'll take a Lyft. Stay here with your son."

"That's very considerate of you," he said.

Then came the inevitable moment when it was time for me to leave. I had left presents on the bed in the guest room—for Meena, the Lunar Chronicles by Marissa Meyer from me, as well as a friendship bracelet from Ophelia. For Sanjay, a piece of driftwood with "The Patels" burned onto the surface. For Monica, a silver necklace, two circles intertwined. Maybe it represented her two children, or her and Matthew. Maybe it represented the two of us, Matthew's mothers.

And for my son, a few framed photos. The two families at his picnic, and another I'd taken of the four of them at Mayo Beach when they'd come to pick Matthew up one day. The sky was brilliant blue behind them, and their arms were around each other. They looked so happy, because they *were* happy. A happy, solid family with a few twists here and there.

And one more photo, though I wasn't sure Matthew would want to display it, or even keep it. I had a copy as well, waiting for me to hang it up back home. Robbie had taken it. It showed Matthew and me, looking at each other, almost exactly the same height. We were in profile—same straight nose, same slightly prominent chin, same curly hair. You could see the wonder in our expressions. *I know you*, our faces said. *I remember you.*

As I came down the stairs with my suitcase, a car horn beeped from outside—my Lyft had arrived ten minutes early. Our goodbyes were swift. I hugged Meena, though it was a bit awkward, then Sanjay, then Monica.

"Thank you," she whispered. "Thank you, Harlow."

I couldn't speak, but as I looked into her beautiful blue eyes, I nodded.

Maybe I would write to her and try to express my gratitude and admiration and love for her, but right now, I couldn't get the words out.

Then it was time to say goodbye to my son. He stepped into my arms, and I hugged him hard and did my best not to sob. Not now. "I love you so much," I whispered fiercely.

"Love you, too, First Mama," he whispered back. "Take care."

Then I left their house and got into the waiting car. The minute we were out of sight of their house, the sobs began. I cried all the way to the airport, worrying the driver, and all through security, and in the bathroom of the first-class lounge. Then I went to the bar, ordered a gin and tonic and sat in front of the window.

There was only one thought running through my head as the planes landed and took off, landed and took off.

I had done the right thing. He wasn't mine anymore.

His tiny hand, his little rosebud mouth. That moment when we had looked into each other's eyes and time had stopped.

And suddenly, I remembered Monica's words all those years ago as I handed her our son. *He'll never forget you*, she had said through her tears. *I won't let him.*

She had kept her word.

FORTY-SIX

HARLOW

Matthew texted me every few days, and we had talked twice in the month since he'd been gone. He'd signed up for Open Book's newsletter, which was sweet. I sent him an email with an update about the family, and my parents told me he had called them. Grandpop received a handwritten letter.

And then, the texts grew a bit less frequent. A little more obligatory, though he always signed off with *Love you!* He had applied to Harvard, Stanford, Dartmouth, UC Berkeley, Northwestern and Georgetown. Hey. Two of those were within driving distance.

Sometimes, I woke up with a throbbing, fiery ache and wanted to call him, hear his voice, schedule a visit. I wanted to book a flight to San Fran and meet him so we could walk around and talk. I wanted to see if he'd grown any taller or if he'd gotten a haircut.

But I didn't. I'd see him again, I knew that. *Maybe you could come to my graduation*, he texted. *I'll see how many tickets I get.*

I, too, phrased an awkward invitation or two. *Let me know when you want to visit and I'll buy your ticket.* Or *If you visit Harvard again, I'd love to see you.*

I had a new awareness now—of my own mother, of Addison and Nicole, Monica, Grammy . . . even of Grady's ex-wife. You can't have a child and not experience terror and heartache in some way. Your little hijacker will hold you hostage for the rest of your life, and there's no getting around that—not by placing the child for adoption, not by abandoning the child, not by being as perfect a mother as possible. Your heart, naked and vulnerable, is now in the form of another person, and your life is never completely your own again.

It was worth it. It was so worth it.

I replaced Matthew's blue-and-gray comforter and sheets with the white quilt I'd always used and painted the guest room a lovely shade of rose. Ollie stopped running up the stairs to look for his boy, which made me cry a little. Darkness came early at this time of year, and the nights were long and good for thinking under the cold, starry sky.

When I was seventeen, I had knowingly broken my heart, and I'd curled into myself, cowering, trying to shield myself from any other anguish. Now, at thirty-six, I had done it again by taking Matthew home. But this time, I decided, my heart had been broken open. The summer of Matthew would make me a better person—a better sister, better daughter, aunt and friend. I was already a perfect granddaughter, so I had that nailed, at least.

I invited my parents over for dinner, just the two of them, and asked how they were still so happy together, then listened without the usual cringing as they talked about their marriage. I offered to babysit for Esme and Imogen and, while they were demons, I told Addie and Nicole I was totally up for doing it again. I asked Winnie if she wanted to take a yoga class with me, and she said yes. I cleaned Lark's apartment when she was at the hospital and left her a note telling her how much I admired her.

At Open Book, I found myself watching the parents more closely—how Alissa DeJonge listened to Pierce so intently, the way Maeve (hater of Pete the Cat) held her mother's hand. One day, Luna and her new nanny came in, and Luna immediately bolted over to see me. "Hello, Miss Harlow! Do you have any good books for me today?" Her cheeks were pink from the cold, and the smile she gave me went straight to my heart. Luna Byrne, this little girl who loved books and story time, who wore a red-and-green-plaid skirt over bright orange leggings and a pink cowboy hat on her head.

"I do," I said, realizing I hadn't answered. "I have some very cozy books for you and your daddy to read, how's that?"

"That's *brilliant*," she said, grabbing my hand. There it was again, that . . . shift inside me. "This is my nanny, Miss Aggie," she said. "Miss Harlow lives here, Miss Aggie, but they let her out sometimes."

"Harlow Smith." I smiled at Miss Aggie. "I own the bookstore."

"I met your grandfather the last time I was here," she said. "Lovely to meet you."

"Where are the cozy books, Miss Harlow?" Luna asked.

I led her into the children's section, her little hand still in mine. "This one is about a dad who takes his little girl on a special walk," I said, handing her *Owl Moon*. It was the kind of thing Gray would do, and the image of them tromping through the snow at night to see owls made my eyes sting. Luna was such a smart and brave little girl, a bit of a thrill-seeker. I remembered her leaping in the waves this past summer at Nauset Light, how she ordered Grady to push her *much* higher. The kind of kid I'd want to be friends with. Curious and confident, friendly and very much an individual.

The kind of kid I loved.

"Here's another one," I said, kneeling next to her. "It's about the animals who live underground when it's cold."

She leaned against me to look at *Over and Under the Snow*. "I think I like this one best," she said, returning to *Owl Moon*. She didn't move away, and I stayed there, careful not to move, her sweet weight warm against me as she turned the pages of the beautiful story. Then Miss Aggie reminded her it was almost lunchtime, and Luna scrambled up, tucking the book under her arm to bring to the counter.

I thought about that sweet, slight weight against my side for a long time. The smell of her hair—baby shampoo and Elmer's glue, a hint of woodsmoke. I thought about that a lot.

Rosie and I met in New Orleans for a weekend and spent the time wandering through the Garden District, eating beignets and drinking coffee. She had a new job as a set decorator, was taking a boxing class and had gained about ten pounds from healthy eating. We talked about Matthew . . . and we talked about other things, too. Her sobriety. Her lonely childhood. She was having more honest conversations with her parents, and had made a friend in AA. I asked her if she'd like to visit in the springtime—like most people from Southern California, she was allergic to winter. She said yes. She didn't bring up Robbie, and I didn't ask. They were both adults, after all.

I invited Destiny, Kate the cute bartender (as we were calling her), Cindy and Lillie over—no book club, just us women—and found myself surprised by how much fun we had, laughing and eating and catching up. Ollie and I went kayaking almost every morning at dawn, both of us bundled against the cold as the good Cape sounds and salt air seeped into our souls.

There was a difference between having a hole in your heart and keeping space in your heart. I had plenty of space, I was learning. More than enough.

One day in mid-December, the Cape hunkered down for a big snowstorm. The local meteorologists were peeing themselves, warning people to stock up on supplies, then warning them to stay off the roads in the next breath. The snow started at two, and this time, the predictions were right. The snow was fast and heavy and utterly beautiful.

I sent Destiny home, since she had to drive to Provincetown, and closed the store early. Made Grandpop cocoa, called Frances to check on her and told Grandpop I'd walk down to the market and pick us up some dinner fixings.

"Ollie will stay with you," I said. "Don't go outside, because it's really slippery."

"Wonderful!" he said. "What a perfect day to snuggle with this *handsome* dog!"

Smiling, I walked out into the snow, sucker-punched by the beauty of it, as I was with every snowstorm. The edges of all the Main Street buildings were soft and clean, any peeling paint or cracked sidewalk covered in white. Christmas decorations and fairy lights twinkled from the windows, and red-cheeked kids were skittering and slipping about, shouting with excitement.

Wellfleet Marketplace was crammed with people buying toilet paper and milk. There was Winnie, talking to Robbie, lecturing him about something, no doubt. I went inside.

"Hi, guys," I said.

"Hey, Harlot," said Robbie.

"Harlow," said Winnie, "I'm trying to convince our brother that now is not the best time to drive to Boston."

"She's right. Winnie's always right, Robbie." I paused. "Boston?"

"Just thinking about a girl in California. Thought I might try to catch a flight."

I started to tell him it was a bad idea, then stopped myself. "Check the flights. I'm guessing they're all canceled," I said.

"So says Winslet."

"Windsor, idiot. Try to learn your sister's name."

"Oh, hey, guys," said Lark, coming upon us with her arms full of various kinds of cookies and chocolate bars. "Great snow, huh? Want to come to Addie's with me? I thought I'd pull the girls around on a sled."

"You walk in her door with all that sugar and Nicole will shoot you dead," said Robbie.

"Oh, this is all for me," she said.

The line was to the back of the store. "Why is Grandpop here?" Winnie asked. "He shouldn't be out in this!"

For heaven's sake. I checked my phone, saw that I had missed the door alarm. He caught sight of us and practically danced over.

"Isn't this *wonderful*?" Grandpop asked. "I feel like a boy again!"

"You're my life goals, Grandpop," Robbie said, brushing the snow from our grandfather's coat. "I've got gummies if you want to hang out and watch movies later on."

"You shouldn't have come out alone, Grandpop," I said. "It's dangerous."

"I'm not alone," he said. "I brought Oliver with me. They wouldn't let me bring him in, so I tied him to the telephone pole." That was fine. Ollie, who feared rain, loved the snow. "Kids," Grandpop added, "you should come back to the bookstore. We're closed, and it's *very* cozy! We have hot chocolate, don't we, Harlow? Robbie, you can make a fire in the fireplace."

I didn't answer. Outside, Grady and Luna stood with Ollie, petting him, my dog's tail swishing wildly.

I had thought, once, that I couldn't ever be a mother because I'd passed at the chance to raise my own son. But this summer had shown me—Matthew and Monica had shown me—that being a mother wasn't one thing. It was an indefinable, eternal state of love and acceptance, sacrifice and forgiveness. And hope. Because being a mother was nothing if not hope.

Since I was seventeen, I had hoped the best for Matthew. I had hoped he would find me, love me, like me, forgive me. All her life, Monica had hoped she could raise her son, love him without limitations, be loved by him. We'd gotten what we hoped for, Monica and I. We two mothers.

And now, I knew, I could be Luna's mother, too . . . if her dad would let me.

Without forethought, I headed for the door.

"There she goes," said Robbie. "We're gonna want to eavesdrop on this one, girls."

I paid no attention. The snow fell heavily, but I only saw one thing: Grady Byrne and his little girl.

"Miss Harlow!" she said, dancing over to me. "We found Oliver Twist! He was right here!" She lifted her arms, as kids do with adults they trust, and I picked her up.

The significance was not lost on me.

Her weight was slight, and she fit right against me. "Thank you, Luna," I said, and my voice sounded surprisingly normal. "Hi, Gray."

As usual, his face was a little solemn. "Hi," he said.

We just looked at each other for a minute, and I felt my face get warm. I should've written something on a note card. I should've planned what to say.

"Gray," I said firmly. "I need to tell you something."

"Okay," he said, not looking away.

"Hello, Luna!" boomed Grandpop's voice. "Isn't this snow *wonderful*!"

"I love this snow!" she said, wriggling out of my arms. "Do you want to go sledding with us, Mr. Grandpop?"

"I wish I could, but I'd probably break every bone in my body!"

"You have two hundred and six bones," she informed him.

"That's a lot to break," Grandpop said. "Maybe you could have hot chocolate at the bookstore with us before you go sledding. Put something warm in your tummy." He caught my eye and winked. "Wingman," he whispered, loud enough that Grady could hear as well.

My siblings were outside now, too. "Hi, Grady, hi, kid," they chorused, more or less in unison.

"Gray, we're headed for Open Book, if you and Luna want to come," Robbie said. He looked at me and raised an eyebrow.

"Can we, Daddy?" she asked, bouncing in anticipation.

"Sure," said Grady.

"We'll just start up the road without you," Winnie said. "Come on, Luna."

Luna grabbed on to Grandpop's hand. "Hold on," she ordered him. "Because of your oldness." Robbie took Grandpop's other arm, and Lark untied Ollie.

"I haven't seen Ollie in way too long," she said, grinning, and she joined the rest of them.

"My wingmen," I said, looking back at Grady.

"Yes. I got that."

People were out on the street, shoveling their patch of sidewalk, scraping off a car. Reverend White was talking with Judith Stiles, and Lillie Silva and Ben were walking down the street, holding hands. Kids ran and laughed, giddy at a day off from school.

"What did you want to say?" Grady asked, and I looked at him, all that goodness and intelligence. All that kindness.

"I love your daughter," I blurted out. "And I love you. You said I was stuck in the past, and at the time, you were right. But it's not true anymore." My eyes filled with tears. "I'm right here, today, this second. I'm not broken anymore. I was, but . . . I glued myself back together. And I'm better because of it. Stronger and braver. And also, I'd let myself be eaten by sharks before I'd hurt you or Luna. Give me another chance, Gray."

Those green eyes were steady on me, and I thought . . . I thought I saw a little ray into them, like the sun cutting through clear ocean water, the light gold and warm.

"Okay," he said.

"Okay?"

"Yep."

"Okay as in we'll date for a while and maybe get married someday and I'll be Luna's stepmom?"

"Yes. That."

My knees weakened in a giddy rush. "Great! Phew! Glad you said it, because—" My words were cut off by his kiss, warm and firm and perfect. His fingers tangled in my snow-crusted hair, and my arms went around his waist, and I kissed him back for all I was worth.

Tears were on my cheeks when the kiss ended. Grady brushed them away. "Should we get some cocoa?" he whispered.

I nodded.

"I love you, too, by the way." His eyes told me he'd been holding on to those words for a long time.

As we stood there, the snow pelting down from the cold gray skies, that little ray of sunshine wasn't so little anymore. Right now, it felt like the entire sun beaming with enough light and warmth to last a lifetime.

ACKNOWLEDGMENTS

What a joy to write about owning a bookstore! In doing so, I contacted RJ Julia, my local independent bookstore, as cozy and bustling and welcoming as every bookstore should be, a haven for readers and a platform for authors. Thank you, Liz, for letting me come and hang out and ask questions and get in the way—Julie, Andrew, Kelly, Sharon and Bridie get a special shout-out and my deepest thanks. Readers, if you're ever in Connecticut, you owe it to yourselves to visit.

Thank you to Alissa and Pierce DeJonge and Meena Jain for the use of their names, and to Irene Labue for the sweet and beautiful Ollie. Thanks also to Clare McCarthy, for friendship, inspiration and for coming to every book launch.

To Christina Hogrebe and the entire crew at Jane Rotrosen Agency, all I can say is holy guacamole. Wow! I mean it! Thank you for all your energetic and cheerful work on my behalf.

At Berkley, thanks to my editor, Claire Zion. I'm sorry you had to read such a crappy first draft, and I forgive you for making me rewrite the entire book in a month. My work is always far, far better because of you. Thanks to Danielle Keir, Bridget O'Toole, Erin Galloway, Jin Yu, Craig Burke, all the folks in art (looking at you, Anthony and Emily!), the amazing sales team who leads the charge, Jeanne-Marie and Ivan and everyone else whose fingerprints are all over my work. You guys are, as one says, wicked pissah.

To my friends in the writing community—Robyn, SEP, Sonali, Jamie, Piper, Kwana, Farrah, Kennedy, Regina, James, Caro, Julie, Lori, another Jamie—your books and your hearts inspire me, delight me, and honor me. And to Abby Jimenez, author and baker, for her special, special cake.

The language of adoption changes often to be kinder and more inclusive—relinquished for adoption, placed for adoption, choosing adoption, first mother. Because the adoptions in this book took place between eighteen and sixty years ago, I used the language that would've been more common at those times.

In researching the many complex emotions associated with adoption, I used many sources including (but not limited to):

The National Council for Adoption
Adoption Institute of Colorado
HelpWithAdoption.com
Adoption: The Making of Me podcast
Adoption Is a Lifelong Journey by Jennifer Eckert,
    Katie Gorczyca, and Kelly Dibenedetto
The Primal Wound by Nancy Verrier
Journey of the Adopted Self by Betty Jean Lifton
Adoption.com
American Adoptions
The many, many people who share their adoption stories
    online
And most especially, my beloved uncle Edward
    Kaminski

On the family front, thanks to my mom, who, no matter what life hands her, manages to find laughter and a reason to smile. How I admire you for that, Mommy! To my sister, Jackie Decker, who never fails to bring sunshine to my day. To Polly, Barry, Brian and Julie—whenever we're together, it's such a happy time. I'm so grateful to have you all. To the sisters of my heart—Catherine, Jennifer, Shaunee, Mary Ellen, Maureen, Christine—I don't know what I'd do without our times together, our lengthy phone calls and many text conversations, and I hope never to find out.

Flannery and Declan, you will always be my heart and soul, no matter what. Forever and ever. Mike, you are damn near perfect in my eyes. Thank you for taking such good care of my daughter. Thank you to my grandson, who is pure and utter joy. I love you so much, little Peeper. And to Terence, my love, thank you for every single day.

And thank you, readers. The fact that you choose to spend time with my books is one of the greatest honors of my life. It really is.

A Little Ray of Sunshine

Kristan Higgins

Discussion Questions

1. Initially, it seems like Monica has a more realistic idea of motherhood, compared to Harlow's idealized concept of it. As the book goes on, how do Monica's and Harlow's expectations about motherhood change, and why?

2. Monica worries that her son is manipulative for the way he blew up both her and Harlow's lives with the Cape Cod trip. Later, he pulls a similar stunt to meet his birth father, and the consequences finally catch up with him. Do you think Monica was right? Why are she and Sanjay upset? Why do you think Matthew felt the need to be so secretive?

3. Many young women are faced with unexpected pregnancies, and they have to make an incredibly difficult decision about what to do next. Why do you think Harlow chooses to give her baby up for adoption? Why doesn't she get an abortion instead? Why doesn't she keep the baby and let her family help raise him?

4. Harlow hid a huge secret from her family for eighteen years. Do you think Harlow's mother's reaction to her secret pregnancy

was fair? How would you react if a family member had hidden the same secret Harlow did?

5.   Harlow's life was comfortable but quiet on the Cape before Matthew came back. Do you think Harlow was happy before her son found her? She claimed everything was fine, but do you think that was denial or the truth?

6.   At the beginning of the book, Cynthia seems self-centered and cynical, especially when it comes to family. How did Matthew's reunion with his birth family affect her character? Do you think Cynthia would have agreed to meet her sisters if not for Matthew?

7.   No one knew that Cynthia had been adopted, yet she still felt like an outcast in the family. Her perspective on the family starkly contrasts with Harlow's. How much of Cynthia's isolation from the Smith family do you think was of her own making, and how much of it was reality? What could Harlow and her siblings have done differently to prevent Cynthia from feeling excluded?

8.   Sanjay's relationship with Matthew is vastly different from Monica's, just as Monica's relationship with her son is different from Harlow's. Each of them has strengths and weaknesses when it comes to Matthew, but Monica's point of view reveals that she is resentful of the others'—Sanjay, who gets to be the easygoing parent, and Harlow, who receives Matthew's love without having done the work for the last eighteen years. Do you relate to Monica's frustrations, or do you relate more to Sanjay's or Harlow's perspectives? Do you think Monica has reason to fear Matthew's relationship with Harlow?

9.   Harlow is surrounded by affectionate relationships: her parents, Lillie and Ben, her Grandpop and Frances. Even Sanjay and Monica seem infatuated with each other—that's why she chose them to raise her son. Why, then, does Harlow keep romance at a distance, and how much do you think the absence of her son influences that? What changes at the end of the novel to convince her to take the leap with Grady?

10.   Matthew's parents did the best they could to be transparent about his adoption, accepting of his emotions, and supportive of his decisions, but they still feel that Matthew betrayed them by staying with Harlow at the end of the summer. Why do you think he made that decision? And why does he decide to leave?

11.   Both Cynthia and Matthew were put up for adoption by young mothers, but Cynthia's birth parents were forced to do so, while Harlow chose it. Cynthia's adoptive parents hid that fact from her, whereas Matthew's discussed it openly. Then, Matthew sought out his birth family, while Cynthia's contacted her. Compare their experiences further and discuss. How do you think their lives might have changed if their parents handled the topic of adoption differently?

12.   Harlow suggests to Grady that they date quietly rather than move toward a committed relationship. Grady rejects that idea and tells Harlow she's stuck in the past, still living a carefully curated life. What did you think of that conversation? How well do you think Grady knows Harlow?

13.   Harlow's family is full of complicated relationships, and Harlow's secret pregnancy and Cynthia's pessimism are only the be-

ginning of them. But there is also a lot of love to go around. Would you want to be part of Harlow's family? What do you think are the good parts of being a member of your family? And what do you think are the hard parts of it?

14. Rosie's alcoholism was a surprise to Harlow, as it can be for many loved ones of alcoholics. Why do you think Harlow never noticed it before? How did you judge Harlow's reaction once Rosie admitted to her addiction?

15. Harlow's romantic life was never more than a distraction from the loss she felt without Matthew, until he finally came back and she let herself fall for Grady. Do you think Harlow's brother is just a distraction for Rosie while she copes with her addiction? Or do you think Rosie truly loves him, and he will be part of her recovery?

16. Matthew's decision to stay with Harlow at the end of the summer was a huge change to his life—and Harlow's. Do you think Monica should have done more to prevent him from staying? Do you think Harlow was justified in agreeing to it?

17. Harlow has to quickly learn how to be a parent to her nearly adult child. Think about the parenting choices she made throughout the book, from their first outing—paddleboarding with a possible shark sighting—to relinquishing him back to the Patels. What mistakes did she make? What successes did she have? What do you think are the most important lessons she learned about motherhood?

Photo by Deborah Feingold

Kristan Higgins is the *New York Times, USA Today,* and *Publishers Weekly* bestselling author of more than twenty novels, which have been translated into more than two dozen languages and have sold millions of copies worldwide. The happy mother of two snarky and well-adjusted adults lives in Connecticut with her heroic firefighter husband, cuddly dog, and indifferent cat.

CONNECT ONLINE

KristanHiggins.com
KristanHigginsBooks
Kristan_Higgins
Kristan.Higgins

Ready to find
your next great read?

Let us help.

Visit prh.com/nextread

Penguin
Random
House